I0662643

THE BERNOULLI AWARD

Published by Tom Sylvester, Inc.
219 Old Pro's Way, Cary, NC 27513
USA • 2009
ISBN-10 0615313337
ISBN-13 9780615313337

First softcover printing (thirty draft copies for editing), March 2009. Second softcover printing (fifty copies for marketing), April 2009. First commercial publication (digital e-book), July 2009. First commercial publication (trade paperback), August 2009. All rights retained by the author.

Tom Sylvester

✈ Acknowledgements

This was a team effort. My sincere thanks to Steve Satre, Jim Herrmann, Wild Bill Stealey, Jack Mohney, Steve Simon, Paula Simon, Joe Dinges, Robert Hensley, and Gail Mahoney for their help in improving this book. Also, my special thanks go to my longtime friend Clayton Davis, former NSA agent, novelist, and command pilot. He gave me my first flying job and continues to inspire me to this day. Thanks, Cap'n Clayton. ✈

"It is characteristic of wisdom not to do desperate things." - *Henry David Thoreau*

Part I

Chapter One

Steve.

Increasingly dizzy and clearly out of options, Steve had no choice but to reach forward and quickly unlatch the tiny canopy on his experimental aircraft. The Plexiglas jolted against the damaged aircraft as it separated and disappeared with the freestream. With the canopy gone, the wind suddenly and violently punched at him, whipping his otherwise perfectly-styled hair in every direction, and upped the urgency of his predicament.

His sweaty *Joe Satriani Crystal Planet* t-shirt flew into his face and slapped at him relentlessly. He grabbed a handful of the shirt, quickly stuffed it behind his parachute harness and resumed the struggle for control. One design flaw that became apparent early in the aircraft's flight testing was its insufficient airflow into the tiny cockpit. Coupled with a bubble canopy, he often baked during the typical forty-five minute test flights conducted in the summer sky of Southern Illinois. Now that the canopy was gone, he half-expected some relief from the hot, stagnant air. But even at three thousand feet above the ground at one hundred knots, he was now being battered by ninety degree Fahrenheit hurricane force winds. This introduced a new set of problems: breathing and seeing. He felt downright nauseous as the lush cornfields below him spun unmercifully into a slimy green blur.

At age twenty-two and only seven hundred hours of flight time, he was hardly a seasoned test pilot. But he knew more about aerodynamics, both in theory and in application, than perhaps ninety percent of all licensed pilots. Yet at this particular moment, he certainly didn't feel like he was one of aviation's rising stars. The world continued to spin toward him from above as he dangled from his upside-down vantage point in the small craft. The mid-summer sweat that moments before had been on his face was now in his eyes, blurring his vision when he needed it the most. Now, all it would take would be a simple twist of the harness latch and seven months of hard work would pull away from him. No time to be angry now. There will be plenty of time to ponder his mistake once he's safely on the ground.

With no time left he yanked the latch handle to the left and it, too, disappeared along with the airplane to which it was attached, leaving him to tumble toward the deep green corn field below. He reached mechanically for the ripcord and jerked on it angrily as he realized how foolish he had been; he had purposely induced a severe negative G on the aircraft, just to see if it could handle it. *Stupid move.*

Everything he had done during the summer's test flights had been so planned and so deliberate—except for this latest maneuver, which was of course not on the script. Big mistake. It was never intended to be an aerobatic aircraft and the required negative one G limit had already been tested successfully. He had no business pushing the envelope beyond the FAA maximum negative load.

He cursed himself as the parachute opened with a series of loud flaps and a forceful bump, just eight hundred feet above the field, which was a few miles north of Kernsville, the home of Dexter University. He would be a senior engineering student this fall—provided he could now explain away this incident to his father. *Boy is dad gonna be pissed.*

Suddenly, the world around him became quiet and peaceful. He looked up at his parachute canopy, then around and below for his falling aircraft. It's a good thing the FAA insists that parachutes be worn aboard experimental aircraft, he reasoned.

Suddenly a low-pitched, resonating boom erupted directly below him, and a huge cloud of dust billowed from where the tiny aircraft impacted. "Whoa," he muttered, *sotto voce*. There was no fire, no explosion, just a hollow metallic thud. A dust cloud seeped upward from beneath the green corn rows surrounding the airplane. Maybe he could rebuild the engine and/or salvage some of the instruments, if they weren't beyond repair.

Rats. All that work and all that money: Gone because of his impatience. *Dad is going to kill me.*

Drifting downwind at the same pace as the cloud of dust below him, he soon slammed hard into the high corn. The stalks slapped him unmercifully just prior to his impact into the hard, dry dirt beneath. He yelped and balled-up to protect himself as he tumbled through the rows. The canopy remained inflated and began to drag him through the field. He tumbled through a few more rows as he scrambled to release at least one of the two harnesses, which would thankfully deflate the chute. He tried twice without success: Each time he got his hand close to the quick-release mechanism, the chute would drag him through another row and he would have to protect his face from being cut from the thick corn reeds.

Finally, he got one line loose and the chute gave up the fight. He stopped with his back arched over a row of crushed greenery, facing the thick, hazy, blue sky that he had owned just moments before. The world around him became quiet as he waited for the pain to set in.

For several moments he wiggled his toes inside his old, filthy tennis shoes and pondered his next move. As the harsh sun flickered on his face through the deep green corn leaves, he felt the flow of fresh blood mixing with the sweat on his now-filthy tee shirt. He knew he was going to be sore once the adrenaline wore off. ✈

Mojo.

The envelope in her student box was addressed to Ms. Monica Joanne Barnes, which usually meant that either 1) the sender didn't know her or 2) she was in trouble again. She paid her overdue rent already; that couldn't be it. So she didn't keep an accurate check book, big deal. Perhaps she was being audited. She did skip a year on her Federal taxes. That was an accident and though she got that cleared up, it was quite costly—which was why the rent was late. No, this was something definitely official, she decided, and it wasn't something good like a sweepstakes winner notification. *Gotta be bad news.*

Even MoJo's close friends didn't know her full name; she was known simply as MoJo Barnes. She hated Monica (rhymes with Harmonica, which—eliding the Kazoo— is perhaps the worst musical instrument ever invented). She used "MoJo" on everything, including her official paperwork at Dexter University.

With one hand she pulled her soft, dark brown hair around an ear as she examined the strange envelope with the other. The letter looked rather official—typed address, sealed and hand stamped—but with only a post office box from Washington, DC in the upper-left corner. No name. *Interesting*, she thought. Even though it was midway through the summer break, her student box was always full of junk every time she checked it. She gathered up the other half-dozen or so notes and papers from her student box and stuffed them into her bag, just as her cell phone rang. She mashed the papers in, took the tiny phone from the bag's side pocket and, instantly recognizing the number she, punched the button with the green icon and said, "Hey."

"*Busy?*" said Steve Brinkley on the other end.

"No. Just checking my mail," she said as she tossed a few of the notes into the nearby waste basket. One of them missed the can and a young, good looking kid appeared out of nowhere, picked it up and put it in the waste basket. Then he leaned against the wall and smiled at her, creating an opening for introducing himself.

She smirked at him with a "buzz off" expression, then turned away and asked, "Why?"

The young man walked away.

"I, uhm—I need a ride," he said slowly.

There was something different about his voice, she surmised. "Why? Where's that old hot black truck?" she asked as she ripped open the mysterious envelope and unfolded the single page within.

"At the airport."

"Then where are you?"

After a short delay, he replied, "Not at the airport."

She paused when she realized that he was grunting the words out. "How's the plane?"

He was still staring at the blue sky above, sweating profusely and bleeding slightly.

"Thanks for asking, I'm fine. Oh, the plane? I thought you were asking about me. Well, uhm, it's gonna need some repair work…"

"Where *are* you?" she asked as she began reading the mysterious letter, still not paying much attention to Steve.

He arched his back and slid down to the bottom of the row. He wiped the sweat off his brow with the same hand that held his cell phone, then brought it back up to his ear. "You know that big corn field north of Dillahunty Road, the one with that single oak tree near the road?"

"Yeah."

"I'm laying in it, staring up at the sky."

"Where's the plane?" she asked as she tore open the letter.

"It's here, too, fifty yards north of the road. The farmer's gonna be pissed."

Reading the letter, she was only half-listening, something about a farmer. Steve's news wasn't sinking in. The letter looked like the break they were looking for.

She finished reading the last of the letter, then asked sardonically, "Now, where are you again?"

He told her again like he normally did, and added, "It's called Attention Deficit Disorder, a.k.a.: A.D.D. Add that to your list of maladies."

"Yeah, yeah, yeah. Where?"

He repeated the location.

"I'll be there in fifteen minutes."

"—oh, and MoJo?"

"Yeah?"

"Better get my truck. I'm going to try to get as much of the plane into the truck bed as possible before dark."

"What's wrong with the plane?"

He closed his eyes and spoke each word slowly, "I. Broke. It."

"Your dad's going to pitch a fit."

"I know."

She paused, then added, "Don't you need to file an accident report with the FAA or something?"

He rolled painfully onto his side and unclicked the other chute harness. "Well, think about it: Flight control failure? Nope. Engine loss? Nope. Substantial damage? I think there's a minimum dollar limit, provided the engine's okay, so I may be all right there, too. After all, it's just a matter of semantics, don't you agree?"

"How about serious injury or death?"

"Negative, MoJo, on both accounts." he said, now impatiently.

She finished reading the letter, then asked, "Hey, got a minute?"

He looked around and saw some bugs crawling around the crushed stalks. "Yeah. Sure. I'd say my flight testing has ended for the day."

"I just got a letter from Mahoney Aerospace. They're sponsoring an engineering contest to build a cheap, efficient, four-seat airplane. Thousand mile range. Yada yada." She skimmed through the rest of the letter. "Best design wins a job after graduation for each team member. Interested?"

No one had to remind him how rotten the economy was, how all of the layoffs were occurring not just at all the aerospace firms, but in every engineering discipline. Most of last year's graduates were still on the street. With an unglamorous dismissal from M.I.T. as part of his official resume, his odds of getting a job were already slim to none.

"Under usual conditions, yes. But it looks like I'm going to be tied up for a while. In fact, I'll probably be writing friggin' software for years to pay off this mess I just made."

She looked at the letter again. "Says here they'll fund each of the top twenty-five qualifying schools fifty thousand dollars for the work."

Steve said, "Jeez that's one and a quarter million. Maybe they're just shopping for some cheap, empirical engineering work from college kids. You know the students will put in more hours than a salaried employee."

MoJo was pleased that he didn't immediately dismiss the idea. "We need to get the school to sign-off on this."

Steve stood up slowly. "I'm listening. Do we get to keep the airplane after it's done?"

"Doesn't say. I'll bring the letter. Might cheer you up."

He looked down at his scratched and bleeding legs. "Hmm. Maybe this will be a way to supplant my broken airplane. While you're at it, bring some Bactine, too. And bring Charms. I need some muscle out here." ✈

Charms.

It seemed unusual now to call Charms by his real name: John Ruess, the third member of Steve's inner-circle. It wasn't a particularly offensive nickname, he reasoned, but it always required an explanation, which was problematic when he was trying to be taken seriously. But for now, Charms was leaning into a well-dressed woman, obviously older than his college age.

She was stunning, hands-down the best looking woman in the bar—probably in all of Kernsville. He was no loser, mind you. Better than average, but on looks alone he was clearly outclassed.

No matter: The only thing separating the two was his occasionally pronating beer mug. She was drinking a phu-phu drink with an umbrella. The bartender had to look up how to make it. She wasn't from around here.

He told her she should consider stretching exercises to loosen-up her tense back muscles. He was, after all, going to be an orthopedic surgeon after he finishes up his residency. The doctor thing always worked well with the chicks, often times better than the astronaut thing. Sometimes the actor thing worked, too, depending on the girl. This one, on first view, seemed intelligent, so he created an appropriate subterfuge to match her fancy.

Maybe he should actually become a doctor someday, he thought. Even with his minimal effort, he was breezing through his college years at Dexter.

The blond lady giggled as she said, "So you're a doctor? You don't look old enough."

Actually, he looked several years older than his nineteen years, which served him well with bar room tales. "I wasn't aware of a minimum age requirement. I did, after all, finish high school at age fourteen."

"Well, I'm glad you're a doctor, because I have a problem."

He took another sip of his brew. "Yes?" he feigned concern, though disappointed that she had been convinced so easily.

"My ears whistle when I run."

He looked at her for a long moment, now understanding why there had been no need for further convincing. Clearly she wasn't as bright as he first thought. Instead, he felt the need to see just how ditsy she really was.

"It's your body's natural warning system, telling you you're running too fast. If you run slower, the whistling will subside." Someday, he thought, he'll meet his match. But it would not be this woman. *Bummer.* He had hoped for Top Shelf.

"Is that kind of like when a sun burn warns you that you've been sunbathing too long."

"Exactly." This was no fun at all. "See that guy over there," he said, pointing to the other side of the bar at a middle-aged man reading a paper.

"Yeah?"

"From just the overt symptoms, I'd say he has a parasite in his bloodstream called *e.sitsonhisasstoomuch.*"

"Wow. I don't know how you doctors do it. You must have a lot of brains."

Charms smirked. He needed out of this conversation; he was sparring with a rookie. Fortunately, from behind him he heard a high-pitched voice call out, "Charms? John Ruess!?"

He turned around and saw her approaching through the crowd of bar patrons.

The blonde said, "Doctor, do you know her?"

Not picking up on the "doctor" salutation, he ignored her and yelled to the woman, "MoJo!" He pushed his beer away and stood, smiling.

"Thought I'd find you here. I need you," she said, breathless.

"Whassup?"

"Steve crashed north of town."

Charms bolted up. "Gawd. When? Is he hurt?"

"No. He said he's okay, but I'm going to need your help."

The blonde added, "Don't forget your doctor's bag."

MoJo looked at her, then back at Charms as she figured out what his game was this time.

Without missing a beat, Charms turned to MoJo and pointed at her. "Listen, Nurse MoJo, call and have Dr. Cramden at County Hospital order twenty cc's of minogranodine and have OCR and OBT consult on the triage. Stat. And I mean ASAP."

"Yeah. I'll get right on it, *Doc*," she added, knowing full well what he had been up to. She wanted to smile, but instead put her arm around his neck and dragged him in the direction of the door. After they were out of the blonde's hearing range, she said, "Was she tough?"

"No. A real bone head. Hugely disappointing. Is Steve really okay?"

"Yeah. Just scratched and bummed. We've got to disassemble the plane and get it on his truck before dark."

"Is it totaled?"

"Appears to be. He said he overstressed it. Went negative with it."

"We already did negative one, plus the safety factor."

"I know. He said he was screwing around at the end of the ride. It'll be recorded in the box. There goes his Aero 311 thesis and my Statics and Materials project. Steve's dad's gonna be pissed again."

"Wonderful. Now, what do we do?"

"We figure out what failed and we fix it."

"The first airplane was a center-of-lateral-area problem—controllability. You're saying this one was structural?"

"Seems to be, since it broke apart in flight. Let's go." ✈

Chapter Two

Mojo and Charms arrived at the field to find Steve at the edge of the dirt road, stacking up some of the smaller pieces that he had managed to disassemble: The cockpit panel assembly, one of the two ballast bladders used for the flight testing, the nose wheel assembly, the pilot and passenger seats, and papers such as the aircraft's radio license, experimental airworthiness certificate, and weight and balance information. He'd now need socket wrenches, a rubber hammer, and possibly a Saws All tool to get the rest of it apart enough for transport back to his dad's hangar.

"That's all that's left?" Charms asked, staring down at the pile near the road.

"It was a small plane. Eight hundred eighty pounds of parts. These are the biggest pieces."

"Guess we won't need my tools, then."

"Oh, I forgot. There's a big chunk of airplane about twenty yards that-a-way," he said, pointing northwest with his arm high. "You might recognize it: It started out shaped like the rear empennage, but I would imagine it looks like Japanese Origami, now. We have to find the canopy, too. That's a three thousand dollar hunk of plastic."

MoJo surveyed the wreckage and said, "I'm told you can't put toothpaste back in the tube."

"I know," Steve muttered. "We may have to use Alan's CADAM *whatchamacallit* carbon thingy. By the way, where is Alan?"

Tossing Steve a can of Diet Dr. Pepper, MoJo said, "Think fast," then added, "I dunno. I called his cell phone and The Pisser, but no answer. Left a message. He could have his Marshall cranked up, hammering out some Steve Vai licks while bossing around the other band members. I don't know how they put up with him. Is the engine okay?"

As he popped the top, the can spewed brown foam everywhere, but he simply held it away from him and responded, "It appears to be in good shape. I cut the mixture before I bailed, so I wouldn't get *Cuisinarted* by the prop." He took a gulp. "And, as luck would have it, the plane hit ass-end first. Not a scratch on the props and it didn't even compress the motor mounts nor yield the throttle riggings. It shouldn't have hit tail first, what with the empennage completely gone, but it did. When I bailed, I pushed it away from me with my feet, which must have induced enough of a side load to get it into a quasi-leaf-tumble. Just a lucky break."

A muffled yell arrived through tall stalks. "I found the Canopy!"

"Good." Steve announced quietly to no one in particular. Suddenly he brought his hands up to his mouth and yelled, "Republican or Democrat?"

"Republican."

MoJo smiled, knowing the answer was good news, but disagreeing with the analogy.

"Mo, the wing comes apart with these four bolts. I've disconnected the aileron linkages and I clamped off the fuel lines. You and Charms can get it into the truck. I have to go fess up to the farmer."

"I just realized where the term 'he bought the farm' came from. How much do you think it will cost to 'buy the farm'?"

"I don't know. This is my first time crashing an airplane. More importantly, I wonder how much it will cost to buy his silence?"

"I thought you said this was an unreportable event?"

"It is, provided we don't report it."

MoJo gave him the look.

Steve had no choice but to add, "Look, I'm the only one with the pilot's license. Who's going to fly the next airframe if the Feds suspend my pilot certificate. No one was hurt. The engine, the prop, the radios, the landing gear—they're all in good shape. The airframe's the only casualty."

"Just the airframe. What do you say to the FAA when they do their next phase check?" MoJo said sardonically.

"I'll just say I abandoned this project and am starting another. Look, it's a borrowed parachute, which is gonna cost me fifty bucks to get repacked, plus I don't know how many ears of corn I'm going to have to buy from the guy in that farmhouse over there. I don't have the money nor the time to push paper with the FAA."

"We'll talk about it later." MoJo said as she searched for a three quarter inch socket.

"Much. It's going to be dark soon." She flips open her cell again and starts to dial. *Come on Alan, pick up.* ✈

Alan.

The music that came out of Alan's guitar was truly mesmerizing. His head was cocked to the side and his eyes were closed tightly. His tall, lean body swayed gracefully from side to side as his left hand became a blur as it raced up and down the fretboard. He wasn't just playing. He was "channeling" the music from a beautiful place out there somewhere that few musicians ever get to visit.

In his garage were the best drummer, the best rhythm guitarist, and the best bass guitarist on campus. Yet he was the one whom the rest of the band revered. His music was a result of both natural talent and thousands of hours of practice. Sure, Alan was a pompous ass, but the others wanted to be with him when he made the four hour drive north to compete in the Greater Chicago Battle of the Bands (GC BoB), an annual drunk-fest held in and around the Charter One Pavilion on the shores of Lake Michigan in late August. With the winning band sharing $25,000, Alan knew his share of the winnings would help fund his new CarbonRenderer, since no one else thought it would—or ever could—work.

Just to make it on the list of competitors at the GC BoB was a big deal, since music agents usually swarmed the place looking for new talent. Alan's band made the list via an MPEG video that they burned onto a DVD and mailed to the event's organizers. Normally, you had to be invited to compete, based on a growing following and a resume of gigs at the better venues, but it was clear to the GC BoB officials that they had found a new talent in this otherwise unknown college band from Dexter.

Three hours of practice and Alan announced, "Okay. We're done." He flipped a switch on the back of his amp, and the red light on the front of the amp faded. "Except," turning and frowning, "Lonnie, you truly sucked today. Be in tune when we start a song, get control of your stomp boxes, quit daydreaming or at least don't act like you're bored to tears, and try practicing the songs beforehand."

He propped his American VG Stratocaster guitar on its stand next to his prized Bullet Proof boutique guitar, stuck the pick between the strings, then grabbed three CDs from behind him and passed them out to the other players.

"This will be the last song in the gig. It's one I made up about a month ago. Beneath the riff, it's simply a twelve bar blues progression, but I mix in both minor and major pentatonics. The triads and arpeggios introduce the chord changes during the bridge. Pay attention to the sudden staccato harmonies during the main syncopated solos. Listen to it tonight and we'll try it tomorrow. Two o'clock still okay?"

The members nodded. It was clear that they supported him. Each felt proud that they were in his band. They were all certainly talented, but they enjoyed playing with him, in spite of his corrosive leadership style. *He* was the band and they knew it was with him where their best hopes for fame and fortune rested. They were music majors. He, however, was a physics major. What they didn't know is that he neither wanted nor needed any of the music fame. He wanted to contribute much more than music. Although, he reasoned, he could foster enough of the fortune portion of Fame and Fortune to stir some interest in his CarbonRenderer project. He had taken the idea to many of the professors in the Mechanical Engineering and Physics Departments, yet the only one who had seemed even remotely interested in it was Steve Brinkley—but Steve was just a student, a pilot, a computer geek with an infamous past. Sure, Steve was a nice guy, but he certainly was not a person who could make the CarbonRenderer a reality. Especially since he had been thrown out of M.I.T. and was still in some sort of trouble, it seemed.

Suddenly, Alan's iPhone rang. He grabbed it off the amp and looked at the picture, recognizing the incoming caller. Touching the green Answer button, he said in a low, business tone, "Hi MoJo. 'S'up?"

"Alan, Steve crashed his plane. He needs your help."

Alan put his guitar in its soft case and zipped it up. "He wrecked it? Hey, maybe now he'll get on board with my idea."

She said, "Well, right now we're all going out to help get the wreckage back to the hangar."

"I'm busy. Can't make it now."

"Listen, Alan, you pompous ass-bite. He's in a cornfield with a wrecked plane. I don't care what you're doing, get your butt out there with us."

"I'll call him." And with that, he hit the END CALL button, then dialed Steve.

Steve answered on the first ring, seeing "Alan" on his Caller I.D. "Hey, Alan. I've got a deal for you."

The Steve/MoJo/Charms trio wasn't yet ready to open its clique to new members. Steve and Alan had a mutual respect for each other's talents. But to both MoJo and Charms, Alan was too self-important, too bossy, and a bit aloof. Steve, however, loved creating new things and improving on existing gadgets, and shared this thrill of invention with Alan.

It was Alan who had initially approached Steve, after Steve's presentation of his "inductive flow" hypothesis to his Fluid Dynamics classmates. Fluids was a particularly tough engineering class, because it required both analytics and imagination. Alan and Steve, however, excelled in the class, and Alan was convinced that he could convince Steve that he could get his CarbonRenderer idea to work. He saw Steve's math on how he could improve on laminar flow qualities of low speed flight and was impressed that Steve was actually building a small airplane incorporating this design. Steve could actually produce things, not just hypothesize them.

Moreover, when he found out Steve's dad was one of the top investment bankers in Chicago—and more importantly tied closely to investors who might be able to finance his invention and a new company—Alan realized the importance of establishing a good rapport with him. It became all the more important when he found that Steve was a reluctant genius when it came to computer programming, and MoJo was a chemist, both critical to getting his CR prototype working. Charms—well—Charms was a bullshit artist. He saw no value in that.

"I'm listening..."

"I'm dragging the Mini-Wolf in pieces out of a cornfield north of town."

"So, what happened?"

"A little 'Steve-induced' metal yield of the empennage."

"Are we talking elastic or plastic deformation?" Alan asked, borrowing the terminology from their Engineering Materials class.

"Went straight from 'no yield' to 'see ya.'"

"The tail came *off*? Like, separated? You screwed up, didn't you?" Alan could only spell the word Diplomacy.

"Yep. Anyway, I need some help lifting the engine block into the truck bed. It's almost four hundred pounds and the three of us just can't handle it. It's gonna be dark in less than an hour and I need to clear the field."

"What's the deal, then?"

Here's Steve, dripping with sweat, scratched and bleeding, pissed at himself, and now being forced to negotiate with the outsider. "I'll give you five minutes with dad to convince him that your CR is worth investigating."

"I can't explain it in five minutes."

"Then I suppose you'll first need a primer on encapsulation."

Alan took a beat. "Fine. Where are you?" ✈

With the AC not working in the truck, the window was cracked open to provide some ventilation, which made the ride noisy. The humid night air had cooled somewhat and had the scent of mildew as it rushed into the cab. They left MoJo at the hangar and the three men were heading back to the field again—this time with flashlights—to make sure they got everything. Steve, Charms, and Alan were each drenched with sweat and grime.

The paper Charms was holding rustled with the wind, making it hard to read, but the interior dome light was on and he did his best. "It says here that Mahoney Aerospace will guarantee us employment for at least two years at seventy-five thousand a year. Who's your daddy!" He blurted, wiping the grit off of his face with his t-shirt.

Alan, seated in the middle of the truck, swiveled his head to the right and asked portentously, "What skill set do you bring them, Charms? Corporate corruption? Sexual Harassment Demonstrations. Levity? You could walk around holding your nuts and smile a lot."

"My engineering degree has more hireability than your physics degree. Perhaps you can dream up some Mr. Spock, plasma-ekto, float-a-gerbil idea, then go to lunch."

"Bite me."

"Empirically?"

"Hey guys," said Steve, both hands on the ancient truck's shaky steering wheel. "Remember that we don't have anything compelling to offer into this competition. No one's gonna get hired by Mahoney if we just build an airplane. It's got to be revolutionary, and we have nothing. Actually less than nothing because of me."

It got quiet for a second as they sped along in the dark.

"Furthermore, we are four college dudes competing against a hundred years of research by thousands of companies who have sunk billions into improving aircraft design. They're smokin' dope if they think someone like us is going to revolutionize anything."

It was quiet again in the truck as they drove along. Then Charms said, "You're gonna need some poon tang, and fast."

Steve smiled slightly, eyes on the road.

They arrived at the field and quickly realized it was a waste of time to try to find anything now. They could barely see themselves and it was going to take daylight to find the rest of the debris. "Well, we're here. Might as well drive to the farmer's house, get it over with."

"You're doing the talking," said Alan as they got back in the truck.

"I know. Hopefully—"

"Hey let me give it a try," Charms offered.

Alan said nothing. Steve gave it a slow nod, then said, "Okay, just tell them—"

"General Patton said, 'Never tell someone how to do something. Tell them what to do and let them surprise you with their ingenuity."

Steve smiled, "Where'd you get that?"

"The Official Charms Bullshit Archives. Need more, let me know," he said as he stepped out of the truck and walked up the gravel driveway to the farmer's house.

Once Charms was out of hearing range, Alan turned and asked, "Why do you like him?"

"For what he's doing now. He's a good friend. Sure, he clowns around and is skirt-chaser *nummer eins*, but he's also got a serious side and he solves problems on the spot. He's also a lot smarter than you give him credit."

The light came on the front porch, the door swung open, and Charms was gestured in by an elderly lady, but he said something then waved her off as being too dirty to go inside. She leaned against the door jamb and they began talking. Her hand went up to her mouth, then he said a few more words, pointed towards the waiting duo at the roadside and laughed so hard it could be heard back at the truck. Soon she was nodding. Then the duo saw her smile, all the way from the roadside. Clearly he was working a solution to the issue of "buying the farm" at his own pace.

They both watched in silence for a few minutes, then Alan turned and asked, "What's poon tang?" ✈

MoJo punched a message into her phone: ENGINE IS FINE. FUEL BLADDERS OK TOO, then she clicked the SEND button. Ninety-five percent of the airplane was on the small hangar floor at Kernsville Municipal Airport. She knew Steve would be getting a buzz on his phone in a second, probably with his flashlight in the other hand out in the corn field. She sat on the hangar's only chair —a folding chair "borrowed" from the small airport office's conference room.

Staring at the mess of what was once a beautiful, tiny airplane, she finally realized what could have happened today if the failure happened too close to the ground or if Steve couldn't get out of it. It sent a shiver through her. She balled-up in the chair, rested her chin on her knees and stared right through the twisted metal and into the past four years....

...He had noticed her first. The Chicago-Area Science Olympiad wasn't the place to pick up chicks, but Steve wasn't going to let this girl get past him. Tall, tanned from a summer-long job working at the City of Orland Park Department of Engineering, and completely self-assured amongst the nerds, he walked right up and said, "Gawd I hope you live on the south side."

She didn't miss a beat, "Why? Are you too lazy or am I simply not worth a drive to drive north side?"

"Yes."

"Yes? To what? Yes, you're lazy? Yes, I live on the south side? Yes, I'll go out with you?"

"Great."

"Great what? You're killing me."

"So far, you know I'm lazy, you live near me, and I'll pick you up at seven. Just tell me where."

She was trying to keep up. After all, he was by far the hottest dude there. She held out her hand and said, "MoJo."

"Yep, I got it going, but only for you. I don't walk up to just anyone and—"

"As in Monica Joanne. My friends and even people like you can call me MoJo."

"Steve. No nickname. Feel free to make one up."

"In due time. What's your project?"

Steve shrugged, then said, "Laminar Flow Optimization Across Dissimilar Competing Surfaces."

She said "Airplane stuff" at the same exact moment he said, "…airplane stuff."

They both smiled.

She said, "Mine's Covalent Orthogonal Bonding of Persistent Carbon Threads."

He shook his head and stated, "Not airplane stuff."

She said, "Nope. But it could be."

"So we need to talk."

"Are you hitting on me or do you really want to talk shop?"

"Yes."

She stared straight at him for a full two seconds, then she leaned into him.

Then she kissed him. Right there in front of every geek in Chicago.

It wasn't just a peck on the cheek. This was the real deal, a passionate one, right on the lips in front of every geek, teacher, judge, parent, janitor, on the floor of the conference center. It went on forever.

The place got so quiet the only thing you could hear were the experiments whirring.

She slowly backed off, looked him straight in the eye with a very serious expression, and said, "Who's in control here?"

Shell shocked, he muttered, "You are."

"Who's the luckiest man alive?"

He was too shocked to even smile. "I am."

"Find my project. It's somewhere on this floor. It will contain the only clue as to where you'll be able to pick me up at seven." With that, she turned and walked away, leaving him standing there, knowing he had just met his match...

…MoJo's iPhone buzzed. She ran her finger across the iPhone and it displayed: "CHARMS WORKED IT OUT WITH THE FARMER BUT WE ARE BUSY TOMORROW AFTERNOON." She knew more details were forthcoming, and it was most likely that it would be something she had never anticipated. She'd known Charms long enough to expect the unexpected. ✈

MoJo hadn't moved in fifteen minutes. Here she was: Friday night, sitting alone in a quiet airplane hangar on the edge of town. She was Ms. Excitement.

She jerked when her phone rang loudly. It was Charms on the other end. He said he was on his way back to the hangar with the other two. She could hear the other two chattering in the background as she listened to him explain what was in store as repayment for damaging the farmer's crop.

Finally she interjected, "A church revival? We crash an airplane into her field and she wants us to sing His praises under a tent?"

"Yeah. And it gets better."

"Better? How, exactly can it get any better than that? Listen, I go to church on Christmas, Easter, and before finals. I don't do enough sinning to warrant much more than that."

"There you go, forgetting that church is not a place to accumulate heaven-admittance coupons. It's a worship center." Charms said pompously.

"How often do *you* go to church?"

"Do as I say, not as I do. Listen, the lady was very nice. Her church is having a revival on Saturday afternoon in a tent they've set up in the parking lot in the back of the church. She needs help with cooking and cleaning up."

"Cooking?"

"It's mostly a pot-luck dinner afterwards. Her husband had taken pride in having a pig-pickin' as the main course. But this year he's slowed down considerably and can't be on his feet all day— he's in his mid-seventies. Anyway he's going to need some help. She's arranging the whole thing, but needs some muscle in getting folding tables set up, getting the slow-cooker going early tomorrow morning, basically filling iced tea cups and busing tables. When I showed up on her door, she was panicked about it but truly thinks God sent me there to help."

"Maybe He did. Is that what you mean by 'it gets better?'"

"No. I talked to her for about twenty minutes while Humpty and Dumpty sat in the truck. The first thing is she asked if Steve was okay. That's when I knew she was cool. Then she asked about us and I told her we were all at Dexter U studying engineering and whatnot. She said, 'What a coincidence. One of the church Deacons is the head of the Engineering Department and—'"

"Zimmerman?"

"Yeah, Dr. Zimm, and that—"

"You know that he'll be the one who will approve the school's team to compete for the Bernoulli Award."

"—and that he'd probably like to meet us."

"So once again you've turned a lemon into lemonade."

"As Benjamin Franklin said, 'Hide not your talents. They for use were made. What's a sundial in the shade?'"

"And as Benjamin Franklin also said, 'He that falls in love with himself will have no rivals.'"

"Oh, stop it! You know I'm a Bennie fan. Don't turn him on me! Fate and faith at work here. At least one of you recognizes my talents. We're pulling onto airport road now. Be there in a minute."

She clicked End Call, blanked the screen, then stuck her iPhone back into her pocket. *Fate*, she thought. To her, Dexter wasn't a bad school, but it wasn't a household name like M.I.T. or Cal Tech. Who knew that because of a simple inflection in the direction of a paper he was working on, that Steve would be asked to leave M.I.T. and that he would later join her at Dexter. She recalled the night he called her from his cold room on the second floor of Stanley McCormick Hall in Cambridge, Massachusetts, almost four years ago…

… "They caught me and they're going to boot me out of school tomorrow at the Faculty Hearing," he had said, holding back tears.

"Who caught you? What did you do?!" She remembered asking him.

Steve had chosen a topic for a paper in his work in the Laboratory for Electromagnetic and Electronic Systems (LEES). His topic was to research the various methods of getting a launch order from the President to the missile silo, then predict the true probability of a message getting through using all available propagation methods in a nuclear-disturbed environment. He got on the Internet and quickly discovered that it was extremely easy: Just about every bandwidth supported the National Command Authority message traffic, and the redundancy was in place and impervious to intervention, even in the most austere (nuclear) conditions. His paper was going to be a one-pager, because communications to nuclear weapons sites is *always* available, he concluded. Period. A one page paper was a non-starter. Any knuckle-head would come to the same conclusion with five minutes' research.

Then he thought, what about testing the methods for interrupting the NCA message streams, thereby compromising the ability to launch a missile? Or, just as critical, stopping the launch of a missile. That was much more interesting. He didn't have to go much further than looking at some pictures of a Peacekeeper Missile Control Room on the Internet. There it was, a Microteka 3200D dot matrix printer, the one that prints out the secret code that authenticates a missile launch message. It was an off-the-shelf printer made many years ago.

Then he reasoned: *Screw up the authentication and you can't launch the missile.* Simple as that. He did some research—all from his dorm room—and found out that the cable from the super-secret communications box to the printer was a standard 25-pin parallel printer cable. All he had to do was to manufacture a new printer cable that looked just like the old one, except he would insert a tiny microcircuit into the cable so that when it saw the Message Header stream pass through it, that it would alter the next nine alphanumeric characters, then return to normal printing as though nothing was wrong. It took him a couple of hours to figure out what the message header format looked like. Then the next set of characters coming through the printer cable would be the authentication codes.

Scramble the authentication, leave everything else alone. No authentication, no launch.

Using a $.49 PIC microcontroller, he wrote a small program in assembler code that would do the trick. The biggest problem was it needed a power supply, so he took a small NiMH camera battery, and wired it up. It was mostly a passive circuit, complete with a tiny voltage regulator costing almost two dollars. But that would make the battery last probably five years. Two nights of soldering and testing and he had a cable ready to go.

He wrote up the paper, submitted it online to his professor, along with pictures of the cable and a program written in VB6 to demonstrate how it worked. He'd drop off the actual cable the next day when he went to lab.

Now that's an "A" paper! he thought. Much better than the one-page, "can you hear me now?" paper he started out with.

Then he grabbed his Economics book and started studying his Keynesian homework, which was, of course, an utter waste of time for him.

Three days later he got the paper back and it was given a C. *Not realistic. Not well thought-out. How do you get the Air Force to switch out the cables? Do they test these cables? Are they MIL-SPEC?*

Steve was pissed. He honestly thought he found a hole in their security net and he deserved a better grade.

The more he thought about it, the more he got motivated to prove himself correct. He spent the long Memorial Day holiday scouring the Internet for information on how to get into a missile silo, who gets cleared-in and how, and what the maintenance protocols are. He was a fast learner. The more he dug into it, the more he pushed himself into thinking he was on a mission to identify a failure in the security structure, something that has worked quite well for half a decade. He started looking up regulations about Airmen policies and procedures, dress code and practices, courtesies and decorum. At three in the morning on Monday night he reached a critical juncture, whether to make a fake military I.D.

Up to this point, it was all fun and games.

By now he knew the maintenance squadron, who the key personnel were, staffing and duty cycles, and most importantly how the work orders and requisitions worked. He documented it all as support material to challenge this C grade.

He could do it. He wanted an A on that paper!

Now, to decide: Who would he be? Again, to the Internet. He went to the Utah DOT web site and found that twenty-six couples were killed on the roads of Utah last summer. Why Utah? Because.....

Fourteen of those couples had children. Ten had teenage boys.

Getting closer.

Mr. and Mrs. Bailey Hubbins of Salt Lake City were killed last August in a car wreck. Their son, Anthony, was just about to leave on a year-long mission to Central America when the accident happened, so he delayed his departure. A few phone calls and Steve found that he left the country last month: April.

Bingo! The kid has no parents and he's out of the country for a year. Tough to hunt down.

Now to the Defense Investigative Service. That took him a full week to hack, mostly because he had to bounce all over West Boston on public computers to do so, just in case he wasn't as smart as he thought he was. But suddenly Airman First Class Anthony Hubbins had the official review records of his personal background investigation to obtain a Top Secret clearance with Critical Nuclear Weapons Design Information (CNWDI) authorization. Everything used to be on paper, with signatures. Now it was mostly online, having gone through the web transformation like most other governmental offices. Only he found out that there were glitches in the system. None that he could hack through, despite his best efforts.

However, all he had to do was fill out a paper report on the DD Form and secure fax it to the Washington Office from the Salt Lake DIS Field Office, along with a cover page saying "Site is down again. Please enter manually."

He looked back two days later and someone in DC unwittingly added a file for A1C Hubbins.

Now all he needed was orders. The Internet had personal web sites with scanned orders showing them leaving for Iraq or as a way of announcing that they had been selected for military pilot training. It was easy enough to create paper orders. However, all orders are managed through the Manpower and Personnel Center in San Antonio. A couple of phone calls, followed by some high-brow bullshit to a Tech Sergeant there was all it took. Anthony Hubbins was "coming in from the cold" from another governmental agency and needed to be placed in F.E. Warren AFB in Wyoming, away from the action. He'd already been sworn in (contact the DIS if they needed proof) and he needed the official records to match the man. After a call back the next day, he was asked to email the Orders to a special number given to him by the Tech Sergeant. Of course, this was done from a masked IP address, with Eyes Only stamped on the scanned orders, plus a note in the email to destroy the Orders once entered into the system. The orders were not signed, but the annotation "PO2992-2" was emblazoned in the signature block in its stead. Paper orders were to be mailed to a Mail Boxes Etc. less than a mile from NSA Headquarters in Fort Meade, MD. That must have been what satisfied the blue suiters in San Antonio—that this person was a spook and needed to hide out for a while. That must have been exciting for the blue-suiters in San Antonio to be involved in hiding a spy!

Steve reckons that the Sergeant must have at least asked his boss, or even his boss's boss to confirm that what he was doing was correct. Nonetheless, in the span of one week and $20 paid to a "mule" kid to retrieve it from his $100 mail box at Mail Boxes, Etc. (bought under another person's name), he now had legitimate orders to match his fake Military I.D. This cost, along with the gas money he spent making two trips from Boston to Baltimore, ate up his whole month's allowance from his dad, but it was worth it to get his grade up. This was the hardest he'd ever worked to get a C grade changed to an A.

He assembled everything together to show that he could, in fact, obtain the credentials to make his way into a missile silo. That he could single-handedly get in, replace a "defective" cable and essentially shut down a launch site. He compiled the whole paper in two hours, with attachments showing the phone logs, orders, files, obituaries, etc.

This was definitely "A" material. Certainly he would get his grade changed with this extra effort. He was typing the cover letter to his professor when he got up to go to the bathroom.

That's when the FBI showed up.

It wasn't pretty. Apparently, a visit by the FBI in this case is not a man who calls and asks if he could come up and talk. It's a full-frontal attack assault, designed that way so no evidence is destroyed. These were large men wearing black, bullet-proof vests and iconic black helmets, bearing automatic weapons. This wasn't a movie. It was the real deal. Steve had never been so terrified in his life. He remembers his saliva dripping onto the polished wooden floor of his dorm room as they mashed his face into it.

The next several hours were the low point of his life as he was shackled and hauled away in full view of his friends, many of whom he would never see again. He was taken to the FBI Regional Office in downtown Boston and given the treatment he deserved as the terrorist he was.

They were eventually convinced of his motives, but he was nonetheless charged with several statutory crimes and spent the next six months appearing before various magistrates and courts, all paid for by his father. The only thing that kept him out of jail was the report and partially completed cover letter he was preparing to send to his professor, showing that it was all done just to improve his grade on that paper.

But M.I.T. was not amused, not at all. They dropped him within two days of the arrest. He remembered them saying, "Don't come back. Don't even try."

Those words resonated to this day. *Don't come back. Don't even try.*

His father essentially disowned him and Steve was ostracized by even his closest of friends. The only one who felt compassion for him was MoJo, ironically the one person *least* likely to show any true feelings about anyone. She was about as sensitive as a Tow Away Zone sign. He went there to visit her at the end of the summer, then found a job at a Papa John's Pizza and made web sites for six months while he got his criminal records "fixed" and endured the wrath of his father.

The next semester, they were together at Dexter University, the only school that was interested in admitting him. Though emotionally wounded, he started to put his life together again....

… "Wake up, Mojo," Steve said softly as he placed his hand on her shoulder.

She raised her head off of her knees, opened her eyes to a squinting sliver, and muttered, "Aw, man, it's Saturday. Can't I sleep in?" She extended her arms all the way out to an exaggerated stretch.

He replied to her, but continued talking to the other two as well, "It's still Friday night. How you can sleep on a chair like that and not fall over, I'll never know. Listen, we're going to close up here, go home, and figure out a game plan for tomorrow. Professor Zimmerman is no dummy. He loves organization and a plan. We've got to act like we're working to our game plan, even if we don't have one yet. We meet tomorrow at Denny's at eight A.M. That gives us two hours before we meet at the church. We can work out details under the tent until Zimm shows up, then we all MUST speak as though we've been at this for months."

"I got my band practicing at two tomorrow," announced Alan.

"Too bad. Put them off until at least six. You're on a mission now." Alan wasn't used to being barked at, but nodded.

"Remind me again what our goal is for tomorrow?" asked Charms.

"Sucking up." Alan was already walking towards the hangar door.

"Later, Alan," said Steve. Alan raised his arm but never turned nor slowed his pace. "I guess that's it."

Steve pulled up MoJo from the folding chair and walked her slowly to the door.

Charms said, "It's still early. I'm gonna get cleaned up, head over to Nookies for a while, maybe find myself a princess in need of a good frog to kiss."

MoJo looked at Steve, then announced loudly so it would echo in the hangar, "Your conscience is your curfew, young Charms."

"Then I shall be out all night!" Charms clicked off the lights and locked the hangar door. ✈

Chapter Three

Some long-haired brunette with large sunglasses dropped off Charms at Denny's twenty minutes after the appointed hour. He kissed her goodbye—the kind of kiss that clearly wasn't their first one. Then he closed the door and gave it a couple of quick thumps as she zoomed away. He was still in last night's clothes. The other three watched his arrival from their vantage point in the circular booth next to the tall windows facing the street. They had been furiously trying to put a game plan together in his absence. They had paused their discussion when Mojo noticed Charms getting out of the car. All eyes were on Charms as he made his way in Denny's.

Alan resumed talking but changed the subject, "You know, we should send him to the CDC in Atlanta, have them put some of his body fluid in a Petri dish and see if it grows out a jackrabbit in heat."

"Is he limping?"

"No, I think he's just sore."

Finally, MoJo spoke up, "Did you guys forget a lady is present? Save your locker room talk for later. You know we still need to get out to the cornfield and clean up the rest of the mess out there."

Charms entered Denny's, slowly walked to the booth, slid into it next to Steve, rotated a coffee cup one hundred and eighty degrees upward, then grasped it with both hands, willing it to be filled with coffee soon. He neither required nor desired a greeting.

In fact, he was expressionless and made no eye contact with anyone.

Steve said, "So, it's agreed that there's nothing we can do aerodynamically to improve on the old design, even though we have to start over with the airframe. The airframe is not a bad design, just nothing earth-shattering about it. We also agree that we can't even begin to make improvements to the powerplant. If Pratt & Whitney can't do it, chances are we can't, either. Thus, the only thing we can do is try to make an airplane super-cheap, and that means change the manufacturing process of the main structural components."

MoJo and Alan nodded, followed thereafter by Charms, who nodded, but while still staring down at his coffee.

"I'm liking this," added Alan. "You need to make a new airframe from scratch and the only way to make it cheap is to consider my CarbonRenderer."

"Okay, I've heard your pitch, but *'splain* it to MoJo and Charms."

Alan's enthusiasm could not be restrained. "It's like stereolithography, but better!"

He was immediately interrupted. "Question from the audience." Charms raised a head and opened his eyes. "What's stereolithography?"

"Basically you build something from the ground up, one slice, one layer at a time. For example, if you were building a pyramid from the ground up, it would be easy. You would add layer upon layer until you got to the top. But there's a problem. If part of the thing you're making is suspended away from that which is below it, there is nothing to support the part that is suspended. Thus, there is a limit to the standard stereolith method. What if you wanted to build an upside down pyramid?"

"What do we do, stick toothpicks in there to hold the outcroppings in place while the layers above it are being layered-in?"

"Nope. You'll like this: You lay down two different materials as a solid sheet, one material becomes the structure, the other material acts as the support. Then when it's all done, you melt-away the support material, leaving the completed piece behind."

Alan still sensed that they didn't get it. "Okay, say you want to build an *upside-down* pyramid. The material in the center of the first layer would be the top of the pyramid. The remaining part of the first layer would have to be made up of another material that could support the layers that are being placed above it as well as be removed later when the upside down pyramid was complete."

Steve said, "So what you're saying is, when it is finished, the overall result would look like pyramid encased in a cube. Then you etch- or melt-away the support material and the result would be an upside down pyramid."

Alan nodded, then said, "The problem is even greater when the structure you are trying to build includes something that is curled under or a portion of which is sticking down. Imagine a lamppost with an arcing arm and a lamp fixture at the end of the arm. Then build this lamppost, from the ground up layer by layer. At some point, before the layers defining the lamppost reach the arcing arm, they will reach the lowest point of the lamp fixture. This low point will appear to be suspended alone, away from the lamppost. Just as with the pyramid, the first layer of material that forms the beginnings of the lamp fixture will have to be supported by layers of material that can be washed or etched away when the total structure is built. As layers are added, the lamppost and light fixture will be complete as will the arcing arm that connects them."

"Aren't there people working on this already?" MoJo understood completely what he was trying to do.

"Yep, but no one's got it working yet."

"I think they do. I've seen building models made by this"

"Yes, but only for one-offs, not for actual production of large quantities of things."

"Patents pending?"

"Sure, but not with my kicker."

"Which is?"

"Ever heard of nanotubes?"

Charms blurted out an obnoxious chuckle. "Yeah, Mr. Spock, we and the Klingons all have." Charms shook his head, looked back down, then muttered, "Physicists…"

Alan ignored him. "Well, they are quite real, but can only be formed in a lab now with extremely small output."

"Okay then, we're done, unless the airplane will fit on the head of a pin. Tell me, do they serve coffee at Denny's any more?" he asked, now looking around.

This time, Alan glared at him. "The same mechanisms that form the lattice structure of a nanotube can be exhibited, albeit with interstitials and imperfections, on a much grander scale. You lose ninety percent of its load-to-weight ratio because of the problems in distributed curing, but it still makes the final product five times lighter and ten times stronger than titanium."

"Shut up! Really?" MoJo, the chemistry major, had read articles on nanotubes, but obviously had not kept up with the latest developments. "So what's the problem?"

"Three, really. The first problem is the second material used to support the carbon lattice during replication must have the same specific gravity as the carbon—it's gotta weigh the same, even at different temperatures."

"Does this involve valence bonding?"

"Normally yes."

This was followed by the other two saying, simultaneously "Question!" "Question from the Audience!"

"Hang on." She punched in some words into Wikipedia in her laptop, then started reading it aloud, "In chemistry, valence bond theory explains the nature of a chemical bond in a molecule in terms of atomic valences. Valence Bond Theory summarizes the rule that the central atom in a molecule tends to form electron pair bonds in accordance with geometric constraints as defined by the octet rule, approximately. Valence bond theory is closely related to molecular orbital theory—"

"Stop! Sorry I asked, Jeez!" said Charms.

MoJo looked at Alan, who began again as though he was never interrupted, "Second, there must be a way to lay down the two materials at nearly the same time, without mixing together or degrading the quality of the bonding action of the carbon molecules. Last, nanotubes are grown all at once. Here, we're talking layer upon layer of nanotubes being bonded quickly. This bonding process needs to be resolved—and not by standard valence bonding."

A waitress walked to the table and poured coffee into Charms' mug. "Finally," he said. His comment was a bit mean-spirited, but as he looked up, he found the waitress to be not unattractive, so he finished the sentence, "…at last, a beautiful Denny's waitress."

Fortunately, she smiled at him before walking away.

"Is there anything without a Y chromosome that you won't hit on?" Alan asked.

"Gotta be a mammal. Everything is else fair game."

"So," Alan continued, "I figure MoJo can get smart with the chemistry research, and Steve can come up with a delivery system to make the layers."

"Looks like a tall order." Steve's mind was already swimming with ideas.

"Attention K-Mart Shoppers," Charms announced, "there's a sale on Electrical Engineers on aisle one." He pointed at himself.

Alan loved the fact that Charms had to remind the others that he was part of the team.

Charms continued, "If it's not valence bonding, then what's the bonding process, Elmer's Glue? Do we need to shoot, whatcha call 'em, *electrical thingies*, at it?"

"It's a chemical process similar to epoxy, but it's very fast. The reagent is a butyl recombinant."

"Won't that screw up the secondary material?" MoJo asked.

"Not if you pick the right secondary material." Then Alan surveyed the group, "So who's primary for talking to Professor Zimmerman?"

Steve said, "I guess it's me."

Alan reached into a satchel and pulled out some sketches. "Okay then. Here are some ideas on what it may look like so you can paint a picture in Zimm's mind as to what we'll be doing."

"Anybody know what Zimm looks like?" Steve asked.

No one did.

MoJo looked at her watch, then announced, "Hey, time's up. We gotta go. We'll clean up the rest of the cornfield after we leave the church. Agreed?" She reached in her front pocket of her jeans and produced a wrinkled five dollar bill, pushed it to her left next to Charms, who made no movement. Then the group slid around the booth and up, the other two flinging five dollar bills onto the tabletop next to him.

Charms, following everyone's lead, reached into his front pocket pants pocket, but pulled out a one hundred dollar bill. Talking to the three other currency notes, "Misters Lincoln, meet Doctor Franklin, the greatest American." He stood the C-note on its side, Ben Franklin facing him, then waved-off the group.

Steve wondered how he came across a C-note, obviously showing it off.

"You're my dog, Ben," he said, staring at one of the inanimate five dollar bills, but still within earshot of the group. ✈

Chapter Four

Asphalt was the first thing they smelled when they got out of the car. It was only nine A.M. and the hot, tar parking lot in the back of the church was already outgassing from the increasingly intense sunlight. It was a new parking lot, deep black with bright yellow lines painted on it. It was almost steaming and felt sticky to walk on. There was no escaping the smell of hot asphalt. A secondary smell was that of barbecued pork, emanating from a large cooker just beyond the bright-white tent at the back edge of the lot. It was a curious and pungent combination of odors, but taken together not wholly unpleasant.

The church was indeed at the edge of town. This brand new parking lot was in the back of the church. Beyond the lot, separated merely by a shallow drainage ditch were thousands of acres of tall corn. There was no shade except for the big bright white tent.

"This is going to suck being out in the heat today," said Charms as he emerged from his own car, having quickly paid the bill and raced to join them.

An elderly man was pushing a rack of chairs on a flat roller out of the back door of the church. MoJo immediately jogged over to help. The three men couldn't delay their work, given that MoJo was already at it. Hers was the first of a dozen racks that needed to be moved from the church's storage room out to the revival tent.

Only a handful of people were there. The event didn't start for a couple of hours, and even then the heat might possibly keep people home.

After the chairs were unfolded and lined up as makeshift pews underneath the tent, they retrieved the podium and rolled it out, followed by a dozen card tables (for the food). Then they were tasked with going to various cars and retrieving tablecloths, napkins, paper plates, cups, plastic utensils, and a couple of extension cords. Last but not least they brought out four huge electric fans from the back of Chevy Suburban and placed strategically on the west side of the tent, since Steve noted that the prevailing wind—what little of it there may be today—would be from the west today.

Alan had had it with the heat and the whole idea of sucking up to Professor Zimmerman to get him interested in investing in their engineering contest. Standing under the tent, with two hands, Alan pulled-up his t-shirt to his face and wiped the sweat out of his eyes. He heard a chair being moved and thought MoJo was walking up behind him, so he asked "What chowderhead decided to have an outdoor revival on August sixth at noon, in hundred degree heat, the Greek god Hephaestus?"

"I did," said a baritone voice Alan didn't recognize. "Bugs will eat you alive after dark."

The sweat was stinging Alan's eyes, so he kept them closed tightly and rubbed them more. "So, what you're saying is some arthropod out there is a better judge of an appropriate climate to congregate than you are."

"Who the hell are you?" Professor Zimmerman asked with impunity.

"Alan Overman," he offered, still not caring to know whom he was speaking. The salty sweat was stinging his eyes. He kept them shut and brought his t-shirt up again to wipe them.

"I've never seen you at this church."

"Nope. I try to sleep until two on Sundays."

When Alan could finally focus again, he saw a tall man in his late forties walking away from him, appearing offended.

"Hephaestus is obviously hot-tempered," he muttered then got back to work. ✈

"Mr. and Mrs. Hellums, I'm Steve Brinkley," he said, smiling, offering his hand. It took little deductive reasoning to figure out who they were. They were working the barbecue grill and were the only elderly couple there.

"Nice to meet you, son. Thank you so much for helping out today," the elderly man said as he wiped a cold, wet cloth across his forehead. Being next to the big barbecue pit exacerbated the mid-morning heat, but he seemed to be enjoying himself nonetheless. "You go to the hospital after the crash?"

"No, sir. I'm just a little scratched-up. I wanted to personally apologize for messing up your field yesterday. I'd still like to pay you for your damages."

"Well, son, last night after Marge here told me about the crash I went out there at the crack of dawn to see just how bad it was, and there were these two kids still cleaning up."

Two kids? Steve was puzzled but tried not to look surprised. *Who could that have been?*

Mr. Hellums continued, "They'd gathered-up the rest of the airplane parts and threw it all in their car. Then they'd pulled-up all the damaged crop, shucked the ears, and put 'em into two big baskets. They were about to drive them up to me when I met up with them. I bet there weren't more than fifty ears ruined total. Crop's 'bout ready to go now anyway. No big loss, really. I'm just glad you're okay, son."

Mrs. Hellums turned toward the barbecue grill and raised the huge metal lid. Smoke went everywhere.

Steve's mind was reeling. It couldn't have been Alan, Mr. Non-team Player. It wasn't Charms. He had been at the casino, an hour's drive away. How else would he have gotten that C-note?

Mr. Hellums then pointed at Charms, who was on the other side of the tent. "That's the boy right there!"

Mrs. Hellums said, "Leroy, clean your glasses. That's Charms. He's the one who rang our doorbell last night."

Mr. Hellums interjected, "But that ain't the girl. The one at the field was a lot taller. Skinnier, too. Looked like one of those uppity New York fashion models. Big sunglasses that covered half her face. Nice enough, though. Pretty thing. I mean a *really* pretty thing."

Mrs. Hellums shook her head in disgust without turning towards them.

"Well, if you like that sort of thing," he concluded, but with a mischievous smile.

It suddenly dawned on Steve that she must have been the girl who dropped off Charms earlier at Denny's. Charms must have come up with a real lulu of a story to get her out there at dawn after having gambled all night!

The old man continued, "Anyways, he said he would like to take the missus and me to the Country Wide Buffet on Tuesday night, in exchange for the bad ears. He had some free coupons for Alaskan King Crab Night. He told me to hold onto them for him. I like crab." He reached in his front pocket and presented them like they were grand prize winning stubs at a raffle. Steve glanced at them; they were gift certificates, not free coupons. Charms, like every other college student, always knew down to the penny how much (or rather how little) he had in his account.   Scratch that: MoJo never knew her bank balance.

Nonetheless, Charms probably blew his entire bank balance buying those gift certificates at the Country Wide Buffet last night. Then he went to the casino afterwards to do some replenishment work at the tables. That's why he had that one hundred dollar bill at Denny's. It made perfect sense now, except for how the girl came into the picture.

"Me, too! They're hard to eat, but good eating." Mrs. Hellums announced, then turned away to check on the pork.

Steve smiled. "May I join you as well on Tuesday?"

"Well, sure," he said, then slapped Steve's shoulder, "Provided you ain't gonna fly us there!" Mr. Hellums laughed loudly, then began coughing and laughing when some smoke filled his lungs. When he got his breath back, he got serious, "Listen, you kids are awfully nice and considerate. I got a boy, fifty years old. He moved out to California years ago. Never married. Works in some big law firm. I hear from him on Christmas and sometimes on my birthday. He never comes to visit. Guess he's just too uppity to come back to Kernsville. I got to say you two young men need to teach my son a thing or two about being considerate."

Steve responded, "Well, sir. I got a *daddy*, also fifty years old. Seems I only hear from him when I've done something wrong. You could teach him a thing or two as well!"

"What could *you* have ever done wrong?"

"Sir, I'll tell you over dinner on Tuesday. Deal?" Steve extended his hand.

"Deal!" Mr. Hellums shook his hand and slapped his other shoulder. That one was really sore, but Steve never let it show. He just smiled, not because of this delightful elderly couple, but because of Charms' thoughtfulness. ✈

No sooner had he turned away to resume working, Steve came eye-to-eye with a tall man who boomed his baritone voice at him, "That boy a friend of yours?" He was not happy.

And he was pointing at Alan.

"Yes, sir, his name is Al—"

"Get his ass off my church property."

"Excuse me?!"

"You, too."

"And you are?"

"Jack Zimmerman."

Rats. What has Alan done?! "Sir, whatever he did to offend you, I'm sure it was an accident. Can I get him to apologize? Would that be okay?"

"No."

"I'll be right back," he announced, not taking no for an answer.

Steve marched right over to Alan, leaving Professor Zimmerman standing motionless, arms crossed. One quick glance behind him and Steve noted that now Zimmerman had his hands resting on his hips. He would not stay there long. Steve jerked him by the shoulder and asked, "What the hell did you do to Zimm?"

Alan glanced at the man twenty-five feet away, then looked back at Steve. "That's Zimm?! Aw, shit. Well, lemme tell you he's a ass-bite."

"Okay, time for damage control. Don't say a word unless it's "I'm sorry."

"That's two words."

"See? Stop it and follow me!"

They marched right up to Professor Zimmerman who had not changed his posture at all, hands still on his hips.

Steve's mind was swimming. He began, "Professor Zimmerman, I don't know what he said to you, but he didn't know who you were and would never have been intentionally rude."

Since Steve used the title Professor, Zimmerman asked, "Are you boys at Dexter?"

Simultaneously they said "Yes, sir," and "No."

No?! Steve couldn't believe Alan just said no and he was left speechless for a pregnant pause.

Alan said, arms crossed, "No, right now I'm standing here sweating in a church parking lot. Later on I'll be at Dexter."

"Smart ass."

"Arthropod."

Steve covered his eyes in disbelief.

"Get your sorry asses off my church property."

Steve said, "Hey, wait a minute. What kind of language is that to use, on church property? Seems like perhaps you may have provoked him a little. Can't we all just calm down and—"

Instantly, Professor Zimmerman took both hands and shoved Steve. Totally unexpecting this, he swayed backwards. His foot snagged on a folding chair and down he went, taking two more chairs and a card table with him. The professor wasn't trying to push him down; he just wanted to let him know he wasn't kidding around when he wanted them to leave. He also immediately regretted what he'd done when the commotion resulted with the clanging chairs.

Alan simply turned and started walking toward the car.

MoJo and Charms turned to see what the noise was all about.

Mrs. Hellums put down her basting bulb and rushed the twenty feet over to Steve, who was climbing up clumsily, making even more noise with the metal chairs banging into each other. "Are you okay, Steve?"

Professor Zimmerman offered Steve his hand. He had to do something, after all. Did anyone see him, he wondered.

He took the professor's hand, rose, and looked at her. "Yes, ma'am. Clumsy me. I tripped on a chair." He looked Zimmerman straight in the eye. He sensed Zimmerman's fear of knowing he had been way out of line. Then he quickly came up with a plan for Zimmerman to save face while at the same time leaving the premises. "Professor Zimmerman noticed my friend Alan was looking like he was about to pass out from heat stroke, so he ordered him home to cool off for a while. I was turning to run over to the car and drive him home, when I tripped. I'll be right back." He nodded at them and jogged away to catch up with Alan.

Mrs. Hellums looked at Zimm and said, "Professor, looks like you're God's hero today!"

He said nothing as he realized Steve saved him from the embarrassment of a distinguished professor of engineering violently losing his temper at a student at a church function. The professor smiled at her and nodded. He looked back towards Steve, but he was already gone. ✈

Alan cranked on the AC to full blast, and was about to put the car in reverse, when Steve ran around the front, opened the passenger door, and jumped in. They exchanged glances. Both were upset on many levels.

Alan wasn't the least bit apologetic. "Look, I didn't know who he was at the time and let me tell you: he's trouble. He's a total whack job. You could charge him with battery, you know."

"He knows he totally lost his cool. But he also knows I let him off the hook, let him save face. Something else must be happening in his life for him to go off on us like that."

"So, what now?"

Steve pulled out his phone. "We call MoJo and Charms. Let them schmooze him. We're out of the game at this point." ✈

Chapter Five

The extra money over and above fifty thousand would be crucial, the group determined. Four hours of working and reworking the spreadsheets, yet Alan kept coming up with the same general amounts. He presented the other three with the bad news: $74,500. Some of the dollar figures had been computed previously, based on some calls that Alan had made when doing his own research on this project. Most of the cost would be associated with the manufacturing of a huge, glass-like plate containing six point four billion dots that could be turned on or off individually, creating an image of each slice, much like the pixels on a computer monitor. However, unlike a monitor, these dots had to withstand being zapped with a large laser, so the material behind this plate would either get "cooked" or not, depending on whether the area was being shielded by a dot that was turned on.

"There's no way we're going to sell Zimmerman on anteing-up the extra twenty-four thousand dollars on an unproven idea." Charms concluded. He rubbed his face and looked at his watch: eleven P.M. Sunday. He and MoJo had been successful in convincing Dr. Zimmerman that the endeavor was worth investigating, but now that they started adding up the equipment and supplies needed to make it actually happen, he realized they had an uphill battle ahead.

"Hey, we can do this in stages." Steve offered. "First, we prove-out the science. Then we demonstrate the build-up process.

Then we present this to the school to finish funding the building of the full-scale unit."

"But if Mahoney Aerospace is going to donate fifty thousand dollars to our effort, we have to at least get past the first step. That's a laser moving horizontally across a movable plane. Basically we'll have to build a CADAM system from the ground up. How much are we talking here?"

"Under a thousand, I'll bet." Alan said.

Charms crossed his arms. "So when we go to the full-scale, plane-at-once method, then none of it could be reused, right?"

"Right."

"So it's really *seventy five* thousand five hundred."

"Look, this thing has to bond carbon pieces together as a single layer as well as bond to a temporary voidable lattice. It has to bond perfectly to the underlying layer as well and these carbon molecules must align properly to get the strength we need. It's going to take a seven thousand degree Celsius shot made simultaneously across an eighty thousand by eighty thousand grid in order to get the resolution we need for the maximum size of the structure. We can't make this thing ourselves. It's going to take someone like Sanyo or LG to do this. I talked to them and they have the means to do it."

"So, what's to keep them from stealing our idea?" asked MoJo.

"They're only making the grid. They won't know how we're going to use it or what the other parts are."

Steve chimed in, "So what are the risks?"

Alan wanted them to understand the degree of thought he'd given to this project. "Look, here's what we're talking about. First, we smear a mixture of Carbon and a secondary material across the preceding layer. Then we zap the whole thing with an intense laser, only there's a grid of six point four billion dots that will either shade the underlying material or let the laser light go through.

Either the carbon power bonds or the secondary material does, due to the residual heat. There are two major issues: 1) the blocking grid has to be completely clean and pure, able to withstand the intense heat generated by the bounce-back from the darkened pixels and 2) we need to guide the laser light evenly across the entire grid."

The three others absorbed these risks for a few seconds, then Steve asked, "So, give me your honest opinion, can we do this? Is this gonna work?"

"Absolutely. But I can't do it without software, chemical analysis, and *electricals*," he added, nodding toward him, then MoJo, then Charms.

Steve closed his notebook with a definitive thump. "Then let's prove it first on paper, present it to the Chem Department, get their blessing, then pitch it to Zimm. I say 'Let's' but I really mean MoJo and Charms. Me and Alan shouldn't get near Zimm any time soon."

Alan said, "You mean, 'Alan and I.'"

"Whatever." ✈

Professor Zimmerman was back in his office. It was late and he wasn't happy. After chumming with the Dean of the Faculty and the Chancellor at that nasty revival all day, he had spent many hours trying to fix the last week's expense records and it wasn't going smoothly. Some of the receipts were illegible, and since these had already been entered into the department's accounting system, it made it hard to duplicate the fake receipts. Two years ago he never thought he'd be skimming funds; but then he never intended to have a gambling problem, either. He would buy junk lab equipment on eBay, then create fake receipts showing the full price, and pocket the difference. His "associates" had created five lab equipment distributors, each with a VOIP answering machine, so if anyone in Accounting ever had a question and called one of them, she would get a message and Zimmerman would be able to get someone to phone back. Fortunately, the scheme was working well over the past eighteen months. He was paying back his debts on schedule. Two more years, he thought, and this nightmare would be over. He would continue sucking-up to his boss by attending their church and contributing to his charities. Long since tenured, he hated every bit of this, but he couldn't afford to have any enemies, should any of this subterfuge surface. He, of all people, knew about the probabilities and statistics regarding generalized gambling. But he thought he was also smart enough to beat the house.

He wasn't. Now, gritty and greasy from hanging out under a hot tent all day, there he sat spending extra time after hours trying to be careful that he won't get caught with a discrepancy in the books. He was on the edge and totally frazzled. He thought, *Did I really shove a kid today? How stupid.* ✈

"Hey, Mad Scientist. I got your secondary material." Charms first checked with MoJo, who validated his research, before making the call to Alan.

"You do?" Alan put down his guitar and walked over to his desk. "You know, Play Dough becomes brittle under intense heat."

"You a funny dude. Listen, how about just plain old silica? It mixes well with the carbon powder and is stable and nonconductive in this environment. It also turns to plasma at the carbon transition temperatures, but coalesces under the dots into plain old glass."

"How the hell do you know about this?"

"I Google'd it. Seems like you're not the only person who has his Junior Chemistry Set opened, doing nanotube experiments." Charms then stopped for a second but when Alan didn't say anything, he finished with, "MoJo agrees."

"I thought you were just an Electrical Engineer."

"Shall I remind you of Benjamin Franklin's achievements? He was just a printer."

"Okay, we'll try it out in the lab tomorrow." Then Alan hung up without saying goodbye.

Charms couldn't contain his smile. ✈

Chapter Six

As Charms and Steve waited outside the Country Wide Buffet restaurant for the Hellums to show up, Charms told Steve about the success he and MoJo had creating glass and carbon nanotubes fused together with a small laser at the Chem lab. They had to explain some of their activities to the lab manager, a nervous grad student making minimum wage trying to keep the undergrads from maiming themselves. Protective eyewear, gloves, emergency procedures and lab protocols—it was dizzying and maddening to have to sit and listen to the lab manager before finally getting the experiment organized. It took all afternoon, but they got the results immediately.

Charms presented Steve with a chip of material about the size of a guitar pick. It was clear on the left side, fuzzy in the middle, and opaque on the right. "This part is glass, and this part is nanotube, sort of."

"What did you shield it with?"

"Well, we tried all sorts of stuff, but in the end it was just rubber from an innertube."

"Didn't it destroy the rubber?"

"Oh yeah, and it stunk up the place. But it wasn't on long enough to burn through immediately. Problem is, it outgasses quickly, which causes the blurring effect. We'll have to find something else as a permanent shielding material, but at least we managed to show the process works."

"Not exactly a crisp transition from glass to carbon."

"No, but then again, we can use better light isolation when we get to full-scale production."

Steve smiled as he saw Mr. and Mrs. Hellums get out of their car. "I guess we need to organize our findings."

Charms said, "I'll put Alan to work on it," then yelled, "Hey there!" towards the elderly couple. They smiled and waved back as they locked the car door and joined them.

Mrs. Hellums wore an outfit suitable for church, as did Mr. Hellums, albeit accoutered with a tattered John Deere hat, obviously emblematic of his farmer's pride. The Country Wide Buffet restaurant was a venerable trough of calories and saturated fat. Everything was either deep-fried or laden with sugar, and that was just fine by them.

"We sure appreciate the dinner invite," Mrs. Hellums said with a smile.

Steve replied, "It's sure nice to have new friends."

"Family," said Mr. Hellums.

"Family," said Steve, returning the smile.

Steve wasn't just feeding them a line to keep them on his good side, given that he damaged their crop a couple of days ago. His own father had been so distant and disapproving of him; it was nice to have someone give him a firm handshake and a pat on the shoulder, extending his trust and friendship so easily.

Steve surveyed the four aisles of food, complete with steam and hot lamps. He was hungry, but always stayed away from the truly bad stuff. He dished up some steaming broccoli, turkey slices, and a basic salad. Charms, on the other hand, went straight for the fried catfish, fried okra, French fries, and cherry cobbler.

They all sat at a wooden booth with high backs separating them from the other patrons. A fat but pleasant lady with a tight-fitting waitress skirt offered some sweet tea from a pitcher. All accepted, though Steve would have preferred water. He regretted his decision when he tasted the sugary-sweet concoction. He could feel his teeth rotting and thought about his insulin level spiking as he drank it. One glass would be his limit.

"So, Steve. What's your big secret?" Mr. Hellums asked, wiping his chin after chomping on a big piece of fried chicken.

Steve's mouth was full, but gave him a "what do you mean?" expression.

"You said at the revival that you had done something wrong."

Steve held a finger up while he swallowed his food, then said, "Well, I used to be a student at M.I.T. and I got in trouble with a report and they threw me out."

"What kind of trouble?" Mrs. Hellums wasn't trying to castigate him; she genuinely wanted to know.

Steve told them the whole story. How he didn't think his grade was fair and wanted to prove that he found a weak link in the Command and Control structure of ICBMs. He admitted he had a tendency to go overboard, but this had been a real mistake on his part because he didn't consider the ramifications of taking it as far as he did.

When he was finished with the story, both Hellums were shaking their heads, understanding the pain and humiliation Steve experienced in being taken from the top of the heap to hitting rock bottom. Charms had heard the story two years before, but had forgotten about the embarrassing headlines in the Chicago papers, how humiliated Steve's prominent father had been. Steve was left with six hundred twelve dollars in the bank, unemployed with a beater truck, and no place to go.

What Charms did remember, however, was Steve's attitude when he first met him: "Stuff happens." He was sure Steve must have had his own private moments where he must have broken down—how could he not have—but Charms had never seen one iota of self-pity. Now, as Steve finished the story of how MoJo had encouraged him to come to Dexter, he realized that Steve was really a first-class person. In spite of all the subsequent rejections and job denials, he was now an honor student with a double major of Aeronautical Engineering and Computer Sciences, without one dime of help from his rich father until last semester. After proving himself again, his father finally loaned him twenty thousand dollars at prime plus two percent so he could build the airplane as part of his senior design project. Just last month, his loan repayment of six hundred twelve dollars per month was reduced to a fixed five percent when he refinanced it through a local bank. He thought his father would have been pleased, but instead threatened to stick him with a penalty for early repayment, even though no early payoff penalty was specified. Charms was glad he didn't have a father like Steve's.

Steve, however, knew his father and understood. Malcolm Brinkley married Lizzy twenty years ago, and nine months later, along came Steve. The three Brinkleys struggled as Malcolm got his MBA, followed immediately by his PhD in Economics from Northwestern all while working full-time at Atcronine, LLC, an investment firm on the thirtieth floor of the Sears Tower. Lizzy, on the other hand, was left to raise young Steve by herself. Malcolm resented Lizzy's attempts to get Malcolm to slow down and enjoy life a little. Malcolm left at five thirty A.M. and usually got back after nine P.M., except on Saturdays, when he was usually home by three. Steve remembered those Sunday mornings sitting in his father's lap as they watched Meet the Press. Malcolm used to explain why the Fed Chairman's job was the most important job in Washington—much more important than the President. He also remembered his father's advice: Become an expert in math and science.

One late night a year or so ago, Charms and Steve were sitting on the two rocking chairs in front of the small airport ops building, sipping on beers as they watched the rotating beacon flash green and white against the black sky. They had worked all day at their nearby hangar gathering together the engine, avionics, yokes, control rods, just about everything they could get out of an old Piper Tri-Pacer they had bought for eight thousand bucks. These parts would become the design specs from which they would construct the sleek fuselage and supercritical wing and stab of Steve's Aero 411 project. Steve was in it for the grade, but Charms was in it for the avionics, and for the fun. Steve had his private pilot's license with an instruments rating since he was seventeen and had about four hundred hours; Charms knew nothing about flying but was a quick study.

It was in the silence of the moment that Steve had told Charms about how his mother had died suddenly. How his father had never cried. How the father had told his eleven year old son he would have to grow up quickly. With no emotion, and less than a week after Malcolm's wife had died, he introduced Steve to a middle-aged Argentinean woman. This woman was to ensure that Steve was dressed properly, fed, and out the door in time to catch the bus to school. She was to be there when he came home, ensure that he got his homework done before doing anything else, and was in bed by nine thirty.

The housemaid was good-hearted, but the sudden loss of his mother left him all alone. It was a point of inflection in his life, as he told Charms, that he could have gone either way. He made the decision to please his dad—his only family—and do well in his studies.

He did of course, but his father was still just there only a few minutes each day, and only gave Steve enough time to skim the headlines of his young life. Most Sundays it was the housemaid's day off and Steve would often pretend his mother was elsewhere in the house. But other Sundays Malcolm was off to New York, leaving Steve to watch Meet the Press alone and fend for himself.

Knowing no other lifestyle, he simply adopted his father's work ethic. He took all of the AP courses that were offered at his high school, yet still managed to excel in his other passion, long distance running. This was his only way he found to clear his mind. As he shaped up, he noticed that many of the girls suddenly took notice of him, but he just didn't have the people skills to turn any of the attention into anything more than just a few dates. Besides, his real passion was the mechanics of aviation, i.e. the mathematics, kinematics, and efficiency of flight.

He finished Carl Sandburg High School—one of Chicago's largest —with a pristine academic record, number one in his class, perfect SAT scores, and a city-wide record in the ten thousand meter race.

M.I.T. actually recruited him. He was just what they were looking for, he remembered them saying. His father seldom complimented him through his achievements, and even grumbled at the cost to educate him at the world-renowned engineering school in Cambridge, Massachusetts. But Steve knew his father and knew that somewhere inside there was a great pride in his son's achievements.

That all came to an end when the phone call came that night from the jail cell in Boston. That he had been arrested for Crimes Against the State, domestic terrorism, you name it.

Charms completely understood Steve, though they had had opposing upbringings.   Charms was the Student Council President, Man About Campus, a chick on each arm as he paraded the halls of his much smaller, more elitist high school near Joliet. He graduated first in his class as well, and originally had thought a law career from a prestigious university such as Harvard was in his future. He had applied and was shocked when he was accepted. But being the last child from a family of six children, he would have to go where the scholarships took him, which was the small but pleasant school in Central Illinois. He framed the Harvard acceptance letter, and decided he would do his graduate work there.

Charms had good counselors at Dexter, who encouraged him to pursue an undergraduate degree in a hard science or engineering field first. Then take those intellectual credentials and broadened perspectives into the field of law at a later time. You can't do it the other way, they explained. So he took a course in basic electronics; you know: Ohm's Law and the like. Most of the other students in this course already knew how electrons moved in a circuit, so he felt like he was already at a disadvantage. But he found he was able to grasp the concepts of potential, amperage, resistance, and capacitance with little difficulty. He was also delighted that everything in "Double E" (electrical engineering) could be quantified precisely with mathematics. Sometimes the math wasn't easy, which is how some of the other students opted into other less challenging courses of study—like Law.

So Steve and Charms had a common bond, that of problem-solving. Each pursued different engineering disciplines, and they certainly didn't share a common persona, but somewhere they clicked as great friends.

The Hellums could sense that the two young men sharing their booth were bright, polite and respectful. Mr. Hellums adjusted his John Deere cap, then tried to lighten the mood after hearing Steve's sad M.I.T. tale. He looked at Charms and asked, "That girlfriend of yours a model or something?"

"No, sir. Much worse. She's a lawyer."

"That pretty thing?"

"Yeah, what was she thinking?" He chuckled.

"She don't look old enough to be a lawyer."

"She's twenty-six." Charms gave Steve the double-eyebrow lift. Steve had never met this woman before. In fact, the only time he'd seen her at all was when she had dropped him off at Denny's on Sunday morning. He obviously had met her at a bar after they left the hangar late Saturday night.

"Actually, we just met. To be honest, I don't know much about her, other than she is *considerably* older than I am. I don't think it's going to turn into anything serious."

Of course not, thought Steve. Nothing ever did with Charms.

"She's so skinny she could slip through a keyhole," Mrs. Hellums added.

That comment put Charms into a trance. His mind started whirling.

Steve noticed.

So did the Hellums.

This frozen expression was quite unnerving to all, like Charms was having some sort of outer-body experience.

The Hellums looked at each other. Steve didn't know what to think or do.

Suddenly, Charms reached into his pocket and dug around for something.

He produced a small sliver of material, about the size of a guitar pick. "Mr. and Mrs. Hellums, do you know what this is?" He asked, rhetorically.

They shook their heads.

"This is half glass, and half carbon material. You just gave me a great idea."

"We did?"

"We have a project at school to make a gizmo that will build any kind of object out of this black stuff," he said, pointing at the carbon area.

"It will make, say, an airplane fuselage by stacking slices of it on top of each other like pancakes until the whole thing is made. The problem is, if any piece happens to curl under some other part, it has to be held there until subsequent layers are added to connect it to the rest of it.

Steve was listening intently, because he knew Charms had come up with something.

"We thought we'd use two different materials, like this. Then when it's done, we'd just melt the glass away, leaving the finished piece."

Mr. Hellums understood the concept perfectly. As a lifelong farmer, he knew about all things mechanical. Mrs. Hellums nodded, but was most likely not as enlightened.

"But Mrs. Hellums, you just gave me a great idea." She smiled. "This carbon stuff has weird molecular properties. When you zap it with a high amount of electricity, it forms a bond, and they glue together. But when you zap it with a super-high amount of electricity, accompanied by a strong magnetic field, the molecules align in a way that they become super-duper strong." Steve tapped his finger on his plate two, then three times, and finished Charms train of thought, "…so we use a single carbon lattice, and zap parts of it more than others."

"Bingo!"

"No need for glass?!"

"No!"

Mrs. Hellums asked, "How in the world did I give you that idea?"

"You said that girl could slip through a keyhole. What if we had a sieve with six point four million "keyholes," each latched with a Boolean bonding gate?"

"Now you lost me," said Mr. Hellums.

"Simple. We squeeze a layer of carbon through a screen, about the same mesh size that you'd have in the screen door at your house. Except picture spray-painting a Smiley Face on your screen door. The squares in the screen that have Smiley Face paint on them get super-zapped while the rest of the screen just gets a normal zap. The normal zap stuff is like thick chalk. The super-zapped stuff is, like, a hundred times stronger than steel. We just sand blast the chalk off."

Mr. Hellums asked, "How do you super-zap without messing up the electrical latch controls?"

Charms and Steve looked at each other. Here was this old man, a simple farmer living on the outskirts of a small town in Illinois. Yet he asked the question of the hour. "Mr. Hellums, are you sure you're not a professor of engineering? You just asked the question that we'll be trying to solve."

Mrs. Hellums grabbed Mr. Hellums hand and gave it a squeeze. The poor old man had a son who never called home, and a body that couldn't put in the hours needed to run the farm the way he used to. He was slowing down, and no exercise, diet, nor sheer will was going to stop the process. Only his wife knew just how depressing it was for him.

Mr. Hellums straightened up in his seat. "KISS. It means, 'Keep it Simple, Stupid." The two young men smiled. "I was about Neil Armstrong's age when he walked on the moon. I followed the whole space race with awe. They came across problems they'd never considered before. And they solved them all, one at a time. I remember watching Walter Cronkite interview one of those eggheads who designed the Lunar Module and he told him that he wasn't really that smart, he just had horse sense. He said the most amazing inventions are made using one simple axiom, 'Keep it Simple, Stupid.' I always remembered that."

"Mr. and Mrs. Hellums, you'll never know just how much this dinner has meant to me," Steve said, seemingly out of nowhere.

"Us, too. You don't treat us like has-beens, and we really appreciate it."

"If it works, we'll call it 'The Hellums Method' in your honor," said Charms. They all smiled, then got up and headed for the dessert bar. Steve came back with a double-chocolate ice cream with hot fudge and sprinkles. He'll run it off later, he reasoned. ✈

"Let's go straight to The Pisser," said Steve as they got into their car. They had promised the Hellums that they would keep them up to speed on their project, and would do their best to have dinner at their farm very soon. He checked the time: Tuesday night, nine thirty. Steve knew Alan's band, "Covalence," would be beginning their set about now over at The Puissant Bar, a.k.a. The Pisser.

"Hang on," Charms said, dialing a number into his phone. "Let's see if our chemist agrees that dual-level bonding will work. I don't want El Jerko dumbing me down if I'm wrong."

Steve started the car, and put it into reverse as Charms began speaking, "Hey MoJo, question. What happens when you give the carbon elixir just a little jolt?"

Steve was only hearing one side of the conversation, but could easily tell how it was going. "So what's the consistency?" "Rubber or chalk?" "Can we add interstitials?" "I see." "How do we isolate the charge to a three micron area and assure bonding to the underlying layer?" "When can you try it?" "No, we're heading to see Alan now." "Okay, bye."

He clicked END CALL on his iPhone, then looked at Steve, smiling. "You want bad news or do you want the truth?" ✈

The band "Covalence" had already begun their first set by the time the two arrived at The Pisser. It was a seedy beer bar at the end of Broadway, just two blocks from the main campus area. The place probably started out as a nice restaurant twenty years ago, but slowly segued into its present configuration as the owner realized he didn't need to serve fine food, only cold beer.

They had just ended a song, and someone walking in reached over and dropped a couple of dollars into the big red paint bucket at the edge of the small stage. Obviously someone either knew the band or the gratuity method. "Feed the Band" was written in black marker on the front of the red bucket. There was probably twelve dollars in it already.

Before the applause died down, a steady, energetic beat of the bassist and drummer began and made Steve and Charms nod their heads in time. A quick look around and it was clear the band had the patrons' full attention.

The rhythm guitarist started playing, melodically syncopated to the main beat, upping the ante of Alan's upcoming solo. More and more heads were nodding to the beat.

Alan used to remark that lyrics were just an interlude between guitar solos. He sang a verse of some unintelligible lyrics, followed by a slight pause as he stepped to the very edge of the stage. A single blue spot light was pointed at that particular part of the stage and Alan knew it. The audience was about to get something good.

When he started the guitar solo, everyone slowly lowered his or her beer mug and focused on Alan's left hand. He played four bars of incredibly intricate music with his picking hand behind his back. He played with only his left hand, creating notes by pounding his fingers down to create the note, or pulling-off a note which resulted in the lower fingered note being played. Of course, this was being orchestrated so quickly it was unclear even how he was doing it. This legato-style solo was simply astounding, but instead of allowing people to clap at the end of the run, he brought his right hand to the fret board and went into a sequence of two-hand tapping, essentially doubling the speed of the Mixolydian run.

"Good. Night. Nurse!," yelled Charms. He had never heard Alan play before and the music was so loud no one could hear him anyway. Steve smiled at Charms and concurred non-verbally.

When Alan finished the first solo, he eased back to the microphone and sang the second verse. But no one could have possibly heard what the lyrics were because the applause was almost as loud as the music.

Then came the second solo. All great composers know that you must have a crescendo followed by a climax. Alan didn't disappoint. He went up twelve frets to an octave higher and began a dazzling speed-picking regimen that included minor to major transitions in perfect concert with the key changes with the other band members, string-skipping sequences, and finally leading to a sustained final note with a huge vibrato, his picking hand pointing to the crowd, who started cheering wildly as he held the note. Suddenly—almost violently—the song ended, and the crowd went wild. People walking down the street stopped, then walked in out of curiosity.

The third song began, but this time at a much slower pace. Alan had clearly worked out a gig list that kept the crowd enthralled but properly paced. Steve, being a big Joe Satriani fan for years, recognized the gift that Alan possessed. Charms, not a guitarist aficionado, nonetheless knew that he wasn't just a typical guitar strummer.

"I had no idea!" Said Charms to Steve, still almost yelling.

"And this is just a hobby for him. He's a better physicist."

"Unbelievable. Unbelievable," said Charms, mostly to himself.

After four more songs, each with a different style and each one a masterpiece, the band took a break. An older waitress with breasts too large for her Def Leppard t-shirt pushed the red bucket through the crowd and it quickly filled with bills. Alan was behind her for a minute, then moved to the side and worked his way through the crowd, doing some low-fives with a couple of dudes at the bar, and made his way back to Steve and Charms.

"So you have a revelation to share?" Alan said to Charms.

"Dude. You rock!" He was actually awe-struck. His ears were still ringing from the volume of the music. The last tune was so catchy that Charms was actually nodding his head as it continued to reverberate in his head.

"Of course I do, but that's no revelation."

Charms realized that once again, he was being mentally outperformed. "Okay, so here's the deal: we extrude the carbonic elixir through a grid, and gate each one with a dual-level charge. We make 'chalk' and 'tungsten,' then we just wipe off the chalk."

"So now you're either an alchemist or you're speaking metaphorically."

"Uhm, I choose the latter. The science is easier."

"Hmm. Maybe we should have MoJo test it."

"She's sneaking into the lab right now. I called her with my idea thirty minutes ago. She said it might be possible. Then she called me five minutes ago to say she couldn't wait until morning. She's heading over there now."

"Then let's go."

"Wait, don't you have a gig going on?"

"I do this for gas money. The bar has an iPod hooked up to those speakers, and a playlist called 'Beer Drinking Music.'"

"Why aren't you on tour?"

"Einstein played the viola. Good thing it wasn't his primary gig, don't you agree?"

"Come on. You're a better guitarist than Einstein was a viola—isst." Charms looked at the both of them, then shrugged-off the sibilated error. "Hey I'd rather listen to more guitar playing and drink some more beers than stand around a lab watching MoJo set up an experiment. She's just going to zap it at different amperage levels and see where the differentials occur."

"Yeah, you're right. We're playing next weekend at the GC BoB at the Charter One Pavilion at the old Meigs Field. First prize is $25,000. Band gets ten, I get fifteen. We don't have many more practice opportunities."

"You've already won it?"

"Probably. We're better than anyone else—I've listened to all of them on MySpace."

"And you keep fifteen of the twenty-five? Won't that piss-off the others?"

"They're coat-tailing me, and I need the money for this project. It's the deal I offered them and they accepted."

Alan truly was arrogant.

Steve said, "That's okay. She's going to call me when she gets some results. This could very well not work, anyway. There's a narrow range of how resilient the secondary lattice must be to support the primary structure."

"Fine," Alan said. Then he got Ms. Def Leppard's attention and pointed to the two. She nodded, grabbed two beer mugs with one hand and filled them from the tap for them. "Sandy will take care of you if you tip her well."

Then he went back to the stage to tune up his Bullet Proof boutique guitar and set up the stomp boxes for the next set of songs. For once, Charms was in no mood to hit on a chick. Even as Sandy leaned her large breasts into them and placed the frosty mugs on the table, he simply nodded to her and started talking about process development. Charms was focused. ✈

MoJo was always nervous around electricity, particularly high voltage stuff. She was alone in the large expansive lab, which was of course against the rules, but rules weren't really elements of her standard operandi.

The school wasn't like, say, Ohio State, where each department had its own fully-staffed lab. The Biology Department, the Engineering Department, and the Department of Physics all used the same lab. It was loosely partitioned into different disciplines, but the consolidation of equipment under one set of fluorescent lights made sense to the budget people.

Carbon was cheap. Really cheap. And it was neither volatile nor hazardous. Thus, it wasn't in a locked cabinet like the mercury. But the abundance of carbon and its peculiar characteristics were reasons why so much attention was being given to the element nowadays.

She didn't need more than twenty grams of it to do four or five runs.

The equipment was easy to set up, too. Just a series of insulators, two probes connected to a variable source of power. She set up the circuit breaker limits, tested the DC voltage, then documented what she was doing. It's always the same method. Keep the process to a single variable, which would be amperage.

It was so quiet in the lab that the lack of noise scared her. She was breaking the rules, but what if she electrocuted herself. What if the carbon sent out molten pellets in every direction?

Why couldn't this just wait until morning? Bad things happen after dark.

Suddenly, a booming voice erupted from behind, "The hell are you doing here?!"

She screamed like a baby, jerked around and threw her ball-point pen at the general direction of the voice. It was a knee-jerk defensive reaction made from pure fear. The pen went high and hit a fluorescent light. The light popped off, then broke into two pieces, one of them dangling from its cradle, the other crashing onto another steel tabletop. The noise was deafening. So she screamed again and almost collapsed from fear, her adrenaline level rising even further.

She didn't recognize Professor Zimmerman as he stepped forward. She leaped to the side, grabbed a Pyrex glass, and held it up in a throwing position. "Back off, dick head."

"Where's the lab manager?" He asked, knowing the answer already.

"Whu—" The room quieted down. Slowly she lowered the glass as it sunk in to whom she was speaking. "I'm—I'm sorry sir. You scared me to death."

"Answer me!"

She jerked again and dropped the Pyrex glass. It shattered loudly and she jumped back into the heavy stainless steel table.

He just stood there. He was menacing. Not an ugly man, moreover a rough-looking middle-aged man with an ugly disposition.

"Listen, I'm MoJo Barnes. We met on Sunday at the revival. I was here to test—"

"I don't give a shit what you're here for. The lab is closed. You signed the rule book. You know it's a two-person safety system we have here."

"I know. Listen, he just stepped out for a minute."

"Who?"

"Uhm, my lab partner."

"Call him."

"Excuse me?"

"You heard me. Call him. All you kids have cell phones. I want to talk to him."

Oh, no. She reached in her pocket, her hands shaking so hard she could barely press the numbers." *God, please let him get us out of this.*

"Don't say a word, just give the phone to me."

She held it at arm's length to him and inched forward. He jerked it from her hand. ✈

As luck would have it, Charms had to go to the bathroom, and the band had not yet started playing again. He was just drying off his hands when his phone rang. It said "MoJo" on the screen, along with a picture of her sticking her tongue out at him. He smiled, clicked ANSWER, then said, "Good news?"

"Who's this?" asked a booming voice.

That's not MoJo. What's going on? "Wait a minute. Who are you?! Is MoJo all right?"

"Where are you supposed to be?"

"Listen, if you don't tell me who you are RIGHT NOW I'm going to call nine-one-one."

"This is Professor Zimmerman."

Charms mind went into hyperdrive. MoJo is supposed to be in the lab. The lab is closed. Zimm is using her phone. She had to have been caught.

"I'm, uhm, downstairs."

"Where, downstairs?"

So he is *in the lab.* Charms had to think fast. "Professor Zimmerman, I swear to you as God as my witness I'm in the bathroom." *Just not the bathroom in your building.*

"Why downstairs? There's one on this floor."

"Professor, she's not doing anything until I get back, I promise. We both signed the rule book. Doesn't she have her ledger open on the table, simply making notes?" He knew she was a stickler for detail and would be documenting everything.

He looked over at the lab table. Sure enough, her ledger was open. She did have a pen in her hand. She had thrown it at him. "You haven't answered my question."

"Sir, I got a severe case of diarrhea coming in here. I never made it to the second floor. I've been in here for an hour. This is so embarrassing, especially with a female lab partner. I told her to just arrange the equipment and start documenting. I thought I'd run home and change. That was a couple of hours ago. Either I get hit with another salvo, or someone's between me and the front door. All she's been doing is waiting on me. She's your best student. Oh, this is so embarrassing. Jeez this is embarrassing..."

He pulled the phone away and asked, "So you haven't done any testing?"

"No, sir," she answered. She thought about saying something else, but it was still unclear to her exactly what Charms had said to him.

He pulled the phone back to his ear and asked, "You need me to call the paramedics?" To this, MoJo would have smiled, had she not still been shaking.

Charms had walked from the sink into the bathroom's stall, then gave it a good flush. He held the phone to the gurgling toilet."No sir, I'm feeling a little better now. I just kind of made a mess here. This is so embarrassing. Can you tell her to just pack up and meet me at seven A.M. back here?"

He didn't say anything. He just hung up, then said, "He's not coming back. Don't let me ever catch you in this lab alone again."

He was already turning to leave before she could say, "Yes, sir."

The room was again quiet. She suddenly burst into tears and began cleaning up. ✈

Steve was waiting for her when she got to her apartment. After she calmed down, she called Charms back to give him the full story, then said she was heading straight home.

He immediately repeated everything to Steve and Alan, and Steve offered to meet her at her apartment. Charms offered to join them, but Steve said he'd take care of it. Just after the initial call, Charms considered running the half-mile from the bar to the lab building, just to complete the story. But one thing he learned was once someone is convinced, don't try to convince them.

So Steve left Charms at The Pisser and walked the four blocks over to her apartment row, sat down on her steps, and waited.

He didn't have to wait long. "Oh, Steve. I'm so glad you're here." She fumbled for her keys. She seemed to be shaking, quite unusual for her. He studied her. He'd never seen her this way.

Suddenly half of her purse's contents spilled onto the floor mat. She began to cry, shocking him at the level of emotion she was displaying. As she started to reach down, he grabbed her and gave her a hug. She buried her face into his shoulder and remained motionless for a half a minute. Suddenly she retreated, saying, "He's such an evil man. I've never been so scared of someone."

He kneeled down and grabbed her stuff. She quickly unlocked the door and they went inside.

She didn't even turn on a light. She grabbed his hand and pulled him through the small studio kitchen and into the bedroom. There was plenty of light in the room, even with all of the lights off. The room was a mess, as usual. The thin plastic window shades had creases in several areas, allowing the street light from across the alleyway to come in and illuminate everything as striped amber light.

She pulled off her shirt, dropped her jeans, and crept into bed. Her white bra and panties seemed to illuminate against her dark skin. He took off his shirt, but left on his shorts and lay down beside her. This was not the time. She rolled into him and hugged him hard.

Though Steve and MoJo had been secretly dating for almost four years now, he was still awkward at both giving and receiving affection. She was no better. Fortunately, it made their affair easier to keep a secret.

Her parents were initially very impressed with him. However, after the M.I.T. dismissal and the front page news stories, she was given an ultimatum: drop him or pay for college yourself.

Later, when her parents found out he had moved to Kernsville, they became enraged. They changed the tuition loans to her name, removed themselves as cosigners, and only continued to pay the monthly installments with the understanding that she was not to have contact with him. The threat worked, or so they thought.

After a few years, she did convince them that she was no longer interested in him emotionally, but she had no choice in seeing him because they shared some classes. In fact, he was good at helping her with her homework and her grades were proof positive. They said okay to the occasional interaction, provided it was just for school-related work. They had been become very adept at keeping their hands off each other in public, even their closest friends had no idea. Both of them knew that eventually her parents would come around, but their secret relationship had worked thus far. It made no sense risking anything at this point.

They were cheek to cheek and she realized he had beer on his breath. That was somewhat out of character for him on a weeknight. She whispered, "How are we going to get anything done through him? He scares me and he hates me."

He stroked her hair and pulled away a little to look at her. Physically, she was very attractive: a perfect body with a flat, thin waist and the curviest hips he'd ever seen, especially when she was laying in bed on her side. Her personality was, however, another matter. She was all business. Even when they were alone, she showed little if no emotion. Tonight was the exception rather than the rule.

She was his first and only. He wasn't really sure what being in love was supposed to feel like, but suspected this was the real deal...

...In fact, when the rest of the world turned on him, she was the only one who still believed in him. The news media had hounded him after the felony charges were filed. His dad flew him back to Chicago after he was released on bail, but was nowhere to be found when he landed. He had to take a cab home from Midway Airport to Orland Park and the gated golf community where his dad lived. The guard at the community's entranceway kept out the press, thank goodness. However, he still felt like he was still imprisoned, not that he had any place to go anyway. He sat around the house for three days watching CNN and eating frozen pizzas, trying to make sense of what had just transpired. Just days before, he had been a rising sophomore at M.I.T. Now his name was being plastered across the networks as a home-grown terrorist. His capture had been a success story for the DoD and the FBI on an otherwise slow news day. When his dad got the lawyers involved, it only took a day to get the major charges dropped and several more months to get him completely exonerated. However, M.I.T. had been given a black eye, and Steve was not to be invited back. Now back home, the phone had been ringing off the hook, and each time he looked at the caller I.D. he hoped it would be his dad, the big investment firm president, who would be there with the good news that he pulled some strings, patted some backs, and got them to reconsider. Instead, it was TV and newspaper reporters trying to get an exclusive with the alleged ICBM saboteur. The story was just too exciting to let die just because all charges had been dropped.

One call came in and he looked at the number: "Out of Area" He let the call go straight to the answering machine, like all the others. A female voice said, "Mr. Brinkley. This is Monica Barnes. If you remember, I was Steve's girlfriend in high school and I need to talk to him. My number—" Steve immediately interrupted the message and said hi. She was still his girlfriend, even though they were a year and hundreds of miles apart. Yet that phone call saved his life, he concluded once. It made him shudder to think what would have happened had she, too, abandoned him....

..."We stay professional with him. We don't lose our cool."

"There's something seriously wrong with him."

"Ya think? Here's a grown man who shoves a student to the ground at a church revival. Here's a guy who scares the daylights out of a female student in a lab at night. He's definitely got a screw loose."

"Who do we complain to?"

"He's the head of the department. He's untouchable."

She studied his face through the dim, filtered light. Her fear appeared to turn to determination. "I'm gonna own his ass."

"Be careful what you wish for."

After a slight pause, she added, "Who's in control here?"

He smiled and said, "You are."

"Who's the luckiest man alive?"

This time he smiled. "I am."

She rolled on top and kissed him. ✈

Chapter Seven

Z immerman took his time. He walked the duo of Ms. Monica Joanne Barnes and Mr. John Ruess over to two small chairs in front of his massive office desk. They weren't late arriving, but MoJo panicked when they had four minutes to go up a flight of stairs, yet Charms said he had to first stop by the printer in the Student Conference Room before heading up to his office. Now Zimmerman slowly paraded around the desk and took his seat in an equally massive leather chair. He pulled a large packet over from the left and slowly opened it, extracting a few pages. Next to the packet was a FedEx envelope, opened. Only then did he look up.

MoJo feared and despised every aspect of this creep.

"How are you feeling, Mr. Ruess?"

MoJo had never heard of Charms referred to as 'Mr. Ruess.' It sounded a bit patronizing.

"Sir, I'm much better. Thank you." Charms was quite comfortable. MoJo, on the other hand, was a mess.

"Where are the other two, Mr. Brinkley and Mr. Overman?"

MoJo only found out Alan's last name when she typed-up the report three days ago. In the premeeting conference, they actually discussed all four of them showing up. However, Steve immediately dismissed the idea, stating that it might be best if he never sees Steve or Alan again. At least not any sooner than at the Bernoulli Award Banquet. They had all chuckled. In all seriousness, Steve said there was no advantage in having the other two present.

"Sir, they are at the lab, further resolving the inflection points where the carbon properties change. Time is of the essence."

Over the past week they had managed to put together a series of experiments that validated their multi-extrusion process. The results were undeniable: they were onto something big, something that could possible cut the cost of manufacturing complex parts by a factor of ten when compared to creating traditional aircraft assemblies. No more stamping, welding, bending metal, rivets. All this took time, and time was money. All of this took human intervention, and humans don't build stuff any more. Not and remain competitive.

Just about anything could be made as one piece or as one completed section, only limited by ensuring that any internal voids were accessible for removing the chalky carbon support material. She was excited as each experiment proved the physical characteristics of the simple carbon atom when exposed to varying levels of heat and electromagnetism. Alan was surprisingly agreeable to abandoning his original ideas of having two dissimilar materials being applied at once as the layers were laid. He also easily abandoned the idea of using an LCD array of on/off dots under a broad, intense light in favor of millions of tiny carbon "water hoses" arranged in a similar-style array over the top of the preceding layer. Each "water hose" would have a microscopic "water heater" at the end that would deliver the carbon atoms at one of two temperatures: 1) Hot and 2) Damn Hot.

No human could produce these tiny hoses and arrange them on a grid, then wire each on to a central processor. Yet, the group delved into a new engineering discipline called MEMS, or Microscopic Electro-Mechanical Systems. Essentially, you take a large working structure that has both mechanical and electrical components, then shrink it down to something so small that it could only be manufactured by a computer. Charms had studied about MEMS technology in one of his EE courses last semester. The electronics in a car's air bag system are a good example. When a car has experiences a rapid deceleration (smashes into something) or acceleration (something smashes into it), then the airbag system deploy the bag. Larger inertia-sensing systems were inconsistent and prone to failure over time. However in the past few years the deploying mechanism had been replaced by a tiny accelerometer about the size of a grain of rice, packaged inside a microchip. Inside this rice grain was a hollow dome with a gas bubble heated to a specific temperature. There were four poles— thermocouples—in each corner of the tiny dome that measured temperature. If a car were involved in an accident, this gas bubble moved toward one or two of these thermocouples. The microcircuit did the math to determine the rate of change of the temperature. At current processor speeds, extremely fast and precise G calculations could be made. Too many Gs, uh oh, deploy the bag. Works great. Lasts a long time, because there were no moving parts inside the tiny structure.

Charms believed a carbon delivery and welding system could be made at this tiny scale, too. Only there had to be millions of them arranged in a grid, so the hard part was still ahead: convincing one of the dozen or so MEMS technology companies that this was worthy of their investigation. A major hurdle was how to superheat the carbon atom as it was being delivered without destroying the delivery device itself. That's when Steve came up with the idea of doing it all in a vacuum. With the distances involved down at the micron level, the energy required to bring the atmospheric pressure down to an acceptably low level would be reasonable. In keeping with Mr. Hellums' axiom of "Keep It Simple, Stupid," Steve envisioned a tiny enclosure surrounding each MEMS device, with the vacuum powered by a venturi from the heat emitted by the mircowelding itself. A quick suck to remove most of the air, zap the carbon, let the air back in as it pulls up to make the next layer. Again, no moving parts at the micro-level.

"You came up with all this yourself?" Zimmerman asked.

Charms said, "We were fortunate to have a group comprised of an Aeronautical Engineer, a Chemist, a Physicist, and an Electrical Engineer, thinking as one. We—"

"Bullshit! The level of detail in this research is too complex for four Dexter undergrads."

Charms didn't raise his voice, he just continued, "While it's true that we didn't just rub two sticks together, we did look at the state of MEMS viability today in terms of what we need it to do. Then we built our system based on those existing capabilities. This is a landmark application of this technology, being created right here at Dexter by students in your department, sir."

MoJo was very impressed with Charms. He had a non-combative style honed from years of negotiating women out of their clothes. He looked at his adversary's needs and desires in order for him to get what he wanted.

"All we need is for you to get us the money from Mahoney Aerospace so we can fund a test fixture. There's a company in England doing MEMS work who agreed to investigate our idea using their facilities and equipment, provided they get licensing rights. I just Skype'd them this morning."

"You did what? You idiot! You told a commercial enterprise about this? Did you ever consider that they would steal this idea from you? I can't believe you are that stupid to talk to anyone about this without consulting me first." Zimmerman looked straight ahead for a moment, then slammed the folder shut and pounded on his desk in defeat. MoJo was ready to flee should he start throwing things. Charms, on the other hand, knew Zimm must have read the entire proposal and was utterly convinced that this could work. Charms wanted to smile.

"Sir, we have made the provisional patent application to the USPTO, and the company has signed the necessary NDAs." Again, Charms never raised his voice. "I have the non-disclosure agreement right here." He handed it across the wide desk to the professor. "We've got a winner here, sir."

Professor Zimmerman took a moment, regained his composure, and said, "I called Mahoney Aerospace late yesterday. They had to scale back their funding. I can only get you thirty thousand dollars. Can you do it for that?"

Charms answered, "Yes, sir. Do you think the university can make up the difference, should we experience any cost growth?"

"Not a chance. Arrange a video conference meeting with this company in England for tomorrow afternoon and let's discuss details with them. That's all." Then he waved them off.

"Thank you," said MoJo and Charms at the same time. They both got up and left his office.

Professor Zimmerman pulled the check out of the FedEx mailer. The return address was from Mahoney Aerospace. A cover letter listed the terms, schedules, rights, and disclaimers. He reread the cover letter, committing the school to provide a 1) general project description, 2) a "reasonable" hardware solution, along with its 3) final design parameters and measured performance characteristics, lastly 4) all supporting documentation. It required an administrator's signature and faxing back of the executed document before the check could be endorsed. He quickly scribbled his name then examined the check. The yellow note was endorsed with two signatures and payable to Dexter University, Department of Engineering Sciences. In the memo section, it merely said, "Bernoulli Award Competitor."

The amount of the check: $50,000. ✈

Chapter Eight

When they got outside and started walking, MoJo phoned Steve. "Good news. We're in. We got thirty thousand dollars." She was so glad to be physically away from that man.

"Why not fifty?" The voice in her phone wasn't angry, just curious.

"Zimmerman said Mahoney Aerospace scaled back the money they were giving out. Zimmerman wants to host a video conference with the London MEMS company tomorrow."

"What *London company?*"

Charms spoke directly to MoJo as she listened to Steve on the phone, "He's probably asking 'What London company?'"

She looked at Charms, stopped dead in her tracks and said, "I'll call you back."

He held up both hands, "Look, we don't have Patents Pending. And there's no MEMS company over there. Alan mentioned "rights and properties" this morning right at the end of our premeeting pow-wow, so I Googled a form, filled in "M.AriahChem PLLC" in honor of Mariah Carey—she's such a lovely woman—then printed it on the Student Conference Room's computer. I signed it and dated it. Good thing, eh? He about went ape-shit."

"So we don't have anyone lined up to do this?"

"Day's early."

She shook her head and started walking again. "How do you live on the edge like this all the time?"

"It's always windy, but the view's great. Which reminds me: gotta make a call. See ya, buh-bye." He yanked out his iPhone, turned to walk in a different direction, and started talking.

"Some day you're going to spontaneously ignite!" She yelled.

He waved his hand, acknowledging the insult, but kept walking and talking into his phone. ✈

"Turns out there actually is a MEMS research company in England, not far from the Oxford campus." Steve had printed out the web site information. "I would have called them, but it's after hours, their time."

Charms sat down and picked up the material to skim. Alan and Steve had been sitting down in the Caribou Coffee since Charms and MoJo began the meeting with Zimm, ready to answer any questions by phone, meanwhile jotting down the manufacturing requirements that needed to match the science. They could already see numerous stumbling blocks. MoJo had not yet arrived.

After a few minutes of reading, Charms reached into his backpack, pulled out his laptop and headsets, logged-into his Boingo account and was online. "Anything you want me to *not* say to this chap?"

"What chap?"

"Bronson Hensley. I'll give you boys two to one odds that he's still at work."

Charms turned the web printout around and put his thumb under the picture of a casually dressed, physically fit, young-looking middle-aged man.

Alan asked, "The chairman of the company? What, are you crazy? Even so, it's almost eleven P.M. in London."

"Put a large cold press iced coffee, touch of cream on it?"

"You're on," said Alan, taking the bait.

The Skype Internet call went through quickly. The two could only hear Charm's side of the conversation: "Good evening. John Ruess calling from the Colonies. Bronson, please."

Steve whispered to Alan, "Charms is always on a first-name basis with people he's never met."

"Okay, Thank you. Love your accent." He wrote down another number, then hung up and called the other number. One ring later and he was talking to the chairman of Hathaway Scalings, PLLC, "Bronson. Hi. John Ruess calling from Illinois. My friends call me Charms." "Yes, it's a childhood nickname, something I can't seem to shake."

He listened for a moment, then laughed hard and loud. "Well, yes, I suppose it *can* be used to my advantage. Listen, the Engineering Sciences Department at Dexter University has finalized the initial science on a carbon-welding process that looks to revolutionize manufacturing as we know it. They look to publish the findings as soon as we prove it under a scaled methodology. However, we're dealing with a bunch of crooks over here—I'm speaking generally of course—but frankly I wouldn't trust the Sunnyvale crowd with my snowboard, much less with our research. We need a MEMS contractor on board to do the FSD and I wanted to start with you first. See what you think."

Steve crossed his arms and laid his head on them. His shoulders vibrated. He was either laughing or crying.

"Dude! Yes." Then he laughed again. "Well, my favorite is the half-pipe at Winter Park in Colorado. My sister has a flat there. Free lodging is a *great* price." "Squared." "Flex, of course." "Well, I'm a step-in type. You know what they say, 'clickers are for kids.'" Now he was really smiling. "Goofy versus Standard? Are you serious? Look, if you have to ask, get out of the way!"

He laughed once again, having fun with his new friend. "L
—Look." The guy on the other end was obviously a snowboarder
and was still laughing at the inside joke. "Look, I want to tell you
all about it, but my partners are going to make me do an NDA with
you first. It's just a one-pager. Then I'll sing like a canary."

Charms winked at Alan, who was mesmerized by his casual
style. Who calls an Englishman, a PhD in Chemistry, leader of a
seven-hundred person research corporation based in Oxford at
eleven P.M. local time and talks snow boarding?

"Great. Gimme your e-mail address. It'll be in your inbox
by morning. Do you chaps actually say 'Tah tah'?" "Okay then,
Tah Tah, Sir Bronson." He laughed as he clicked END on his
computer screen.

"*Sir*, Bronson?"

"He said, 'Only if you're a knuckle-dragging boarder
minion of the Ruling Class.' Looks like we're in."

"How did you know he was a snowboarder?" Asked Alan.

"Didn't you read the box on the right side of the article?"
Charms pointed to the gray box on the right side of the corporate
window. It read: "HATHAWAY'S PERSPECTIVE ON THE
CUSTOMER: 'Most of our business focus is on US West Coast
time, so we sleep in late and all come in at four P.M. That's perfect
for me, too, as I now work out of my office at the base of
Grindewald and always find time to carve-out a little exercise
before work.' —Bronson Hensley, Chairman Emeritus."

"Grindewald?"

"Sure, big boarder resort not far from Geneva. Carving is
snowboarding."

"But you don't even snowboard."

He put down his headsets and closed the lid on his laptop.
"But I watch the Winter X-Games. Don't forget, I always put just a
little cream in with that large cold press." ✈

"Hi Mrs. Hellums. It's Steve Brinkley." He sat at the crossroads a few miles north of town, a couple hundred yards away from where the airplane bought it a few weeks ago. The heat inside his old, hot black truck was immense. Even zipping down the dirt road with the windows open didn't help. He would have to get his AC fixed sometime if he could ever find the time. Now that he had stopped, the heat intensified almost immediately. He stepped out to try to find a little breeze.

"Well, how are you?" She asked.

Steve could picture the broad smile she was wearing. "I'm just fine, ma'am. In fact, I'm great. We've been doing a lot of stuff in the laboratory, testing out this carbon thing to see if we can make that contraption we talked about. We've had nothing but success thus far. We're all really pleased."

"You kids sure are smart."

"Mrs. Hellums, I just called so you wouldn't get spooked by seeing a black truck at the edge of your property. I'm parked out at the southeast corner of your east field again. I'm still missing a few pieces to the airplane and didn't want Mr. Hellums to run over them and possibly mess up his harvesting equipment. I won't be too long, I hope."

"Aren't you nice. Do you have time to stop by and visit?"

He didn't. He needed even more hours in each day. But he thoroughly enjoyed their company. "Why sure, as long as you don't mind my being all sweaty."

Thirty minutes later, he found the rudder cable assembly. It had separated with the empennage, but when MoJo was disassembling everything, she had also disconnected it from the rudder, too, leaving two long wire cables laying alone in the field.

He remembered Mr. Hellums describing his John Deere 70 Series Combine with a 600C Series Corn Header at dinner a few weeks ago. It was a huge green tractor valued at over one hundred thousand dollars on the used market, a quarter of a million for the new models. It was his pride and joy. To have him describe it, this thing was an engineering marvel. He used very complex terms in describing the method for shucking the corn from the stalks, via internal auger that separated the stalk from the ear. Everything was about the transfer of the fragile ear from the plant to the hopper at the maximum speed possible. He wasn't a member of John Deere's design team, but he was a man who thoroughly understood the machine's capabilities and limitations. This man was no dummy, Steve thought. Nowadays a farmer had to be a chemist, an accountant, a mechanic, and a commodities manager if he were to succeed. Many farmers didn't.

One thing Steve knew, if this Corn Picker had sucked in either one of those cables, it would have either destroyed the auger or the gathering assembly. The repair cost would have bankrupted Mr. Hellums, not strictly due to the cost of the repair, but more importantly due to the down time. There is a narrow window of time when his fields must be harvested. A few days of rain or mechanical malfunctions at the wrong time and the crop was at great risk. *Catastrophe averted*, he thought.

Only when he was convinced he had every last piece removed from the field, he got in his truck and drove the short distance to the Hellums' farmhouse. The hot black truck absorbed the sun's intense rays and collected the heat inside the cab. In the two-minute drive to the farmhouse, he was completely drenched in sweat.

Steve walked up the wooden steps under the front porch, and knocked on the screen door. The inner door was closed because it was so hot that even the Hellums were running their air conditioner. They preferred to leave the doors and windows opened rather than live in a stuffy but cool home.

Mrs. Hellums opened the door, summoned him in with a big smile and gave him a huge mother-like hug. He tried to explain that he was sweaty, but she didn't care.

They went into the small kitchen and sat down. She had made iced tea, sweetened of course. Kernsville was far enough south of Chicago that it could be considered part of the South, not the Midwest. It was a confusing location: plenty of snow in the winter, but steaming hot in the summer with all of the deep-fried and sugary-sweet amenities of the Deep South. Of course, farmland friendliness knows no region. Perhaps the best way to describe the people of Kernsville was "middle America."

"Did you find the rest of your airplane parts?" She asked.

He drank down the entire glass. The super-saturated solution of one part tea/one part sugar had melted most of the ice away. "Yes ma'am. And it's a good thing, too. They would have damaged Mr. Hellums' Combine if they had been eaten by it."

Suddenly Mr. Hellums appeared in the doorway. He looked much older than he did a few weeks ago. Steve rose from his wooden chair, "Hi, Mr. Hellums."

"Hi there, Steve. Good to see you!"

Steve walked towards him and shook his hand. Mr. Hellums smiled and gave him the familiar shoulder slap with his other hand. This time, it didn't hurt. There was something about that man-to-man gesture that gave Steve a feeling of "family" and trust.

Over the next twenty minutes, the three sat at the kitchen table, drank sweet tea, and talked about all that had happened over the past week: the success of the experiments, the lack of complete funding, the temper of Mr. Zimmerman, etc.

Mr. Hellums completely absorbed each word that Steve uttered. Steve got the feeling that anything he said was being stored in a powerful, perhaps underutilized old man's brain. However, when Steve described how terrified MoJo had been back in the lab when Mr. Zimmerman confronted her, Mr. Hellums shot a quick glance at Mrs. Hellums. Steve noticed, but kept on talking. He realized that they must have known something about this, and decided that full disclosure was probably best, "Another thing, sir. I'm not sure it's appropriate to tell you this, given that I've only had contact with him once, but..."

He paused. He didn't know the true relationship between Professor Zimmerman and the Hellums. Was it important that they know everything?

"Go ahead, son."

Again, that word "son" was an unaccustomed descriptor. His father had never referred to him as "son." It was always "Steve," or "Steven" if he was in real trouble. Steve swallowed, glanced at both of them, then said, "Remember when I fell into those folding chairs at the revival?" The two Hellums nodded. "Professor Zimmerman had just had words with Alan. When he found out I was a friend of his, he told me in fairly vulgar terms to leave the church lot *immediately.* That put me in a really awkward position, because we had just shown up to help. I tried to discern the reason why he had become so angered, when I think he just lost it and gave me a shove. I felt like I was back in grade school, being bullied. I went backwards, caught my foot on a chair, and went down."

The Hellums exchanged another glance.

"Anyway, I think Professor Zimmerman may be going through some sort of personal crisis. Both Alan and I have avoided seeing him again since then, but inevitably we're going to have to face him again, and he's not going to be happy to see us."

"You know, son, "Mr. Hellums said, nodding, "Professor Zimmerman is only going to our church because the Chancellor of Dexter University goes there."

Steve understood, but now felt terrible. The only reason the four of them had gone to the revival in the first place was to meet Professor Zimmerman and smooth it over with the Hellums for crashing the plane into their field. "Mr. and Mrs. Hellums, I think you should know something, but I hope you'll let me finish my thought before you ask me to leave." The Hellums could sense the sudden seriousness in his voice. "When Charms banged on your door the night after the crash, we went to you out of fear. We knew we had damaged your crop and we didn't want to upset you, so we were prepared to empty out our bank accounts to pay for the damages."

"That's nice, but—"

"But," Steve switched his eyes to Mrs. Hellums, "when Charms discovered that Professor Zimmerman was going to be at the revival, he thought this was a real opportunity to discuss this Bernoulli Award contest with him face-to-face. In a way, I felt like we used you to get to him." Steve suddenly felt more ashamed than he had felt since he had when he was kicked out of M.I.T.

"For this, I'm completely ashamed and I apologize. I firmly believe that none of us are naturally selfish nor self-serving. But we just lost our senior project out in your field, the economy's rotten—all of the engineering jobs are being outsourced to China and India. We were suddenly a desperate group in need of a break."

All of a sudden, he got choked-up. Perhaps it was his own reflection of everything that had transpired over the past couple of weeks. Perhaps it was that he had gained their trust and now that trust was shattered. Perhaps he really liked them; that they were becoming the parents he never had, and this might be the end of what was a great beginning.

"I'll understand if you don't forgive me." His dad never did, after all. "I just want you to know that—that I truly value our friendship, that I feel more comfortable talking with you now than I ever felt with my own father."

Mrs. Hellums got up, and Steve took this as a hint that their conversation was over and rose as well.

"Again, I'm so sorry." He turned and started in the direction of the front door. However, Mrs. Hellums quickly caught him, swung him around and gave him a big motherly hug, something he had not expected at all. He put his arms around her and returned the hug. Everything was okay.

"Son," Mr. Hellums said, never having risen from his chair, "we're not done talking yet."

A combination of sweat and tears was on his face. He raised his shirt in a motion he'd done a thousand times on the track team, unknowingly exposing his flat belly, and wiped it all away. He nodded and sat back down.

"Zimmerman has a gambling problem." Mr. Hellums said, crossing his arms.

Steve stared at him as he absorbed this new fact. Mrs. Hellums topped-off everyone's tea glasses, then sat down again.

"Doctor and Mrs. Carlock like to go out to the river to the casino."

Mrs. Hellums added, "They say they like the buffet, but I think they like the craps table more."

"Anyway, they were there about six months ago. Apparently Zimmerman must have had a pretty big losing streak going. Something set him off at the dealer or someone because they saw him hand-cuffed and being hauled through the casino lobby and into a waiting squad car."

Steve's mouth opened slightly, trying to imagine the scene.

Mrs. Hellums said, "You know, Dr. Carlock is a big blabbermouth."

Mr. Hellums shook his head, then continued, "Well, I have to admit something to you, too, son."

Steve's mind was swimming with this new revelation, but nodded.

"I saw Zimmerman push you at the revival. Mrs. Hellums here was facing the other way, but I saw the whole thing. I sent her over there because I didn't want to talk to that guy—I'm a little too old to be trying to stop a fight anyway and I figured he wouldn't be hauling off and punching her."

"You mean you sent me over there knowing he just pushed Steve?"

Mr. Hellums brought his arms up and feigned some shadow boxing moves. "Hey, you're tough. You can hold your own with anyone." She shook her head as he turned to Steve. "When she said you told her you tripped, I knew you were covering for him. That man is, indeed, troubled. After the incident, I went to the county tax assessor's web site."

Steve would never have considered that the old man even knew how to turn on a computer, much less use it with purpose.

"I had a feeling something might be going on with him, so I cross-referenced his home address and in big bold red letters it showed that he has not paid his property taxes for the past year."

Mrs. Hellums added, "Yeah, Dr. Carlock is seldom wrong when it comes to knowing what's really going on in this small town."

Mr. Hellums looked over her, then continued, "My VFW buddy is the bank president. Earlier this week at the Daybreak Restaurant I pulled him aside and told him about this Zimmerman guy."

Steve realized that the worst place to keep a secret is in a small town.

He continued, "He said, you know these days we have all of these privacy laws and he really can't tell me anything. Then I told him about him shoving a young college kid and he sang like a canary, saying he had to call him on a delinquent house payment. He paid up a couple of days later, saying he was working through some issues with Dexter's payroll system. My buddy said he has hundreds of Dexter employee loans and no one else reported any problems, but didn't call him on that fact."

Steve connected the dots. He certainly didn't rejoice in someone else's problems, but at least he thought he understood the reason for all of this trouble. "I'm glad it wasn't anything we had done. Maybe he'll get everything sorted out, get control of his temper, and give us a chance."

"I think he's trouble. Listen, if he gives you any more flack you just call me up. I'll sick the Missus on him. Meanwhile, if I were you I wouldn't give him too many details about this new thing you're making. He's the kind of guy who would steal the idea for himself."

"I think you're right."

"You using Dexter's email system? If so, I'd open up a separate Google Mail or Hotmail account when you're passing project information around to the others—at least until you get it patented."

Steve was again taken with how computer literate Mr. Hellums was. "That's a very good idea. In fact, I may create a little program that will encrypt/decrypt messages. This really might be a major breakthrough in manufacturing. I'd hate to have someone steal the details just because we were lazy when it comes to security."

Mr. Hellums smiled, which made Mrs. Hellums smile, too. She hadn't seen much happiness in him of late. "Well, I bet you're busy. We won't keep you."

Steve rose. "Mr. and Mrs. Hellums, I can't tell you how much I appreciate your encouragement and ideas. I'm serious when I say that we're going to name the process after you."

"Just don't forget about us when you become rich and famous."

Steve laughed, hugged Mrs. Hellums, shook Mr. Hellums hand and received the shoulder slap, then left. He got into his hot, black truck and immediately started to sweat for the drive home. Just then, he thought: *Hot black truck—dot com.* www.HotBlackTruck.com. He wondered if the name was available. If so, he was going to buy it. He could create a dummy web site and post a blog so Charms, MoJo, and Alan could communicate with him with total anonymity. He switched on the AM radio to catch the news at the top of the hour and it said, "…Franklin Templeton Funds is up four basis points in late day trading" when he immediately switched it off again. "That's it!" he said to himself loudly. He now knew how to communicate using some simple rules that everyone could understand. "Mr. Hellums, you are a genius!" He exclaimed. ✈

Chapter Nine

S teve finished the software project in less than an hour. It went very smoothly with no glitches. He had also looked up the web site name **www.HotBlackTruck.com.** It was available. He bought it immediately for under eight dollars and hosted it for a year for less than fifty. It was already up. He had put the tiny software program on three USB thumb drives and flung them across the table at Starbucks to Charms, MoJo, and Alan. Each picked one up and examined it. MoJo and Charms stuck it into their laptop's USB port. Alan laid his down.

"Take the software on the thumb drives and install it. But don't make a shortcut on your desktop, and delete it from your Programs list. The only way you should be running this is from the executable file in its installation folder."

"What's it do?" Mojo asked.

"It's kind of like a secret decoder ring. We'll use it to encrypt messages and paste them into an innocuous blog, then use it again to convert it back to plain English again."

"Why don't we just e-mail stuff like we've been doing in the past?"

"I went to see Mr. and Mrs. Hellums. They brought up a good point: Zimmerman is not to be trusted. It's best that we not show all of our cards to him. So I checked the EULA license. Any Dexter dot com mail address is subject to review by a Dexter administrator in order to ensure that no cheating nor illegal activities such as file sharing are being done under it. Bottom line:

they can snoop into your mailbox any time they want to, because it's theirs, they own it. They are simply letting you use it."

"You mean the mail in **MoJo@Dexter.edu** can be viewed by the university?"

"It probably already has been. Zimmerman, being the head of a department, can certainly qualify as an administrator."

"Then we need to get HotMail accounts."

"That's fine. But remember, most intercepts are made through open systems. If we end up with a winner here, this is something that will be worth stealing. Let's use HotMail and GoogleMail for normal email, but if there's something that's specific to the design, encrypt it and post it. Just text everyone and say, 'One's out there' and you'll know to go there and get it. I'll remove the posts after we've read them."

"How does it work?"

"Easy. All you need is a stock symbol and a date in the recent past. It looks up the stock price on that date and uses it as the key to encrypting the message."

Charms got it immediately. "So let's use 'BEN' as the stock symbol. Yesterday, it was way up."

"You trade?"

"Dabble. Sometimes I have money left over from poker challenges at the casino. I have a Roth IRA and keep buying YUM, BEN, and AAPL shares. Dollar Cost Averaging and the Miracle of Compounding Interest. I get a kick out of Cramer on *Mad Money*."

Alan asked, "By the way, how do you get in to this casino? You're only twenty."

"Please," he replied as he removed the thumb drive, having successfully installed the small encryption program that Steve made.

While studying the thumb drive, MoJo said, "So let's use a date that is two days prior to the posting date of that particular blog. You post a message on the eleventh; use the ninth as the date to look up the price of BEN shares."

Steve said, "Obviously it's important that we not tell anyone which stock we'll be using and which date. After you're done, please reformat the thumb drive or give it back to me. Alan, you want to install yours?"

Alan finally spoke, "This is stupid. You guys are paranoid." MoJo said, "Well, don't come cryin' to me when we find out we've been a victim of corporate espionage."

Alan thought about it for a second then said, "Fine. I'll play your spook games." ✈

"Hi Dad." This was the phone call he'd dreading. In fact, in the past three plus years, he dreaded all the phone calls to him, but this one was going to be exceedingly unpleasant.

"Steve. What's wrong?" Malcolm Brinkley was a busy man and had little time for small talk.

"Nothing. But I do have some news." He swallowed hard.
"Go on."

Steve could hear some papers being shuffled. He knew that his father couldn't just lean back and give you his undivided attention. He was still working.

"There's an engineering contest sponsored by Mahoney Aerospace. They are giving twenty-five schools thirty thousand dollars each to come up with a design for a small aircraft. The winning team of students is guaranteed a job after graduation."

"So you're going to enter your airplane?"

"Yes and no. The airplane is efficient enough, but it's not revolutionary in any way, so I scrapped it."

"You did what?"

Here it comes, Steve thought. *Quick, start talking.* "Dad, the fuselage, wings, and stab all are made from stringers, bulkheads, and sheets of aluminum, all riveted together. It's very labor intensive. We have discovered a way to make each section all at once using a material with a carbon base that behaves with many of the physical characteristics of nanotubes. Basically you give it the Three-D parameters of the assembly, turn it on and go have lunch. When you get back, it's done."

"Have you done it? Made a part?"

"We've done the science. We know the process works, but there's a significant capital investment required to take it to the next phase."

"Which is?"

"We would like to demonstrate building a lines of this material, producing a single sheet or slice of it. If we can do this, then the next step is to do an entire plane of the material at once. The difference is a line of this involves eighty thousand tiny MEMS devices—spigots if you will—dispensing the molten carbon out in a line. To do it in a plane involves eighty thousand lines of these eighty thousand spigots. That's six point four billion tiny on/off valves arranged in a plane. There's a company in England that does a lot of MEMS-related work."

"Hathaway Scalings."

"You've heard of them?"

"Yes."

"And?"

"And I can't give you my opinion of them. We have been chatting with them about helping them with some acquisitions and have access to potentially internal business financials and secrets.

Whether I say, 'they are out of ideas' or 'they have a new product coming,' either way open myself up to insider trading even if I am just talking to my son."

"Understood," i.e. there'd be no money coming in from dad. "I just wanted you to know we think we discovered something that will revolutionize manufacturing—*all* manufacturing."

The elder Brinkley tapped his pen a few times, loud enough to be heard over the phone. A second or so later, he said, "Listen, Steve. Jot down this phone number…." ✈

The proof-of-concept test apparatus contained eight valves. They were essentially heaters, creating a spark right when the carbon was being spit out of the valve. The spark had two settings according to Charms: hot and damn hot. The arc of the spark was across an area that was wider than the point where the carbon actually came out, a machined part in the shape of a rocket nozzle. Only the carbon didn't expand to the edge of the nozzle. Instead, the shape of the nozzle caused the spark to heat the area around the carbon and form a little molten cannonball that dropped onto the previous layer.

Making one valve assembly took an entire day. They were going to make twenty-four, but in the end decided that eight days' work was enough. Imagine making six point four billion of them by hand, at one thousandth the size: impossible.

So the test bed was nowhere near as small as it would ultimately be. It was perhaps one thousand times larger than the final MEMS assemblies would be. But, they were as small as Charms and Steve could make them by hand and they were still trying to prove the science. Steve had constructed the physical nozzles, which only took an hour or so each. Then it was up to Charms to wire in the "spark plug," power leads, and switching electronics to each one, which took the rest of the day for each one. It was tedious and exacting work. While Charms was squinting through a magnifying glass, Steve was hard at work designing the computer code to generate the series of on and off zaps as the contraption built the eight-bit wide structure. An "off" zap wasn't really off, it was simply a zap half as powerful, which arranged the carbon atoms into a much less organized structure—and thus it made the material much less strong.

Now, after almost two weeks of work they had it ready for the first test. A hopper of carbon material was above each of the eight valves, under one hundred PSI of pressure to assure an even flow of material into the nozzles. Below the nozzles was a metal board that was connected to a stepper motor that lowered the board ever so slightly each time a line of carbon was electrically zapped and dropped onto it. The whole contraption was about three feet high, including the twelve inches of movement that the board could move down.

The first test was a dry run: just three zaps, each followed by a lowering of the base metal board to simulate building three lines of carbon.

"Ready?" Steve asked Charms. All he had to do was connect the 220V line to the apparatus, then hit ENTER on his laptop. The laptop had a USB wire extending from it into an assembly that had twenty-four long wires extending from the other end, three for each of the eight valve assemblies.

"Hang on. I'm backing up a little. By the way, what should we call this thing? I hate the name 'CarbonRenderer.'" Both were wearing smocks and eye protection. But this was a lot of amperage.

"You'll come up with something, I'm sure."

"Okay. Go for it."

Steve hit ENTER. A quick DAT-DAT-DAT sound was heard in concert with three bright flashes. The metal board underneath was a dark red color, obviously very hot—very quickly.

Both Steve and Charms erupted in tremendous shouting and high fives. Two weeks' work *not* wasted!

Then they smelled something. It was burning wires.

They went back and worked out a solution.

It took another two days.

Their solution was to spray each nozzle assembly with cold distilled water to cool it.

Then they made their projections on how slowly they would have to build this thing and initially got the bad news: one inch per hour! Then they realized that due to scaling and the degree to which they could isolate the spark in a MEMS configuration, they could build it at six inches per minute. Much better, provided the water cooling system worked. A drip-pan of sorts was fashioned around the eight valves to catch the water.

"Three. Two. One." Steve announced, then pressed the ENTER key.

DAT-DAT-DAT, and this time accompanying the light was a tremendous amount of steam emanated from the device. They ran up to it, and quickly realized the drip pan was both charred and unnecessary. The water was completely vaporized. So they removed it, cleaned up the soot on the nozzles created by the incinerated areas of the drip pan, then did another round of three zaps.

Still, lots of steam, but it worked fine.

Then they tried sixteen layers (zaps).

Perfect.

Then a hundred twenty eight zaps in a row.

Looks like the thing was going to hold together. They took a break and documented their findings in terms of temperatures, electricity usage, byproducts, etc. They had shot video of each experiment with Charms' camera. They would have to remove the audio from it because there was a lot of unprofessional "aw crap" and "friggin'" language being spoken as they tweaked the assembly.

Of course the big tests were still ahead, that of actually shooting out the carbon. After an hour of writing up the test results and organizing the videos into a library of .WMV files on Steve's hard drive, they decided to take a break and wandered down to the lab's canteen.

"You want to do this tonight or call it a day?" Charms asked Steve as a Diet Coke rumbled inside the vending machine, then clunked out the bottom. Steve grabbed it and twisted off the cap on the bottle.

"It's all set up. I say we find out tonight. But let's shoot out some carbon with the *bug zapper* deenergized first. We may have to calibrate the head pressure."

"Okay," said Charms as he got some M&Ms from the other machine. Then they went back upstairs to the lab. Food and drink weren't allowed, but it was eleven P.M. and they were the only ones there.

At least they thought.

When they arrived back, they saw a tall man hunched over the assembly.

"Hey, pal!" Steve yelled. "Back off!"

The man continued to look closely at the assembly. "Where's the lab manager?"

Zimmerman. Rats.

They stood there, slowly lowering their food into a nearby desk drawer.

"Well?" he asked, still with his back to them studying the wiring, the water hoses, the machined nozzles, the hopper full of black powder.

"He went home at nine, sir."

"That's it. You're done. Two strikes and you're out. You will both meet with a disciplinary board tomorrow at eight A.M. in the Engineering Conference Room." He turned to them, removed his bifocals and put them in his pocket. "You know the safety rules."

Charms started to say something, but Steve held out his hand in front of him.

"Listen, Zimmerman," Steve said. One shove in the parking lot. Another incident with the terrorizing of MoJo, which was the real reason that Steve had had enough with this man.

Charms noted that Steve had not prefaced his last name with "Professor." What Charms *didn't* know was that Steve had the goods on Zimmerman and his gambling problem.

Steve moved towards him. "Here's the deal. First you threatened me, then you shoved me—I believe the legal terms are 'assaulted and battered'— three weeks ago in a church parking lot. There were two witnesses, my friend Alan and a senior member of the church. That Saturday I came back, took statements from both, had them notarized at the UPS Store, then marched right into the Kernsville Police Department and filed a complaint. I told them I'll wait to see if you apologize. If you did, then wouldn't file charges. If not, I told them I'll sign it and send your sorry ass to jail. The police don't cotton to that kind of behavior at your age. I won't even get into how you have verbally terrorized Ms. Barnes."

Charms had never heard Steve talk this way. Or lie for that matter. What had gotten into him? He kind of liked it.

Zimmerman now recognized him. So the other two students on this project are the ones who he had banished from the revival. He tried to maintain his composure. "Who is the other witness?"

Steve ignored the question. "I give you my word that I will not sign the complaint if you promise to treat us with more civility. Simple and straightforward. Agreed?"

"You're lying."

Steve moved forward. "Is that your answer?"

Steve was now toe-to-toe with him. Charms got the sense that mild-mannered Steve was now truly pissed.

"I think I'll take my chances. Now get this shit out of my lab."

Zimmerman turned toward the apparatus as though he was going to lift it up himself, when Steve landed a crushing blow

across his chin. It was sudden and so powerful that it lifted
Zimmerman off his feet. Steve yelled at the top of his lungs as he
delivered the blow, filling the room with adrenaline. Zimmerman
was caught totally off-guard. Charms couldn't believe what had just
happened and moved back into the table behind him.

"Jeez," uttered Charms. Even as Zimmerman went flying,
Charms wheeled around to see if anyone else was within earshot of
the commotion. He didn't notice the security camera above the
door.

Zimmerman went down hard onto the linoleum floor. Steve
flew in formation with him and leaped on him ferociously, grabbed
him by the neck, yet managed to say in a controlled voice, "Look,
I've had just about enough of you. Now we're even. Screw with me
in any way again and I swear you'll show up at Kernsville
Community Hospital with my size eleven shoe lodged up your butt.
Agreed?" The professor's eyes were bulging with fear. Steve
wasn't even breathing hard.

He nodded.

Steve release his grip and pushed on his chest to stand back
up. Zimmerman made the proper choice and stayed down.

Now what? Steve thought. He turned his back to
Zimmerman, grabbed the heavier part of the apparatus and
unplugged the wires. Charms closed the lid on the laptop, threw it
in his backpack, then grabbed the USB assembly. Steve carried the
apparatus out of the lab, followed by Charms, who stopped to grab
his M&Ms from the drawer.

Zimmerman weighed his options as he rubbed his chin.
Then he noticed the security camera with its red LED illuminated.

✈

They walked in silence for a couple of minutes. Charms spoke
first. "You're golden. What can he do to you? You were just

defending yourself. And he was going for our test bed. And, plus, it's his word against ours."

"I don't know what possessed me to do that." Steve said softly.

"I got it! Let's call it the 'HeyPal 9000'!" said Charms, referring to the bulky test apparatus Steve carried as they walked back to Steve's apartment. It was only two small buildings down from MoJo's. "Your first words to him were, 'Hey Pal.' Them's fightin' words. Yeah, 'HeyPal 9000.' That's a catchy name."

Steve wasn't interested in frivolity. It was late and his heart was now pumping with adrenaline. "That was a bad move on my part." His right knuckles were sore. He could only imagine how sore Zimmerman's jaw was. "Do you think Zimmerman will go to the police? What happens when he finds out that I lied about taking statements? I think I'm in big trouble."

"Trouble? You eliminated the threat. That guy is just a big bully. Those kind of people back down when confronted."

"But how do we work with someone like that?"

"We don't."

Steve stumbled a little on a cobblestone but caught himself. The HeyPal 9000 was bulky and starting to get heavy. "What do you mean?"

"Have we taken any of the thirty thousand from him?"

"No."

"Have we signed into the lab even one time?"

"No, but that's what he's pissed about."

"What did we use the school's equipment for, documented as part of this project?"

"Nothing."

"So we were never there."

"I don't follow."

"Remember what you said that FAA told you, 'It's the paperwork that always gets you.' Well, screw the contest. Screw

Zimmerman. I say we proceed ahead with this, then get it patented and license its use ourselves. We don't need the school anyway; we have Hathaway Scalings' ear, and they are in a much better position to help out than the school is."

Steve nodded and they walked in silence the rest of the way. They arrived at his apartment and walked up the stairs to the second floor. He put the HeyPal 9000 on the floor mat and reached for his keys. He felt a piece of paper that was commingled with his keys in his pocket, but couldn't recall what it was.

Steve finally said, "So, we form a small company, just the four of us, and license this manufacturing method to anyone who wants to build one for themselves."

"Exactly."

Steve examined the piece of paper he removed from his pocket.

"We'll need seed money. And it just so happens that I have a phone number of some private investors that my dad gave me earlier today." ✈

Zimmerman finally got the security office to make him a copy of the video from the lab cam. Initially the lone security guard was unwilling to do anything for him. "Wait until morning, when the boss is in," he had said.

"I *am* the boss. I run this building and three others just like it. Either make me a copy of the E-301 Lab security cam tape now, or lose your job tomorrow. Your choice."

He backed up the tape on the screen marked "E-301" until he saw movement, then slowed the rewind, then pressed PLAY. When the guard saw the student strike Zimmerman, he understood the man's urgency. The images were black and white, and the clarity was less than ideal. Yet, there was no doubt who these people were and he had the lab logs already doctored to back him up. "You want me to arrest him?"

Magnanimously, Zimmerman said, "No. I don't want to make him a criminal out of a temper tantrum, but I do want him to know that this kind of behavior is unacceptable. I'm going to share this with his parents," he lied. He was going to keep it as insurance.

Within ten minutes he had the video copied onto a CD-R. Zimmerman grabbed it without so much as a "thank you" and was out of the building. Only then did he smile, even with the sore jaw.

✈

Chapter Ten

E veryone was present in Steve's garage when the HeyPal 9000 produced its first two-dimensional part. It took two hours to fashion a 220V, three-phase cable from the dryer socket in his laundry room, out the door, and into the garage, so Steve, MoJo, and Alan had time to talk about creating a company and getting funding, should this work.

At last, everything had power, and appeared to be connected together well. They all stepped back and donned their protective eyewear. First he turned on the air pump to pressurize the carbon hopper. It made a loud buzzing sound. The garage held the excitement of a rocket launch. Steve mouthed a short countdown then hit ENTER on his laptop.

MoJo, who rarely got excited about anything, was literally jumping up and down as it loudly created the thin slice of carbon. Steam filled the garage, adding a visual effect that intensified the drama. If it had been a whole grid of valves, it would have made a 3D part, but it was just a line of valves. Thus, there was no depth to this piece. It was a slice of carbon rather than a block of carbon. But then again, this was only a test. Plus, with only eight valves, or "bits" as Steve referred to them, it wouldn't make anything more than just a checkerboard-looking plate.

Slowly, a sheet of black carbon emerged to the sound of a fast tapping sound. However, the more the piece began forming as the base began dropping, the less that MoJo began jumping. MoJo and Alan thought it had failed, and couldn't hide their disappointment. It was a blank sheet of carbon. Their shoulders slumped as the machine became silent and the steam subsided. But Steve and Charms exchanged winks. They knew that their system worked.

The sheet cooled very quickly. Steve touched it carefully to be sure, then popped it loose from the base, which had been lined with a thin layer of graphite so it wouldn't adhere to it. He picked it up and banged it very hard against the garage floor. Black dust went everywhere. He banged it again, then again—violently—as hard as he could, then held it up for all to see. The lettering inside the plate simply disintegrated, leaving only the outline around it. It read:

WE DON'T NEED YOU, ZIMMERMAN.

The plate lettering wasn't very crisp due to the granularity of just eight bits, but the uncalibrated heat of the application smoothed-out the lettering somewhat. They would have to work on that. Also, there were no external connections to the voids inside the letters D, O, R, and A, so these internal structures of the letters fell away with the banging. But no matter: the group cheered, hugged, and gave high-fives. They passed it around. The long, rectangular plate was light as a feather, yet as strong as steel, as evidenced by the pounding that Steve did to it. Pictures were taken, and a video camera was passed around, showing four college students at a critical juncture of their lives.

Steve went to his fridge and got a six pack of Miller Genuine Draft, passing bottles out to the other three. Tops were popped as he exclaimed, "A toast!"

The bottles were held high.

"To the Hellums Process, proven last week. And to the HeyPal 9000 here, which is the first practical test of this new process that may very well change manufacturing in a way not seen in a hundred years!"

"Here, here!" They cheered and laughed for a while, then they vacuumed the dust from the garage and got back to documenting the event. ✈

The phone didn't even ring when a lady on the other end answered and said, "Good morning, Evo Financial. May I help you?"

Steve said, "Yes, Steve Brinkley here. May I please speak to Mr. Harold Talone?"

"One moment." *Click.*

As he was on hold, he thought about how he should react to the questions of a technical nature. Should he discuss the method in terms of Joules and bonding properties, or simply use terms like energy and glue? He decided he would start off with the more proper terminology, then dumb-it-down depending on how Mr. Talone responded. Yesterday afternoon's e-mails and phone calls to Hawthorne Scalings in London had been very promising. They were very impressed with the results, although the group had quickly decided to keep the actual process and methods confidential.

Click. "Talone here."

"Hi Mr. Talone. I'm Steve Brinkley, Malcolm Brinkley's son."

"Steve. What can I do for you?" There was no emotion. Just seven words spoken in response and Steve quickly surmised that this man would be a good poker player.

"I have a business proposition to offer you if you have twenty minutes on your calendar. It involves a new and potentially revolutionary new manufacturing process."

"Sure. How…about…tomorrow, Friday, at nine A.M.?" Steve got the sense that Mr. Talone wasn't asking. Instead, he was jotting the meeting down in his agenda or desk calendar as he was talking, regardless of whether the date and time were acceptable to Steve.

"That would be fine, sir."

"You know how to get here?"

"1000 Wisconsin Avenue, Fourth Floor?"

"That's it."

"Thank you sir. See you tomorrow morning."

The whole phone call lasted less than a minute. Now his mind began filling with questions: 1) Who should go with him? 2) When should he leave? If he left today, should he stay at his dad's home, which was an hour or more away from the Evo Partners' offices, or should he get a hotel room nearby. He could always get up at two A.M. tonight and drive straight through to Chicago. No, he'll want to be fresh and alert. 3) What documentation should he bring, in addition to the non-disclosures? 4) Should he bring the HeyPal 9000?

But, most importantly, 5) What licensing or royalty terms should he agree to if they decide to fund their venture? He'd never been involved in this sort of thing before and his dad was on a plane to Amsterdam now, not that he had any time he could really devote to teaching Steve about these things. These were decisions that the group should help with. Steve sent a text message to everyone: EMER MTG CARIBOU COFFEE ASAP.

A few minutes later, everyone had gotten back with him except for Charms. Things were already getting complicated. Dexter University, Mahoney Aerospace, Hawthorne Scalings, now Evo Financial. There were a lot of people who could declare an interest in this—and potentially try to claim it as their own if they don't do things properly. He made a note that the first thing he should do with Evo financing is to hire a patent attorney. He should get MoJo to ensure that any records of their having used the lab or lab supplies for this project be destroyed. They never got a dime of that thirty thousand dollars, so that's shouldn't be an issue. It was Charms who reminded Steve of the FAA Examiner words during his Instrument Rating checkride, "It's the paperwork that always nails you."

In turn, he reminded himself that he must officially notify the FAA that he has permanently "disassembled" and abandoned his experimental aircraft and surrendered its registration and airworthiness documents. It's starting to get complicated.

Steve's phone buzzed with a text message from Charms: GOT INVITE TO COZUMEL WITH :) CONXTN VIA STL. BACK TUES AT NOON. NO CELL THERE. MAY SWIM IF I LEAVE ROOM. WILL DEFINITELY PLAY.

Rats, Steve thought. He quickly sent a reply: 911-CALL ME B4 LEAVING STLOUIS. Then he put the phone back in his pocket. What if they ask electrical questions tomorrow?

Charms must have anticipated a reply, because another message appeared, sent out at about the same time he had sent Charms his message: BTW ALL EE DOCUMENTATION IS ON BLOG.

Steve smiled, then flipped up his laptop and logged-in to www.HotBlackTruck.com. There were ten messages posted, all in gibberish. The first one read:

```
Tvhwg=!"Wig#og{u"pfuvbiht"fppwbkq!
com"rg"wig#fnhdvujedm"hoiloghskqh"gbvd!vkbv#zqx(no!
phff#uq#gwom{#egvdtlcg#ujh!fxbn0mgyfn#dcucqq!drofloi1!K#hqw!
kqwkwff#uq#Dq}vohm"dof#J"zpp*u"kbxh!
ehmn#qjrog#dqyftdhg#ujhsg1!"Epcuekqh"d!robph!
prx"lo"Hwcqtxlmnh!*figdqgvu"ibth*0#!K*mn#dcom"|pw#xjho"L!
rdtu#ujupwji"Vu"Opwlt0#!Gyft|pph!ehmgescwfu#jp#ekiggufpw!
ydzu1!"L!fr!kw!pdlgg!yluj#b"jjto!kq!qqf"dso#bpg!vhrwlmc#jp#ujh!
qwigu/"#Sgjbtgt.#.Ekbtpt0
```

He COPIED the above text to his clipboard, opened his HotBlackTruck software, entered the date from two days ago, and the stock code of BEN, then hit the COMPUTE button. It generated the encryption key and enabled the text boxes and other buttons on the window. Then he PASTED the above text into the bottom text box and hit the DECRYPT button. The following appeared in the upper text box:

Steve: The next series of messages contain all of the electrical engineering data that you'll need to fully describe the dual-level carbon bonding. I got invited to Cozumel and I won't have cell phone coverage there. Boarding a plane now in Evansville (cheapest fare). I'll call you when I pass through St Louis. Everyone celebrates in different ways. I do it naked with a girl in one arm and a bottle of tequila in the other. Regards, -Charms.

Steve smiled, both at the content of the note and the fact that his encryption idea was successful and easy to use. ✈

"Where's Charms?" MoJo asked as she sat down at the wooden table at Caribou Coffee.

Steve, always the gentleman, rose for the lady, but was late with the gesture because she arrived and sat down so quickly. He sat back down, and said, "He got invited by someone to go to Cozumel for a long weekend."

"You're kidding! Who just darts off like that? Fall semester starts up again next Wednesday. He has to in-process, get his books, yada yada. When does he get back?"

"Tuesday at noon."

MoJo said, "Jeez, he just drifts along. Never stumbles."

"I think he's like a duck: cool and calm on the surface, but paddling like hell underneath."

Alan got down to business, "We don't need Charms. Listen, Saturday is the Chicago Battle of the Bands. We'll most-likely win the thing and my take is fifteen K of the twenty-five thousand dollars for first place."

MoJo shook her head at the arrogance he exuded. "Two things. One: do you really think you'll win the whole thing and

Two: how come you get sixty percent of the take?" She did the math as she was talking.

Alan said, "It's all about research. Music is subjective, but why not play the style of music the judges like to hear? There are five judges, all identified online at the Battle of the Bands' website. I Google'd them and call around, found out who each one of their favorite performers are, and even which specific songs they like best. Three of them are Joe Satriani fans, all admire Hendrix, four mentioned Clapton. The odd-ball one liked Yngwie Malmsteen. So I wrote five songs, each with a mix of Mixolydian and blues riffs, all with magnified expression. One of the songs has a classical tempre, even though Yngwie's not my style. My onstage act will consist of the head-bobbing smile of Joe, the front and center of Clapton, and the showmanship of Hendrix. Basically, you cook what the judges will eat."

MoJo was astonished, "You mean, you wrote five songs and created an on-stage persona just for this concert?"

"It's a fifteen thousand dollar performance. By the way, to answer your second question, *I* am the band. The other three guys are just food coloring."

MoJo said, "Just hope the stage door's big enough to squeeze your big fat ego through it."

Alan was all business, "MoJo, just accept the fact that I'm one of the best guitarists alive today. While you were playing with Barbie dolls, I was practicing Dorian subdominant scales. But who the hell cares? Did Simon and Garfunkel really change the world? I need cash for this project. I could work at Wendy's for a year or do one Saturday at the BoB Festival."

Steve intervened, "Cash is what we're talking about here with my meeting tomorrow morning. And it's a lot more than fifteen K."

Alan suddenly became agitated. "And what are you offering them in terms of ownership?"

"That's what we're here to discuss. If we're going to convince Hawthorne Scalings to make the MEMS lattice for us, we're going to need to bring bags of cash with us." Steve pulled his chair in closer and leaned forward. "I saw an article earlier today in an IEEE publication. It takes about fifteen to twenty million dollars to bring a new MEMS product to production. It's our job to share the risk—with the lowest bidder—without giving up significant ownership. If Evo Financial offers us a the standard deal, they will want to have a convertible debenture with lots of restrictions on us.

"Convertible debenture?" Mojo asked.

"I'm sorry. Too much time with dad over the years. Our goal is to negotiate a buyout of their interest downline and limit the amount of restrictions they put on us for the money. We just need to find out what kind of returns they have been getting on their investments.

"However, if we can get Hawthorne Scalings to absorb the cost of tooling and setup in exchange for exclusive manufacturing rights at for a period to recover their investment it would be better for us, because we wouldn't need Evo at all. I say we let both of them know we have competing funding sources and let them each give us their best offer."

Alan said, "Either way, we have to give up ownership."

"For the short term, we give up some ownership to EVO with a buyback clause if we take their money or we give more profit to Hawthorne Scalings for their investment and no ownership to them. You have to understand that you can win every Battle of the Bands competitions for the next twenty years, and you still won't generate the kind of money we need to make this CarbonRenderer a reality. This prototype we built has just eight jets on it, which will make a plate. We have to make a three-D cube, not a plate. We have to shrink it down one thousand fold, something we can't do. Then we need to make a grid of eighty thousand by eighty thousand, or six point four *billion* jets. How far do you think your fifteen thousand dollars will go in that effort?"

Alan folded his arms, "I'm not selling out. It's my invention."

MoJo folded her arms, mocking him, "It's my invention, too. If I had not computed the crossover temperatures and validated the mass properties, Charms would not have come up with the EMF restraints and amperages required to do the zaps."

Steve folded his arms in support of MoJo, "And don't forget the CADAM. Can't build a part if you can't control the process. That would be me. Bottom line—"

Alan interrupted and was adamant, "This was my invention. You guys are just support."

MoJo banged her fist on the table. "You little weasel. Don't you know that without us, you'd still be trying to do it with electrolysis and Silly Putty?"

"Screw you."

MoJo raised her hands to him and leaned back in her chair.

Steve said, "Alan, everyone knows it was your original idea. However, there's no doubt at this point that you were heading down the wrong path and your original idea was doomed for failure. We were all there during the trial and errors and it's fully documented. We'll give you first billing if you need an ego boost. But you need to accept the fact that we are all equal in terms of equity and ownership of the working solution. You also need to get over the fact that we're not your band members. In fact, you do not possess the personality traits needed to deal with the overall management of this project."

"Screw you, too."

He started to get up when Steve demanded, "Sit down!"

Alan stood there. Steve leaned slightly toward him and repeated the command, this time at a lower volume but with considerably more authority, "Sit down."

He did, but not immediately.

Steve continued, and didn't mince words, "Here's the deal: you couldn't have made it work without us, and we can't make it work in true scale without big bucks. Now, we must work intelligently on getting the proper funding without relinquishing ownership of the patent. So guess what the very first step is: get a patent. An hour ago I set up an appointment with a patent attorney on Tuesday morning at nine A.M. That's the earliest he could meet with me, but he said he would give us his undivided attention. By the way, that's when I was going to buy books and try to get into the Aero 433 course, but this is important."

Alan just sat there listening.

"This attorney said to not make a move without having any other parties first sign an NDA—a non-disclosure agreement. Even with one, he said we are not to discuss any details of the design solution until the patent paperwork is formalized, which could take a week depending on its complexity. It's not something you throw together and submit. Every word in a patent claim is important. He said it should be general enough so copycats don't come in with something slightly different, yet not so general as to be unpatentable. It's a fine-line we have to walk.

"Which brings me to tomorrow's meeting with Evo Financial. I need to get them interested in investing in our project without telling them too much. I need your input. Charms is gone until Tuesday. Alan, I know you have to be in Chicago this weekend for the BoB Contest. But frankly, even though I value your input at this moment, I don't want you at the meeting tomorrow. You've not yet grasped the concept of sharing and I don't want to babysit you amongst those vultures."

"So now you are managing my destiny?"

"I'm not going to decide anything tomorrow. First of all, I'll be leaving at two thirty A.M. to get there and even though I could call England enroute and let them know we have a possible financial partner in works, it's probably best that I leave that up to Charms when he gets back. My position is that Evo Financial should feel damned lucky that we have offered them a chance to invest in this. They will be told we have other investors interested, i.e. Hawthorne Scalings. Though I'll be quite careful not to mention who they are. I will also tell them that my partners are concerned about giving up too much equity and we will want a buy back clause of their equity at an agreed to return for them. We would be quite willing to give them an above their average return as long as we can repurchase any equity they have. They will not think we will have the ability to purchase their shares back from cash flow and are likely to go for the buy back provision. We just need to find out what their expectations for a real ROI on their investments might be. I would be willing to give them at least five points over their average return. Agreed?"

Alan decided to back down. "I'm okay with that."

"Me to," added MoJo. "I'm not doing anything tomorrow. I'll drive. You can sleep on the way. You need to be at your best when you meet with these people. That hot black truck of yours won't make it there, anyway. I have air conditioning."

"Good idea."

Then she added, "And we can sleep at your dad's house, then go to the BoB Contest and root for Alan the next day."

We can sleep at your dad's house? Alan looked at the two of them, trying to read anything into her last statement, then asked MoJo, "Don't your parents live in Chicago?"

As soon as she said it, she realized she screwed up and had already formulated a response, "Yeah, but they're way north and I just saw them two weeks ago."

Alan looked at Steve, who remained composed and said, "Good idea. Alan, when does the Battle of the Bands start and where do you want us positioned?"

He looked at MoJo, then at Steve, still not convinced there wasn't something going on between them. "Obviously near the judges, within cheer-shot of them. MoJo, wear something tight and sexy that shows off your boobs, put on some slutty red lipstick, and don't cheer for anyone but us." Then he looked back at Steve for a reaction.

There was none. He should have at least winced if she were his girlfriend. Either there was nothing going on between them or Steve was a good poker player.

After a short pause, MoJo said, "Okay, but only if you'll stuff some socks in your crotch." ✈

Chapter Eleven

The text messages and emails sent to Charms remained unanswered after checking again at two A.M. Then he kissed MoJo awake so she could pack while he showered for his long day ahead. MoJo only needed fifteen minutes to shower and clean up. Steve always went into the bathroom first; it was their normal routine. They would be out the door by two thirty A.M. as planned.

Shaving, Steve looked at himself in the steamed mirror and suddenly felt alone, underprepared, and anxious. A lot was at stake today. Charms was out of the loop and of no help. Alan would be negative help. MoJo agreed she would be a distraction in the meeting, and would wait nearby. Steve would be flying solo. It was all up to him, and he would be dealing with professionals.

His one and only suit was a bit wrinkled, but fit well. She ironed his dress shirt after arriving at his place at nine P.M. Less from a lurid and more from a logistics standpoint, MoJo had spent the night with him. She broke one of their clandestine rules and parked her car directly in front of his apartment, since they would be leaving in the middle of the night anyway.

She hadn't considered that Alan would walk right past her car at midnight after returning home from The Pisser. Alan certainly took notice. In fact, after seeing her car he stopped in his tracks and stared at Steve's darkened apartment window. He wondered if they were laying together, naked in bed at that very moment. It didn't bother him that they were a romantic couple; it angered him that there were alliances forming in the midst of the group. He always felt like he was the late addition to the group. Yet now he was convinced that he was being further alienated: Charms was certainly no ally. In fact, they had a mutual dislike for each other. Now, this pair of lovers up on the second floor beyond the darkened window would prove to be a formidable adversary, if crossed. He had no way of knowing that the only reason they were being secretive was because of MoJo's unapproving parents. To him, he was now powerless in the group, and the more he thought about it, the more angry he became.

Brooding, he continued walking home. ✈

Friday, August 12. Press Release, Dexter University. For Immediate Dissemination. Subject: Revolutionary new manufacturing process discovered....

Five-thirty A.M. and Professor Zimmerman was already in his office, typing the press release for the Dean of the Faculty's review. He wanted in print—fast and first, which would 1) protect the claim, 2) ensure the kids don't try to undermine his ownership, and also 3) keep his gambling "lenders" at bay with the prospect of a new revenue stream.

It was a good thing that Zimmerman had access to all of the student's university email in-boxes. Otherwise he wouldn't have known that they had been successful in creating a working prototype on Wednesday. He had collected pictures and experimental notes that the girl had sent to the three guys following their debut test. He even downloaded the video .WMV file that she had uploaded to a web folder for them to download for safekeeping. At first he wondered why they hadn't bothered to tell him, but after the incident in the lab he guessed at an answer. His jaw was still sore. His next clue was when he saw the video of the Brinkley kid pound the plate against the concrete floor and the words "WE DONT NEED YOU ZIMMERMAN" suddenly appeared. His final clue was when he went back this morning to check for new message traffic, and everything was gone. All the messages had been deleted from all of their email storage, and the video file was gone from the web folder. They were obviously trying to protect their invention. No doubt they were going to try to claim this as their own invention and had probably made other efforts to remove any affiliation with the school or the competition.

No matter. These were amateurs. These were adolescents who would probably talk to their parents this weekend about hiring a patent attorney, then sometime—if they're really on the ball as soon as the end of next week—they'd finally get the documentation submitted. Too bad. He'd have it done by the end of today.

The image of "WE DONT NEED YOU ZIMMERMAN" appeared in his mind. He didn't give a rat's ass what they thought about him personally. In fact, a rare smile appeared on his face when he realized what a nice piece of evidence this video would be. They actually admitted that "ZIMMERMAN" had been the project manager right there on the carbon plate and their plan was to steal it from him!

No, what mattered was getting his personal financial affairs in order, and this was going to be a gold mine. It was the school that invented this, with Professor Zimmerman as the project leader. It will be Dexter University that will own the patent, that will reap the benefits, that will share the spoils with the true inventor. Today, the patent lawyers will be readying the documentation. The only thing they needed were the carbon bilateral properties, and the kids' initial project prospectus had most of this information, which he had forwarded to the lawyers late yesterday. He would enlist some chemistry graduate students to fill in the rest. Now, with the university's patent attorneys' blessing, expected sometime around lunch, he would be ready to tell the world.

There were matters of privacy as to why he would not mention any of the students' names in the initial press release.

Eventually he would credit these miscreants in the footnotes, but he would let them beg a little first.

After completing the first paragraph of the press release narrative, a box suddenly appeared in the lower-right portion of his computer screen: New Message. He clicked on it and a message appeared from S. Brinkley:

Fri, 05:32
Dear Professor Zimmerman:
Sir, we decided that it would be in the best interest of both the students and the faculty to no longer compete for the Bernoulli Award. We have not used any of the $30,000 that were provided by Mahoney Aerospace. This competition gained us no scholastic credit and we are better served by concentrating on our core curriculum. Thank you for your time and assistance.
Sincerely, Steven Brinkley o/b/o Margaret Barnes, John Ruess, and Alan Overman
Sent by Steve's iPhone.

The veins in Zimmerman's temples raised. He knew this email would be coming eventually based on the "WE DONT NEED YOU ZIMMERMAN" quote on the carbon plate. But he had plans for liquidating the entire fifty thousand with this Bernoulli Award competition. Hell, he had already drained about five thousand from it. This was not good. He sat silently for a minute, then typed a response. He didn't care whether they placed in the competition. His only concern was giving himself enough time to properly launder the money he got from Mahoney Aerospace. He'll resell some equipment, reorder some tools, relist some inventoried items. Fifty thousand dollars was easy enough to hide. But for now, his focus must be on getting possession of this new new manufacturing process on behalf of the school, so he could start a royalty revenue stream for himself. ✈

Steve lay prone in the back seat of MoJo's car, going over his notes for the meeting with Evo Financial as they reached the outskirts of Chicago. The sun had not yet risen, but there was enough morning light that he no longer needed his pen light to read. He hadn't slept much during the long drive to Chicago.

To pass the time, Mojo had plugged her iPod into the car's stereo and played a couple hour-long podcasts of *This Week In Tech*, better known as *TWIT*, a weekly news roundtable for geeks and techies hosted by Leo Laporte.

In the back, Steve organized all of the hundreds of documents and files and put them in his *C:\Documents\My Pictures\Meissa* folder. After the various Excel spreadsheets, Word Documents, Adobe Acrobat files, and PowerPoint presentations were assembled in there, he ran a small program that he had created that renamed all of the files, beginning with "BeachPics" concatenated with a four digit number, incremented, then a final letter was added that indicated what kind of file it originally was. The small program then changed the type of file for all of them to a JPEG photo (.JPG) and modified the Date Created and Date Modified properties to five years ago. The original document name was ASCII-shifted and stored as the Author property. Now all of these files were hidden in plain sight. If anyone tried to open them, it would simply show up as "corrupted." He went back in that folder and checked it. The Word document originally created as **"HeatDissipationAnalysis.DOC"** was now renamed to a five year old picture, innocuously called **"BeachPics0021w.JPG"** with an author of "IfbuEjttjqbujpoBobmzjt." He would use the same home-made program to convert them back to the original Word document when needed. With millions of dollars at stake now, he couldn't afford to have these files simply laying around his hard drive for all to see.

Yesterday, they discussed the idea of letting Zimmerman know that the best solution was to no longer work on this on school property and school time. They had already removed and stored all of the documentation from online locations, thanks to a suggestion from Charms before he left town. All lab records had been either vanilla in nature or completely exhumed. There was no paperwork trail left to cover, so rather than delaying the inevitable, he composed a message and sent it from the back seat of MoJo's car, thinking that would be the end of it. Within five minutes of sending the message and getting back to his notes, his iPhone buzzed. He picked it up and opened his GoogleMail (to which his school email account autoforwarded). The message was from Zimmerman and read simply:

Brinkley: You signed a legal contract. Don't embarrass the University. Honor it and give me your best effort. -Zimmerman.

He frowned. "Hey MoJo?"

"Yeah?" She replied from the front seat.

"Zimmerman's not going to let us out of the competition." He sat up in the back seat and looked at himself in the rear view mirror. His hair was uncombed, but otherwise he appeared well-rested and ready for the meeting. All he had to do was throw on his dress shirt and tie. He'd dress, shave, and brush his teeth at a Burger King somewhere on the south side.

"But if we continue with the project, either Dexter or Mahoney Aerospace will claim some or all of the ownership of the CarbonRenderer."

"Yeah. But if you think about it, we still hold all of the aces. At this point they don't know we actually got the HeyPal9000 to function, that the whole CarbonRenderer idea really works."

"I'm listening."

"So we try a bunch of dead-end ideas and never conclude that the solution is a bi-level energy application to a single carbon component."

"I don't like failing, even in jest."

"Just think about it: while you're failing, you're winning."

"Kind of like you at M.I.T., eh?"

That was the old MoJo persona rearing its ugly head again. She didn't intend it as an insult or dissing. In fact, she probably meant it as a compliment, given what they had just accomplished. However, the memory from several years ago was still bright and in full color in his mind. Often he had considered reapplying for admission, or perhaps trying to enroll in a masters program there someday. But their parting words were "Don't come back. Don't even try." It was a pain that just wouldn't go away.

MoJo saw his expression in the mirror and realized that she was being insensitive again. This recognition was, in itself, something new for her. "Won't those bastards at M.I.T. be surprised to learn that one of the greatest innovations in large-scale manufacturing was invented by a student they threw out. Talk about egg on their face."

"Nice recovery," was all he could say. The vision of him being slammed face-first into the wooden floor in his dorm room by the FBI came back. He remembered watching himself on Fox News and CNN, being labeled a terrorist. Where were they when all charges had been dropped? He didn't need these thoughts going through his mind now. His mission at the moment was to win-over some high-powered investors so they could turn their garage prototype into a massively more complex solution.

"We need to be at the deli on the first floor of Evo's building by six thirty A.M. I have one final chore to attend to." ✈

The moment Zimmerman hit the SEND key to reply to Brinkley, he realized that it was imperative that he initiate the first salvo. In order to ensure the kids wouldn't sandbag him with non-working experiments, he decided to put them in a position where they could not hide their success. At eight A.M. he put in urgent calls to both the Dean of the Faculty and the Chancellor of Dexter University.

After forwarding the video he stole from the kids of the successful test, each called back. Each also questioned, "WE DONT NEED YOU ZIMMERMAN," and he said it was an inside joke of professional bravado, indicating they had completed the test apparatus without his final assistance and ahead of schedule. "I'm so proud of these young people," he lied.

With their concurrence, he contacted the St Louis and Chicago TV and newspapers, stating simply, "A major industrial innovation will be unveiled at Dexter University in Memorial Auditorium this evening at six P.M. This manufacturing innovation will put the United States back in the venerable position as the world's leader in manufacturing, and will suddenly stop the exporting of manufacturing jobs to China, Taiwan, and Indonesia. This is the single most important news you will report this year."

It must have been convincing, because within an hour news vans began appearing in front of Memorial Auditorium. A naturally competitive business, each new organization spied on the others, and a race for the story ensued. The phones rang throughout the front offices of the University for some early insight into what this announcement might contain.

Brenda Hinson, the executive assistant to the Dean, had been handling many of the calls, saying "show up and we'll tell you all about it," as ordered. After an hour of putting off reporters, she stormed into his office and said, "Okay, what's this all about? I'm getting ten phone calls an hour."

The Dean, seated at his desk facing her, looked up from above his thick bifocals, put down the material he was working on, signaled her to come over. He swiveled to his keyboard, typed a few keystrokes, then turned the monitor around so she could see the display. Windows Media Player popped-up and an hourglass replaced the cursor. She looked at the top and saw the web link, something short like **"www.Dexter.edu/engr/zimm/1.wmv."** But then the word **Buffering** caught her eye, along with a series of periods repeating in an animated fashion to the right of the word. In a couple of seconds, the screen filled with some young students in shorts and tee-shirts.

They looked like they could have been at a barbecue rather than a lab, except each wore protective eye goggles. One wore thick, oversized gloves. On a card table in the middle of a mostly-empty garage, was a machine of some sort. The machine was attached via rollers to four, yard high legs which were welded to a rectangular frame at the top. A small tank was suspended above the main part of the machine, and above it were also several wire bundles protruding from the top, extending into a box. This box, in turn, was connected by a USB cable to a laptop. A grinding electrical noise was heard as the machine was obviously being turned-on, followed by someone uttering "three...two...one..." and the sound of fast tapping. Steam began enveloping the device and it began a slow ascent up the four legs. The girl on the screen began jumping in place and the others smiled. The video, though obviously shot with a home video camera, was compelling. Once it reached three-quarters the way up the legs, the machine's tapping and upward motion stopped, followed by the buzzing sound. As the steam dissipated, a plate appeared underneath the risen machine. One of the students walked over and touched the new plate, obviously testing to see if it had cooled. The group all started talking at once closed in on the now-silent apparatus. No one was smiling. It appeared to be a failure. Then a handsome young man took the plate from the other man and smashed it several times on the concrete floor. Black dust flew everywhere, and the students suddenly screamed with joy. When the video ended, both the Dean and his assistant were smiling, almost laughing.

"It's made of a high-strength carbon, stronger than steel and lighter than aluminum," the Dean told her as he closed the window and rotated the screen back towards him. During the sentence his smile had vanished. "But I can't deal with this right now. I have do do criminal background checks and run down references for four new instructors in two departments before Monday. It's a big deal, no doubt, but this gadget they made is, perhaps, Bullet Item Twelve on my list right now." He then pulled his paperwork back to the center of his desk.

She nodded and left.

After taking calls from a half-dozen or so more press inquiries, she was about to go to lunch. Some guy named Bruce called from the Fox 20 van, which was already parked outside, he said.

"We are being told this isn't that big a deal. Please give me some encouragement to staying here. I have other things to cover and I'm not sure this is worth my time," he lied.

Brenda said, "Oh, I've seen the video of it. You'll like it."

Bruce wrote down the word "video" on his pad, then asked, "Can I see the video?"

"No. I'm not authorized."

"Can I buy you lunch and see what it takes to get you authorized?"

She wasn't sure what he meant by that. Then she thought, *My gosh is it lunchtime already.*

Before she could answer, he said, "Listen, I've got an expense account just for this kind of stuff. I'll never use your name. I just want the news one minute before the others. That's all. No harm."

She reasoned, it's not like she'd be giving away military secrets. He sounded cute.

What the hell. "Okay. How about Red Lobster?"

"How about The Empire Room?" He really wasn't asking.

Wow. Dexter wasn't a big enough town to have a chain like Ruth's Chris or Morton's Steakhouse interested, but The Empire Room was by far the fluciest place in town and rivaled it in terms of accouterments and price. "Oh, that's too expensive, and I only have an hour."

"Not my money, and your plate will appear when you sit down. What kind of salad would you like and what would you like to drink? I'll preorder."

"A salad will be plenty for me for lunch, thank you." She didn't care if it wasn't his money, she wasn't going to take advantage of him. She was a lady.

"And to drink?"

Then she thought, *oh whatever—it's Friday.* "Do they serve Chardonnay at lunch?" ✈

"Come in, Mr. Brinkley."

Steve wasn't sure who was doing the talking, but it sounded like a giant in a cavernous cauldron. He had been told by the lady outside the conference room to go ahead and go on in, that they were waiting for him.

He wasn't expecting a dozen men, all his dad's age, seated around a large mahogany table, all staring at him as he entered. Some smiled. One had his arms crossed. Most looked simply solemn, as though they had been discussing funeral arrangements. The room was brightly lighted, yet dark in appearance. The floor was covered by a deep maroon carpet that absorbed all non-essential sound such as his rapid breathing. The walls were all solid mahogany, slightly darker in color than the table. The chairs, all high-backed black leather, were all oriented towards him. A lone seat was available at his end, so he moved in that general direction, his backpack in hand contrasting with his well-tailored suit.

"Have a seat." It was the same booming voice, and associated with a cigar stub of a man in a jet-black suit sitting at the end of the table in a chair larger than any other. His thick, black eyebrows were the only hair on his head. The shadows on the sides of his round head gave evidence that he wasn't a bald man, but perhaps one who was going bald and decided to just shave it all off. He noticed a microphone on a base in front of him, which probably added some ethos to his voice.

"Whadda you have for us?" The voice did, in fact, come from speakers around the room, and he wanted to look around. But Steve kept his eye on the man. Just like in his phone conversation yesterday, this was a man who had no time for small talk.

Before he even got settled in the chair, Steve began talking, "Mr. Talone, I represent three exceptionally gifted students who, with me, have demonstrated to our satisfaction that we may be able to produce extremely detailed and complex parts using high strength carbon."

He thought someone might interject, but no one did, including Mr. Talone. Steve quickly looked around. He noticed all of the water glasses in front of each person. None had been consumed. In fact, condensation had formed around the area below the glasses up to and level with the common water lines. The ice water had been there for some time. Clearly these were people who didn't move unless directed to by the man at the head of the table.

He continued, "We have completed the preliminary testing of the material, and a rough test of the process."

He produced an object twice as long as a license plate, albeit narrower, wrapped in brown paper. He tore the paper off of it. The tearing of the paper seemed particularly loud to him, since no one else in the room was even blinking, much less moving or talking.

He handed it to the gentleman on his right, who took it and immediately passed it to the guy on his right. It worked its way right up to Mr. Talone. Interestingly, Steve noted that no one bothered to examine it. They didn't even read the message, "WE DONT NEED YOU ZIMMERMAN." They simply passed it up.

Mr. Talone, on the other hand, put on his glasses and looked at it as though he was studying a prized work of art.

It was a very interesting dynamic in this room. Steve dismissed the others as unimportant and focused on Mr. Talone. Steve spoke again, yet this time more confidently and deliberately, "This is the product of an eight-bit digital rendering, half the clarity of an old nineteen eighty's dot matrix printer and magnified perhaps a thousand times. We had an eleven percent overdispersion of heat in the junctions, thus the smoothing you see. This sample is expressed as a single plane. We intend to produce three-dimensional shapes, or blocks, at a resolution not of eight bits, but of eighty-thousand bits by eighty-thousand bits, or single layers at a time of six point four billion bits. We estimate we can make one truck fender in less than five minutes. We're not just talking the fender itself, which is normally stamped out of a steel alloy. I'm talking an assembled fender, including the flanges, crossbeams, wire holder assemblies, holes, even die cut recesses, all assembled as a single unit, ready for painting, in five minutes. Anything that had been previously riveted together including aircraft fuselages with its internal firewalls and articulated stringers—five minutes. Let me correct that. Aircraft fuselages would no longer require any internal structural hardening, because that material in front of you is at least ten times stronger than steel. It's also half the weight of aluminum, is non-conductive, and it's almost as plentiful as dirt."

Mr. Talone took off his glasses and laid them down next to the plate. He closed his eyes for one second, then opened them right at Steve.

"MEMS?"

"Yessir."

"Who?"

"Can't say—yet."

"Why not?"

"You know the answer to that already, sir." Steve stared him down. He could almost hear the men around the room inhaling.

Perhaps no one had ever dared to stand toe-to-toe with this man before.

"What are your terms?"

Steve had been expecting to hear something condescending like "So, let me tell you how this works." or "We don't have a lot we can do for you." This was encouraging. He was being neither eschewed nor trivialized.

Steve decided to be slightly conservative, "It's a twenty-nine month plan to break even, including paying you back your investment plus a reasonable return above your average normal return. We have done a market analysis and—"

"I don't need details."

"Yes, you do."

His comment reverberated like a stun grenade. The room could not have become more quiet. Some of the eyes turned to Mr. Talone, then right back to Steve.

"Why?"

"Because in less than five minutes I'm going to ask you for a huge sum of money, and I want you to be confident that I am capable of obviating your risk."

"Because you think I'll take a smaller return if you can convince me that you can deliver."

"No." Steve then shook his head once so there would be no misinterpretation.

Again, silence ensued. Steve was convinced that the other men around the table were perhaps the best-dressed crash test dummies ever made. Talone must have given the order: don't talk unless spoken to.

"No?"

"No, because you already know I can deliver or you wouldn't be wasting your time with me. I'm here to offer you your normal equity position for investments you have done like this in the past but want the option of purchasing the equity back within five years at precisely ten points above your average annual return your company produced over the past five years."

"And what would that be?" He leaned slightly back in his chair. This was a private investment company. It was a secretive company. No one except Talone knew the full breadth of their portfolio. None of the gentlemen surrounding Steve had a clue what the others made in terms of salary or anything about the others' individual investment portfolios. None of them knew the true ROI for the whole company, and certainly not over the past five years.

"Thirty-six point four six percent."

The number resonated with Talone for a second, then something clicked with him. "What the..." Talone jerked forward and flipped up the lid on his laptop. This was the most animation that Steve had seen thus far. Talone spent a full two minutes in silence, tapping away at his keyboard. At one point he looked up at a man to Steve's right, pointed at the door and said, "Clayton, close that door."

...By midnight last night, Steve had acquired Talone's wife's name, his home town, his kid's name, and their school names. Nothing's private any more in the Information Age. Armed with this personal information, he was in search of possible passwords. One hundred twenty-eight bit encryption and a firewalled server is nothing when you have the proper passwords. The hacking itself was quick and simple.

That's why he had been sitting in the corner of the deli on the first floor of Evo's building at six thirty A.M. with his laptop open and pretending to be reading his USA Today. He had two and a half hours.

He didn't get a nibble until seven thirty, when a man came in, plopped his laptop on another table, put his briefcase on the other chair, then lifted the lid on the laptop and went to get some coffee. He wanted it fully-booted by the time he returned.

Thirty seconds later a window appeared on Steve's computer: "New connection..." He smiled.

Quickly, he gained remote access of the other man's computer and copied a tiny executable file into the man's C:\Users\Owner\AppData folder. If the man somehow noticed the file and simply ran it, doing so would make it disappear. And it would *completely* disappear—never to be seen again, not even in his computer's Recycle Bin. But running the file with the tag "-MoJo," it would immediately start sending out packets of keystrokes to Steve's www.HotBlackTruck.com/_Priv private folder. Then, all he had to do was recover the man's keystrokes, and it would send him flying through Evo's corporate firewall. He'd be halfway there. He was simply fortunate that the man didn't know his laptop was vulnerable.

He ran the file remotely and then guessed that a message, "Would you like to run this file? Some files can harm your computer." had appeared on the other screen. Steve clicked "Y."

Then he guessed another window, "You need to have Administrator privileges to run this file" would also pop up. So he allowed another few seconds, then this time Steve chuckled as he again clicked "Y."

Steve actually had a few minutes to spare, as the man was still in line. So Steve walked casually around the back of the deli and grabbed a napkin. He wiped off his face and turned to walk back, glancing at the man's screen.

Good. No pop-ups or warnings.

Soon, the man sat down with his coffee and began typing and clicking his mouse. Obviously there were no messages on his screen to alert him of any trouble.

Steve read the business section of the paper while the other man worked. After that, Steve closed the lid on his laptop and got another coffee, occasionally glancing in the man's direction.

Steve flipped up the lid of his laptop after he returned to his small table. Steve grabbed the key log file off his server from his own laptop. After retrieving the keystrokes, it turns out the man was checking on a camera he was selling on eBay.

Not good.

Then, he went through some more of the key log and discovered the man had typed-in the access link to get into the company servers, entered his username and password, then got on the site and checked his email.

Steve wasn't the least bit interested in this man's email. Already, he had everything he needed. Now all he had to do was clean up his mess. He could have simply left the Trojan Horse on that man's computer. Chances are he'd never see it. Even if he did, it would vanish if he tried to run it.

But as luck would have it, the man got up to get a refill of his coffee. Steve went into the man's active processes, remotely of course from his own laptop, stopped the execution of the small applet, then deleted the file completely from his computer. Done. No evidence whatsoever.

After the man left, he logged into the server himself, using the man's username and password. Once in, he hacked into the list of folder names, found a "TALONH" folder and then presumed that must be his username, too. Then he went through the usual suspects of passwords, and almost let himself get disappointed when the log-in procedures required a combination of letters and numbers. Then he thought, it was probably no more than two numbers, like a high school football number or a day of the month. Nothing worked.

He was so close.

He had twenty-nine possible password names, and four best guesses at numbers (street address, birthdays, jersey number). After that, the odds of finding it within the time frame needed were too low. Counting reversing the numbers and the alpha characters, he had two hundred thirty two combinations to try. Scratch that. He added "51" as a possible number, just because. Make that two hundred and ninety combinations. Now it was down to simple grunt work and patience.

He had been at it for almost an hour when he hit it: **Fetch51**

Fetch was his dog's name and 51: well, that was a fortunate afterthought. 51 is the usual percentage of ownership for legally maintaining the controlling interest in a corporation. He almost thought 51 would be a waste of time trying.

Once he was in, he simply looked through Talone's folders and grabbed some spreadsheets. One, entitled, "CorpAll5Yrs.XLS" was password protected. He tried **Fetch51** and got right in....

Steve said, "Sir, the number you are looking for is on Line 512, Column G of the third page of your spreadsheet. Twenty one point four six two three nine—to be exact. I simply added ten percent to it."

Talone didn't ask the rhetorical question of "How did you get this?!" Talone simply said, "I won't do it for less than thirty-five percent, compounded per annum over the period I'm sure you were about to divulge."

This man was cool under pressure. Steve had just unraveled the entire corporate portfolio in front of him. This was surely the biggest corporate spying event that Talone had ever witnessed. Steve just wanted to know that he was every bit his equal.

Steve said, "Okay Harold. Thirty-five percent per annum equivalence. Two phases. First, design, twenty-nine million, thirteen months. Second, initial production, one hundred units, sixteen months, thirty-one point six million."

"We'll write it up."

That was it. They were done. *We'll write it up.*

Then the room went silent.

With that, Steve rose from his seat. "Thank you sir. Can I have my plate back?"

Talone pushed it in front of the man directly to his right, who picked it up and passed it down the five men on Steve's left and back to him. As he stuffed it in his backpack, he said, "By the way, none of the peripheral information discussed today has or will leave this building. However, I would suggest that you disable Remote Computer Connections on your employees' laptops." ✈

Chapter Twelve

Bruce was leaning against the red brick alcove, watching women exiting the Dexter University's Administration Building. The Fox 20 van was running with the air conditioning set on high with the cameraman sound asleep in the back seat. Bruce didn't know what Brenda Hinson looked like, but he had been a news investigator long enough to mark her, he was certain. She would walk out the door at one minute before noon, because it was her job to be punctual. She would most likely be thin, wearing something nice but inexpensive. Her hair would be in perfect shape and she'd be wearing just enough extra makeup to cover those mid-thirties complexion changes.

He smiled as a lady emerged through the double-glass doors, scanning the parking lot in front of her. Her eyes weren't accustomed to the bright sunlight and was squinting, displaying a few wrinkles. He was off to the side, out of the sun and just sticking out of the alcove enough to catch the breeze.

"Hi Brenda. Bruce." He said, pushing off the brick wall and in her direction.

She shuddered a bit, mostly from the nervousness associated with this blind lunch date, and what would be expected of her in exchange for lunch.

Once she saw him, however, she smiled. He was, indeed, nice looking and dressed in a coat and tie. There was no Fox 20 baseball cap nor microphone in hand. She would never have guessed him a news reporter. She also glanced down at his left hand and confirmed: no ring.

Bruce noticed the glance. After all, he was a professional noticer. He never wore the wedding ring at work; it was often an impediment, as was the case here he concluded.

He shook her hand and flashed the whitest teeth she'd ever seen. "Shall we?"

She nodded, then thanked him for the lunch invitation as he gestured where the van was parked.

"My cameraman is asleep in the back seat. He's kind of a lazy hippie throwback. He is perfectly content on sleeping through life."

"Is he joining us?"

"Him? Heavens, no. He'd rather have chicken fingers, and I'll give him the van to run get something more to his palate while we dine in style."

"Are you two a team?" She asked, not knowing what else to say.

"We share them. He's one of three full-timers. He's lazy, but he gets the basic job done. He'll have the camera set up for the press conference and he won't miss a word. But he won't go out on his own and take any campus shots or dig up any file footage without prodding."

The van's side windows were darkened by the station's logo, which covered not only the windows, but the entire side. He opened the passenger door and yelled, "Wake up!" to which the man grumbled a little, then sat up and stretched.

Bruce pulled the door open wide and said, "Brenda, John, my cameraman."

She peeked in the door and looked into the back seat. A Lilliputian creature with a bald head and a big gray beard smiled and said hello. He wasn't the least bit threatening, but he wasn't the least bit handsome, either. She smiled and hopped in.

Bruce ran around the front and harnessed himself into the driver's seat. "How about chicken fingers?" He asked, looking at John via the rear view mirror.

"Great. I'm starving."

"Here's the deal. We're going to the Empire Room. Then you take the van. Just be back at twelve forty to pick us up. She has to be back by one."

"'Kay, fine."

Bruce wasted no time, and even before he got the van in gear he glanced at Brenda and said, "Now, of course I'm on the clock and I only have a few precious minutes with you. Just tell me what's on the video and then we can talk about something more interesting, like you."

He flashed that brilliant smile again.

She had already decided that there was no harm in letting him in on what she had seen. It was no doubt going to be played at the press conference at six P.M. anyway. "There's these four college kids—engineers and scientists—who figured out how to make super-strong parts out of carbon. I'm told it's a whole lot stronger than steel, but weighs less than aluminum."

"Thanks. Well, looks like that's all I need. Back to the office you go." He put the van back in park.

She gave him the look of someone betrayed.

"Just kidding," he said, then he reached over and squeezed the top of her shoulder.

She smiled and shook her head, acknowledging the quip. "I'm sorry, I feel like I'm doing something illegal here, like taking a bribe."

"You're just helping out a stranger. I get a bonus when I scoop the others. It's not much, but the thrill of knowing I beat out the others to a story is, like, second only to sex."

She giggled like a schoolgirl, then started to reply, but wasn't really sure what to say. His comment was a bit crass, but at the same time she wasn't offended. On the contrary.... ✈

MoJo always talked with her mouth full. It never bothered Steve, but he always noticed. This time it was a Caesar Salad muffling her words, "You mean he didn't even balk at your terms?"

Steve, on the other hand, finished chewing the bite from his tuna salad sandwich, then said, "Yeah, that's weird, isn't it? Here I was, thinking that since they would be assuming all of the risk that they would require a huge return on their investment, much more than the number I threw at them."

"I'd like to have seen the expression on his face when he found out you hacked your way through his files."

"That was strange, too. I would have called security. In companies like this, privacy is important."

"Yeah, he didn't even acknowledge the fact that I got into their files. Little weird." ✈

Mr. Talone was ready to adjourn the morning-long meeting, which had been delayed significantly while they hunted down the IT director. While they waited, Mr. Talone sent out an Urgent Action email to have each and every employee do a full system scan of his/her computer with the latest virus definitions—now. Talone then went around the table to each manager and asked repeatedly and dogmatically, "Do you have the file 'Corp All Five Years dot XLS' on your computer?"

He told each of them that they would merely be fired if they admitted having it. Otherwise, when the IT guy shows up and scans each laptop, if he subsequently finds the file, that person will be fired, sued, and charged with theft.

It was close to noon when the CTO of Evo Financial appeared before the group of men. He was halted just inside the doorway and asked where he'd been. He had no idea he had walked into an inquisition. The man was now standing in the conference room door, being ostracized in front of the senior managers of the company. Mr. Talone barked, "How is it that I know our files have been compromised, and yet you don't. You are our computer expert and you're not doing your job. By the end of the day, I want every single computer stripped of its capability to be connected to remotely. Got it?"

"Yes, sir," the man answered.

"Get out of here. And next time I want you, you got two shakes to make yourself present."

The men around the table were relieved that Mr. Talone didn't follow-through with his threat to have the IT guy search their computers. Once the man turned and left, Talone put both hands flat on his desk and rose from his chair, leaning into the group. "Some kid in his early twenties compromised our entire company today. That will never happen again. Got it?"

They all nodded.

"Dismissed—except for Lamley." Then he returned to his sitting position as they quickly rose and vacated the room.

Talone said, "Close the door, Lamley."

The man's face looked like a bald eagle's: unemotional, with a hook nose and piercing eyes.

"You're my special projects guy and it's time I turn you on to this Brinkley kid."

"Fine." Once the door had been shut, he acted more casual with Talone, a sharp contrast to the other lemmings that had surrounded him all morning. "I've been thinking about this since he left. You want me in his face or behind the scenes?"

"How'd you know?"

"You accepted his offer. It was way too low."

"He could have offered anywhere from a stick of gum to the Queen's jewels, and I would have accepted the offer. I was just sizing him up. Twenty six percent my ass."

"I figured. The others must have been thinking, 'what the fuck?'"

"Watch your language. Every waking moment, you are a senior manager at this company. Regardless of why you're really working here, you will present yourself as a professional at all times."

"Will do, boss."

"Good, now steal every fuckin' thing you can find on this carbon project. Papers, videos, equipment, I mean everything. You better also ransack his place. Make it look like a robbery. Steal his fuckin' TV and his iPod while you're at it. And I don't want to see your fingerprints on anything. Use your friends, like before. And find out everything about the other students. I'll give them an offer they won't be able to refuse. It's up to them. But either way, this is mine. I'm either buying or I'm taking, but by close of business on Monday I want Evo's patent submission completed."

"So when the police investigate the break-in, don't we become their number-one suspect?"

"Why? He came to us, gave us everything, and we didn't sign any NDAs. Why would we steal something he already gave us? At this point, it's our word against his as to what transpired here this morning."

"Shit, you're right!"

"I said watch your language." ✈

The Chardonnay went right to her head. It was twelve forty, time to leave, but she said she didn't have to be back right at one. Her first glass was poured as she sat down at nine minutes past twelve. Now, thirty-one minutes later she had finished her meal and her second glass of wine.

Even at high noon, the light was low in the Empire Room. All of the shades had been lowered to keep the intense sun from baking the tables next to the windows. However, the shades were quite opaque, giving the entire dining room area a cozy feel. Candles were lighted at each table, and the flame danced between the couple.

"This is a business lunch, right?" Bruce asked.

"Yes, it is. And a nice one at that."

"I want you to work for me. Scratch that, I'm just gonna tell it like it is: I'm about to offer you a bribe," he said with a smile.

"Uhm, okay," she said as she sipped the last of the white wine.

When she put the glass down, he softly grabbed her hands. She hadn't had her hands held this way in a long time.

Then he transferred a wad of bills to her. Wrinkles appeared on her face.

Before she could say anything, he said softly, "Let me say a few sentences. Then you can talk, okay?"

She wasn't liking this.

His smile vanished as he became serious. "I haven't had a good story in months. I've been given notice by the news director at the station: I'm on their Watch List. I'm worried they are going to fire me if I don't start producing. This story looks to be big, so I want you to have my commission on it—five hundred bucks. This will give me job security for a year if it's as big as you say it is. I need all the details you can provide me by three o'clock so we can get it on the air by five, an hour before the press conference."

She rotated her palm up. It was five, one hundred dollar bills.

He continued, "One last thing. Will you have dinner with me tomorrow night? Not business, all pleasure."

She said yes before she could really gather her thoughts.

"Thank you, Brenda. You are an angel. Buy yourself a nice dress with that for dinner tomorrow night."

He had no intention of taking her to dinner. He and his wife already had plans. ✈

Zimmerman had the briefing completed by two o'clock. The lawyers had completed the patent search and it looked good. In his rush to get the announcement made, he had forgotten to do this essential step. Good thing the Chancellor had asked if anyone else already had the process patented. There were many similar patents, almost thirty, but none with the dual-carbon process. He had noted that there were no lab logs filled-in by the students. He checked every entry over the past two weeks: nothing. However, he had the e-mail messages that told him the full story. It was a good thing he mined them when he did, because earlier today when he went to get more, it had been wiped clean. They were smart, he thought, but not as smart as he was. Twice already he had put the student's names in the briefing. But in the end, it was best that he just identified them simply as four gifted Dexter undergrads. Bastards and bitches, they were. ✈

It was the best five hundred bucks that Fox 20 had ever spent. Stations don't advertise that they buy information, because the price of information would go up. But all Bruce had to do was file the expense report and he would be reimbursed. He just needed his cameraman's co-signature that it was a valid claim, that he wasn't just sticking the money in his pocket. A 1099 tax form was to have been given to Ms. Hinson so the payment would be properly recorded. But, like most transactions like this, it didn't happen. Somewhere in the bowels of Fox 20 offices, an accounting clerk had to figure out how to expense it.

The video link given by Ms. Hinson had already downloaded into the producer's computer, one floor above the station's news desk. Good thing she remembered what folder it had been in on Dexter's web site. The editing staff was busy pasting photos, sequencing video, retrieving archived footage, making font selections and writing script. It was business as usual until one of the editors yelled the cliche, "Stop the presses!"

The young editors clamored around her desk, amazed at what she just discovered: one of the four kids was that boy who had been arrested at M.I.T. several years ago and charged with everything from domestic terrorism to treason. This was huge.

They all scrambled back to their desks and began to Google "Steve Brinkley." There were over two hundred thousand pages on the world wide web that mentioned him. It was old news made new again—the best kind of news!

Bruce's cell rang in rapid succession as they each wanted to let him know the new stuff they had dug up on this Brinkley kid. Bruce couldn't believe his good fortune. Two hundred miles from the station, sitting in the back of the news van at his laptop, he smiled. This was Pulitzer-quality research. The press conference was still a few hours away, but the most innovative manufacturing process discovered in the last seventy-five years was invented by some ex-M.I.T. whiz kid turned criminal. Dexter was the only school that would enroll him. ✈

"Rats," Steve said, looking at his dead phone after waking from the ride to Orland Park, about forty minutes from downtown. "I forgot to bring my phone charger. Mistakes happen when you're bereft of sleep."

"I'm going to bereft you of more things when we get to your dad's," she mused, handing her phone to him. "Use mine."

"Do you have Alan's phone number?"

She grimaced. "No."

"I think I have it in an email. We'll look it up when we get to dad's."

"You sure your dad's not home?"

"Positive. Europe somewhere."

"Good, because I can get pretty noisy during sex."

He looked at her. "I've heard."

"Forget make-up sex, this is celebration sex, and it's going to last until we leave for the BoB contest, twenty-six hours from now."

"I would say we're having a good day."

The black Camry, that had been trailing them since leaving the Evo offices, continued past the entrance to the gated community where Steve's dad lived. MoJo, on the other hand, drove up to the gatehouse and stopped. Steve was in the passenger seat and the gate guard immediately recognized him. Fortunately the driver of the Camry had plenty of time to decide to continue driving straight rather than making the turn behind her. Had he made the turn, he would have pulled right in behind MoJo's car, and would surely have been spotted. Now, they would reverse course, pull over, and wait until they came out through the gates again.

Others were already enroute to Kernsville. They had their instructions as well. ✈

"Ladies and gentlemen, thank you for attending. As you know, Dexter University is the three hundred ninety-fourth largest school in the nation and has a rich forty-six year history."

Some scattered laughter was heard throughout the sea of reporters and cameras. The self-deprecating humor didn't work. He glanced behind him. Seated were the Chancellor of Dexter, the Dean of the Faculty, and four other members of the school's administration. None of them were smiling.

Professor Zimmerman opted to skip the next paragraph in his prepared text: "We boast no alumni who are Nobel Prize winners, no astronauts, no senators...."

He continued, "But today, the research done here at Dexter will change how we manufacture complex parts forever, changing the face of manufacturing in a way not seen since plastic extrusion was introduced in the nineteen fifties.

"We have devised a method for arranging the orientation of the carbon element into two different physical properties. One is a structure that, when properly treated, is up to twenty times as strong as steel. The other has the consistency of a dirt clod.

"Why two different manifestations of the same element, you may ask? Because we have devised a way to create three-dimensional objects made of super-strength material, using the other material as, say, scaffolding during the manufacturing process. After the part comes out, we just remove the scaffolding. This enables us to build parts with outcroppings and internal folds, something not possible except for prototyping. This is not just for prototyping, this is for mass production, and we demonstrated it this week on a small scale."

Zimmerman hit the enter key on his laptop and the screen behind him suddenly displayed the video stolen from the students.

"As you can see, this is our device making the very first part, a flat plate. Future parts will be created as large cubes or blocks and will have a resolution over a six by six foot plane of six point four million units, or a resolution of over eleven hundred dots per square inch. It's a relatively new science called MEMS, or micro electro mechanical systems, and allows extreme miniaturization of electrical and mechanical parts, which is exacting enough to create threads for screw holes and incredibly tight tolerances.

"The part created here was created using only eight dots, not eighty thousand. We are working with a company to produce these jets at one ten thousandth the size of the jets shown here."

The video was now showing Steve banging it against the garage floor, and holding up the finished plate for all to see. The cheers in the video were broadcast over the auditorium's sound system, and the photographers in the audience started flashing cameras and the crowd began talking and smiling. The video was quite entertaining.

When it was over, the audience understood and seemed enthused. Zimmerman was quite pleased with his performance. "Now, I'd like to answer any questions you may have."

Several hands went up. Zimmerman pointed at the good-looking chick in pink dress in the back.

"Professor. Kate Jackson, Channel 8 News. Are these kids graduate students, and how many were involved?"

"No, they are all undergraduates. There are four of them. The team leader is a double major in aeronautical engineering and computer sciences. One is a chemistry major. One is an electrical engineer. The last one is the one who came up with the idea, and is a physics major. However it took the whole team, plus the expertise of the faculty here at Dexter, to make it a reality."

Another hand shot up. Zimmerman acknowledged him.

"John Bateman. Were they working on this as part of the Bernoulli Award competition?"

Zimmerman froze.

How could this man know about The Bernoulli Award? He couldn't admit that, yes, that was the case. Doing so would invite a lawsuit that could result in sharing the patent with the competition's sponsor.

"And you are with?"

"I am the CEO of Mahoney Aerospace, the sponsor of the Bernoulli Award. I have a piece of paper here, signed by you that you have four students, an aero engineer and computer scientist, a chemist, an electrical engineer, and a physicist enrolled in our little competition. You also cashed our fifty thousand dollar check. In fact, if you glance down at the sixteenth paragraph, just a few above your signature, you'll see that it reads," Bateman paused to adjust his glasses as all of the cameras turned to him. "...conclusions and engineering remedies shall become and be retained as property of Mahoney Aerospace, including all rights to patents and processes created herein. That's an interesting legal phrase: 'All Rights.' Wouldn't you agree, professor?"

A murmur came over the crowd. Zimmerman didn't say a word. He never read the fine print.

"Perhaps I should be up there on stage, celebrating with you, professor."

"Mister Bateman, we will—"

"It's Doctor Bateman."

"Doctor Bateman, we'll look into it. Next question." Zimmerman quickly pointed to a man with bright white teeth in the front row. Quick, change the subject, he thought.

"Professor Zimmerman, Bruce McPort, Fox 20 News. I reported on our five o'clock segment today—just about an hour ago—that the student's team leader is Steve Brinkley. Is that correct?"

How did you know this?! No names had been listed anywhere. Zimmerman was gathering a response when the reporter continued, "He's the guy with the double major in Aeronautical Engineering and Computer Science, correct? I understand that this is the same young man who was charged in federal court with treason and for planning on taking out a nuclear missile site in Wyoming almost four years ago, is that correct?"

"Well, he was—"

"He used to be a student at M.I.T., Massachusetts Institute of Technology, right? But he was dismissed, thrown out, is that correct?"

"Well, yes, but—"

"No one else wanted him, yet Dexter enrolled him, is that correct?"

"He was never convicted." Zimmerman then tried to think of something else to say, but the silence was deafening. "He's a talented young man who made a mistake. A formal press release is available at the door. Thank you for attending."

With that, he turned and quickly walked off the stage. He didn't dare look at those seated behind him. ✈

By the time the press conference ended, two small men had already emptied Steve's apartment. Even if the police had been called, most were on the other side of the campus managing the news vans and satellite trucks.

They simply jimmied the apartment unit's garage door open, and backed in their minivan. Most of the apartment complex was empty during the summer, as it was a haven for college students. No one took notice of the break-in and once inside they were free to look around without the worry of being discovered.

Taken were a small metal filing cabinet as well as his stereo system, his answering machine, his alarm clock, and his coffee maker. In the garage, the HeyPal9000 was wrecked, presumably to make room for the van to get in. It was not taken, intentionally. This was just a standard burglary. They did, however, take the air compressor, his tennis racket, and Nerf football from the garage.

The filing cabinet contained both school work and documents such as his electric and cable bills. They took it all, again to hide the real reason they were there. One of the eight jets from the HeyPal9000 was removed from the debris in the garage, for further examination. It would be a while before anyone would notice it missing.

The whole event took less than ten minutes. What they really needed was his laptop, but that was up to the crew in

Chicago to handle that. They would stop by the Kernsville Solid Waste Disposal Center and dump everything except the small jet taken off the HeyPal9000 and the papers from the filing cabinet. Then they would drive to Kernsville Airport and give it to a crew waiting in a twin-engined Cessna 310 who would fly it all back to Chicago. Time was of the essence. ✈

"Finally, drama at a small college in Southern Illinois," announced Dana Bergman, desk anchor at CNN in Atlanta. Sixty million people were tuned in, according to the account executives upstairs. In her lively delivery, she continued, with video being played synthetically behind her.

"Dexter University officials held a news conference that, well, didn't go exactly as planned." Then the screen filled with Professor Zimmerman showing the video. Then came the question about patent ownership from the back. A confused expression showed as a camera zoomed-in on Zimmerman's face. Then came the Steve Brinkley revelation.

Lastly, it showed Zimmerman shuffle quickly off stage. The camera panned back to the senior Dexter officials, left on stage in bewilderment. It was nice editing work by CNN.

The camera was back on Bergman who was smiling and shaking her head in amusement. An off-camera person laughed, which made Bergman chuckle and say, "And you thought you had a bad day. Back after these messages." ✈

Mr. Talone's limo service dropped him off at his downtown condo on the Miracle Mile. He would be attending the symphony tonight with his wife, then take the jet to Lake Okoboji tomorrow morning. The reports back on his "carbon project" were looking favorable. Looks like they had the documents needed. He scolded the team for taking the part off of the test apparatus, and had them drive back and throw it back in the garage. Steve, he noted, was smart enough to figure out that if any of it would have been taken, that would have been the part to take. The rest of it was fully documented, which was what they were really after.

As for the Chicago unit, they were still in place at the Comfort Inn, one mile from the entrance to the gated community. They had dropped a wireless web cam on the ground across the street from the gatehouse, which relayed the images to a laptop placed in the shrubbery nearby. The web cam's battery was good for twelve hours. The laptop was good for about seven, they estimated, because the screen was disabled. The only big drain was with the wireless Internet card, which was used to feed the pictures to a protected page on Evo's web site.

If the girl's car came out of the gate, it would most likely turn south, and they would have plenty of time to get in their car, drive out to the road, and wait for it to pass.

If the car turned north, then they would have to rush. There were many stop lights on the road north, but most turned into residential areas and the odds were that they would stay on the road. Still, both men remained dressed to dash from the hotel at a moment's notice.

Suddenly, a message flashed on Mr. Talone's phone: CALL WHEN SECURE. -L

He stepped out of the limo, then turned up the street and dialed a number.

"What?"

"Dexter University just announced that they have the patent for the carbon project."

"Did Brinkley lie to us?"

"Gets worse. The patent is already being challenged by a company named Mahoney Aerospace because it apparently was being worked on with money provided by them as part of an engineering competition."

"Feed it all to my secure page. Then remove it in one hour."

He closed the lid on his phone, stood there for a minute, then called the number that Steve had left with his executive assistant a few days ago.

It quickly went to Steve's voicemail, indicating that either the phone was off or he was not in cell coverage. He hung up before the beep.

This was not good. He walked back to the entranceway to his condo's foyer. He would have to tell his wife he'd be late for the performance, that something urgent came up and for her to take the limo without him. ✈

"Leroy, get in here!" Mrs. Hellums was frantic. She called for him again from the living room, but he was out of earshot. She stood and watched the rest of the news segment, then went outside and yelled, "Leroy? Hey, Leroy! Where are you?!"

A moment later, he emerged from the barn, fifty yards away, wiping his hands off on a rag.

"Come in here!" She yelled.

He didn't panic. He just started walking. He had two speeds, stroll and walk. The emergency would still be there regardless of how fast he got there.

When he got within speaking distance, she said, "Dexter's on the national news. Steve's project!"

"How 'bout that."

"Yeah, but it looks like Zimmerman was trying to claim it as his own, just like Steve said he would."

"No kidding." Mr. Hellums wiped his sweaty forehead off on his shirt sleeve; the rag was oily. They both went inside, except they diverged: Mrs. Hellums went straight for the TV and turned up the volume. Mr. Hellums headed for the sink to get a glass of water.

"You're going to miss it."

"Headline News? Six segments per hour, three minutes of commercials, seven minutes of news per segment. We have a few more minutes before it comes up again."

He then went to the bathroom. A few minutes later he was dried-off and seated next to her watching the national news.

The report came on after the sports segment, but wasn't as animated nor entertaining as CNN's version. It was simply that a small college in rural Illinois laid claim to a new invention and an aerospace company was there to challenge it, and one of the whiz kids was that guy from four years ago who had put the nation's ICBM fleet at risk.

After the segment finished, Mr. Hellums smiled. "Steve's gonna get his chance to hang Zimmerman after all. You hear him mention fifty thousand?"

"Yeah, so?"

"Steve told me he was getting thirty thousand. I bet Zimmerman was going to stuff twenty thousand in his pocket. Go gamble."

"Maybe you should call him."

"Good idea."

He got up and walked over to the phone on the wall. Next to it was a small chalkboard with a few flowers printed around the black area. On it was Steve's cell number. He dialed it, then after about thirty seconds, said, "Hi Steve. It's your buddy Mr. Hellums. Listen, I don't know if you're aware of this or not, but Zimmerman just had a news conference and said he got fifty K for your project, not thirty K. Just thought you'd like to know. Oh, and that aerospace company says the patent is theirs. Anyway, talk to you later. Bye."

He hung up, looked back at her, and said, "No answer." ✈

Chapter Thirteen

The webcam went blank at midnight. The two men scrambled from the Comfort Inn and raced back to the entrance to the gated community, even though it was midnight. The one with the laptop in hand got in the driver's side and threw it in the back. Either the wireless webcam failed or the relaying laptop failed, but it was probably the latter. The webcam was designed for outdoor use, and was very frugal when it came to power consumption. The laptop, on the other hand, was not intended to be left outside.

One of the men jumped out of the car, which was positioned a couple of blocks from the street leading into the guardhouse, and walked along the periphery of the community's hedge line to get the laptop they had left there the night before to relay the wireless webcam images to a private web page that they viewed from the hotel room. The laptop was covered with a layer of dew and was, in fact, dead as a doornail. He grabbed it, walked back in the darkness along the hedge line and tossed it angrily into the back of the car through the open rear window, where it bounced off the other laptop.

"Well, it was good while it lasted," he muttered as he jumped back in the passenger seat. He had no intention of retrieving the webcam, since it was across the road in plain sight of the guardhouse. It was a throw-away item anyway.

They complained about having to be in the car the rest of the night, with the windows all down so the windshield wouldn't steam-up from the humid night air. They positioned the car out of sight as much as they could and waited. Occasionally, car lights would appear and they would roll up the windows and duck down. This regimen continued all night and they quickly became agitated.

Once dawn arrived and the sun came up, they could finally roll the windows up because window fogging was no longer an issue. However, the next issue was whether to start the car and run the air conditioner, because it was going to be a scorcher.

They began questioning whether they had somehow missed them leaving the community. They also wondered whether they would be staying the whole weekend. They were both miserable. Absolutely miserable.

However, positioning themselves within view of the neighborhood entrance turned out to be fortuitous, because when the two finally left the enclave at noon, their car turned north rather than south like they had expected. Plus, the woman was driving at breakneck speed. Surely they would have never caught up with her had they started their pursuit from the hotel. ✈

The night before had been wonderful. MoJo and Steve stayed up late, drank his father's good wine, watched movies in his home theater, and honed their lovemaking skills in just about every room in the expansive home. The hours passed quickly. They talked about everything, and nothing. They treasured each other's company and shared a common interest in so many things. How lucky they were to have found each other. After four years together, they couldn't imagine a life apart. Soon, their hide and seek game would conclude and her parents would come to love him again, too.

They never once turned on the news, which would have changed everything.

With a chance of thunderstorms, Steve thought it might be a good idea to stop by the CVS on Cicero and grab a few panchos, just in case. The Greater Chicago Battle of the Bands was an all-day, outdoor event at the site of the old Meigs Airport. It promised to have a huge crowd of people and lots of Chicago Dogs and thick pizza slices.

Alan's band "Covalent" was already listed as a favorite and would be playing as one of the final bands of the evening, so leaving his dad's home at noon was perfect, her fast driving notwithstanding.

As they turned into the CVS parking lot, MoJo said, "Hey, why don't you pick me up some really obnoxiously red lipstick? Alan would get a kick out of seeing me wearing it next to the judges."

"Your shirt isn't exactly what he had in mind, though."

She looked down. It was a very nice blouse she got a few weeks ago from Banana Republic. She brought, along with a black skirt, just in case she had been invited into the meeting at Evo. Today, she wore it with very stylish denim shorts. "Hey, it's all in the attitude."

"You got that right," he said, then leaned over, kissed her, then swung open her door and jumped out.

He emerged with a bag of stuff and as soon as he got back in the car, he grabbed a small plastic container from the bag and threw the rest in back.

"Whatcha got there?"

"iPhone car charger. Cost me twenty bucks but I can't go until tomorrow afternoon without a cell phone. I hate this industrial packaging they put stuff in nowadays." He twisted and folded the plastic until it gave way, then tossed the packaging into the back seat. Then he lifted the center armrest and found the car charger receptacle and plugged it in.

"The armrest doesn't close with the charger wire sticking out, does it?"

"Beats me. I've never used a car charger."

He saw that the phone was taking a charge, so he tucked the wires and the phone in the compartment under the armrest and closed it. "No matter. I'll let it charge up on the way to the BoB before I turn it on and call Alan."

"Use my phone and call him now."

"We don't have his number on it, remember?"

She reached in her front pocket and pulled out her iPhone. "I got it off my computer when you were in the shower last night. It's stored under 'Alan' because I can never remember his last name."

"Overman. I'll put it in."

He edited the entry, then dialed him.

Alan answered quickly, but the background noise was incredibly loud. *"Alan here."*

Steve found himself talking loudly into the phone, "Your fan club is enroute. We'll be there in an hour."

"You're not missing anything. The bands that have been playing this morning suck."

"Good. See you soon."

MoJo and Steve never noticed the black Camry behind them. ✈

They arrived at Meigs Field, paid the exorbitant parking fee, then MoJo drove across the grass to the extreme end of lot, right at the fence line just in front of a large building used for maintenance of the Charter One Pavilion grounds. It meant a longer walk to get into the BoB, but the car would be in the shade as the sun worked its way westward. It was still early and the largest crowds weren't expected until the heat of the day began to dissipate. Even at the edge of Lake Michigan, it was still a punishing day to be outside.

Steve and MoJo began the walk to the entrance of the outdoor Pavilion. Since they were going to be seeing Alan, they reverted back to their hands-off-each-other mode. They had been so intimate over the past twenty-four hours, it now seemed unnatural not to be holding hands as they walked.

As they worked their way closer to the venue, the music became louder and less muffled.

Alan had set up a small portable canopy at the far corner of the grassy area, far away from the covered seats and stage. Under it were beach towels and their three guitars, each one in its own hardshell case. They were chained together and locked to a common stake, should anyone decide to try to make a dash with one while they weren't looking. The rest of their equipment (drums, amps, stomp boxes, cables) were grouped together, inventoried, and guarded behind the stage. Security was tight, but they weren't taking any chances with their guitars and kept them within sight.

"Hey, guitar god!" MoJo shouted from thirty yards away, over the noise from the stage.

Alan was laying down underneath the canopy, his head against his backpack, one foot on a guitar case. He was wearing Ray Bans and seemed to be staring straight at them, but he was sound asleep. The other band members were no where to be found. Good thing the guitars were secured.

They stepped under the canopy and sat down on the towels, flanking Alan.

"He seems nervous," said Steve, smiling.

"He'll never be able to relax before the show," replied MoJo.

"I'm awake." He lifted his sunglasses. "The heat is melting Eric's drumsticks."

"Where are the rest of your band?" Steve looked around.

"I think they took off for a couple of hours. We don't play until eight forty tonight."

"Is that good or bad?"

"Very good. Only three bands play after us. The judges know the top five bands are on stage last, so we're already at an advantage, psychologically."

Suddenly, MoJo remembered, "Jeez, I forgot the lipstick."

Alan said, "I was joking. I didn't think you'd really consider wearing it."

"No, we stopped at CVS and Steve bought me some really bright and slutty red lipstick. I better go get it because it's going to melt in the back seat of the car and I know I'm not *ever* going to wear it again!"

"Want me to go with you?" Steve asked.

"No, conserve your strength. It's going to be a long, hot afternoon of rock and roll."

With that, she left.

For some strange reason, Steve felt uneasy. Something wasn't right. Perhaps he should run to the car instead of her. "You want me to go? You can hang here."

"Naw. I'll be right back." She waved him off and jogged away. ✈

Most of the cars were parked as close as possible to the Pavilion gates. However, one long row of cars were parked along the western edge, just like MoJo's. Apparently they all had the same idea: capture the shade as soon as possible. All of the cars coming in were now parking with proximity in mind, versus shade. She walked across seventy-five yards of open space and arrived at her car. Reaching for her keys, she though she saw a dog move behind her car.

She smiled and leaned back to see.

That's when a large, shiny revolver emerged, pointing straight at her.

There was a man rising and moving toward her. "Make one sound and I'll blow your fuckin' head off."

She noticed there were two men. The trunk of her car was open slightly. They had Steve's laptop open and a small black thing connected to it with a USB cable.

Then she collapsed.

As soon as she hit the grass, her adrenaline kicked in and she tried to regain her balance and move away from them. She managed to get to her knees.

That's when the man swung his gun at her with all of his might, hitting her across her right temple. Her lifeless body bounced off the adjacent car and crumpled in place. A streak of blood on the white car recorded her flight path. He grabbed her feet and pulled her body behind her car. It all happened in the blink of an eye.

The other man continued copying files. He didn't look up, but managed, "What'd ya do, kill her?"

"Yeah."

He kept working for a few more seconds, then said, "A bit high-strung today, are we?"

"I just need some sleep. That's all." ✈

Part II

Chapter Fourteen

The music from the band playing at the moment was very catchy. If this was "crummy," as Alan had portrayed the early bands, then he was in for a treat as the day progressed. With only ten minutes allowed between gigs —five minutes to tear down and five minutes to set up—it was also fun to watch. If a band took more than five on either end of their performance, they were penalized one point per minute. Obviously, no one took more than five minutes to set up and five minutes to tear down. Some of the bands brought their own friends to act as roadies. Others simply pushed out their amps and plugged -in. A huge artificial clock appeared on the big-screen TV, so everyone knew how much time they had before the penalties started kicking in. It was part concert and part athletic event. The crowd had begun a countdown before this last group started. The band timed it perfectly with the crescendo of the countdown and hit the downbeat right at zero seconds left on the clock. The crowd then went wild at their perfect timing.

Steve had never been to a battle of the bands and clearly liked the way it was being orchestrated. He was watching the band on the big screen because Alan's canopy was so far back. However, it was a very pleasant location, away from the bulk of the crowd.

An ambulance chirped in the distance, which Alan thought was pretty rude of them. Then the ambulance chirped again, this time closer, then a third time, as it swung into lot.

"Somebody O.D.'d. Always happens," said Alan.

Steve stood up. Something was wrong. *Where is she?*

The ambulance continued straight ahead, towards the back of the Pavilion. The lights were on, but no constant siren. Just an occasional chirp.

Steve looked in the area where MoJo's car was parked, but the lot was slightly convex and the area was obscured by several big pickup trucks. He sat back down and looked back at the stage.

He didn't notice the ambulance as it reached the end of the lot, then veered right, then right again, stopping directly in front of a group of people near MoJo's car. ✈

The pundits manning the weekend business shows on CNBC and Bloomberg had some fun with Friday's news conference. They repeatedly showed the repartee between Zimmerman and the chairman of Mahoney Aerospace. "We should get Bateman on our show when it's a dull day," one mused.

Then the mug shots appeared of a nice-looking young man from M.I.T., along with the stories ending with either "he was eventually cleared of the charges" or "his rich dad got him off." In no case was the description of Steve Brinkley endearing. Fortunately, the masses didn't normally watch the weekend business briefs. However, the seventy-hour workaholics—the ones who really mattered to the business community—did watch these weekend wrap-ups, and phone calls were already being made. Beneath the drama was an invention that caught the attention of the right people. ✈

"What do you keep looking at?" Alan asked Steve. Alan was perfectly content to lay under the canopy and stare at the cumulus clouds forming overhead.

"She's been gone for thirty minutes." He kept looking for her to walk back up.

"She's fine."

"Borrow your phone?"

"Where's yours?"

"It's in her car, charging."

Alan reached in his pocket and tossed it to Steve. He dialed her number and it beeped at him. Call Failed. He looked at it and saw it flicker between one bar and no bars. "You got no signal."

"Yeah, you'd think it'd be better this close to downtown."

Steve held the phone high overhead to see if it showed more bars. It did, so he turned to walk further away from the stage to a slightly higher elevation.

That's when he noticed the police cars near MoJo's car.

"No," he muttered to himself. "God, no."

Then he started sprinting all out towards the gate, then across the grassy field-turned parking lot.

When he got there, he knew. There were people standing behind to the yellow Do-Not-Cross tape. Breathing heavily, he pushed his way through a thin section of people. Three policeman were taking pictures and pointing at things around her car. The fourth policeman was charged with crowd control.

"Oh, God," Steve said this time louder, then pushed his way toward the the lone policeman. "Where is she?"

"Cook County—and how did you know it was a she?"

He ignored the officer's question. "Is she okay?"

He just shook his head.

"Oh, God, no..." He looked around, then back to him. "Take me there?" He wasn't asking.

"No. This is a crime scene. You want to tell me what you know about this?"

"Her name is Monica Barnes. Oh, God. Please. No." Then with that, he started running for the main road next to the pier. The policeman was yelling something at him, and he suspected he knew it was something like "halt," but he had to get to the hospital. In no time flat he was through the parking lot entrance and saw a line of yellow cabs about two blocks away. They were there for those who had the good sense to decide on taking a cab home after drinking all day rather than driving. To keep you from ending up at a hospital.

He ran to the front one and got in. "Cook County Hospital. Please hurry. It's an emergency."

As the cab pulled away, he glanced over at the crime scene. Neither police car had moved. He guessed they didn't need to. They knew where he was going and they had radios. ✈

As he neared the Emergency Room, he saw no less than three police cars there. No ambulance. Maybe that came and left. He had a flashback to four years ago, being roughed up and questioned by people who presumed you were guilty, in spite of what the law of the land presumes.

"Stop here," Steve commanded.

The cabbie asked, "Here? The hospital is right there!"

"Just wait."

The cabbie pulled over next to the curb.

If she was in bad shape, he wouldn't be allowed anywhere near her. If she was only minimally injured, she might just answer her phone. He still had Alan's. Yes, that was the best course of action for the moment.

The cabbie started tapping his wheel, then said, "I have to charge you wait time."

He looked up and said, "Fine." as he dialed her number. It rang three times, then a male voice answered, "Hello."

His heart sank. Must be bad. It was either the police or an emergency room technician. "This is Steve Brinkley. I was with her at the concert. Can you tell me how Monica is doing?"

He heard the man muffle the phone and say, "It's him" to someone else. But, the man didn't cover up the microphone properly. Then the man said, *"She's dead,"* although it appeared that he was eating something while he talked.

Dead. A flood of emotion came of him, but he managed, "How?"

"Boyfriend bludgeoned her."

Steve could barely understand him. It really appeared like the man had food in his mouth.

"Listen, I'm her boyfriend and—"

"Well, then it looks like you have some explaining to do." The phone went dead.

Dead. Oh, dear God in heaven....

His head filled with flashbacks from last night. Then his thoughts went to her parents. Suddenly a jolt of reality hit when the words "Boyfriend bludgeoned her" reverberated. A policeman wouldn't be so informative about the status of a victim with an unknown caller. A policeman wouldn't try to scare away a suspect. A policeman wouldn't be talking non-nonchalantly and unprofessionally. Was the man actually eating?

He called the number back but got a busy signal.

What's going on, here?

He looked back towards the hospital's emergency room entrance. Then he wheeled his head around in every direction, finally stopping over his right shoulder. "Can you back up a hundred feet and drop me off?"

"Back up?" The cabbie was now totally confused.

"Yeah, there's an ATM back there."

"Can't you just walk back?"

"Not if you want more than a two-dollar tip."

The cabbie shook his head, then waited for a car to pass and backed around a parked car, then straight back another forty feet and stopped.

Steve stared straight ahead during the risky back-up maneuver. His eyes welled-up. Dead. She can't be. When the cab jolted it to a stop, Steve gave him two twenties; the fare was only twenty-nine. He swung open the door, saying "Keep the change" then headed for the ATM.

The cabbie drove off quickly. Once he was gone, Steve jogged ahead fifty feet and looked again at the ER entrance. The police had not noticed the idling cab. He turned back and went to the ATM.

He took a beat. Now what? He was considerably west of Meig's Field and the BoB Contest. He doesn't have a car. He doesn't have his own cell phone. He only had thirteen dollars in his billfold now.

He had to find out about MoJo, but the pragmatic part of him said get some cash. He took three hundred from the ATM. Then he put the card back in and tried it again. It said, "Daily Withdrawal Amount Exceeded. Please visit the nearest branch office one block north of West Harrison."

Steve knew the area because he had once tried to find a parking space at a Bulls game at the United Center, but didn't want to pay for stadium parking. He had ended up parking near Cook County Hospital but ultimately paid the same and gave himself a fifteen minute walk.

So he circumvented the hospital and walked ten minutes to a manned branch, where he withdrew another five hundred. He knew, ultimately, he might have to buy a bus ticket home and the banks were closing soon for the rest of the weekend. He was fortunate that this branch was even open on Saturday afternoon.

He decided to walk into the hospital's main entrance rather than the ER entrance, avoiding the police. The phrase "boyfriend bludgeoned her" kept repeating itself in his mind.

An elderly lady was manning the reception desk. She was wearing a uniform that set her apart from the other staff, identifying her as a volunteer. She had deep blue eyes encased in a face full of wrinkles. He put her at eighty years old.

"Ma'am, I'm trying to check on...my wife...Monica Barnes. She was just admitted less than an hour ago."

"Sign-in, please, and I need to see your ID."

He reached in his billfold and presented his Illinois driver's license to her. She held his license under her glasses, then said, "Oops. Wrong ones." She took off one pair, let them dangle from the string holding them around her neck. Then she grabbed the other pair and put them on. "I wish I had just one pair for close-up and for distance."

"I know what you mean, ma'am." He didn't.

She wheeled-around a large ledger that was clipped to a rectangular board atop a lazy-Susan. He stared at it, slowly picking up the pen, and thought, *It's the paperwork that always nails you.*

She asked, "What's her name, please?"

"Monica Barnes."

"That's not your last name," she was quick to conclude.

"I know. She's got a high-powered job and didn't want to change her name."

"You mean her job was more important than her husband?"

"Except when something needs fixin' around the house." He then smiled.

She smiled back, then typed "BARNES" into the Last Name field and "M" into the First Name field, and hit <ENTER>.

As she typed, he signed-in as "Stanley Bringle," making up the name as he was writing. He wrote it in very sloppy handwriting, close enough to look something like Steve Brinkley, but not on close inspection by people later. Under the patient's name he wrote "M. J. Bringle" and the time-in. She may be old, but this receptionist was quite sharp and a good gatekeeper.

"All I have here is she was admitted at one forty in the Emergency Room." Then she reached in a drawer full of plastic clip-on badges. "Here." She handed him one with a big yellow "V" on it. "You'll need this to get to the ER. Go that way and follow the signs."

"Thank you, Ma'am." His smile was long gone, ever since she confirmed that she was here. He pictured MoJo's lifeless body sequestered in a closed, darkened room with a sheet over her head, awaiting further processing.

So it *was* true. She was here and she was dead. Soon she would be taken to the morgue. Sometime today her parents would be told. He thought about the pain that they were about to endure. Suddenly another wave of emotion came over him, but this time it was too much. He saw a chair at the edge of the large foyer, sat down and put his head in his hands and wept.

He was there for several minutes. Tears seeped through his fingers. One moment he was as happy as he's ever been in his life. Everything was going their way. Now, he had never felt so lost and alone. His only real friend, his only lover, the only one he could completely confide in, was gone forever. He had experienced a similar loss when his mother died, but he had been so young at the time he didn't feel the full gravity of the event at once. This time he did.

A man in shiny shoes appeared in front of him and asked, "Can I be of help, sir?"

He never looked up. All he saw was his shoes. He waved the man off, motioning that he would be okay. But the thoughts of MoJo's short life kept roaring back, angering him at how unfair this was. Why her? She was incredibly smart and quick-witted. She had so much to offer the world.

She was oddly callous to others when it came to empathy and compassion, which gave many the impression that she was uncaring. Yet, he understood her better than anyone. She *did* know what love meant; she just didn't know how to express it sometimes. She was beautiful, yet she was also a nerd. He loved every bit of her.

Now she was gone. How could he possibly go on without her. As far as he was concerned, his life ended an hour ago. ✈

Stuart Varney loved Chicago. After having worked at various FBI assignments from Washington DC, New York, and Houston, this town finally felt like home to him, even though he was no longer a federal agent.

He was on his second career and was loving it. They worked you hard at The Bureau, to be sure, but in kind you are put out to pasture earlier than with other jobs. Now drawing a retirement from the federal government, he had joined the Illinois State Bureau of Investigation last year after seeing an opening just prior to his retirement in DC. So he took the job, never having spent much time in Chicago.

They had every bit as much work as the FBI did. Always more than the staff could handle. But the pace somehow seemed more manageable. Though he was much higher up the ladder when he retired from the FBI, he was just a staff investigator at the SBI. Maybe it was the fact that he didn't have to both investigate crimes and manage others that made it more enjoyable and rewarding. He probably would move up quickly within the SBI chain of command, but he really didn't want that. This level was his choice. He always enjoyed the grunt work more than heading up teams of investigators. But, even though he was working at ground level investigations, because of his ties in Washington, he still had to travel more than he wanted to when it came to coordinated investigations with the FBI and other state agencies. He had spent a considerable amount of his career at the Hoover Building and still knew everyone well there.

He married long after his career had blossomed, and was older than the other dads by as much as ten years.

Work had always been his passion, and he still enjoyed it immensely. But as he grew older, that passion was now more oriented towards his family.

In fact, at the moment he was on the golf course with his twelve year-old son, Drake, playing in a father-son scramble at Hickory Oaks Country Club.

Drake was so radically different than his father. Dad was the scholar and the perfectionist, with great attention to detail. Drake wasn't anything of the sort.

Dad stayed in good shape, but was a klutz when it came to sports in general. Drake could already out-drive his dad, and out-chip and out-putt him as well.

As far as music was concerned, Stuart couldn't begin to tell you who wrote *Swan Lake*. Drake was the consummate musician. He knew the musical styles of everyone from Dbrenyn to Dr. Dre, from Handel to Hanna Montana. Stu couldn't tell a major scale from a minor scale, but Drake could tell you that E flat was the fourth note on a Mixolydian A progression. But Drake would also forget his lunch money, never clean his room, and would wear the same shirt to school for five days, if his parents would let him.

It bothered Stuart that Drake was neither self-regimented nor had any interest in science or math. Drake was much more interested in playing soccer or jamming with his friends in the basement, or playing Grand Theft Auto on his XBox. He was a good kid, but this boy simply wasn't predisposed to be a second generation G-man.

Stuart's phone rang as they approached Drake's ball on the middle of the eighteenth fairway. They were having a good round. It would have been a great round if the elder Stuart had held up his share of the shots. "Nice drive," he said to Drake, then spoke into the phone, "Varney here."

"Stu, I know you're not on call, but I got a pop-up for you. We got a girl beaten at the Pavilion at Meig's Field, rushed to Cook County. They say she won't survive, if she's not dead already."

"Why SBI and not Chicago's Finest?" Stu motioned for Drake to go ahead and hit first, then turned away to talk.

"She was visiting from Kernsville. Parents live in one of the burbs around here. But the reason why it's ours is apparently it was Steve Brinkley who did it."

He motioned to Drake with his thumb tapping his other fingers that he would be yapping on the phone for a minute and for Drake to go ahead and hit first. "I give up, what's a Steve Brinkley."

"He's the guy who tried to take down the US's ICBM fleet a few years ago. He was at M.I.T."

"Right. You know, I just heard about that again really recently. Then, isn't it the FBI's jurisdiction?"

"No, he's enrolled now at Dexter down in Kernsville. Yesterday, they announced a new invention down there and—"

"Wait, I think I saw that last night on Fox News. Is that where that professor got slammed by that guy in the audience? And —now I remember—it was the M.I.T. kid who was one of the students. Now you're saying he killed a girl?"

"Yep. But not just a girl. She was a member of the team that invented the thing they announced yesterday."

"Hang on." He nodded at Drake, who had finished his practice swings and was lining up his shot. Drake had a very slow and deliberate back swing, and smoothly swung his six iron, hitting the ball perfectly, taking the divot in front. "Just one sec," he said into the phone, then, "Nice one" to Drake. The ball sailed beyond the pin, bounced on the back of the green, then rolled back to within a foot of the pin, his best shot all day. "Woo hoo!" he yelled, then "We'll use yours. I can't beat that."

He then brought the phone back to his ear and said, "I'm just finishing up a round of golf with Drake. Sounds pretty cut and dry. I'll do the interrogation. Where's he being held?"

"He's still at large. He bolted from the Pavilion. They thought he might show up at the hospital, but no one's seen him."

"All right. I'll be out of here in thirty minutes—we have to see if we placed. Then I'll run home and change. Where first, Pavilion or Cook County?" ✈

He rubbed his face as he waited for that son of a bitch to answer. This was not part of the plan. It should never have come to this.

Click. "Yeah."

"What in the hell were you thinking? I said steal their information. I didn't say kill anyone."

"Hey, she came back to the car. Her mistake."

"No, *your* mistake. You're on your own. I'm not a murderer."

"No, you're just the guy who paid the murderer. Listen, I'm going to give you some advice. You're running with the dogs now. Don't turn on the dogs. They'll eat you alive."

"Don't you fuckin' threaten me."

"You feel threatened? You'll know it when you've been fuckin' threatened." *Click.* ✈

Chapter Fifteen

When he finally composed himself, Steve wiped his t-shirt across his face, and looked around. People must understand that hospitals are an acceptable place to break down, because no one had really noticed him, except for that one man five minutes before. He still needed to go to the emergency room and face the fact that she was gone. He should also be the one to contact her parents. She would have argued against it, but no matter now. He had to let them know that he loved her more than anything. That if there was anything he could have done...

A flat-screen TV was installed in the corner of the reception area. It caught his eye. It was the Headline News channel. The screen showed someone who looked familiar to him. At the top in bright yellow, it read, "This Just In.." The larger caption along the bottom read, "...and now, murder." Underneath, in smaller text, it read, "Student inventor kills fellow student." Steve sat upright, then stood as he recognized Professor Zimmerman speaking to a crowd of reporters. *What the..?*

The volume on the flat-screen was way too low, so he raced closer to the TV to hear, "...embarrassed by the CEO of Mahoney Aerospace yesterday when he tried to claim the patent as his own. Then, another reporter puts the professor further on the hot seat when he reveals that the student leader was none other than the young, former M.I.T. student who was charged with trying to sabotage an ICBM launch center in Wyoming four years ago."

He stood dumbfounded and listed to more, "...found bludgeoned to death at an outdoor concert in Chicago just hours ago. Our sources say the young lady was Monica Barnes, a member of the team of inventors headed by Mr. Brinkley. Police say Brinkley should be considered armed and dangerous...."

No. This can't be. He looked around to see if anyone else saw either him or the TV. Only a handful of people were around, but were too far away to have seen it. A man in shiny shows wearing a starched blue shirt was talking to the elderly receptionist. He recognized the shoes. She rotated the register towards him and he turned slightly, revealing a badge.

It was a policeman and he's looking for him! It had been that very man who asked if he was okay! If he had looked up, the man would have arrested him on the spot.

Steve scanned the area, then decided against trying to go out the front entrance. The ER entrance was no good, either. Surely it would be guarded as well. He slipped into the lobby men's room and intended to go into a stall and wait. A man washing his hands made eye contact with him. That's when both of them heard the loud "psshhht" of a police radio outside the door, followed by "He went to the ER five minutes ago." The voice faded as the policeman rushed by the rest room door in the direction of the Emergency Room.

Steve had to get his act together quickly. His girlfriend was dead—not an hour ago—and already his name was on the *national* news as a suspect! Who had reported him? Who had answered her phone? He thought, *Don't panic. Just wind your watch,* which was an old saying when you're airplane is on fire or the engine quits.

So he slowly turned and glided over to the urinal. Then, facing the wall, he considered his options. There were but two: run or surrender.

To surrender meant giving up his chance to find out what really happened, since someone had obviously been laying down a path leading straight to him. Only then did it occur to him that perhaps the CarbonRenderer may have been the motive. Otherwise, how could the news agencies have possibly put all of this together in short suspense. Someone was organized. *Jeez, they had my picture on TV,* he thought. This attack had been planned, this was no random act.

But who? He had told Zimmerman that the group no longer wanted to compete for the Bernoulli Award, but that's no reason to commit murder. Hawthorne Scalings didn't know much at this point. Couldn't be them. Mahoney Aerospace: no, because Zimmerman wouldn't have been stupid enough to let them know the team was resigning from the competition. They wouldn't have a claim anyway; none of their money had been used yet, i.e. no receipts, no paper trail that they could use as a claim. Agreeing to compete is not a material contribution nor work for hire. As far as he knew, Zimmerman didn't even have their money yet.

The obvious person was Mr. Talone. He sensed the head of Evo Financial could be ruthless. Talone must have understood the gravity of this invention across several industries. But murder? And *Why?* Unless the ROI over the life of the patent was in the hundreds of millions. Perhaps Steve, himself, didn't understand just how important this manufacturing method was. Yet this seemed extreme, even with those dollar amounts.

Then a thought came to mind. If she had been targeted, then the others must be in peril as well. He grabbed the phone, but remembered that it was Alan's. And there was no way to contact Charms until Tuesday.

No, he needed time to find out what was going on. Sitting in jail was not a place to conduct an investigation. If he did get caught, he would be let go eventually anyway, because he was on the good side of justice.

So the option was to run. But where? He couldn't go back to the concert. He had Alan's phone, not his. He had no laptop. Charms was gone. MoJo---*Oh God, please bring her back to me.*

The one thing he did know was he needed to get away from the Cook County Hospital. ✈

Stu Varney rubbed his face with both hands. He was now dressed in a suit, immaculately tailored and pressed. He had taken a quick shower because of the mid-day sweat from golfing with his son. But over the years he had learned to dress with the speed of a soldier in boot camp. Within an hour of getting the call, he was at the small precinct downtown near the music pavilion

"So let me summarize what you just told me. Man in early twenties hits girl with something—you don't know what it was—but it crushed her skull. After you arrive this man approaches a third officer and asks him for a ride to the hospital. When he says no, the young man runs away and catches a cab. He was spotted at the hospital, but now has disappeared. My first question is, why would he commit a heinous crime, then ask the police to drive him to see the victim? That tells me it's gallows guilt or he didn't do it."

The two officers who had first arrived on the scene were seated directly across from him at the precinct. They should have clocked out an hour ago, but Stu didn't care. He had their report in his hand, but didn't read it—it would have just made him angry. The more recent, the more memorable, and they simply didn't do their job with the short narrative.

"Yep. It's all in there," said the shorter one, pointing to the report. Each squad car had a laptop in it. They filled-in the information at the scene, then hit the PRINT icon and it printed it out back at the precinct.

"I want to hear it from you first, then I'll compare what you said with this report." He held it up like it was contaminated. "How did you know that the perp was her boyfriend?"

"Came in on the call."

"The perp called in to report it himself?"

"No," the shorter officer said without offering anything further.

Stu just sat there.

Finally, he leaned in and said, "Look, you're wasting my time. You know the procedure. Your written report is worthless."

"You haven't even read it."

"You telling me that you completely described everything in four paragraphs? I want you to paint me a picture, here and now. What was the caller's phone number?"

"He used her phone."

"Is that in the report?"

"Uhm, no. I don't think so."

"This is going to take all night. Did he identify himself as her boyfriend?"

"Wasn't the perp who called."

"Well, don't you think that's something I should know? Start at the beginning. Your dispatch gave you a call, saying a girl had been beaten severely in the parking lot?"

"No, we were there and somebody ran up and told us."

"Then how did you find out about the phone call?"

"We got it after we were already on the scene."

"And when was that, precisely?"

"I dunno, around two twenty."

"So, some guy using the victim's cell phone calls to report the crime, but you're already there. That means whomever called didn't know you were there, yet. Right?"

"Yeah, I suppose."

Stu held up the one-page report, crumpled it, then tossed it into the garbage can about five feet away. "You guys either need a vacation or a boot up your ass. You are not Chicago's Finest. I'd be embarrassed to sign my name on a four paragraph report. Go back, sit down, write down everything you know, including the critical timelines for everything, and the exact words the caller used when he called in. The report you wrote represents a lazy, half-assed attitude. Do me a favor and tell me everything, including the location and orientation of the body, how quickly you secured the area."

The other one spoke, "That's in the homicide's notes."

"I want it in your report, too. Tell me, did you check her pulse and administer CPR? How long until the crime team showed up? Start off with telling me who your shift supervisor is. There's a young feller whose face is on every national news channel at this hour, and the first-on-scene respondents gave him just four paragraph's worth of their time."

They told him their boss's name in unison.

He stood up, flung a business card at each of them. "Email me a *real* report the moment it's done. I'm heading to Cook County Hospital." ✈

A covered walking bridge crossed over the Interstate north of the hospital. He had taken a good look at it before he walked into the main entrance because it was such a grand expanse. It had a square stepcase on either end, which must have been frustrating for those who traversed it with bicycles. Even more appealing was its shady pathway leading from the northern-most edge of the hospital grounds up to the staircase. The thick trees and foliage meant that he would only be visible from the main entrance, currently unmanned by the police.

He waited a grueling five minutes for the old lady to entertain another visitor and put on her near-vision glasses. When he saw her switch-out her glasses, only then did he waltz by her and out the door. He scanned both directions along the outer walls for any policemen, then jogged casually to the darkened pathway. Once there, he ran at full speed to the staircase and flew up the three flights two steps at a time.

Reaching the top, he held his head low and walked casually over the great expanse of the bridge, since he was again visible from most areas of the hospital. No doubt the police were on high alert. He was playing the odds that their search was focused primarily throughout the hospital's interior.

Reaching the other side, he dashed quickly down the steps and into one of the poorest and most neglected parts of the city of Chicago. He began running, putting a maximum amount of distance between him and the hospital.

Fortunately, it was the hottest part of the day, and few people were outside.

He was in great shape, but the late-afternoon heat was still omnipresent, and the mile run north of the hospital was done at a near-sprinter's pace. The whole way, he half-expected someone to yell, "Freeze, maggot!" like the police did on TV. But no one followed. No sirens. Nonetheless, every twenty seconds or so, he whipped his head around, looking for the authorities. He slowed his pace when he saw the campus of Malcolm X College. It's facilities seemed like an oasis amidst the squalor of matchbox homes, weeds, and broken concrete. The building in front was also the one with the most promise: Memorial Library. He thought he'd get lost in the crowd while he figured out his next step. Wiping his face with his shirt, he walked into the library. He was sweaty, out of breath, and the only white person in there: not good if you're trying to be inconspicuous. He saw a vestibule labeled "Rest Rooms" and headed that way.

He went through the door, into a stall and took inventory of himself. He had a cell phone and a little over eight hundred dollars in his pocket. What he needed was information, and fast. At least they wouldn't think to look for him on a predominantly black college campus. Then he glanced at Alan's phone. *Idiot!,* he thought, then quickly turned it off. By now, they must know he had Alan's phone and were triangulating his position. *Stupid. Stupid. Stupid.* He pictured a handful of policemen at that very moment huddling around a computer screen, watching a small white circle moving on a map north from the hospital, then stopping.

He didn't have much time.

After he made himself more presentable, he walked out and up to the front counter. No one took notice. A young girl smiled and said, "Can I help you?"

"Yes ma'am. I'm a student at Dexter here for the weekend." He handed her his Dexter Student ID. "Can I use your computers to look up something on the Internet?"

"Sure. It's five dollars an hour for visiting students."

"Thanks." He reached in his billfold and extracted a five. "Here y' go."

She took the bill, then wrote down a username and password on a slip of paper, then handed it to him. "Computers are on the second floor on the left. No food or drink."

"Thank you." He nodded, they both smiled, and soon he was upstairs and online, but not before first noticing where the red EXIT signs were located. His credited his flying experience with thinking ahead of possible scenarios. He thought of this situation as a long-running flight emergency, and tried to remain calm and think ahead. This is where the discipline of being a pilot was going to pay off. Some of the best flying adages were also mixed metaphors: "Don't paint yourself into a corner" and "Never be out of both airspeed and options." Knowing more than one way out of the building might come in handy this afternoon.

He typed "murder" and "Dexter" and "Brinkley" into Google and to his horror he saw over a thousand matches! "Oh, no," he muttered in the quiet of the second floor. He looked around, but no one had looked up. He clicked on the FoxNews.com link and his picture covered a quarter of the screen. He looked around again, then minimized the window and clicked on the BBC link. This time, it was mostly text and the picture of him was much smaller, so he began reading:

Just one day after a small university in the central United States announced a breakthrough discovery in manufacturing, one of the students credited with this invention was brutally murdered while attending a concert in Chicago. Miss Monica Barnes, was transported to Cook County hospital where she is reported to have died of massive trauma to the head. Police have not commented, but sources say they are trying to find Steve Brinkley, the student team's leader, in connection with this killing. It is unclear of the true motive for this killing, but it is believed to be due to a disagreement in ownership of the patent.

His eyes glazed over as he was again reminded that she was gone. He finished the article, then read another, then found one which referenced a press release from yesterday at Dexter. He clicked on it, then placed the computer's headsets over his ears and listened. After listening in amazement to what had transpired yesterday, he hit the REWIND button on the screen, then grabbed a score-card pencil from the corner of the computer desk, reached in his wallet and pulled out a deposit receipt, and began jotting notes and he replayed the press conference. He wrote Bruce McPort, Fox 20 News, then drew a swooping line underneath his name. This man knew about him even before the news conference started. *But how?* He had become invisible over the past four years. McPort must be good.

He hit the REFRESH button on his browser and the number of Google matches jumped to eighteen hundred. This was a growing story. He could have spent hours combing through all of the articles, but he concluded he knew everything that he could at the moment. Now he had to hide, and this was not the place.

Looking around, he emptied the computer's memory cache and closed out his session, then moved with purpose down to the lobby and outside. He looked at an angle down the street and saw a really old Toyota with its hood up, an elderly black man leaning into the engine block, pouring in a quart of oil.

He walked across the street, then down the uneven sidewalk another seventy-five feet. Reaching him, he said, "Isn't it too hot to be working on your car?"

The man looked up, sweat running down his face in streams. "Yeah, but I need sunlight. Can't work on it after dark."

"I used to have this car. Celica hatchback," he lied. "What year is it?"

"Eighty-one."

"No kidding. Does it run?"

"Barely."

"Sell it to me?"

The old man looked up, puzzled.

Steve may have been too quick with his pitch. Time to slow things down. "It's just that I rebuild old cars, and this one may be salvageable. It would be kind of nice to work on a car I used to own."

"How much you willing to pay?"

"I'll give you three hundred here and now."

"A thousand."

"For that? You got the title?"

"No."

"No title? Then the most I can give you is four hundred."

"Five."

Steve walked all the way around it. The old man twisted the top off a second quart of 10W30 and poured it in.

"Deal, provided it runs."

The old man looked away, wiped his face, then slammed down the hood. Steve's heart jumped. He wiped his face again, then looked back at him. "Cash only."

In less than a minute, the man was paid and Steve was driving away in a 1981 Orange Toyota Celica, headed for Palwaukee Airport. ✈

Fortunately for the Barnes' they were told about their daughter by their next door neighbors. Otherwise, they probably would have tried to drive to the hospital themselves. That would have been dangerous given their state of mind. Mrs. Barnes' best friend had logged into her Yahoo! Account and noticed the news headline regarding the murder of a Dexter student and clicked on it, moments later screaming to her husband. The good neighbors they were, they sent the kids to another neighbors, then walked next door and told MoJo's parents the news.

It was very confusing at first—it must have been a mistake. MoJo would never have come home to Chicago without calling them. However, when they turned on Fox News, her picture was being shown, and their worst fears were confirmed. The shock, which turned to grief, transformed into rage when they learned that Steve Brinkley was being sought in connection with her murder. The neighbor wife hugged them and stayed with them while the neighbor husband tried to find out where MoJo had been taken. When he found out, he ran next door and wheeled his car into the Barnes driveway, then collected the other three and sped away towards Cook County Hospital.

Detective Stu Varney presented his credentials to the policeman patrolling the area just outside the emergency entrance only a few short minutes before the Barnes foursome arrived. He had been taken to the room where MoJo had been wheeled, and was surprised and shocked at what he saw. You never get used to seeing young people like this. He began taking notes from the doctors on call when a knock on the door interrupted them, letting them know that the parents arrived.

Stu looked down at MoJo, then said to the doctors, "Let me handle this."

He thanked the doctors, then stepped out of the room and looked down the hallway. He could see a group of people near the entrance. One man was hugging a lady. Closer to him, a perky ER Technician smiled at him as she approached. He nodded—not returning the smile, then spoke softly, "Ma'am, where can I have a private moment with the girl's parents? They just got here."

The tech became serious when she concluded which girl he was referring to (MoJo wasn't the only one brought in that afternoon). Dealing with family and friends was the worst part of working in the ER. Her head swiveled around, then back to him. "Sir, just use this room." She reached in her pocket and unlocked an adjacent door leading into a small office.

"Thank you. Are you busy? Could you please bring them to me. I don't want to meet them in the lobby." He needed to gather his thoughts and didn't want to answer a single question until they were all alone. This was never easy. He thought of his own son Drake and wondered whether he could keep it together.

"Sure." She reversed course.

Moments later, he was pacing slowly as they rounded the corner and came in. Expecting two, four appeared, which meant someone would be left standing. Based on the body language and flushed faces of the couple in front, he extended his hand first to the lady and said, "Missus Barnes, I am Stuart Varney. I am a detective with the Illinois State Bureau of Investigation."

He thereafter shook hands with the father, introduced himself to the other couple, then said, "Please close the door." ✈

Chapter Sixteen

The noise was so intense, Stu could hardly converse with the investigation team. Compared with the ER an hour ago, it was a three-ringed circus of events at The Pavilion. Two hundred yards away, a band was playing to a cheering crowd. Closer in, a small crowd had gathered and was gawking from behind a long bright yellow "POLICE. DO NOT CROSS." tape, which had been moved further away from MoJo's car. A team of reporters mixed with the crowd, each trying to find out what the investigator's knew.

Stu had left the Barnes with the hospital's minister until their own preacher arrived. His mind kept wandering back to Drake, who was safely at home.

Now the sun was setting, so Stu ordered floodlights from the CPD Armory to illuminate the crime scene. The lights would arrive within the hour. Saturday afternoons were usually slow for CPD, but turns into utter havoc once darkness envelops the city and the unwashed emerge. This crime promised an early start to a busy evening for the crime scene investigators.

"Everything inventoried?" Stu asked.

"Yes, and we have thoroughly swept the grounds. Fortunately, the area was not well worn. We found that someone made field-grade imprints in the grass behind the car. If this had been an asphalt lot, we wouldn't have been able to deduce some things."

"Imprints? What kind of imprints?"

"Here. Look." The impish investigator with thick goggles for glasses led Stu around to the back. Four stakes were stuck in the ground enclosing a three by three foot area. Wrapped between them at the top was more "POLICE. DO NOT CROSS." tape.

"I don't see anything."

"Those two indentations at the back, moon-shaped?"

"Yeah."

"They're the front of two hard-soled shoes. And see where the grass is flattened in front of them?"

"Yeah."

"The guy's knees."

"How do you know they aren't a woman's knees?"

"The ground's soft, but it ain't *that* soft. Of course it could have been a two hundred fifty pound woman wearing men's dress shoes."

Stu smiled. This was the Chicago PD he knew and loved.

"What was he doing, praying for forgiveness?"

"Doubtful. He has studying or examining whatever he removed forcibly from the trunk. Look." He pointed at a jagged hole in the trunk door, which was raised. "The trunk's keyhole was smashed with something akin to a jackhammer, given that it had been ejected inside the trunk, leaving nothing but a hole where the keylock assembly had been. Somebody must have gotten something out of the trunk and was reading it or examining it out of sight. They obviously didn't care that the break-in would be noticed later."

"You think this was done today?"

"Yes. They would have been driving with the trunk up, otherwise. It's spring-loaded up. No evidence that it had been tied down, and the parking attendant said he would have noticed a raised trunk."

"Hmm."

"That's an utterance often conveyed during these kinds of investigations."

Again, Stu smiled. He liked this guy. "You know, if I was Brinkley I probably would have simply opened the trunk with her key."

"Unless he didn't care whether she knew he was snooping or wanted to take something from the trunk and have her *think* it was theft. She obviously surprised him, except one thing bugs me."

"Just one thing?"

"Yeah. The blood splattered on the car from about waist height. She was down on all fours when she was hit. Look at how these marks hit the other car's door panel. See how the streaks extend *upward*? Someone delivered a real haymaker to her. Looks like we'll be putting gravity on the witness stand. Gravity is always a good and consistent witness."

"Any other physical evidence?"

"Sure. His prints are all over the car. Recent prints. Fortunately, his prints were on file from his terrorism charges several years ago. They came back positive within fifteen minutes."

"Anything in the trunk?"

"Nothing of any consequence. Typical kid's car. It's nasty back there. This girl had ancient Burger King wrappers, dirty clothes, a Frisbee, a beat-up John Lescroart novel, a rag with car wax on it, etc." The man adjusted his glasses, then turned and walked to the front of the car as he continued, "We did, however, find his phone being charged in the car."

"More proof he was here. These kids don't go anywhere without there cell phones."

"Well, she did. Her cell phone is nowhere to be found."

"Can I have his phone?"

"Yeah, I suppose. It's been cataloged and my tech guys have already gone through it's files thoroughly. Just sign for it over at the van." ✈

If either of the two codes had changed over the past four years, Steve would be screwed—maybe even caught. The trip to the large general aviation airport had only taken an hour, including a stop for gas and some fast food—who knows when he'd be able to eat again. More importantly than gas and food, in the convenience store he saw that they still sold Pay As You Go cell phones. They had been popular when he was in high school and thought they were just a fad. He bought one, along with five hundred extra minutes in addition to the one hundred that came with the phone. Minutes were a lot more expensive than his normal phone, but the important thing to him was it got him reconnected, since he couldn't turn on Alan's phone without risking being tracked. As he laid down the dwindling cash he wondered whether drug dealers and miscreants used these types of throw-away phones. If so, the authorities must have some sort of way to track them. Still, it was better than Alan's. Now he was at the security gate at the Williams Air Center FBO (Fixed Based Operator), the place where Mr. Herrmann kept his airplane.

Mr. Herrmann was a workaholic friend of his fathers. During his senior year in high school, Steve obtained his private pilot's license at Palwaukee Airport and had gone flying in Mr. Herrmann's airplane a number of times. Impressed with Steve's flying and decision making skills, Herrmann had told him, "Steve, I probably put no more than fifty hours a year on that airplane. I'm barely keeping my landing currency and these airplanes need to be flown regularly. Keep it topped-off and it's yours when you need it. Just let me know if you want to keep it overnight somewhere."

That had been four years ago. Since then, Steve's life had taken a number of reroutes. Although his year at M.I.T. was spent without once grabbing a yoke, once he arrived in Kernsville he went straight to the airport and hooked up with an instructor who got him his instruments rating, commercial privileges, and CFI (certified flight instructor) rating. He used his dad's credit card. Fortunately, Mr. Brinkley never balked at Steve's flying aspirations. Steve needed fifteen hundred hours in order to get his Airline Transport Pilot rating. The ATP is the one rating he thought he needed to either get a job with the regional airlines or simply to gain the respect of his fellow aviators. He was several hundred hours of flight time away from even being eligible to get that one.

The FBO looked much improved. He guessed that business was good. They even renamed the airport to Chicago Executive Airport, but it was still known as Palwaukee. A row of well-manicured perennials lined the edge of the new asphalt road leading from the side of the main entrance out to the ramp. Herrmann's hangar used to be the sixth one down on the left. Hopefully it still was. The key code to get on the ramp had been 0415 (tax day) plus the two-digit hangar number, in this case 06. He drove up to the wrought iron gate and punched #041506# into the keypad and the gate began sliding open.

Good. He drove onto the ramp and down the row of hangars until reaching Hangar Six.   He looked around. Two rows of hangars flanked a common taxiway that lead out past an outdoor tie-down ramp, then out to a parallel taxiway to the main runway. Easily a third of the hangar doors were open and empty. After all, Saturday was the day when people pull their airplanes out and go fly. It was a trusting environment. Even though many had thousands of dollars worth of tools, spares, and equipment in their hangars, they left the big doors open when they were out flying, unless they would be going on an extended trip.

He hopped out of the car, only then considering that perhaps Mr. Herrmann had sold the airplane and the hangar was no longer his.

Sure enough, the lock was different. *Rats.* The previous lock had been a small attache lock with a combo of 7-2-2 (Mr.

Herrmann birthday was July 22nd). This was a much larger lock with four digits.

Now what? The hangar would have been the perfect place to hide and regroup. He couldn't go to his dad's house. His dad was in Europe, but the police would be watching the house. He couldn't go to Kernsville. He couldn't check into a hotel. He had no one to call. At this point, he really had no back up plan. He was about to hop back in his car. Just for kicks, he entered 0722 on the dial and yanked.

It opened! He stared at the lock in amazement for a moment, then quickly removed the lock and pulled on the large roller door enough to peek inside. He was relieved to see Mr. Herrmann's plane: a white Cessna 182 with a blue and red stripe along the length of the fuselage. The hangar wasn't large—just big enough to contain the airplane, a work table and a tan storage cabinet at the left corner. The place was organized, but dusty. He glanced to the right and knew there was enough room on the right to park his car, albeit under the wing.

So he clicked on the lights, swung the door all the way open, pulled his car in, then closed the hangar door completely. Once safely inside, he relaxed. Now he had a place to hide, at least for the night.

Staring at the airplane, it brought back fond memories of flying MoJo up to Lake Geneva for a "hundred dollar hamburger," i.e. five bucks for the burger and ninety-five dollars getting there and back. Nowadays, it's probably called a two hundred dollar hamburger, given the price of aviation fuel.

He smiled at the airplane. The first time MoJo complimented him on anything was after a nice landing in that very aircraft.

Alone and quiet, he realized that today had been the longest and most difficult day of his life. How could he ever get any sleep. He crawled into the hatchback of the car, moved some old road flares and jumper cables to the side, laid down and closed his eyes. Within minutes he drifted off. ✈

Chapter Seventeen

An airplane engine roared to life just outside the hangar. Steve was instantly awakened, became reacquainted with his surroundings, stretched, then looked at his watch: five A.M. He jumped out of the back of the car and stretched again. His mouth was dry and he needed a shower. This was not a safe place, he reasoned. What if today just happened to be the day that Mr. Herrmann decided to go flying? How could he pass through the gate again without being noticed?

He waited for the airplane to taxi away, then he opened the hangar door, got in his car, drove it out, hopped out, yanked the hangar door closed. He fumbled with the lock, first clumsily, then almost panicked when he couldn't get it closed. He was exposed now. He jiggled it like his life depended on it. Finally he got it closed. Scrambling to his car, he drove to the gate where a sensor opened it automatically for exiting vehicles.

Ten minutes later he was walking into a twenty-four hour Wal-Mart. Ten minutes after that he was back in his car with a new laptop purchased with his father's credit card. He drove a quarter of a mile to a Comfort Inn, parked next to the lobby, then logged-in to their open Internet connection.

He couldn't call Alan—Steve had his phone, so he sent Alan an email, hoping that no one had yet figured out his email address and obtained a court order to obtain access to it. The email itself was intentionally vague:

Please upload the program you thought was worthless onto the site. Create a folder called "_program" in lower case and put it

there. I'm on a new computer and don't have it. FTP user ID is
"MoJo" and password is "mach1" and are both case sensitive.
When it's there, I'll get the program then I'll send you a note to
remove it. Then I have a lot to tell you.

Steve hit the SEND button, and felt himself relax a little.
Yet a lot of unknowns existed: Did Alan even know about MoJo? If
so, had he been taken into custody for questioning? Was he
anywhere near a computer? Were the police already waiting in the
wings?

Then he thought, *The Hellums!* It was Sunday morning, not
yet six o'clock. Surely they would understand, so he looked up their
number on the Internet, then dialed it into his throw-away phone.

"Hello," answered Mr. Hellums on the first ring.

"Mr. Hellums, it's Steve Brinkley." He wondered what
response this would bring.

"My God, Steve, are you okay?"

"Yes, sir, but have you heard?"

"Yes, last night. We stayed up until after midnight. It's on
the national news, but it's on full-time on the local channels. What
happened?"

"We were at the Battle of the Bands and had just met up
with Alan. She went back to her car to get something and never
came back. When I went to go find her, the car was surrounded by
policeman. They said she had been beaten and an ambulance had
taken her to the hospital. I guess I panicked and ran away to catch a
cab to the hospital. When I got there I saw the news that not only
had she died, but that *I* was being sought in connection with it."

"Where are you, son?"

He thought about it for a minute, then said, "Mr. Hellums, I
don't want you involved. Matter of fact, please feel free to call the
police after we hang up. I don't want you to be evasive at all with
them—just tell them that you talked to me but I wouldn't tell you

where I am for your own sake. I just called because I needed to talk to someone."

"Thanks for thinking of us. You're in our prayers. We know you loved that young lady."

Steve was again reminded of how insightful the old man was. "She was everything to me. I can barely function. I have to find out who did this. The only reason I'm still on the run is I can't figure this out from a jail cell."

"How can we help?"

"Just please believe in me. I met yesterday with Evo Financial in Chicago. They are the only ones who had any reason to do something like this. Once I get my ducks in line, I'll contact the police and let them try to close the gaps."

"Evo, you say? Never heard of them. Son, listen, you sure are mixing metaphors, a sure sign that you aren't thinking straight. Just calm down. We're here for you. What about Zimmerman?"

"What do you mean?"

"He made the news conference on Friday without any of you there. He didn't even mention your names until that pretty-boy reporter brought up your name. I suspect he's pretty greedy and focused. He's also hot-tempered and prone to violence."

"It's a stretch that he would make the leap from pushing a student to killing one. Was that reporter named McPort?"

"Yeah, he's been reporting like crazy since this started. At this point, don't rule anyone out, son. Oh, by the way, Charms is back in town."

"He is?! I have to talk to him."

"Get in line. He called me using his one free phone call from jail." ✈

After an hour of research, a call to the news director on call at Fox 20, followed by one confirmation call, Steve placed the most important call of the day.

"McPort here."

Steve was really laying down his cards at this point by calling him. The previous calls had been anonymous. This call was not going to be, and the conversation could go in many directions, just like the one with Mr. Hellums. He had stared at the phone for a good two minutes before making the call. Now he wasn't sure what to say.

"Hello?" McPort asked, since no one replied.

"Bruce, it's Steve Brinkley."

A moment of silence ensued, followed by, "Cut the shit." Then *click.*

Rats. Maybe it was a good thing that he thought it was a crank call.

Then his phone rang. *Jeez, how stupid could I be.* He should have hit *78 to hide the caller I.D. like he did on the previous two. He needed zero mistakes. Now he was committed. He knew who was calling and skipped the formalities. "Bruce, it's really me."

"What's MoJo's middle name?"

"Joanne."

"Her birth date?"

He told him.

"The hell are you calling me for? Do you know you are the most wanted man in the country right now? Appears you are both dangerous and stupid."

"I've seen your reports. I think you're bright—or at least persistent—and I think you can be of help to me."

"Why should I help a murderer who's on the lam?"

"Because you can either report the news with everyone else or be part of the news. Maybe win yourself a Pulitzer or something. You can hang up and call the police and I'll smash this phone, then you can report that you talked to me. Big whoop. Here's a travel tip: don't do it. It won't help your career. Or, we can start a dialog, develop some trust. You can help me find the people who did this to MoJo."

By now, McPort had left the room where his wife was still sleeping and had walked downstairs to his home office in the back. "It's called aiding and abetting, Brinkley. Perhaps with your personal history you've heard that phrase before."

"Nice. I thought opening a dialog might benefit us both. Have a good day." This time, he hung up. He shook his head, knowing that he'd now have to buy another phone, only this time the police would be investigating all new pay-as-you-go cell phone calls.

He was about to turn the phone off and throw it away when it rang again. He clicked ANS and said, "Look, we're not getting off to a good start here. You may have misunderstood me. I'm not begging, I'm offering.. You stand to be the focal point in the number one news story in the nation, so don't screw with me. Understand this, Bruce. I may be only twenty-two, but I'm smarter than you. I may need help, but it doesn't have to be from you. Understand?"

"Fine."

"Fine is not definitive. I want a 'Yes, sir' or a 'No, sir.' You must also know that you'll have to do some deep-level research with some pretty seedy people to get to the truth. You're not going to turn white on me are you?"

"No, sir."

"Good answer. You stand to become known with the ranks of Woodward, of Krackaur, of Armanpour. But it's not without risk. Agree to do this and succeed: you'll be the envy of your peers and the world will be your jelly donut. Agree to this and fail: I'll take you down."

"And just how are you going to do that?"

"I'll start with your wife. You know, you were a no-show for dinner last night with Brenda Hinson down in Kernsville. You've got good taste; she's pretty cute, but she's pissed. You won't be dealing with one scorned woman, you'll be dealing with two. Shall I continue?"

In a defeated tone, he said, *"No."*

"'No' what?"

"No, sir."

"Good. So we've agreed that I'm smarter than you. Are you willing to help?"

After a moment, he heard the answer he wanted: "Yes, sir."

"The first thing I need to know is the lead investigator's name and his phone number. Can you handle that?" ✈

After he finished with McPort, he made one more call, one that was incredibly short: "Check your email." *Click.* He was done with the phone and smashed it so he wouldn't be tempted to use it later. ✈

Chapter Eighteen

Risk Analysis was a phrase Steve recalled from a 300-level course in Engineering Management. It was a process, a methodology for measuring actions along a risk/reward scale. The more you can quantify, the better chance you have of knowing the probability of success. He kept a spreadsheet open and had various groups of things listed under the "Evasion of Capture" heading, such as Locale, Traceability, Anonymity, etc. He concluded he could stay under the radar for several weeks, if necessary, provided he didn't violate any self-imposed rules like using any more credit cards, logging into known email or web sites, using "tagged" phones or calling any of his circle of friends.

The other column was equally important: "Murder Investigation Success" This one had no groups, only items such as "Company Firewall," "Internal Contacts," "Police/FBI Involvement," etc. Obviously if he could get the authorities interested enough in considering Evo, then that would be a level of effort and resources available that he could not match. Each time he looked at that column, he concluded that he would have to do the lion's share of the legwork, at least initially. The two columns, "Evasion of Capture" and "Murder Investigation Success," were diametrically opposed. The more he investigated, the more exposed he would be. The deeper he hid, the lower the chance of finding evidence that Evo had murdered MoJo.

Steve looked around the dark hangar. The only light came from the work table and his laptop. He recognized he did have a stroke of luck when it came to the aircraft hangar. To boot, there was a weak Internet signal emanating from the FBO, a bonus. With the first of the five new cell phones he bought at five different quick shops, he called Mr. Herrmann's office and the answering service told him he had left for his annual trip to the North Carolina Outer Banks for some beach time with the family. The hangar was his, but he was also down to less than a hundred in cash out of the original eight hundred. He couldn't just hang out there indefinitely. The police or FBI only had one suspect—him. He needed to help them exonerate himself.

The spreadsheet also contained entries under the Evasion of Capture column regarding the cash withdrawals. By now, the FBI would have looked at his banking transactions and noticed the two withdrawals, one from the ATM next to the hospital, and the other from the nearby branch. Yes, they had to have concluded, he had been to the hospital yesterday.

The Celica would not be a liability unless the old black man had seen the news *and* recognized him as the guy to whom he sold his car. He assigned a "2" value (out of ten), but as the week progressed, he would raise it to a much higher value because eventually the man would see a picture of him.

So, too, were other entries in the list. The laptop purchase with his dad's credit card would eventually be noticed. Any more purchases with that card would have to be done quickly, because his dad would be contacted very soon, even though he was overseas. *Boy is dad going to hit the roof.*

Bottom line: he had to investigate Evo quickly, because eventually he was going to be caught—so says the Risk Analysis.

He pushed the laptop back and thought about what communications methods available.
It was basically the Internet and his five throw-away phones. Yet the Internet was, for now, only good for gathering information, not sending. It had been a few hours since he logged into

HotBlackTruck.com to see if Charms had gotten the message and uploaded the encryption software so they could start communicating. The new laptop didn't have the encryption software and the only way he could get it was via Charms. But the last he had heard, Charms had arrived back from Cancun only to be detained and questioned regarding MoJo's death. Eventually he would get the message and check his email—but the risk now was that so would the FBI. Of course it would take full disclosure by Charms. Steve knew him well enough to know Charms wouldn't 1) think he had anything to do with MoJo's death and 2) wouldn't cut off his only chance to hear what Steve had to say. He was about to start digging into Evo's web pages—basically starting from nowhere—when he thought he'd try the encrypted site again, just in case.

  This time when the site window came up, a new advertising button appeared, "Refinance your home!" Steve almost laughed out loud and said, "Yes!" even before he clicked on it. No one clicks on banner ads. *Typical Charms*, he thought. Hidden in plain sight.

  He clicked on it and a small, official-looking pop-up window appeared.

> "Warning. The file you are attempting to open contains virus 301-D (The "Daisy" virus). Please close this window and CANCEL the download."

"Ha!" Steve said to no one. That Charms is good. He had put in a second "fence" to stop anyone who would casually find the site, then casually click on the link. Steve knew it was a ruse and immediately clicked SAVE to save the file on his hard drive. Then he ran the file and installed the encryption software. After it was installed, he logged into the site as the administrator and check the download statistics: Downloads: 1 Number of visitors: 212. *Good.* The search engine web spiders were finding it already, but these numbers probably indicated that no one else knew about the site.

He immediately removed the encryption program, and the banner ad. Then he logged out. *Got it!*

Now, he looked into the blog on HotBlackTruck.com and saw a new post:

```
Tvhwg/!K#dcq(v#cgojgyf"vig*t"jpph/"#Zqx!
oxtv#cg#egybuwbvhe.#bpg!ufbthe.#bpg!
cqht|/"#J)yf"noqzo"ipt#gqxs"|fcut"dcqxu"wig#uyr!qi!{rv0#!
Jdoi#jp#ujhsg1!"Dmcq(u#pp#cqdsf/!
vrp0#J"pfv#xkwi"kjo#bhwft#ujh!
rrmkff"ofv#ng#hq1!"Zf"zfpw!hrs"d!tleg#jp#ikv!
eds"vp"wig#qqojeh!ervngo)w!gyfugsqs/"### L(o#xkwi"|
pw/!dxe0#!/Ficunu1
```

He copied the text into the offline program and it revealed:

Steve, I can't believe she's gone. You must be devastated, and scared, and angry. I've known for four years about the two of you. Hang in there. Alan's on board, too. I met with him after the police let me go. We went for a ride in his car so the police couldn't eavesdrop.

Here's a start: We called the Hellums (no, we didn't dare go there) from my girlfriend's phone. They had already gotten a hold of their son in California, who called Evo. He said he was with the law firm of Yada Yada and told the answering service that he needed to reach Harold Talone immediately. She told him he flew out to be with his family at Lake Okoboji this weekend. Well, Mr. Hellums got the address on the Internet somehow. It's in Northwest Iowa. Here it is: 29921 East Trailfoot Road, West Okoboji, Iowa. I don't think you'll get anything if you show up at his doorstep, but maybe you can park out next to his house and get into his wireless or something. I know you must have a phone by now--leave me your number in RPL back with me.

I'm with you, bud. I'll check back here every hour.
-Charms.

Steve sat back and re-read the message. Then he sent back the phone number—backwards as requested by the "Reverse Polish Logic" acronym, along with a thank you. Then he logged out, closed the lid to the laptop and closed his eyes.

What could he possibly gain by meeting Talone face-to-face? It's not like he could simply walk up to him and ask, "Hey Harold, did you kill my girlfriend?" That would be reckless—obviously if Talone had anything to do with it, it would have been carried out by people who didn't even know who the original "customer" was. This man was the leader of a billion dollar investment firm. Talone wasn't stupid. On the contrary. No, he need to establish goals, devise a plan, and measure the probability of success against the risks.

He looked at his watch: ten A.M. on Sunday in a darkened aircraft hangar, with precious few options. He had no choice, so he began to formulate a plan. The first was to get Talone's itinerary for his return to Chicago. If he couldn't match the timelines, then he'd simply abandon the whole idea. Thirty minutes later, with a plan in mind, he was on his way to Radio Shack, then one more trip to Wal-Mart. Within an hour and fifteen minutes, Mr. Herrmann's Cessna 182 was airborne and climbing out on a VFR flight westbound.

But he had a lot to do before he landed in Spencer, Iowa, in order for his plan to work. In the passenger seat were five elbow-length chains, a lock, an LED flashlight, a 370 Ohm resistor, a small DIP-sized solenoid, a road flare, a model rocket fuse, a three and a half millimeter stereo headset jack, a throw-away cell phone, a nine-volt battery and clips, and a couple rolls of electrical tape. Hopefully he didn't forget anything. Once he leveled at twenty-five hundred feet and leaned the engine, he trimmed the airplane and began assembling the contraption. He only had an hour and a half to put it together. ✈

"Stu Varney here." He hated the way that phone rang, especially on a Sunday morning. He didn't get home until almost three A.M. He also had nothing in terms of leads. It was like Brinkley disappeared into thin air. He always gave himself at least six hours of sleep. Otherwise, he'd make mental mistakes. Adequate sleep was just as important as being on duty.

"Mr. Varney?"

"Special Agent Varney. Who's calling?"

"This is Bruce McPort, Fox Twenty News down in Kernsville."

"I don't speak to reporters."

"You'll speak to me. I just got off the phone with Steve Brinkley." ✈

Chapter Nineteen

Steve was flying the plane with his knee while twisting two wires together when the phone rang. He put down the apparatus, and grabbed the phone. He didn't recognize the number. He wasn't sure if the phone had voice mail and right about the time he decided to answer it, it quit ringing. He started to call the number back, but then thought twice. He was juggling too many tasks. *Get your mind straight.* Then it rang again.

There was a better than even chance he knew who it was. *Aw, screw it.* "Hello."

"Steve, it's Charms."

"Thank God. I didn't recognize the number."

"It's Mrs. Hellums' phone. You okay?"

Good thinking, Charms. "Yeah. I'm glad you called."

"Jeez, you sound like you're in an airplane."

"I am. Heading west out of Chicago. Listen, I need a couple of things from you. Call a guy at Fox20 named Bruce McPort and tell him you need him to give you the lead murder investigator's name and phone number. He should have it by now. Then, if all goes well, I'm going to need you to make a call to three people in a couple of hours."

"Okay"

"I'm sorry, but I'll fill you in later. I've got my hands full here. Thanks for trusting me."

"What's not to trust?" ✈

With each passing moment, he got more angry with the prospect of meeting MoJo's killer face to face. He also thought of his father. Did his father know that Talone was a cold-blooded murderer? *Impossible.*

He considered this evil creature, and felt his chest tighten. Anger was a certainly a motivator, but could also make Steve do something foolish. He tried to allay those feelings and stay focused on the mission. He called the Flight Service Station on VHF Frequency 122.2 megahertz and asked if a certain tail number had filed an IFR flight plan from Spencer to Chicago. They said yes. He asked what time they were expected to depart, their ETD. When they told him, he looked at his watch.

He didn't have much time and he needed to practice a number of contingencies in his mind, should things not go as planned. ✈

The Hellums watched their TV, virtually in tears. On the screen, a distraught couple came out of their house and faced a crowd of reporters. The husband proclaimed to the world, "This man murdered our daughter. Over what, some invention? Listen, if you're out there watching this, Brinkley, we're going to find you and we are going to watch you fry." The husband hugged his wife, who looked like she had been crying for weeks.

"That poor couple," said Missus Hellums, getting up slowly.

"Yeah, I understand how they must feel. But how is anyone going to look beyond Steve for suspects?"

She went into the kitchen, still talking, "It's not like we can call the police and say, 'I know that boy. He couldn't have done it.'"

Mister Hellums raised his voice so she could hear him. "You know, I can call Doc Carlock. He'd know something about Zimmerman."

From in the kitchen, she almost yelled, "You still think he could have done it?"

"No, but we might as well find out all we can. You never know."

She walked back in, walked right over to the phone, picked it up, and handed it to him. "Okay *Detective* Leroy. If you think it'll help." ✈

Chapter Twenty

Somewhere over Western Illinois, over two thousand feet in the air, the Cessna 182 caught fire. Now it wasn't just that the plan would have to be abandoned; Steve was now struggling just to stay alive. He had finished assembling the electrical connections on the apparatus he was going to use on Talone. However, as soon as he attached the second wire to the model rocket fuse inserted into the roadside flare, it ignited. The leather passenger seat seemed almost pyrophoric; the conflagration that ensued was sudden and intense. The cockpit filled immediately with dense smoke. Steve tried not to panic, but the worst thing a pilot can face is a fire. Engines can quit, you can get a stuck landing gear, but a fire is a big deal.

He reached behind his seat and blindly located the fire extinguisher, yanking it out of its cradle. Then he pulled the pin, squeezed the trigger, and sprayed it at the base of the flare. The force of the extinguisher blew the flare onto the passenger floorboard. He put out the seat, then leaned over and redirected the spray onto the flare which was now burning the floor mat. However, it wouldn't extinguish. He popped-open the passenger window and the noise level in the cockpit doubled. Now, a mixture of smoke and Halon was blowing everywhere. The net affect was that it created even more smoke in the cockpit. Forcing himself to remain calm, he continued spraying the extinguisher on it as he pulled the engine to idle and began a descent, though he couldn't see anything and was coughing uncontrollably.

He couldn't open his eyes because the smoke stung them. He should have tried to throw the flare out the window, but instead opted to obey Rule One: Fly the Airplane. Blindly, he pulled back on the yoke, judging by the wind noise that the plane was slowing, then he reached over and selected the first notch of flaps. The plane pitched up and he added some down trim.

The survivability of a crash landing is directly proportional to the speed of impact, he recalled. *Slow it down. Don't panic.* He added another notch of flaps. He reached up, felt for the fresh air vent, and yanked it open.

As the fire extinguisher bottle emptied, he realized his persistence worked. The fire went out. Through the fading smoke, he saw his attitude indicator and knew his wings were level. Then he saw the altitude indicator and was horrified: nine hundred feet and descending at eleven hundred feet per minute. The nine hundred feet was the height above average sea level. Yet the actual height above the ground was only three hundred feet. *Three hundred!* He had only a few seconds until impact. Instinctively, he added full power and pitched the nose to the horizon. The smoke cleared enough to now see and he gained speed and retracted the flaps on schedule. As he regained full control, only then did he pick up the hot flare by its other end and throw it out of the open passenger window.

Calming himself, he looked at the seat. It was charred. The floor mat was also in ruins. He reached into the back seat and dumped his half-consumed bottle of Gatorade on both areas, just in case.

He climbed back up to two thousand feet and flew straight and level for a few minutes, willing his adrenaline level down. This plan was not going well.

On the ground, at least three 9-1-1 calls were made to the Rockford Police Department of an aircraft on fire and descending behind a grove of trees. ✈

"Stu Varney here." He looked at his watch: three thirty P.M.

"Sir, you need to investigate Professor Jack Zimmerman at Dexter University regarding the murder of Miss Barnes. He has some gambling debts and quite a temper."

"I will. Whom, may I ask is calling?"

"I'm just a citizen seeking the truth. Thank you." Click.

Stu looked at the phone's Caller ID. It was blocked, of course. He pulled out his pad and wrote, "Anon call: elderly man's voice. Prof Jack Zimmerman—Dexter. Gambling. Temper. 3:32 P.M. Sun." Then he sighed and rubbed his eyes. He could sure use an iced coffee. ✈

Steve looked at his right hand as he slowly pushed in the mixture control, preparing for his descent for landing at the Spencer Municipal Airport in Northwest Iowa. The hand was shaking. The right seat and floor mat were charred from the incident over Rockford. There was trash all over the two back seats from where he had thrown things as he assembled the IED (if Charms were there he would have called it "The Truth Encouragement Device.") He would not be testing it—not after the incident earlier in the flight. He actually didn't care whether it worked. It's sole purpose was as a motivator, to get an admission of guilt.

He had assembled the first one in a hurry while flying the airplane. It wasn't really complicated, but he wondered whether the minuscule voltage coming out of the headset jack of the cell phone would be sufficient. It had to trigger the solenoid switch and light the model rocket fuse stuck into the road flare. None of the parts were soldered, simply twisted together and taped.

In fact, the entire device had been bundled and ensconced with electrical tape, then attached with even more of the tape to the center of a yardstick-long chain. Four more chains were attached to that chain with small padlocks. One large padlock was available to complete the unit once it was donned.

The second unit went together much faster, because, well....

The final item bought at Wal-Mart was a pellet pistol. It would be the "incentive" to get Talone to wrap the Truth Device around his waist.

So he had a plan. He had timelines. He had the exit strategy. He had the will. Yet, he had already had complications, including an airborne fire which almost killed him. He also had the uncertainty of who would be with Talone and where this would all play out. At any point in time until Talone spotted him he could abort, he concluded.

Yet his hand was still shaking as he retarded the throttle and began his descent.

"Spencer Traffic, Cessna Two Five Echo, five east, airport advisory please," he announced to anyone on the airport's common frequency. This was a small town airport with little traffic; there was no control tower.

After a moment, a voice came over the airplane's speaker, "Cessna Two Five Tango, Spencer Unicom. Spencer is using runway three zero, left traffic. Are you R.O.N.?"

"No, I'm not staying overnight. Just getting gas."

"Okay. Just pull up next to the building. We'll top you off."

Rats. He had already screwed up. He referred to himself as "Two Five Echo" which was the aircraft's registration number he had always known. However, he had taken masking tape and black paint and changed the "E" to a "B" and should have called himself "Two Five Bravo."

He could not afford any more errors, no matter how insignificant.

Flying overhead the airport, above the traffic pattern altitude, he spotted the single jet on the south end of the ramp. It had to be Talone's. The door was down and two guys were standing next to it. *Must be the pilots.* He scanned the airport road leading out to the highway, then north to Lake Okoboji which he could easily see from his vantage point two thousand feet above the ground. No cars in sight. The sun was getting low in the sky. Actually if he arrived after dark, that would probably be to Steve's benefit.

"Spencer traffic, Cessna Two Five Bravo, overhead for standard entry, runway three zero, Spencer."

He took the airplane west of the airport, descended to traffic pattern altitude, then came back towards the airport, and reported, "Spencer traffic, Cessna Two Five Bravo, forty-five for a left downwind, runway three zero, Spencer."

He entered the downwind, did a mental landing check, then descended on the base leg, scanned the final for any straight-in traffic, then turned final and landed.

Pulling off the runway, he saw a guy come out of the building and head towards the gas truck. There were several parking spots in front of the building, but he chose to park outboard of the jet, a Gulfstream G-150, way in the back of the ramp. As he pulled to a stop, he could see the man had jumped out of the truck and was frantically motioning him to pull up to a spot closer. *No way.*

The guy got in the fuel truck and drove over as Steve yanked on the mixture knob to shut down the engine.

The propeller stopped, but before he turned off the master switch, he entered "KEST" into his GPS unit, for Estherville Airport, an airport even smaller than Spencer located twenty-five miles to the northeast. Then he stored it and turned off the master switch.

It was quiet now in the cockpit, except for the buzzing sound of the attitude indicator gyro that was spinning down.

He looked at his hand. It was no longer shaking.

Shoot. He forgot. *Stay focused!* He flipped on the master switch again. Forgot to check the range back to Kernsville from Estherville. He entered it as Leg Two, then checked the estimated time enroute. After a moment, the screen displayed "2:48." The tanks had about three and a half hours' worth of gas. Should be enough. He flipped the master switch off once again and was startled to see a young man standing right outside the cockpit door.

Steve opened the window on the cockpit door.

"I figured you might want to park a little closer. I was waving at you."

"I'm sorry. Didn't see you. I thought those spots were for overnight parking."

"That's all right. Bathroom's in the FBO."

"Thanks, I'm fine." Steve reached in his billfold and pulled out his dad's credit card. He knew he was leaving a trail, but had no choice. Handing it to him, he said, "Please top it off with your finest hundred low-lead."

"My pleasure, sir. You smell something burning?"

Rats. He turned into him and sniffed, concealing the passenger seat from view. "Oh, that's my Hibachi. Can't do a road trip without it."

The young man must have thought how cool it must be to fly somewhere with a portable barbecue grill because he said, "Now that's traveling in style!" With that he left and started pulling the hose from the reel on the side of the truck. Steve relaxed and continued looking to his left, reading the tail number of the jet. *Good.* It was Talone's. The pilots were back in the airplane, though only one was visible in the cockpit. Steve organized his plan once again. The pellet pistol was at his side. The Truth Encouragement Device was ready. He got out of the airplane and gave it a walk-around inspection. Then he got back in the airplane, pulled out his enroute sectional chart and pretended to be planning his next flight.

Five minutes later, the card was returned to him and the gas truck had pulled away. Now, all he could do was wait. Surely the guy in the jet's cockpit had noticed him parked to his right. Now, he wondered how long he could sit there without drawing any more attention to himself. He spread the chart out across the glare shield and feigned a detailed review. After about five minutes, he put it away and pretended to talk on his cell phone for a while. He couldn't just sit there indefinitely. ✈

He rang the doorbell, then wiped his forehead. Moments later he heard a man approach the door from inside. "Professor Jack Zimmerman?" Stu stood at the professor's front door, sweating, awaiting a response. The sun would be setting soon, but it was still oppressively hot. He had his Starbucks iced coffee in his left hand, half consumed. His right hand was free out of habit, in case he needed to reach for his weapon.

"Yeah, who is it?" The voice came from behind the closed door.

"This is Detective Stuart Varney, Illinois Bureau of Investigation. Got a minute?"

Oh no. "Uhm, yes, detective. Just hang on a sec."

Varney waited but the door didn't open. Seconds passed. He had been in this position before and he didn't like it. The local Kernsville police were already at the back door, should he try to make a break for it. But at the moment, he was exposed. Instinctively, Stu stepped to the side and unclipped the leather holster, placing his hand flat against his weapon.

"Professor?"

Nothing.

He was about to make a call for back up, when the door opened. Stu was shocked at what he saw and moved his hand away from his gun, asking, "What the hell happened to you?"

Zimmerman's right eye was almost swollen shut and a large cut traversed the bridge of his nose. The area around the eye was a mixture of yellow, black, blue, and purple tints. It was a nasty sight.

"Brinkley. He nailed me as I got out of my car this morning."

"Brinkley was here? You saw him?!"

Zimmerman's right eye shifted. "Well, I never actually saw him. Next thing I knew I was on the ground."

"Why did he attack you?"

"He thinks it's all my fault—everything. Yet I was the one who encouraged them to get the patent paperwork submitted and to not enter the Bernoulli Award competition at all. Now he feels like Mahoney Aerospace has stolen their idea."

"Listen, I'm not a patent attorney, and I don't know about these claims and rights. But don't you think he would have taken his frustration out on, say, Mahoney Aerospace?"

"Well, I guess he also thinks that Dexter University stole it from them, too."

"Is he right?"

"Not that we stole it. It would have been a shared patent and they knew it. They developed it in our labs, at our cost. We gave them help and assistance. In the end, they were upset when they found out it wasn't all theirs, which shouldn't have been a surprise to them. They were pretty cocky, though. Did you see what the first thing they made read?"

"It said, 'We don't need you, Zimmerman.'"

"Exactly."

"So, if he killed Ms. Barnes, why didn't he kill you, too?"

"I don't know. Lucky, I guess."

"Call me crazy, but a call to the police may have been warranted, don't you think?"

"Yeah, but his parting words were, 'You are going to get me out of this mess, or you'll die a slow and painful death.' I'm scared, detective. Until he's caught, I thought I'd just stay inside with the door locked."

Stu Varney looked him square in his good eye. It didn't blink.

Stu then changed the subject. "Tell me about your gambling problem, professor." ✈

The more he sat there in the aircraft, sweating and watching the sun fade, the more he thought, *I can't do this.* Too many variables, too many ways that this could fail. As soon as he confronts Talone, his whereabouts will be known. Even in an airplane, you can't run and hide. He thought about the possible limits to the Air Traffic Control radar coverage in rural Iowa. If the authorities knew what to look for, even with his aircraft's transponder turned off, they could review the radar "tapes" and see where he went, simply based on the secondary returns from the metal on the aircraft.

Yet he knew he had the wherewithal to go through with it. Talone should be dead, not MoJo. Steve had no one, now. Where could he go? What did he have to lose? This man killed the only person in his life and he's not going to get away with it.

Almost dark now on the ramp. The light was out at the FBO. The fueler must have gone home.

Suddenly, a black Lincoln Town Car appeared on the ramp and turned towards the jet next to him. This is it. He grabbed the chains, the lock, and the pistol and opened the Cessna's door. He noticed the captain strapping himself in and the aircraft beacon started blinking.

Steve stood there for a minute, out of view of the car which stopped on the other side of the jet. He walked to the front of his airplane, pretending to look at his propeller, his back facing the jet. Mr. Talone emerged from the car from the driver's door. He was alone. The family must still be at the lake. *Good.* The copilot hopped in Talone's car and drove it away, presumably to park it in front of the main building and run back.

He saw Talone's feet disappear up the jet's staircase.

It's now or never.

He ran around the back of the jet, dashed around the left wing, and sprinted to the jet's stairs, chains in one hand, pistol in the other. He bounded up the stairs, did a one-eighty turn and yelled at the captain, "Turn the Master Switch off and get out of the cockpit—NOW!" He leveled the gun at his head. The captain, a young man with a crew cut, stared at the gun, then at the man holding it: unshaven, disheveled, with wild eyes.

"What the hell is—" Talone said from the leather chair in the back.

Steve swung around and fired a shot into Talone's leg. He let out a guttural grunt and doubled-over.

Steve swung the pistol back at the captain. "I'm not going to tell you again."

The captain slowly reached and killed all electric power to the aircraft. All interior lighting went dark, but there was still just enough daylight to see—at least long enough to get everything done here. "Now, put this on him." Steve handed the captain the chains as he slid by him and went back to Talone. "First wrap the chain with the electrical tape on it around his waist. Taped part in back. Now two chains go over his shoulders and down. The other two, under his crotch and up. Clamp them all together with this padlock."

Then Steve looked at Talone, who surprisingly said nothing, despite the fact that he had been shot in the leg and was about to be shackled to something wrapped in electrical tape.

The captain muttered something to Talone. Steve said, "Talk all you want, but if you try anything stupid, we all die. Right here." He held up a cell phone, his finger on a key.

The captain simply nodded. He got it.

About that time, the copilot came bouncing up the stairway. Steve lowered his pistol from view and motioned him to make a right-turn and sit down in the cabin. He seemed confused as he topped the steps. When he turned and saw his boss being shackled by the captain, he looked back at Steve, who now had the pistol pointed squarely at his head.

"Have a seat."

The copilot didn't say a word; he simply obeyed.

"Now, here's the deal. Talone, you're coming with me. I'm taking you to the police. As for you two, after we get off the aircraft, I want you to come off the aircraft as well. At the bottom of the steps, you will remove your cell phones and walk to the end of runway twelve where you will stand there and stare at the paint on the asphalt for one solid hour. I will not hesitate to inflict an immeasurable amount of pain on your boss if you do not comply. Understood?"

The pilots nodded. Talone sat there, emotionless.

"Talone. You first, followed by you two."

Surprisingly, Talone stood up. Then he said, tugging at the chains, "Is this thing shock sensitive?"

"You bet it is. And when I press my speed dial on this phone, it will light a road flare and literally burn your ass off. It may not kill you, but it will be the worst pain you have ever endured and I promise you'll never have another normal bowel movement for the rest of your life. Furthermore, if you overpower me or somehow take me out and I don't ping my contact at least once every ten minutes, *he* will light your ass on fire remotely."

Talone rose and walked towards Steve, who backed down the stairs and onto the tarmac. After Talone exited, the two pilots emerged. They were conformists and each put his cell phone on the ground and began walking. Once they were a comfortable distance away, Steve said, "Let's go for a ride." And began walking to the Cessna.

"You going to throw me out?" He walked with a slight limp from being shot with the pellet, but did not complain.

"No. Your going to be taken to the authorities where you are going to confess."

"Fine."

Steve was expecting an argument, but Talone walked around the front of the plane and opened the door. Then he saw the charred seat and froze.

"My other flare failed on the way here. Hopefully you'll be more careful than I was. I advise you to not make any wrong movements and set your flare off, too. Ever been burned? First, you're afraid you're gonna die. Then you're afraid you *won't* die." Steve flipped on the master switch and the lights came on. He held the cell phone in the other hand, his finger on the "1" key, ready to press it. "Don't screw with me, because I used up my fire extinguisher putting out the first flare. You'd be amazed how intense the flame is." He started the engine and immediately began taxiing. "And frankly the only thing I have to live for now is to see you punished for your crime."

For the first time, Talone looked scared. Shooting him in the leg with a pellet had no measurable effect, but seeing a freshly-charred airplane seat was quite illustrative.

Within thirty seconds, he turned onto the runway at the midfield intersection and gunned it. No run-up checks, no performance charts, no weight and balance. He just turned and took off. The two pilots never made it to the end of the runway behind him. ✈

Climbing out, Steve told him to not say a word until they were back on the ground, which would only be about ten minutes. Then he remembered to have Talone hand over his cell phone, which he did. He seemed genuinely concerned about being chained to a road flare.

Once safely on the ground in Estherville, he taxied all the way to the end of the runway, turned the airplane around, and shut it down, including all external lights.

"Get out."

He did, quite slowly and carefully. He had no idea where this airport was, only that it was shown as "KEST" on the GPS unit. They were surrounded by fields of corn. Not a sole around. A small building was three-quarters the way down the short, narrow runway, with a single taxiway leading straight out to it. The airport was so tiny that departing aircraft had to taxi down the runway, then turn around to take off.

With his right hand, he used Talone's own phone to dial his father's home, allowing the answering machine to pick up. He held the phone between them. The phone's screen was the only illumination. He began talking, "My name is Steve Brinkley. I have Mr. Harold Talone with me, and I am holding him against his will until the authorities arrive. Mr. Talone, do you have anything to confess?"

"I broke into your apartment and stole documents pertaining to your invention."

Steve didn't know this; he was expecting a murder confession. "What about the murder?"

"I broke into your apartment because you broke into my computer files. Tit for tat. You actually got more information from me than I did from you. We'll call it even."

"Who killed MoJo?"

"You did."

Steve hung up the phone. This was not what he had hoped for. "Listen, Harold. They're going to find out about you anyway. You can either go to jail or you can go to jail severely burned, because frankly I don't care either way."

"I don't know what kind of stunt you think you are pulling here, but the news
reports say *you* murdered her, not me."

"Look, you obviously hired someone to do it. Just tell me who they are. Maybe the police will appreciate the gesture."

Mr. Talone leaned slightly towards Steve and spoke softly, even though it was deathly quiet anyway, "I don't murder people. I don't hire people to murder people."

He faced Talone in the near total darkness. "Okay, fine. We're done." Steve turned and walked back to the plane. "This cell phone works in the air, because I'm not getting above a thousand feet. I can set you on fire from anywhere. Try taking that off and it will ignite on you. Just do yourself a favor and wait for the police. Once you are in their custody, I'll tell them how they might be able to disarm it."

"You're not going to kill me?"

"Not that I don't want to. Have a seat at the edge of the runway. Your best chance of not incinerating your ass is to sit on it and wait until the police arrive."

Steve got in the plane, started the engine, then began a slow taxi down the runway to the other end. He tossed the "detonation" phone in the back seat. Good thing the flare burned the seat, because the device Talone was wearing was a total fake. It wasn't even wired and there was no fuse in the flare. He simply ran out of time to make another one and didn't want to risk another in-flight fire, either.

As he taxied, he called 9-1-1.

"Emergency Response. What is the nature of your emergency?"

"My name is Steve Brinkley. I'm the guy on the news."

"Sir, it is a Federal offense to abuse this number. It is for emergencies only."

"Ma'am, as you know, this is being recorded. If you do not follow-through with my request, you will be impeding a murder investigation. Please have the police go out to Esthersville Airport. There is a man wrapped in chains who should be placed under arrest in connection with the murder of Ms. Monica Barnes. Please write this down. The lead investigator's name is Special Agent Stuart Varney, Illinois State Bureau of Investigation. Are you ready to copy down his phone number?"

After she agreed, he gave her the number, then he said, "Please have them hurry. He is sitting at the far end of the runway. By the way, the device he is wearing is completely harmless."

"What device?"

"Got all that?"

"Yes. What device?"

He never answered her. He hung up and dialed another number as he continued his slow taxi to the other end of the runway.

"Stu Varney."

"Agent Varney, this is Steve Brinkley."

There was a pause. Then on the other end, Steve heard, *"Says on my Caller I.D. that you are H. Talone."*

"I'm using his phone."

"Where is he—and who is he? And where are you?"

"Sir, I'm in Iowa, but I'm about to head back to Chicago," he lied.

There was a slight pause, followed by, "Well, what can I do for you, Steve?"

Steve got the sense that Agent Varney didn't yet believe he was actually talking to him, yet was the kind of person who would be willing to listen. "I thought I might get a confession out of Mr. Talone for MoJo's murder, but all I got was a confession that his thugs broke into my apartment and stole my papers."

"Wait, just how did you know about the break-in? This was not reported to the media."

"I just found out about it myself. Mr. Talone just told me."

Stu's phone beeped with Call Waiting. "Can you hold on a second, Steve?"

"Sure, it's probably the Esthersville Police Department." Steve turned the airplane around and faced the full length of the runway. He turned off the taxi light and flipped on the much-brighter landing light. There, at the far end of the runway, sat the president of Evo Financial. He turned the light back off so his eyes could readjust to the darkness. He looked towards the airport shack and the road leading to it. No sign of the police.

Click. "*Steve, I'm back. Okay, can you tell me what's going on?*"

"Believe me now?"

"Well, at this point I believe you have phoned the police in Iowa."

"You'll get your proof soon enough. I met with Mr. Talone early Friday morning. I thought we came to an agreement for him to invest in our invention. However, he sent someone to Meigs Field to murder MoJo. Or maybe it was me he was after. Or maybe all of us. I don't know. The only thing I know for sure is my dearest friend and the most wonderful person in my universe has been taken from me. It was all I could do to not beat him to a pulp moments ago. When you interview him, please understand that he's very shrewd. The only thing I could get him to admit was to breaking into my apartment and stealing all of the documents."

"How did you get him to admit that?"

"I chained a fake incendiary device to him and pretended that I would weld his ass shut if he didn't talk, pardon my French."

"Steve—may I call you Steve?"

"Yes, sir, of course."

"Fine. Please call me Stu. You probably don't know this unless you watch *Law and Order* on TV, but a coerced confession is not a confession."

"Thank you, sir. Noted. I just wanted to face the person who murdered the only person I've ever loved; watch him squirm a little before I handed him over to you, a *real* professional," he said sardonically. "If you're interested, his confession is on my father's answering machine at his home phone number. I'll give it to you if you're ready to copy it down."

"Go."

He did, then he said, "The access code is pound two-two to listen to the messages. Lastly, and I hate to trouble you, but do you have any way of flying to Esthersville *tonight*?"

Stu now was starting to believe it really was Steve. *"Why tonight?"*

"Because I have, in fact, seen *Law and Order*. The police won't be able to hold him. As far as they are concerned, he's the *victim*. So, without your intervention they will have to let him go— and good luck talking to him at a later time without going through a gauntlet of his lawyers. One of my favorite episodes is where the blonde investigator says, 'rich guys always skate.' Maybe you could go there and, like, interrogate him or whatever you call it."

"Touche'. Any chance I could talk you into giving yourself up?"

"Thank you, no. Not until I can prove he did it. No one is looking beyond me for suspects. I'm on my own."

"I promise to keep an open mind."

Steve chuckled, then got back to the business at hand when he saw blue lights approaching, no siren. "I'm sure you will, sir. Listen, I see the police are here. Please come out here and beat a confession out of him or whatever your current methods are. I don't think for a moment that he's the trigger man, but I know he ordered it."

Steve ended the call, then opened the door and threw the phone in the grass at the edge of the runway. Then he revved the engine and took off with all of his lights off. The police never saw him leave. ✈

"Police department."

"This is Agent Stuart Varney, Illinois Bureau of Investigation. Can you tell me if you have a man in custody at the Esthersville Airport?"

"Yes."

"Is his name Harold Talone?"

"Hang on....Yes."

"What's he wearing?"

"Chains, mostly. When I say he's in our custody, I exaggerated. We're not getting near him while he's wearing a bomb. The guy peed his pants. I guess I would, too."

"Relax. The I.E.D. is fake. I'm in Southern Illinois. Wait as long as you can before you give him his one phone call—and definitely do not release him. I'm flying there tonight to arrest him and have him extradited."

He hung up, then rubbed his eyes and face. Sometimes he had to break his must-sleep rule. ✈

He hit ANS on his phone and immediately heard the noise of something like, perhaps a lawnmower. "McPort here." He was just finishing dinner. The center of the news universe was in his own backyard. The national correspondents had been calling him. All was well with him. His wife smiled. Perhaps it was Charlie Gibson on the line.

This time Steve blocked the number. *"Hi Bruce. Steve Brinkley."*

No way. "Steve. Didn't think I'd hear back from you."

"I just wanted to thank you for getting me Agent Varney's phone number. Now I'm returning the favor."

"What do you mean?"

"Agent Varney is about to fly to—write this down—Esthersville, Iowa to arrest Mr. Harold Talone, President of Evo Financial of Chicago, in connection with the murder of Miss Monica Barnes. You, sir, are the only one who knows it, except for perhaps the Illinois State Police helicopter pilot who is about to fly him there."

"No way!"

"Trust. It's all about trust." Then Steve hung up and thought, *Take that, Stu. Pressure's on you, bud.* Law and Order *my ass.*

Within fifteen minutes, Bruce McPort, Fox20 News, was on the air. Within twenty minutes, it was on the national bureaus. Stu had not even boarded the helicopter before his bosses began calling, asking him what's going on. ✈

Chapter Twenty-One

Kernsville airport was a typical municipal airport. Manned like the one in Spencer, from dawn to dusk, it was certainly vacant and quiet at this hour. And, just like street lights, its runway lights came on automatically at dusk, albeit at a dimmed setting. A pilot landing at Kernsville merely had to click the microphone switch several times to brighten them if needed.

Steve would leave them on dim. In fact, he wouldn't be using his landing light and his rotating beacon will be switched off once he began his descent for landing, in clear violation of the regulations. He knew it's just as important for other aircraft to see him as it is to see others, but he couldn't afford to be spotted, regardless of the increased risk of collision. At about seventy-five miles out he began a listening watch on Kernsville's common traffic advisory frequency (CTAF), the one that all the aircraft use at that airport—not that anyone would be using the airport at one A.M.

Occasionally he would hear another aircraft announce that they were landing at some other airport, since many airports shared the same CTAF as Kernsville Municipal Airport. There was no traffic at Kernsville, and he didn't expect any.

However, that did not calm him down. Not normally paranoid, during the long flight he was convinced that by now Air Traffic Control had been watching him. Of course, his transponder was off, but their radar systems were powerful enough to track an aircraft simply by bouncing a radar pulse off the metal of the aircraft. They wouldn't have a tail number nor an altitude, but they'd get a ping on their screen.

Even if they hadn't been able to react quickly enough to know to track him, there was a chance that some officer might have been dispatched to the airport, since they must have found out about his hangar by now.

He thought about flying over the field at two thousand feet for a look, but at one in the morning, it would probably draw attention. No, his plan was to swing wide to the northeast of the airport and land straight-in on runway two-two. That way, he wouldn't overfly the city, located a mile to the southwest. He also had one additional task to accomplish, provided he could see well enough on the approach.

How many laws had he already broken? He had stolen an airplane. He had operated it carelessly and recklessly. He had kidnapped and terrorized a rich and powerful man. He shot him in the leg with pellet pistol. He had drawn a deadly weapon on two others. And, of course, he was evading the police in a murder investigation.

He tried hard not to feel sorry for himself. But during the three hour late-night flight from Spencer to Kernsville he had a lot of time to think about all that had happened over the weekend. It had started out wonderfully and held the promise of being the best weekend of his life with MoJo. She was the best thing that had ever happened to him.

He had good friends, too—particularly Charms—someone who would never abandon him in a time of need.

Their new invention meant financial security for him, forever releasing him of his father's financial dependence.

Most importantly it meant redemption from his past errs.

But he ended his weekend as a fugitive—again—except this time for murder. No amount of his father's influence and bevy of lawyers would be able to fix this. Moreover, after the events in

Iowa he was having his doubts about Talone. He got the feeling that Talone wasn't lying when he said, "I don't murder people. I don't hire people to murder people."

If he was telling the truth, it would put Steve back to square one. But if he was lying, then he was probably smarter than Steve had originally presumed and his tracks would be covered completely. In any event, his only hope was that Agent Stu Varney could cull the truth from him.

He looked at his watch: one ten A.M. He should have been on the ground ten minutes ago, but the winds must have been stronger than forecast. The gas gauges were showing a little more than an eighth of a tank each. He had never allowed the tanks get this low before and wasn't sure how reliable the readings were. He had done everything he could to conserve his fuel in order to make the long flight Kernsville, but the worst thing he could have done now was to stop somewhere for fuel. So he flew slower, and leaned the engine as much as he could. The synergy in both the slow speed coupled with the stronger headwinds meant he would be landing on fumes.

Worried about simply getting to the airport, the option of diverting to another airport was completely out of the question should the police be there waiting for him. With a deer fence around the entire perimeter of the airport, he would never get away on foot either. Besides, the state police helicopters all had infrared cameras on board. He'd be a sitting duck in the middle of the corn fields, even at night.

Bottom line: if the police were at the airport, the game was over.

All of the fears and frustrations were exacerbated by the fact that he was both painfully saddened and completely exhausted. The airplane had an acerbic stench from the fire that seemed a distant memory. Was this all worth while? He thought how easy it would be to simply push the yoke forward and end it all. No, he quickly dismissed that thought: no one would be around to punish the guilty if he took himself out. Still, he was so sad and so tired. His defenses were down.

He sat there listening to the drone of the engine, pondering his next move and realized he was bereft of any real plan. What was he thinking? How could he possibly outsmart the authorities when he was the lead story on every national news channel. He was the most wanted man in America.

When he saw the lights of Kernsville appear near the horizon, he snapped back to the matter at hand, which was to fly over Lake Stealey, then land and disappear again. Taking one last glance at the gas gauge, he practiced his deadstick technique in his mind: 1) slow to best glide speed, 2) turn into the wind, 3) add full flaps when below five hundred feet, 4) turn on landing light. Then, as the joke goes, if you don't like what you see ahead, 5) turn the light back off.

But the engine continued to run smoothly as he began his descent. He saw the green and white airport beacon first. Instinctively, he turned to a heading that would put him on about a five mile straight-in, even though he had not yet seen the runway lights. He saw the beacon, and the glow of the town to the airport's southwest.

Lake Stealey was about a two acres' worth of catfish and canoeing, but at the moment it was going to be the permanent home of the pellet gun, if he could spot it in time and his aim was good. It was easily spotted from the air during daylight, just slightly to the left of a three-mile straight-in to the runway. Turning onto about a five mile final, spotted the dim runway lights. He turned and moved slightly to the left of a long straight-in final approach and popped-open the window. He descended to about one thousand feet above the ground and suddenly saw the lake right below him, catching him totally by surprise. He was so sleepy. In one sweeping motion he grabbed the pistol and tossed it out the window. He never saw it once it left his hand, but there was still a chance it would splash and disappear forever. He closed the window, lined-up with the runway lights again. Nothing he could do about it now.

On short final, he looked to the dimly-lighted ramp a half-mile down on the right. No police lights. He wasn't expecting any, even if the police were there. His eyes scanned every direction, since all of his external lights were off and he had made no position reports to any other aircraft that may have been there. He really didn't expect any other aircraft. He did, however, still fully expect to be arrested upon landing.

His wheels touched down softly and he rolled ahead to the taxiway just south of the airport office, then a quick zip-zag and he was on the ramp and next to his hangar. He quickly shut down the engine, then turned off the electrical master switch and looked around.

A low-pitched buzz from the slowing gyro instruments was the only sound. After three hours of the constant drone of the engine, he welcomed the near silence.

No one here. *Good.*

He jumped out of the aircraft, ran twenty feet over to the hangar door, removed the lock, and lifted up the large, balanced hangar door. He left the lights off and quickly moved the wrecked aircraft parts around, then a few minutes later was pushing the much larger Cessna into the hangar. Only then did he close the door and turn on the light.

He looked around. His ears were still ringing from the drone of a three and a half hour flight, but it was otherwise quiet. Too quiet.

He had two throw-away phones left. He could only make one call, and thought about it for a minute before he making it.

"Hellums." The voice was that of Mrs. Hellums. She was alert, almost expecting a call at one twenty in the morning.

"Mrs. Hellums, it's Steve. I'm sorry for calling so—"

"You poor child. Are you okay?"

"Yes, ma'am. Listen I completely understand if you hang up on me and call the police. Please understand that I don't want to be any trouble—"

"Don't be silly. You must be exhausted. Can we pick you up?"

How did they know I just landed? "Well, I thought I might sleep in your barn until I can come up with a plan. You can deny everything if I get caught."

"Don't be silly. No one has been here. No one has called us. This has to be the best place for you."

"I'm at the airport. Thank you so much."

"Leroy will be right there." *Click.*

Only then did he wonder if the police were standing right beside her, listening on the extension. ✈

Chapter Twenty-Two

Stu sat across from a man who continued to scratch himself as he talked. Hours before, Mr. Harold Talone had sat at the edge of the runway for no more than ten minutes, tops. However, afraid to make a move and possibly igniting whatever the boy had chained to him, he had been eaten alive with mosquitoes. He had been every mosquito's dream: a stationary, hyperventilating, carbon dioxide-emitting dinner entre.

Stu rubbed his eyes under the strong florescent lights of the tiny office that doubled as both the Esthersville Police Department and the Esthersville Chamber of Commerce. It was the only office with a light on in the four block area comprising the central downtown. Three people were in the small, quiet room: Varney, Talone, and the lone local policeman who had been on duty at the time of the 911 call. The young policeman scratched his Marine Corps high-and-tight scalp. Clearly as irritated as the other two, he had also endured the mosquitoes—albeit fifty yards away from Talone—until he was advised the device was a fake.

Stu was tired and tried not to show his irritation. Talone was willing to sit there and talk and scratch as long as it took. Stu and Talone were two competitors in a proverbial log roll competition. Though each was showing signs of wear, clearly Talone was the one with the better balance.

Stu looked him straight in the eye. "Why would he go to so much trouble to fly out here and do this to you if he wasn't absolutely convinced you did it, Mr. Talone?"

"Because he needed someone else to divert the attention away from him. He must have thought I had motive." With both hands under the table, he looked down and scratched his ankles. His leg throbbed from the welt he got from the pellet pistol earlier.

"Do you?"

"No. And, as you recall, I told you I would hold nothing back from you. We went into his apartment and took some of his notes. Mind you, it was in response to his hacking into our most sensitive corporate information, stuff that even some of my senior partners are not privy to. We couldn't let him go unchecked." He was still looking down at his feet.

"Still, both were unlawful acts. He's a college kid. You are a corporate executive. Perhaps you could have shown some restraint."

His right hand came up to scratch his neck, which had a few raised bite marks. As his hand came up, so, too, did his head. He was serious, his game face on. "It was a volley, a tit-for-tat, nothing more. And he's an adult and should be treated as such. Don't underestimate his intellect and resolve." Talone's skin was crawling. He felt like he was going to pass out if he didn't scratch his ankles again. Yet he willed the itching away as he returned the stare. Neither man blinked.

Suddenly, Stu's phone erupted. Neither man blinked, but the young officer in the back jerked at the loud ringing.

The phone had startled Stu, but he casually flipped open the phone, brought it to his ear, only then looking away from Talone. "Varney."

"Agent Varney. Matt Thompson. FAA, Chicago Center. We spoke a few hours ago."

"Yeah, Matt."

"Look, we marked the airplane that took off from there several hours ago."

"Took you long enough."

"Sir, we work in the *now*. We keep airplanes from hitting each other, in real-time. We don't just hit some sort of rewind button from a master screen. This guy went through three separate radar regions, all of which have separate backups. We had to get time signatures and lat-long coordinates to find him as he went from sector to sector. He wasn't squawking a code. All we got were skin returns. Much harder to track, especially between the radar screens."

"So where'd he land?"

"A place called Kernsville, Illinois."

Stu's head dropped. He closed his eyes.

"You still there?"

Talone looked down at his ankles beneath the tabletop. His right hand was on the table.

Varney noticed the downward glance and wondered what had his attention under the table, but continued his phone conversation. "Yeah. I left there several hours ago. We swapped locations. How long ago did he land?"

"At oh-six-thirteen-Z. That's one thirteen A.M. local time. Forty minutes ago. I took the liberty of calling the Illinois State Police just before I called you."

"Thanks. Sorry I was short with you. It's late."

"Tell me about it."

Stu hung up, hit RECALL a few times, then hit SEND to call the helicopter pilot, who was probably sound asleep.

"Fire it up. We're heading back to Kernsville."

Hanging up, he then looked at the policeman in the corner. "Can you drop me back off at the airport, then drive Mr. Talone back to Spencer?"

It was as though he had been asked to cut off a favorite appendage. "I'm not supposed to leave my jurisdiction."

Varney didn't want an argument at this time of night. He gave him a *you can't possibly be arguing with me* look. "Official business and professional courtesy."

The officer stood, "Well, of course. It'd be my pleasure."

Stu rose. "Thanks. Mr. Talone, you're free to go. But don't disappear or I'll you'll see what it's really like to be a suspect."

"Is that a threat, Agent Varney?" Talone remained seated.

Stu took a beat, then said, "Mr. Talone, I resort to threats only with those who fail to comprehend the breadth of my authority, intellect, and resolve."

"Did you win your golf match earlier today with your son, Drake—is it?" Only then did Mr. Talone unveil the cell phone he had been looking at underneath the table. His team had been sending him text messages since Steve left him alone on the runway. He got the phone back when an alert policeman saw it glowing in the grass, five feet from the edge of the runway. He was alert, but missed a step in giving it back to him rather than keeping it as evidence.

Stu smiled. "Oh, you a funny guy!" he said in Asian accent. "Quick, what color's my underwear?"

"White, of course. By the way, I not only recorded this interrogation, by I also recorded my conversation with young Steve Brinkley on this phone, too, after we got out of the airplane. Would you like to hear it, or are you smarter than me and don't need my exculpatory evidence?"

Stu rubbed his face with both hands. "Some days, Mr. Talone, I guess I just don't get enough rest." Stu sat back down as Mr. Talone slid the phone across the table to him.

"Oh, by the way, thank you, gentlemen, for the offer for a ride back to Spencer, but I have a car waiting outside." He sat back in the chair, relishing the successful denouement of their meeting.

Abruptly, Varney looked up at nowhere in particular and yelled, "John?"

"Yes, Agent Varney." The voice was coming from the speaker phone on a nearby desk.

Talone looked over at the black phone. He had not noticed it before.

"Go back a couple of minutes and play back that part where Mr. Talone said something like, 'I told you I would hold nothing back from you.'"

"Sure. Hang on."

Stu smiled at Talone, then said, "We record everything, too. Let's talk about withholding evidence. Now call me crazy but I think that's a crime" just as *'No. And, as you recall, I told you I would hold nothing back from you. We went into his apartment...'* was played back over the speakerphone.

After the recording playback stopped, Stu turned to the phone and said, "Thanks, John."

"My pleasure."

He looked straight at Talone and smiled. "It's a mystery to me that smart people like you think I don't know what I'm doing. Listen, I have to go catch Mr. Brinkley. Please sit there in that chair and ponder for a few moments about the benefits of full disclosure. I'll leave it to this fine officer to determine whether you should be further detained."

Talone nodded, in the same gentlemanly manner as having lost a chess match. ✈

The room was totally dark. A t-shirt had been thrown over alarm clock; even its LED display was illuminating too much light. He had planned on sleeping for the foreseeable future. Since the world tipped on him late Saturday evening it was nothing but talking to the police and avoiding reporters.

Before turning in, Alan considered turning off his new phone. It was a cheap phone—ten bucks at the T-Mobile store, replacing the one borrowed by Steve. Obviously Steve would never use it again, but eventually he hoped to get his original phone back. At least he got to keep his old number.

But for some foreboding reason he opted to leave it on. Turning it off meant delaying any news and he needed to know everything. Moreover, only a handful of reporters had gotten his number. Most of the calls had been from his parents and siblings and from Charms. The police had his number, of course, and were most likely listening.

So when the phone rang, he simply felt around for it, then squinted at the display. The number on the phone was blocked. Then he shook his head against the pillow as he saw the time display on the phone. Alan thought it was probably another reporter. It was less likely that it was an investigator, he reasoned, unless it was something critical. As he clicked the ANSWER button, he decided the caller would decide his temperament. An investigator: the response would be polite—albeit forcibly. However, if it was another reporter, he would really let him have it for calling at almost two A.M.

"Hello."

"Well, hi Alan. It's Steve. How ya been?"

Alan felt a rush and his alertness ratcheted up a notch. "Gawd, Steve. Before you say another word, you need to know the Feds spent ten hours interviewing me. They are probably listening in as we speak."

"Yeah, I know. Hey, remember that cheesy method for keeping others from finding out about our test results?"

"Yeah."

"Good. Please just be honest with the investigators. I don't want you in trouble for aiding and abetting me, even though I'll eventually get out of this. Tell them the truth: you don't know where I am and I'm not going to tell you. Agent Stu Varney is probably interrogating Mr. Talone now and it all may be over already if he beat a confession out of him. However, I still have to assume that I'm the only one on their radar screen and I need you to stay in the game."

"You're mixing metaphors."

"You're the second person who told me I do that. I haven't had much sleep, so I hope you'll excuse my being bereft of erudite thoughts at the moment. By the way, did you win?"

"Yeah. Sorry you weren't there for it."

"Tell me. I wish I had gone to the car instead of MoJo. I'm sad and angry and vindictive and scared and just plain lost. I still can't believe it. However I can't turn back time. Nonetheless, my mother once told me, 'Find at least one modicum of treasure in each day.' My only treasure is the limited freedom I still have in being able to hunt down the murderer. I can't do it from jail."

"Agent Varney was one of the last guys to talk to me. He's sharp. I don't think you have much time before they round you up. Just don't do anything stupid. I don't need two dead friends."

"Thanks. I will. You take care."

"You, too, bud."

Alan hung up, then tossed the phone back on the bed. *Poor bastard.*

In less than five minutes, the police arrived, confiscated his new phone and began a two-hour interview that centered on "that cheesy method" the two had talked around. The young, deputy investigator was high-strung and had given Alan all of the warnings regarding evidence withholding and aiding and abetting a fugitive. Yet, all he got out of him was the team's referring to the device as the HeyPal9000. If the young deputy investigator hadn't been so obnoxious and overbearing, perhaps Alan would have been a little more forthcoming.

Alan, in the end, chose to keep the single line of communication open with Steve, unknown to the detectives. But to protect himself from prosecution, he opted to print out everything and stuff it between his mattress. It was unlikely his room would be torn apart for evidence twice in the near future. The first time they were quite thorough. ✈

When Steve saw Mr. Hellums' truck approaching the airport, he grabbed the throw-away phone and did just that: he tossed it on top of the hangar. It was still on, which was deliberate. He wouldn't, *couldn't*, use it again anyway. He turned on his remaining phone, but it didn't come alive. He pressed the ON/SEND button several times. Nothing. *Rats.* He needed that phone! All he had now was the laptop, his only connection to Charms and Alan, thanks to the encryption software and dummy web site. It wasn't real-time, and things were happening too quickly to rely on the two others constantly checking the blog.

Standing in the darkened area around the corner from the street light that glowed the ramp in a dull yellow hue, Steve emerged as the truck reached the chain link fence and stopped. Mr. Hellums was the only occupant.

He jogged over to the truck as Mr. Hellums leaned over and opened the passenger door. The cab light came on. Mr. Hellums was wearing his signature outfit, blue overalls and a green John Deere hat. It was strangely comforting to Steve. As he hopped in, Mr. Hellums extended a hand. He probably would have slapped his shoulder with the other hand had he not been strapped-in.

"Good to see you, son."

"Sir, I can't tell you how good it is to see you. Thank you so much for believing in me."

"We'll get you through this. I saw on Fox20 that there was an arrest in Iowa regarding MoJo's murder."

Steve thought it was unusual that he had referred to her as "MoJo." Previously, it had been "Miss Barnes." He surmised it was because of all the news coverage. "I called that reporter and put him on it, just to ensure that the detective didn't simply dismiss the man."

For the next few minutes, all was quiet. The truck hummed along the asphalt road leading out to the highway, followed by a right turn and a mile into the outskirts of Kernsville. Mr. Hellums then drove on a cut-off route to another highway that took them north of town.

Steve pierced the quiet and offered, "I slept in the hangar of a family friend. Then I flew his airplane to Iowa where I kidnapped the president of Evo Financial and tried to force a confession out of him." Steve looked at the shards of light moving across the floorboard of the truck as they passed under some street lights. "He was either pretty tough or a good liar, so I left him there for Agent Varney to see if he could get anything out of him. You know, try to make him slip up."

Mr. Hellums continued driving for a few minutes. Steve just stared at the darkened floorboard. They were both exhausted.

Out of the blue, Mr. Hellums said, "You know Zimmerman did it."

Steve looked over at him and replied softly, "He's a mean guy, but a college professor murdering a student? Sounds unlikely."

"Doctors have committed murder. Policemen have, too. Even preachers. This is not a big stretch for me. Maybe he didn't do the actual act, but he could have arranged it. Think about it: he's a man deep in debt and just got put on leave because of his awful press conference. A friend of mine told me he's not coming back, at least until this whole thing runs its course. There are some who hopes he never comes back. People do crazy things when their lives fall apart. The university has to be hopping mad by the news conference he made on Friday. He humiliated the university on a national stage."

Steve realized that he had been out of touch from any news since two o'clock the day before. He had trouble keeping up, even when connected. His mission to Iowa, then on to Southern Illinois isolated him from the stream of information being released by the news. "Maybe you should fill me in on what you've discovered." ✈

The state and local police quickly surrounded Kernsville Municipal airport. However, they stayed in their vehicles because of the omnipresent humidity and mosquitoes. Once perimeter checkpoints were in place, as additional police arrived on the scene, they were dispatched to conduct a detailed search of the area enclosed by the checkpoints. They were the unlucky ones who had to go out on foot.

The response coordinator, Kernsville Police Chief Ron Dulaney, was back on duty, although he had only made it home a few hours earlier. He had crawled into bed, still in his clothes. He knew better than to wake his wife, other than to say the inevitable "sorry I woke you." They had a long-standing agreement that he would fill her in with any news over coffee the next morning. But when the call came in a half-hour ago from Agent Varney, he crept into the bathroom, washed his face, threw on a clean uniform, and headed out to the airport. Initially, he set up a headquarters location at his car outside the tiny airport office.

Once the airport manager, Rick Cuda, was awakened and summoned, he too arrived in his Ford Bronco and opened the airport's only building, which was used as both the Fixed Base Operation (maintenance, aircraft fueling, flight planning, etc) and airport manager's office. Then the group moved inside and Ron established the headquarters at a flight planning desk just inside the front door.

The airport manager made some coffee and tried to engage the police for a little inside information, as he knew the Brinkley boy well and had been glued to the news like everyone else. But they largely ignored him as they hustled to get everyone in position. He had a large key ring in his hand, but given that they were treating him with no more respect than a coffee server, he dropped them on his desk in the same spot where he had retrieved them moments before.

All of the police were given a common frequency for the search and each checked in. The first thing they did once the perimeter was secured was a visual survey of the ramp for a Cessna 182 with a certain tail number. No luck. There were only a dozen aircraft on the ramp, so it didn't take long to look.

The group came in and the airport manager tried to interject once more, but was quickly silenced again by Dulaney, "Rick. Please. Relax." Personally, Rick Cuda liked the Brinkley boy. Earlier in the summer he had watched proudly when Steve made the maiden flight of his homebuilt airplane. But Rick wasn't going to jail for him, in spite of the shunning he was getting at the moment from the authorities in his office. He grabbed the key ring that had been on the edge of his desk since he first saw the news reports. Underneath the keys was a note written the day before, simply stating: "Brinkley's Hangar." Rick walked to the door, then announced in the voice of a simpleton, "You professionals hang tight. I'm uh gonna go check out his hangar. Any uh y'all wanna come along?"

The room suddenly became quiet. A few officers moved laterally, allowing an unobstructed line-of-sight between the airport manager and the police chief. Dulaney, seated at the flight planning table, barely moved his head. Instead, he shifted his eyes up through the thin area above his eyeglasses and his bushy eyebrows. After a pregnant pause, he said slowly, "You gotta be shittin' me."

The day before, the airport manager had received a call from the state police asking if anyone had seen Steve. Rick had said no, but nonetheless said he would leave the key to Steve's hangar on his desk. For whatever reason no one picked it up to check it out. The airport manager certainly wasn't going to obstruct justice, but he wasn't going to go out of his way to help them catch him, either. It was the state police who dropped the ball.

Suddenly, a chirping sound went off on the base frequency, followed by "Ron?"

Ron never took his eyes off the airport manager, who continued to stand there motionless. He pressed TX and said, "Yeah."

Chirp. "Strong cell phone signal inside a hangar out here." Phone company says it's a throw-away purchased in Chicago yesterday.

Dulaney looked at Rick again. The police chief and the airport manager were both in the Kiwanis Club and were otherwise good friends. However, at that very moment the airport manager returned the stare, then said, "Otherwise I'll just continue making coffee for you expert investigators." ✈

Stu was airborne, midway over central Missouri at a seven thousand foot cruising altitude. The steady drone and cushy leather seat was a sedative. He fought to stay awake. The helicopter was a Sikorsky S-76, one of three state-owned helicopters. It was used primarily for executive transportation largely between Springfield and Chicago. It was also used less frequently by the Illinois State Police and the SBI. The lone pilot told him he was "turning into a pumpkin at two forty-five A.M." and under no circumstances would fly a minute beyond his duty limit imposed by the FAA regulations. The pilot then gave him an ETA, and Stu flipped open his phone to illuminate the display on his watch. *Good.* They would land with fifteen minutes to spare. Before closing the phone, he glanced at the reception and realized he had five bars. He quickly dialed Ron Dulaney.

"Dulaney here." His voice was a whisper. *Strange.*

"Ron, it's Stu."

"Hang on a minute." The tone of his voice was as though here were in a library. Then Stu could hear some strange, erratic sounds, then suddenly a large commotion followed by, "Police! It's over, Brinkley. Move out into the open—now!" followed quickly by "Stu. Gotta call you back."

Stu closed the phone, sat back in the plush helicopter seat, then exhaled. *Finally.* ✈

The first officer flipped on the hangar's interior lights as no less than a dozen officers rushed in behind him. Within a few intense minutes they ascertained that the hangar was empty.

"What the hell?" Asked Dulaney as he stared at the remains of a destroyed aircraft, in front of the Cessna 182 they were looking for. "Rick, get in here!"

Rick had been told to stay back for his own safety while they conducted the raid. He secretly hoped they wouldn't find the Brinkley boy in there.

When Rick walked in, he saw the wreckage and muttered, "Dear God." Every piece of the airplane was laid out neatly on the hangar floor.

"No blood. He wasn't in it when it crashed."

"Thank God."

Dulaney looked at Cuda. "You know about this, too?"

"No. But it looks like you found your one eighty-two." He walked over to the Cessna and put his hand on the engine cowling. "Still warm."

Dulaney then turned slightly away from the airport manager and spoke into his walkie talkie, "We got Brinkley's plane. He's here, probably in the corn. Perimeter, you're on high alert. Let's get this kid." ✈

The shower felt wonderful. The bed was soft. The room was quiet. He was exhausted and should have been sound asleep. Yet, the dim red LEDs on the alarm clock read four fifteen A.M. and Steve was wide awake. He stared at the digital read-out until it changed to four sixteen, then flung off the sheet, crept out of the guest room and into the Hellums' living room. He hunted for the TV remote in the darkness. He felt around the recliner, found the remote and turned on the TV. He quickly turned down the volume.

The TV illuminated the room now. He sat on the edge of the sofa and surfed through the channels until he landed on Headline News, but it was nothing but commercials. He remembered the channel number, then surfed the cable guide channel for either CNN or Fox News. As he surfed, his mind raced as he again retraced his actions over the past month. Could there be anyone who might infer that he knew the Hellums? He concluded that he was probably safe at the farmhouse, at least for the moment. Mr. Hellums had confirmed that he had talked to no one, other than gossiping about Dr. Zimmerman. He had no cell phone now to trace. He had not used the Internet.

He rubbed his eyes, then flipped the channel back to Headline News. Still commercials. He surfed in the other direction and landed on Fox News, which had "This Just In" in big red letters across the bottom. A video inset was showing above it, with a black and white video, obviously from a security camera. A caption between the two areas said, "Brinkley Attacks Professor." He leaned forward in disbelief.

Three people were on the video inset: two young people in shorts and a tall, middle-aged gentleman in Dockers. The man leaned towards one of them, which Steve instantly recognized as himself. Steve knew what was coming next. *Zimmerman gave them this.* Even though there was no audio, it was clear by the body language that they were arguing. Then the man turned and attempted to pick up some equipment off the aluminum lab table and in a blur Steve slugged the man, sending him flying to the ground. The video was quite dramatic. Steve didn't remember it being so violent. Then the image of Steve was seen jumping on Zimmerman and grabbing him by the neck. Five seconds later he pushed off the man and rose to his feet. The man stayed down as the two young students grabbed the apparatus and left.

How could this possibly get any worse? There was no doubt who the people were on the video. And videos don't lie. Maybe Mr. Hellums was right. Zimmerman must have had some involvement. This was more than piling-on, otherwise it would have been given to the police who would have kept it from the media. No, this was deliberately released by Zimmerman. It had to have been.

"You want some coffee?" came from the edge of the room.

Steve jerked up and looked around. "I'm sorry. I didn't mean to wake you."

"You didn't. I've been thinking about Zimmerman."

Steve first needed to know just how bad it's gotten. "Have I been on the news non-stop?"

"Yep. And it's been picking up steam. You are a household name. It's a polarized group, like the whole O.J. thing was. Most people want you crucified, but there are some who insist you're innocent. You even have an online fan club and a MySpace site. Girls say you're too handsome to have done it."   Steve thought about the old farmer using the word "polarized." "Although I wouldn't be signing autographs if I were you. You have a lot evidence against you. Want some coffee? I'm going to make some for myself."

"Are you up for good?"

"Sure. I'm a farmer. We tend to get up early."

Steve smiled. "Thanks, yes. Coffee would be great." He rarely drank coffee.

From the kitchen he could hear some clanking and water running, yet Mr. Hellums was still standing there. Obviously Mrs. Hellums was up, too. Mr. Hellums turned and went to join her.

Steve flipped channels and was astonished at the coverage on him. He was clearly the most wanted man in the country and was the lead story on every cable news channel. He stopped on Fox

News where he saw a reporter in front of a familiar scene, but it took a few moments for Steve to recall the precise location. Then it hit him: it was the home of MoJo's parents. He hadn't been there in years, ever since the M.I.T. incident. The segment had been filmed earlier, since it was daylight. He turned up the volume to hear the end: *"...family members have not been back home since the murder. Barnes' neighbors have speculated that the family probably left the area in order to grieve in private and come to grips with this horrible murder."*

Murder. The word kept repeating in his mind, and he hoped that he would soon see details of the news that the man arrested in Iowa had confessed and at least he could put the fugitive part of this nightmare behind him. His thoughts then became focused on traceability. Alan and Charms must have their phone and email tapped. They probably have the authorities tailing them, too.

The two Hellums appeared, Mrs. Hellums carrying two cups. Steve put down the remote to receive one, saying, "Thank you ma'am." Mrs. Hellums sat beside him on the couch and Mr. Hellums sat in his Barcalounger.

"You ready for this?"

The suddenness and seriousness of the question from Mr. Hellums made Steve put down his coffee. "For what?"

Mr. Hellums put down his coffee on the small table next to his chair. "I'm taking charge, and here's why: you're on the run with no plan. You've had no sleep. You've had more mental trauma in the last couple of days than most people have in a lifetime. You've made some mistakes already. It's time you start taking orders from someone who can think things through methodically, if you know what's good for you. You can't be a coach and a player at the same time. Agreed?"

Steve knew he was right. Hiding was not a plan of action. It would get him no closer to resolving the murder. He nodded.

"Good. First thing—forget about Mister Talone. If Agent Varney interviewed him, rest assured the truth will come out. As smart as you may think he is, he's no match for a professional crime investigator. You handed Talone to them on a platter. Let them handle the rest. No sense treading over the same turf." Steve nodded, amazed at the thought Mr. Hellums had put into this already. "Second, if Zimmerman had something to do with this, the path most likely extends from him through his gambling debts and straight to MoJo. My guess is with his job now at severe risk, the casino's 'collection agency' was probably putting added pressure on him. He probably struck a deal with these thugs to steal the details of your invention. I think they followed you to Chicago. You should know that I had breakfast yesterday morning at the Sharecropper restaurant, where Police Chief Dulaney usually stops by. Ron and I are in Kiwanis Club together. He looked like he hadn't had much sleep either. Anyway, he told me privately that the back of MoJo's car had been pried open. She must have wandered over to her car at the wrong time."

"What about the president of Mahoney Aerospace?"

"I asked Ron about them. The guy has been completely cooperative and although they can't really rule them out, they're not really treating him as a prime suspect right now. His lawyers looked at your patent filing, the fact that your names were, in fact, forged on the The Bernoulli Award application, and decided they were beaten."

"What patent filing?"

"What do you mean?"

"After all this, I doubt Alan and Charms ever got to it."

"Here it is." He reached down and pulled up some printed pages from a leather folder next to his chair. He handed it to Steve, who began perusing them. "Look at the submission date."

He studied it and his eyebrows furled. "That can't be right. One, Charms was in Mexico at the time and two, I don't even know who this lawyer who signed it is."

"It's Charms' girlfriend."

Steve's mind was swimming. Charms went to Cancun with a girl—the lawyer girl. He must have made the patent submission before he left. That was days before the others made their claims. Charms did it. "You mean he—"

"Yes. He beat them to the punch."

Steve smiled slightly, not because of the patent itself, but because of Charms' effort.

"Mahoney Aerospace was the first to realize they had been defeated. But they didn't admit defeat until they investigated the signatures of the four of you and realized that the contract for The Bernoulli Award was forged and, thus, unenforceable. You weren't working for them."

"So the authorities must know that Zimmerman was behind this, because they must know that he forged the signatures."

"Sure, but with all of the actual and circumstantial evidence that is stacked against you, as far as they are concerned, it's two different and unrelated crimes. Here are the other patent submissions." He handed Steve more papers, all printed from his searches on the Patent and Trademark Office's web site. "This one is from Dexter University. This one is from Mahoney Aerospace. This one is from Scientech Partners."

"Who? Who's that?"

"They are a wholly-owned subsidiary of Evo Financial. Apparently, all three of them raced to get the patent submitted on Friday, not knowing that Charms had done so several days before. You clearly own the patent, thanks to Charms."

Steve was still reading through the paperwork, but uttered, "I don't want it. I'd give anything just to get MoJo back."

"Well, the best you can hope for now is to find the truth."

"I don't get it. There are plenty of suspects with plenty of motive. Why am I the only one on the news?"

"Think about it: you're the only one on the run. If you're running you must be guilty. You were with her when she died. You had both motive and opportunity. You have committed several crimes since then. You purchased a firearm. You shot a man in the leg. You stole an airplane. You had a history of malfeasance from your M.I.T. days. You are a one-man menace with nothing to lose. Can you blame them that you have made yourself the most wanted man in America?"

It was silent for a moment. Steve looked down and shook his head. "My God. Why on earth would the two of you put yourselves at risk for me?" He looked at the both of them, his eyes watering.

Mr. Hellums looked at Mrs. Hellums, then back to Steve. "That lady sitting next to you is a good judge of character, and I concur with her assessment. We knew from the first time we met you that you were an honest kid, but one dealing with demons from the past. I saw the way you looked at MoJo. You clearly adored her." Steve's red, swollen eyes began to tear. "We knew in our hearts you were a good kid. It's in our nature as Christians to help the disadvantaged, and I'd say you are clearly disadvantaged at the moment."

"But the two of you are harboring a fugitive!"

"We're old and senile." He winked at the missus. "When you reach a certain age you get a sort of tacit immunity from crimes. We couldn't have possibly known what was going on beyond our farmhouse gate. We didn't know what we were doing. We forgot to take our medicine. Whatever. Old people rarely get convicted."

Steve smiled, almost chucked, and wiped his eyes. "So what's next?"

"We need to get the truth out of Zimmerman. But time is *not* on our side. It's not going to be easy and it's going to take more than just the three of us." ✈

Stu had been speaking to the crowd of law enforcement officers for only a few minutes. The meeting began ten minutes late due to stragglers. When he finally convened the meeting, it took him several seconds to get the room settled, which annoyed him even more. Now he was being interrupted again. As he was talking, a pair of officers came into the small room, laughing and talking, obviously not knowing the meeting was in progress. After they sat down, they stopped talking and irreverently gave him attention.

"You two." Pointing at the two uniformed men.

They gave Stu a "who me?" expression.

"Yes, you. Get out of this room—now!"

"We just got here," said the larger officer.

"You're late, and you're off the case."

"You don't make my assignments."

Everyone quit breathing.

Stu, still dressed in yesterday's tailored suit, stood there for a split second. Then he slowly placed his laser pointer on the podium and stepped to the side, exposing his whole body. He raised his chin, ostensibly becoming the alpha male. "Who's your boss?"

"Chief Dulaney," he said as though it meant something.

Stu looked over at Ron. "Ron, these men are impeding a murder investigation. If they are not out of my sight in five seconds, I want you to fire them, arrest them, and charge them with obstruction of justice. If you won't do it, the state police here will."

Ron, seated on the front row, immediately turned back towards them and yelled, "Boys. He's not kidding."

Then men, embarrassed amongst their peers, nodded and stood to leave. Stu picked up a piece of chalk and continued the briefing as though nothing just happened, "...I'm talking about his friends, no matter how distant. His barber. His apartment manager. If a person in this town has ever even bumped into Steve Brinkley or stood in line at the grocery store with him, I want that person revisited and reinterviewed." He turned and began writing names on the chalkboard. "He's here, in this town, and *someone* is hiding him. Feel free to add names to this list. The list will remain here for all to see."

He jabbed the chalk into the dark green chalkboard at the small briefing room in the Kernsville Police Station. The room was completely quiet, except for the tapping made by Stu on the chalkboard. He wrote "John 'Charms' Ruess" in small uppercase letters, then underneath it wrote "Alan Overman." He then wrote down a list of clients that Steve had produced web sites for over the past few years. He wrote down the airport manager's name, which was still a sore spot for Ron Dulaney, having screwed up and not sent a patrolman to investigate Steve's hangar the day before. This list grew steadily. He wrote down "Ed Spaeth," the geek from Radio Shack who often called Steve when he couldn't answer a customer's technical questions. Stu, continued to speak, louder than before because he had his back to everyone as he wrote, "...and don't forget for a minute that this fellow, wearing shorts and a t-shirt, has been all over the great states of Illinois and Iowa, visiting hospitals, stealing and flying airplanes, buying cars, computers and cell phones. Yet with all of our combined resources and experience we have continued to stay one step behind him. I, for one, am professionally embarrassed. I want this kid caught. Let's end this, and let's end this today. Got it?"

He continued transcribing names from his list to the chalkboard, but no one responded. He finished writing "Bruce

McPort- Fox20" on the board then turned and looked at the thirty men in the room.

"That was not a rhetorical question. Can everybody hear me?" Nothing. "Got it?" he asked a little louder.

A couple of men were listening and nodded, but no one replied. Fully a third of them were looking down at briefing sheets or daydreaming—he couldn't tell. A few were whispering and smiling, not paying attention at all. Now he was truly pissed. He picked up the felt chalkboard eraser, and spotted a uniformed policeman who was obviously bored. First, he was looking at his fingernails. Then the young, acne-faced officer closed both eyes and with elbows extending out rubbed his forehead with both hands.

Stu hurled the chalkboard eraser at him with all of his might. "Wake up, people!"

The eraser impacted on the officer's left bicep, then bounced inward and off his chest. In even more dramatic fashion, the officer pulled in his arms in a knee-jerk reaction to the sudden assault, sending the eraser upward, spraying chalk everywhere. Chalk dust covered the front of his uniform. Stu didn't care.

The "Wake Up" command echoed throughout the small, crowded room. It was such an unexpected event that a few of the policemen actually reached for their weapons. The rush of adrenaline he interjected into the room resulted in their immediate and rapt attention. Stu looked directly at the chalky, stunned officer and said specifically to him, "He ain't no jaywalker; I need you to at least *pretend* like you're interested."

Stu, dead tired and out of patience, threw his hands up and turned to the rest of the attendees. All eyes were riveted on him now. He said, now barely above a normal volume, "Listen, this is not a social gathering. This is not a break room. I've been chasing shadows since Saturday afternoon and I need your help. He may be young, but he is smart and he is inventive. Right now he is smarter than anyone in this room, including me, because he's still at large. That should piss you off. I haven't slept. Many of you haven't either. We're all at wit's end. But, I give you my solemn promise, if he slips through again because of any inaction or miscalculation on your part..."

He turned his body slightly toward the man covered in chalk dust, and finished the sentence as a one-on-one message, though clearly making the point to everyone else in the room: "...then I'm going to make it my personal mission to end your law enforcement career and get you a job taking movie tickets at the Malco."

He backed up a little and looked around, "I'm not here to make friends. I'm here to catch a killer. You have precisely one minute to write your name next to one of these names," pointing over his shoulder to the names on the blackboard, "then get out of this room and get to work. Don't go home, don't run errands, don't see your kid's baseball game. Consider yourself on duty until we catch him. Meeting adjourned."

The crowd uniformly rushed to the chalkboard. Stu sidestepped the stampede and walked over to the chalky policeman who was brushing himself off. Stu handed him his card, and spoke softly, "Thanks for helping me motivate the rest of them. Send me the dry cleaning bill. After you change into another uniform, please join me. I need a local partner. I want you to be with me and personally experience the thrill of arresting a murderer like Steve Brinkley." ✈

The sun was already heating up the air as Mr. Hellums and Steve walked out of the back door, across the grassy backyard and towards the combine, parked next to the barn. Steve squinted, in part due to the bright sunshine, but also because his eyes were already red and irritated from a lack of sleep.

The big green machine was much larger than he remembered. A new one costs a quarter of a million dollars, twice as much the average family home in Kernsville. Probably three times the cost of the Hellums' home. It was the John Deere 70 Series combine with a 600C series header. It was also the lifeblood of the farm and Hellums' pride and joy. It had an air-conditioned cab with stereo surround-sound speakers (though he never listened to FM stations; he only listened to The Clark Howard Show, Paul Harvey, and The Daily Farm Report on the local AM station).

The vehicle had the latest portable GPS equipment, including the optional autopilot, which he rarely used. Most of the time he enjoyed manually driving the rows.

The main purpose of the GPS as far as he was concerned was to gather data location data just prior to the planting. He would take the GPS out of the combine, and connect it to the laptop in his much-smaller planter tractor. The laptop was also connected via a USB cable to a device that would gather soil samples and record them for moisture content, weed density, and the previous-years' crop yield into a computer spreadsheet. In the Spring he would purchase and import satellite data on drainage and moisture content. He would combine all of that information into a software program that would meter the proper amounts of fertilizer and weed control for each specific location in his fields. He also had software that imported real-time futures and predictive functions for determining the best crop rotation. For an old man, he was clearly with it.

They came up to the rear of the combine. Mr. Hellums stuck his finger at a place to peer into the corn hopper. "See that long green metal plate on the bottom in there?"

Steve moved his head to peer into the bin of the huge combine farm vehicle. "Yes I do."

"That thing covers access to the accessory gearbox. It weighs about a hundred pounds, but it just lays flat on the floor of the bin. You climb in there, lift up on that plate, and squeeze down onto the carpet remnant that I just stuck in there. It's tight and it will be lumpy and uncomfortable, but you can probably stay there for a few hours, should anyone come out and search the farm."

"What happens if someone decides to start up the combine while I'm in there?"

Hellums yanked off his John Deere cap and gave the top of his head a really nice scratch. He replaced the cap as he spoke, adjusting it just right. "The drive shaft to the accessory gearbox is exposed from the housing to the universal joint at the front. Part of the carpet is laying directly on that drive shaft. If it turns it will most likely grab the carpet and take you with it." Mr. Hellums thought about it for a moment, nodded like he had just won an argument with himself, then added, "Yeah, there's enough torque on that shaft that it'll probably squeeze you through a space no wider than a beer can. You'd come out the other side as hamburger meat. But don't worry: I disconnected the ignition system and removed the battery cable before I stuffed the area with the carpet. It won't even turn over."

"What if they use dogs, you know, catch my scent?"

"I spread paprika all around the ground out here this morning. Dogs' noses are something like fifty times more sensitive than human noses. But dogs hate the smell of paprika and will shy away from it. The handlers won't know what's going on. I'll do it every other day, or after a big rain. We must have bought out the whole town's supply of paprika."

"How do you know about this kind of stuff?" Steve asked, smiling and shaking his head.

"Son, you get to be my age, enough stuff has been hurled at my brain that some of it was bound to stick."

Steve nodded, then asked, "What if they use sophisticated stuff like infrared detectors?"

Mr. Hellums scratched his belly through his coveralls. "Well, young man, if you think about it, it's pretty simple. I backed it out of the barn this morning and parked it in the direct sunlight for good reason. During the heat of the day, the interior of the cab is going to heat up to probably a hundred and fifty degrees, because it's enclosed in glass. That reminds me, I should crack the windows a bit."

He walked Steve around to the front and continued talking as he began the long climb to the cab so he could open the windows slightly. "Other parts will heat up at different and varying degrees based on the various metal alloys, and they will cool at varying rates, too. Lots of different kinds of parts in there. Probably looks like a kaleidescope to the guy scanning it. The area where you will be hiding will probably be close to the ambient temperature, since it is shielded from the direct sunlight by the roof of the bin. The sides of the bin, the hopper, are just a metal gratings, so air will flow freely underneath. What's the high temperature supposed to be today?"

"I dunno, a hundred and two?"

"So the average temperature during daylight hours will be, what, say ninety-eight. What's your body temperature?"

"Ninety-eight point six." Steve smiled, knowing that Hellums knew he knew. He also now knew where Mr. Hellums was going with this, but let him continue.

"Yep. Those IR devices work best when showing contrasting temperatures. If you were hiding there in the dead of winter, you'd light up like a Christmas tree. Heck, even if they searched the combine tonight when everything around you has cooled to seventy five degrees, they'd still notice you. But if they're searching for you in broad daylight, which they probably will, you'll be perfectly camouflaged. You're gonna sweat a lot if you're in there, though. It'll probably be pretty hot and stuffy. Keep yourself hydrated, just in case."

Suddenly, a voice yelled from the back door of the farmhouse, "Steve! Phone call." Mrs. Hellums was now out of her housecoat and dressed for the day.

Steve looked at Mr. Hellums, who said, "It can only be either Charms or Alan."

"Hope so." Steve said as he ran across the back yard and into the house. ✈

He dialed the direct line. It rang once.
"Any word?"
"Nothing."
"Let me know." *Click.* ✈

Alan was sitting low in the driver's seat of Charm's girlfriend's car. He was, perhaps a block away. "He's getting out of the squad car now. Looks like there's a patrolman with him, I guess driving him around."

Steve was relieved to know Alan was now a team player, having stayed in constant touch with Charms initially via the HotBlackTruck.com blog site. Now he was either seeing Charms in person or talking via their new phones. At the moment, he was talking—finally and comfortably—to Steve."

"Good. Hey, how did you know I'd be at the farm?"

"I didn't. I just called to keep the Hellums in the loop. They are plenty worried about you and I couldn't call them on my own phone. You know, it's probably tapped."

"So who's phone are you talking on? The number is blocked." Steve was plenty worried about traceability.

"Long story. But don't worry, it's secure," said Alan.

"Humor me."

"Okay. Charms went down with his new girlfriend to Evansville and—"

"Evansville, Indiana?"

"No, Evansville, Texas. Or was it Evansville, Costa Rica. Could have been Evansville, Antarctica."

"Smart ass."

"Well, then let me finish. They went down to the USI campus and into the Southern Indiana Cafe. Two girls came in and his girlfriend went up to them and asked if she could use their cell phones for a week. She said the two were planning to elope and wanted it to be totally secret. She offered them five hundred dollars plus two throw-away phones to use during the week. She even gave them her own cell number for them to call and showed them her ID to prove it wasn't some crazy scheme. I guess they still weren't convinced until she told them they could always check the minutes used and who they were calling at any time. Both were on the Sprint unlimited plan, though, and must have believed her, because we now have two phones completely and utterly unconnected to any of us."

"Wait. What happens when they trace every call that happens through a Kernsville node? Won't they trace it back to them, then to you?"

"Sure, but talk about a needle in a haystack. Have you seen this town? It's a circus. First it was just the local news crews. Then the big boys started showing up. Then when it became such a super-big news event, the national news anchors flew in and ran their nightly anchors from the scene. Brian Williams, Katie Couric, and Charlie Gibson are all here."

"I didn't see any jets at the airport."

"Runway isn't long enough. They need six thousand feet. They flew into Evansville and drove up. So that started filling up hotels and the KOA motor home campsite. Then the rock stars came in."

"Rock stars?"

"Sure. Anderson Cooper from CNN and Shepard Smith from Fox News. The pretty boys. The chick magnets. That's when the kids from the other area colleges started making road trips. You know, catch a glimpse, be part of it. It's a big party here in town. The bars are packed. Five to a room at the Holiday Inn. The rest sleeping in their cars. Some of the townspeople have rented out their homes for a week and have left town. You're a real boost to the local economy. You think the police are going to notice two college girls' phones from the University of Southern Indiana?"

"Perhaps you're right. So what's with you two? Have the press been hounding you?"

"No, we both left our phones in our apartments and haven't been back. I'm sure there are news vans parked outside. I've been in Charms' girlfriend's house out on Pecan Way. By the way, how have you been contacting the police?"

"The lead investigator is Stu Varney. He's with the state bureau of investigation. I've also been talking with a knucklehead at Fox 20 named Bruce McPort. Speaking of the police: I'm sure they told you to keep in touch."

"We did. We each got the third degree from Stu Varney. We thought they were done with us, until we realized they were tailing us. That didn't go over well with Charms, so we climbed out the bathroom window at The Pisser. Driving away in her car, that's when they got the idea to drive to another campus and borrow some phones. So they dropped me off at her house and went straight there. Yesterday I faxed a note from FedEx Kinkos to Agent Varney, care of the Kernsville police, saying we are still in town, just hiding from the press, as he had told us to do. We swore to him that we didn't know where you were and have not seen you, which was true. We promised to check in with them periodically. I just didn't specify how often."

"Well, now you know where I am. You are officially aiding and abetting."

"I guess you're right. Listen, Zimmerman let Varney and the uniformed cop inside. They're now in Zimmerman's house. I'd love to be a fly on the wall."

"Okay. Here's what you're going to do. I need to take things down a notch. Leave a note on his car. Make it from me. Tell him I am, indeed, in town and that I have not seen Charms or Alan since I got back, which is true. Tell him that Mr. Talone probably didn't do it. He probably knows that already, or he wouldn't have had him released this morning. Tell him to give me twenty-four hours and if I don't bring him proof that Zimmerman did it then I'll turn myself in."

"You really want to turn yourself in?"

"No, I just want to plant some doubt in his mind. I sure don't want to get gunned down if I get spotted and cornered. I get the feeling everyone is trigger happy right now. I don't want some yokel cop mowing me down because he thinks I'm gonna go postal on him. I've got to reduce the pressure. Be sure to write it in neat block letters. They'll probably analyze the handwriting."

"Charms girl has a thermal printer and car power adapter behind me in the back seat. She prints out directions and stuff with it. My laptop's in the trunk. I'll fire it up and just print out the note."

"Perfect. Just don't be seen. And if you get cornered, just tell the truth. I've got a pretty good hiding place and I'll tell the Hellums to tell the police I had held them hostage."

"Ain't gonna happen. We're all with you. MoJo was our friend, too. Hey, did you really shoot Mr. Talone?"

"Yeah, in the leg with a pellet pistol. He's still a sleazy crook. When I threatened to light a flare in his ass, he peed his pants."

"Cool." ✈

Stu was standing, rubbing his eyes as the two others took their seats. The pimple-faced city cop was seated in one high-armed chair. He removed his hat, revealing a buzz-cut of peach fuzz for hair. His head was several shades lighter than his face and neck, indicating a fresh cut, way shorter than it had been. It was not an attractive sight. Zimmerman was in the other, separated by an elegant coffee table. Zimmerman looked terrible, too. He was dressed in an old dress shirt, untucked over Dockers. No shoes. He was unshaven and the eye was still heavily bruised and swollen. Stu had bags under his eyes, but was clean-shaven. It was day two on his suit, but he steamed it before the meeting to take out most of the wrinkles.

Stu smelled coffee, but the professor didn't offer any.

"Professor, let me tell you where I've been since I last saw you yesterday. I was just up in Iowa. Seems Mr. Brinkley was there yesterday, too."

"Okay. So?"

"Okay, so if he was there, he must have had quite a reach to punch you in the eye, since he can't be two places at once."

"He had an airplane, didn't he?"

"Yeah."

"So he punched me, then flew up there and shot that man." Zimmerman's tone was totally dismissive.

"Now how do you know that?"

"It's on every channel. You know that." Again, the tone was *get to the point; you're wasting my time.*

"Well, we know he purchased some stuff in Chicago the night before he allegedly punched you. So you're saying he flew all night down here just to punch your lights out, then flew all the way back up to Iowa, then all the way back here last night."

"Did he have a curfew I'm not aware of?"

Stu rubbed his eyes. "Tell me, is Brinkley right-handed?"

"Beats me."

"Actually, he's left-handed. He writes right-handed, but everything else is left-handed. He throws left handed. He bats left handed. He golfs left handed. We examined his sports equipment. We've seen his papers and notes. How come your left eye is blackened? You'd think that if he was left-handed that he'd punch you in the right eye."

"Unless I was turning away, which I was."

"Good one. I like that." He didn't. The response was well thought-out and perfectly logical. This was not going well. "So, professor. What possessed you to give the video of him hitting you in the lab to News20, rather than to us?" Zimmerman fidgeted. "Perhaps we might have more of a vested interest in it. Why are you avoiding us? First he beats you up here and you don't call us. Then you fail to disclose you had a physical altercation with him in a lab, instead giving the video to the news hyenas. Why are you afraid of us?"

"Listen, I just lost my job here. I needed to let the administration know that I was not at fault. My hearing is tomorrow. They could can me, but now I've got a slim chance of actually saving my job. Had I given you the tape, you would have held onto it for months, preparing your case against him. Meanwhile, I'd be without a paycheck for months. I'm sorry, but it was for selfish reasons. Besides, you got it minutes after they did— big whoop."

"Professor, I don't investigate cases via news reports. I don't like reporters. They are in a competition for getting the story first. I, on the other hand, want to get the story to convict. Big difference." Stu moved towards the door. "Well, thanks for your time. If you decide to take a trip somewhere, please do me the favor of letting me know so I can deny it."

"Excuse me?"

"In case there is any doubt in your mind, you are more than just a person of interest. There's something you're not telling me. I think I'm gonna go get some sleep and come back to give you some questions you may not have thought I might ask. You see, I have to be well rested to be at my best, and I'm clearly not. I don't yet know what you've done, but I can smell a liar a mile away." He motioned for the uniformed policeman that it was time to leave.

"Yeah, you call me a liar again and I'll file defamation charges against you. And you have no right to restrict my travel, unless I'm arrested."

"All in due time, sir."

He walked out. The door slammed behind them. The young policeman put on his hat, brim almost touching the bridge of his nose, giving him the look of a true Prussian and said, "Agent, you're right. This is fun. You did a fine job with him, sir."

"Bobby, that was awful. He shot me down. This guy is no dummy. Hell, he is the head of the engineering department at a university. There's nothing tougher than going up against someone who is logical and prepared. Engineers are professional problem solvers. I am a professional investigator. He's trying to slither out and I'm trying to cover the exits. This is not going to be easy."

They both noticed the note on the car at the same time. Instinctively each one scanned the area for cars or other movement. The street was empty.

Stu read the note, then gave it to Bobby. "I am so sick and tired of being hoodwinked."

"Well, sir, why don't we just go pull him over?"

Stu looked confused.

"When was the last time you were actually in a squad car?"

"It's been a while."

"Here." The young officer took off his hat and began pushing some buttons. A video screen on the dash started rewinding. The view was out in front of the squad car from the camera just in front of the steering column. A large white object was in the middle. "There's your note," he said. To the right of the note, a car suddenly appeared in the distance, quickly traveling backwards from a side street, turned their way, and rushed back the street towards them, disappearing behind the note as the car neared. Suddenly it zipped to the left and stopped. The front of the car was lined-up with and parallel to the front of the squad car. The note disappeared quickly. He pressed stop.

"Okay, let's see who this is," said the young officer in a matter-of-fact tone.

Stu smiled at him.

He pressed a button that made the video play forward at one quarter speed. The hand of a young man lifted up the wiper blade while another hand brought the note down into view. He released the blade and it slapped the note against the windshield.

The car accelerated forward and he hit the stop button. He was a little too late because the license plate was already hidden by the note. He rewound it slowly until "MEEF82" appeared clearly. "Got it?"

"Got it!" Stu grabbed the microphone and said, "Kerns Control, Car seven. Place APB on a white Lexus, license plate number Mike Echo Echo Foxtrot Eight Two. Hold for a ten twenty-nine foxtrot." The last was standard police code that the subject driver was wanted for a felony.

The officer began typing in the license plate number as the APB was released over the dispatcher's radio, "All units, be advised: white, late-model Lexus, license mike echo echo foxtrot eight two. Last seen heading north on Elm Drive. Proceed with caution. Code twenty-nine fox."

The license information popped-up in green letters on the squad car's screen, indicating no arrest warrants had been issued for the owner of the car. "Here ya' go. Car registered to Deborah Burge. Jeez, I know that lady. She's a lawyer here in town. Dan Burge and Associates. She's his daughter, Debbie."

"You sure?"

"Yeah, we see her in traffic court sometimes. She's hot. Wicked hot. Wait 'til you see her. She has these killer legs and—"

Stu shook his head. "Thanks, Bobby, I get it. The real question is, why is Brinkley driving her car?" ✈

A news van suddenly appeared next to Alan, straddling the yellow line in the road, honking wildly. He glanced over at it and a man in a tie was frantically waving at him. The back door of the van was wide open and a cameraman was video taping him.

"Aw, crap," he said to no one in particular and rolled down the window.

"Yes?"

"Brinkley. Steve Brinkley! Why did you do it!?"

"I'm not Brinkley."

"Sure you are. The police scanners are going nuts. White Lexus, M-E-E-F eight two. That's you."

Alan took a deep breath, then made two fists and pounded the steering wheel. Then Alan pulled the car onto the shoulder, put the car in park, and turned it off. He grabbed his laptop, stuck his cell phone in his shirt pocket and opened the door. "Let me in."

The news reporter suddenly screamed, "Let him in. Let him in!"

He got in and said, "Drive and I'll talk."

The van drove off, leaving the car just beyond the intersection.

"Where to?"

"Just move. First I gotta make a call. Turn that damned camera off or you get nothing more."

The reporter almost came out of his seat and yelled at the cameraman in the seat behind him, "Turn it off. Turn it off!"

Alan was furious as he dialed the number. After one ring, Mrs. Hellums answered.

"It's Alan. I've been spotted. They got Debbie's car. I'm toast."

"Wait, let me put Steve on."

Alan's mind was racing. The three people in the news van were holding their breath.

"Hey Alan, it's Steve."

"Hey, bad news. They spotted Debbie's car after I left the note. I abandoned it when a news crew pulled me over after hearing an APB on the police scanner. I'm with the news crew now in their van. I'm screwed."

"Wait, let me think. Who do they have? They don't have you, but they do have Debbie. They'll go straight to Debbie's house. They have to be on their way there now. Where's Charms?"

"Jeez, what am I thinking? Call you back." *Click.*

He frantically dialed the other girl's cell phone. *Please answer.*

"Hey, what's going on?"

"Go. Go now! They just found Debbie's car."

A half-second later he was hearing his own voice repeated back in the background of Charms' phone.

"What the—"

After a short delay, then *"What the—" resonated in his phone.*

"Alan, what's going on. Why are you on TV?"

Alan looked at the cameraman. A little red light was on steady. They were broadcasting him live over the television. In less than one minute, he was being seen by millions of people around the world, saying "Turn it off. Turn it off now!" ✈

Chapter Twenty-Three

Fortunately they weren't home when the call came in from Alan. They were in Debbie's father's minicamper, parked near the front lobby of the Red Roof Inn out near the interstate. They had been using the hotel's Internet connection. The minicamper was perfect: a portable command center complete with a small shower and kitchenette. Her father seldom used it. He also knew she never had any interest in it, either. It sat for months in a storage lot. If he remembered, he would go out and start it occasionally. But when she explained she was renting out her house for a few days to some news crews, he understood and handed her the keys.

"That's it!"

Charms mind had been racing since he saw Alan's face on the minicamper's tiny TV moments before. "What? What's it?"

Just then, her cell phone rang. It was not unexpected, given that she knew her car would soon be as famous as O.J. Simpson's Ford Bronco. She looked at the number on her phone, then said to Charms, "Follow me on this: start the camper and head towards daddy's office. We have no time." Then she answered the phone, "Deborah Burge."

"Debbie, this is Ron Dulaney at the police station."

A chill went through her. She had been out of law school for just a year or so, and most of her time was spent with contracts, deeds, minor torts, the occasional traffic violation. Nothing like this—and certainly nothing where she was becoming a defendant.

She barely knew Ron, although he and her father had been friends for years.

"Ron, how are you? I'll bet you're busy," she said cheerfully.

"Listen Debbie, who has your car?"

"A news crew. Why?"

"Why does a news crew have your car?"

"No rooms anywhere. I rented my house and car to them for two thousand bucks a week. Enough of this lawyer stuff. The real money is in slum lording," she said jokingly. Hopefully she was convincing.

"What channel are they with?"

"They're the cameraman and producer from Court TV. That cable channel must be doing okay because they paid me in cash and didn't balk at my price."

"What did they look like?"

She thought for a moment. What did he know? Was he feeling her out? "I only met one of them, the cameraman. He was young, skinny, about my age."

There was a pause on the other end.

A scary pause. Ron was thinking.

"Where are you, Debbie?"

"I'm at my office. Actually I'm around the corner, but walking back. Be there in two minutes. What's going on, Ron?" She motioned urgently for Charms to step on it, which he did. She wasn't kidding when she said they had no time.

"I guess that explains it. You see, I called your office first and when you weren't there, I asked for your dad. He said he gave you the keys to your minicamper."

Her heart sank. "Yeah. Not exactly luxury living, but I'm still accustomed to college dorm life, so it's not so bad. I was a little wary about them renting my car, too, but they said there are no rentals to be found within three hundred miles of here. I have to park that big thing a few blocks away because it's too big for those tiny spaces out front."

Charms nodded, knowing exactly where to go. They were now homeless and he, specifically, had to disappear quickly.

"When you get back to the office, give me a call and I'll have someone pick you up and run you over here. Then we need to go to your house."

"Sure. Level with me, Ron, is my house okay? What did they do to it?"

Charms smiled. She was every bit as smooth as he was.

"I'll explain when you get here." *Click.*

She hung up and asked, "You up to speed?"

"Yeah. Here's where we stand. I'm to park the van somewhere near your office and give you the keys. You walk back and do your thing with Dulaney. I'm going to take the phone and laptop. I guess I'll just go back to my apartment and check back in with Stu Varney. Things are happening fast, so it's best to keep it simple. Remember, you had no idea. Act surprised."

"How are you going to get home?"

"Walk. That's what they'd expect." ✈

Alan said, "You violated my trust."

The producer said, "Hey, I didn't know he was filming."

"Then who ordered it on the air, live? Drop me off at the police station."

The producer said, "Are you going to turn yourself in?"

"For what? You don't even know who I am."

The producer thought, *he's right.* They had seen enough pictures of Steve Brinkley on the news to know this was not the guy they wanted to film. Yet they knew he was involved by virtue of the Lexus. He must be part of the story. Yet, he wants to go to the police. *Why?*

"Fine. We'll take you to the police. But we want two minutes of you on air to answer questions."

"Agreed. Get me there first."

The ride was quiet. The producer was busy texting messages to his news coordinator in Saint Louis, formulating his plan. The cameraman had the big HD camera on his lap at a ninety-degree angle to Alan, his eyes staring down the road.

As they got to within a few minutes of downtown, Alan saw the little red light on the camera come on again. *They're recording audio!*

Just after the light came on, the producer made a non-verbal gesture to the cameraman and said, "Before we start recording, tell me who you are."

Alan was done with them, so he decided to see just how stupid and overzealous they were. "I'm Ron Dulaney. People at the station already know me. I'm ready to turn myself in as the murderer."

The producer was amazed at his fortune. This was the story of a lifetime.

Alan continued. "I guess my conscience has gotten the better of me. I need to set the record straight. Steve had absolutely nothing to do with this—it was all me. I know that I'll have to face the music, but—but, wait: are you recording this? What's this red light doing on?" He feigned shock at being recorded.

Alan pointed down at the camera. "Stop the van. Stop it now!" It was a magnificent performance. He should have been an actor.

As the vehicle slowed, Alan pushed the shoulder of the cameraman as he reached for the door to the minivan and swung it back. They were one block away from police headquarters.

Stepping onto the pavement, Alan pointed at the producer. "You are perhaps the most untrustworthy people I've ever seen." As he spoke, Alan noticed a perfect exit strategy, just beyond the front of the van. He almost felt sorry for these guys.

"That's twice that you recorded me. You're not getting anything else from me. I'm walking the rest of the way." He turned and pointed to the cameraman. "Follow me and I promise to shove that great big camera so far up your ass you'll be able to videotape your pituitary gland."

With that, he yanked the van door closed. He started walking. The van started moving at his same pace. In less than fifty feet, a UPS truck blocked their view of Alan. Emerging from the other side, he was gone. Directly behind the truck was an alleyway.

"Where'd he go?"

"I don't know. Is he still behind the truck? Did he go down that alley?"

Instantly they were at a standstill. They couldn't possible catch him on foot.

"Great. That's just great. Hang on." The producer prepared a message and sent it. The message to their news desk was just a few lines of text: "We picked up a guy in a stolen car who identified himself as Ron Dulaney. He asked us to drop him off at police headquarters so he could plead guilty to the murder of Barnes. He said, 'They know me there.'"

One of the researchers back at the news desk in Saint Louis did a quick Google and was shocked to find out that Ron Dulaney was the chief of police. After confirming the "they know me" comment, they decided to put the short story out on AP, with a promise of a follow-up.

In less than two minutes, Kernsville Police Chief Ron Dulaney was reported to have admitted to killing Monica Joann Barnes.

Almost immediately they knew they'd been had. Not only had they instantly become the laughing stock of the news crews for allowing such a story to be aired with such reckless abandon, but they were in more trouble because they actually allowed a real suspect to get away. The only thing that saved their jobs was the the fact that they got him on video earlier via a live feed, and the name Alan Overman became the next person in Kernsville to be put on their Most Wanted list. ✈

Alan made one more call back to the Hellums. "Steve, once I tell them where you are, they'll be showing up within fifteen minutes. Sure you want to do this? Are you sure you can hide?"

"Yeah, we're all set for them. Have at it."

"Good luck. I'm tossing the phone, because they'll be able to trace Charms' number on it. The only thing I'll have is Hot Black Truck dot com, provided they don't take my laptop."

"My guess is you'll be charged with aiding and abetting. You won't see your laptop anytime soon. Just confess to everything, except where Charms is. I'll handle their arrival."

"Sorry I let you down. Oh, by the way, let me give you Charms' new cell number."

Alan gave him the number.

"Thanks. And you haven't let me down. You're doing the only thing you can do. I can't thank you enough for your trust." *Click.*

Stu tossed the phone into the dumpster he had been hiding behind and emerged from the alley, rounded the corner and walked right into police headquarters.

The middle-aged woman behind the glass was rugged looking, with pale-white skin and jagged black hair, closely cropped. Her nose was encased with parenthetical lines extending down around an unattractive pair of lips which were smeared with reddish-black lipstick. Ugly, for sure, but it was an unattractiveness amplified by a sour disposition. "Help you?" she asked, clearly not wishing to help him. It was interpreted to him as "The hell do you want? We're busy here."

"I'm Alan Overman to see Ron Dulaney." He placed his laptop on the narrow countertop, smoothly sliding it right up next to the glass.

Her head canted slightly. After a good stare-down, she continued looking at him as she picked up her phone and uttered, "Hang on."

He looked around. Given all of the world-wide attention being directed at Kernsville, the police headquarters lobby was quiet and empty. The news crews either knew or had been warned to stay away, because none were found loitering. Not that there was any place to loiter. The barren lobby was so quiet he swore he could hear his heart pounding. He put his hands in his shorts' pockets so she wouldn't see them shaking.

She hung up the phone, looked him in the eye through the bullet-proof glass and said, "I'm going to need you to turn around and hold your arms out wide."

Just as he was about to comply, the door to his left burst open suddenly and two uniformed policemen emerged, each with his hand on his holstered weapon. The younger one said, "Arms out. Turn around."

Alan immediately extended his arms and swung around. His heart was racing so fast he thought it was going to explode. He imagined what a gunshot must feel like. Or perhaps a good clubbing. One officer patted him down, saying, "Are you armed in any way?"

"No, sir," he managed.

The pat-down was over as soon as it began. After all, he was only dressed in shorts and a t-shirt. "Follow us." There was an urgency to their command. He dropped his arms, turned, and had to jog a couple of steps to keep up with them. The older officer held the metal door open as he walked into a larger room with several desks separated by waist-high partitions. Most desks were unoccupied. Everyone must be out looking for Steve, he presumed.

A couple of officers who were in the room looked up, then went back to what they were doing. A man in his mid-fifties approached wearing a uniform with considerably more stuff on it than the other two.

"Alan. Ron Dulaney. Thanks for coming in." He extended his hand.

"My pleasure, sir."

"Shall we go to my office?" It wasn't a question. He turned back around and headed to the only enclosed office in the larger area. Alan followed him closely, now accustomed to their tempo. One of the two officers became the caboose, the younger officer parting at the door. He had been in the police station for perhaps no more than a minute. These guys didn't believe in keeping people waiting.

"Have a seat," Dulaney said, motioning towards the heavy wooden chair in front of his desk. Dulaney sat in his high-backed leather chair and rolled-in, elbows landing softly, followed closely thereafter by his clasped hands. "Where's Brinkley?"

"At the Hellums' farm, north of town. At least, as of ten minutes ago."

Dulaney tried to not act surprised. This was too easy. "How long have you known that he was there?"

"About an hour, I suppose."

"Care to elaborate?"

"Not really, but I guess I must. They—the Hellums—have been very concerned about Steve. I called them to tell them that I hadn't heard from him, and Mrs. Hellums said, 'Well he's right here," and handed the phone to him."

Dulaney held up a finger, interrupting him. "Hang on." He pressed a button on his desk phone and spoke at it. "Call Stu Varney, patch him to me now—pronto."

"Will do," emanated clearly from the phone. Dulaney looked back at Alan from across his desk and leaned onto his forearms. "So, just why are you here?"

"Because as much as I would have liked to have helped Steve, I was discovered while staking out Professor Zimmerman's house."

"Why were you staking him out?"

"If he met with anyone, I wanted to find out who they were. In all honesty, after they put out the license plate on the car, I couldn't be of any help to him if I was also on the run. Plus, it was better to bow-out now than be gunned-down in some alley by an overzealous policeman." *Oops, maybe that was a mistake.*

"Did you warn Steve to leave the farm?"

"No, sir. In fact, he was the one who said I should turn myself in."

"How magnanimous."

Now he was starting to get riled. "Listen you people need to quit focusing on Steve. The only reason he's on the run is he's the only one looking for the real murderer. He can't do it from a jail cell." *Don't start an argument. Get him on board.* Alan shifted the topic. "You know that we are all convinced that Professor Zimmerman is responsible for MoJo's death, don't you?"

"We have interviewed him several times already. And who is *we all?*"

Did I just screw up? "Uhm, the team. Me, Charms, and Steve."

"Where's Charms?"

"Haven't talked to him today. Last I heard, he was at his apartment," he lied. Now he'd crossed the line.

"Has he talked to Brinkley?"

"Doubt it. Unless he called the Hellums too."

"So you haven't talked to Charms today?"

He had to keep Charms in play. He had no choice but to lie again. "No sir."

"I'm going to need you to hand over your phone."

At that moment, Alan knew he was screwed. At least make it sound plausible. "Chief Dulaney, I'm sorry but I don't have it anymore."

Dulaney leaned back and crossed his arms. Alan knew his response to Dulaney's question was incomplete at best.

"Sir, I was shocked by how incredulous the news crew was when they picked me up. Steve is innocent and is my friend. Imagine how you would feel if your best friend was the subject of the largest manhunt in the country? Before I decided to do the right thing and turn myself in, I destroyed the phone. I guess, in retrospect, that was a bad decision on my part." Nice. He'll buy that.

"Yeah. I see." Dulaney looked at the other officer in the room. "Ted, lock him up. Read him his rights."

Jail? Me? A prisoner? A criminal? Fortunately, the normally explosive Alan was too blindsided to throw a tantrum. *Am I really going to jail?*

"And book him under his real name, Alan Overman. Not as Ron Dulaney, like the news was reporting." Dulaney made a knowing but unamused glance at Alan.

"Sorry. Those TV news guys deserved it. Just goes to show they'll report anything you tell them."

Then it suddenly hit him. *That's it!* But how could he tell Steve? "Sir, just one request: do you guys have one of those 'You get one phone call' policies here?"

"Sure." Dulaney popped a button on his phone and swung it around.

Alan hoped he wasn't too late. ✈

Chapter Twenty-Four

Mr. Hellums walked up to the big John Deere combine and spoke through the metal grating to the bottom of the seemingly empty hopper. "Steve, I just got off the phone with Alan. He was talking in code, like the police were listening in."

"Yeah?" Steve replied, safely concealed in the shucking mechanism beneath the combine's huge hopper. Alan's now completely out of the picture, he concluded.

"He told me to ask you, 'What does Zimmerman need the most right now?'"

Steve thought about the question as Mr. Hellums continued, "And he also wanted to know if you have a good working rapport with that news guy."

In the dark, greasy, dirty confines deep inside the combine, Steve smiled.

Steve was about to answer when Mr. Hellums noticed a dirt cloud rising above the tall corn approaching from the main road. He said, "Well, here they come. Last thing Alan said was 'use your last remaining asset to help.' I suppose you know what he meant by that. Got enough water?"

"Yes, sir."

"Good. Stay still in there, son, and if I call for you, don't answer."

"Okay." Steve adjusted the carpet remnant underneath him. Mr. Hellums was right when he said would be uncomfortable. The carpet was the only thing between him and a cam shaft with two bars connecting to small gear housings, which in turn, powered some other part of the combine. Some slits on the sides allowed a tiny bit of sunlight into the long, narrow crevasse that would be his home for who knew how long. He thought about the engineers who designed this assembly. Perhaps space was not at a premium in farm equipment. Perhaps it was an inefficient design. Regardless, he was glad there was enough room for him to hide there.

As Mr. Hellums walked deliberately back to the farmhouse he notice the dust cloud stopped about halfway down the dirt road leading from the main road up to his driveway. He presumed they must be waiting for backup. As he got to the back steps, he heard a helicopter approaching. He seldom heard helicopters around here and it caught his attention.

"Momma, they're here," he said to Mrs. Hellums.

She turned off the TV. "Okay. I'll get the fuse box." She walked over to hall closet and opened the door, then opened the door to the small metal fuse box in the inside wall of the closet. She took the needle-nosed pliers and extracted the good fuse. Then she walked over to the medicine cabinet in the bathroom and grabbed the bottle of Advil. She shook out a burned-out fuse, then dropped the good fuse in there and returned the bottle.

Back to the fuse panel, she carefully inserted the bad fuse, closed both doors, and walked back into the living room. The lights were now out.

"Did you get the TV?"

"Yes. I don't like sticking metal pliers into there. You all set?" Then she noticed a mess of parts were atop the kitchen table. "What's all this doing in my kitchen?"

"I need to stay near the phone and look busy at the same time. It's the carburetor assembly from that old Johnson outboard in the barn."

She rolled her eyes. "Leroy, you don't even have that boat anymore." She closed the window. It was now too hot to keep them open. She would let it get really warm before turning on the AC, according to their plan.

"Don't worry. I'm not gonna scratch your table."

They didn't act the least bit nervous. You would think they did this every day. ✈

Charms had to wait for a few cars to pass, then he hopped out of the minicamper and darted into The Pisser. Debbie looked at her watch as she hopped into the driver's seat and sped away.

It was only ten A.M., but someone at The Puissant Bar had to be there when the beer and other wholesale trucks arrived. He was relieved to feel the cool air conditioning hit him when he entered the unlocked front door. It was going to be a scorcher today. The place was dimly lighted, a stark contrast to the bright sun outside.

"We don't open until eleven," came from a female voice in the rear.

"My name is Charms. I'm a friend of Alan Overman."

A female form approached him as he adjusted to the dark bar room. She was the waitress back when he first heard Alan perform.

"Did he win?"

Win what? Then it hit him: the contest in Chicago. That seemed to be such a long time ago. "Yes, but he's just now turned himself into the police."

"The police? Alan? What in the world for?" It was the waitress from last week. She had a clipboard in her hand, like she was taking inventory in the back.

"In connection with Steve Brinkley."

"The murderer?!"

"Oh, gosh he's no such a thing. Steve is a good friend of both Alan and me. The three of us were trying to find out who really murdered MoJo, since the police obviously won't focus on anyone else." She looked at him and studied his face. She had been a bartender for almost twenty years. She could read faces and tell in an instant if she was being fed a line of crap. "Alan said if I asked you nicely you'd let me use your Internet connection."

"He did, did he? Why don't you use the school's? Don't you have the Internet at home?"

"Yes, but everyone is looking for me. The press is parked outside my apartment. The police would probably like to snoop-in on my surfing, too. I probably won't find anything—haven't found anything yet—but I can't sit around and do nothing and not help. You can check me out: I'm not wanted by the police, at least not yet anyway. Alan talked with Steve this morning and the police found out about it. That's why he's being held. He actually walked into the police station and surrendered to them. I haven't talked directly with Steve, but that doesn't mean I can't help him. Look, I know you don't know me and you don't know Steve, but you do know Alan. MoJo was the love of Steve's life and has been since they were in high school. I've known Steve for years and know for a fact that he could never have done this. I've only known Alan for a short period of time, but you and I know he wouldn't hang out with anyone he didn't trust and respect."

She finished sizing him up then said, "The kitchen's not open for another hour, but you can park yourself over at that booth. There's a plug on the wall next to it. The wireless link is called 'puissantbar,' all spelled together. The username is 'pisser' and password is 'pisser' too. Everything is lowercase."

"Thank you so much," he said, scurrying over to the booth, pulling out his laptop en route.

For the better part of an hour, Charms Googled through the web trying to find out particulars about Zimmerman. He found out the man was married to a woman named Lizzie, but she must have been invisible because Alan never reported a woman coming or going from his house. He tried logging into his Dexter account using "Lizzie," "Lizzie," "Liz," and other various forms of "Elizabeth" with no success. He also searched Gmail and HotMail accounts with Zimmerman in them, but they were too numerous to possibly determine which or if one belonged to him. Then a thought came to him. He called a friend who worked for the MIS contractor at the school.

"Dixon here."

"Cullen, it's Charms."

"Well, hey Charms. What's new?"

"Oh, I'm in a world of hurt. You know Steve Brinkley?"

"Not personally—thank God."

"I do. He's one of my best friends and one of the smartest guys I've ever met." *Like that will impress him...*

"Are you saying you don't think he did it? Then, why's he on the run?"

"MoJo was his girlfriend of five years. He's devastated. Can you imagine what it must be like to lose the only person you've ever loved? I knew them both like they were family. The police aren't even looking for anyone else but Steve."

"Didn't they arrest some other guy in Iowa?"

"Yeah, but it turns out he was just a crook bent on stealing our patent."

"Holy sh—that patent was yours, wasn't it? They mentioned John Ruess, and I thought that name was familiar. I've only known you as Charms."

"Yeah, talk about a turn of events. Last Friday we all thought we'd be rich from this patent. Now MoJo's dead and Steve is on the run. Alan just turned himself into police for aiding and abetting. I'm the only one left, really."

"So now you're aiding and abetting, too?"

"Yes, I'm trying to aid and abet the police into investigating the real killer."

"And that would be?"

"The head of the engineering department."

"Zimmerman? What an ass. I saw that clown on the news."

Good, thought Charms. "Yeah, but he is a dangerous man. He had MoJo in tears not long ago. He is also deep in debt with the casinos and I think this patent was his ticket to freedom. I want to find out who the thugs are that are pressuring him. Maybe he used them to steal the patent details from the back of MoJo's car."

"Why not let the police handle it?"

"Because they are convinced it's Steve since he won't turn himself in. They've talked to Zimmerman a couple of times already. But I honestly think he is outsmarting them. He's not going to give them any reason to believe he's in any more trouble than forging some student names on The Bernoulli Award competition application and making an ass out of himself at a press conference."

"You want access to his email account, don't you?"

"Well, yeah. If you don't mind."

"You know I can't do that."

Charms sighed. "I kind of figured. Hey, what about this: how about if someone who looks like me and talks like me tries to create an email account like 'password dot admin at Dexter dot ee dee you' and you don't find out about it immediately?"

"I see where you're heading with this. He's too smart to be phished. Furthermore, abuse of the Dexter University email system is grounds for revocation of your privileges." The last sentence was said sardonically.

"Hey, if you can't give me access to his account, perhaps he can."

"Did you know you can rename your own e-mail account?"

"To any name I choose?"

"Yes, but your identity is still visible to us. In fact, all changes are subject to review by the MIS department, which we do on a daily basis. I have meetings until two o'clock. If I find any nefarious email accounts set up when I get back—at two o'clock—I'll suspend it."

"Thanks, Cullen."

"My pleasure. Listen I've got to go to a meeting now. If you need me, leave a message and I'll call you back after—"

"—Two O'clock. Yeah, I get it." *Click.*

Charms went to work. First, he went to the Dexter University website and right-clicked on many of the image files and saved them to his hard disk. Then he went to his web presence provider and registered a phony web site called **SecurePasswordAdmin.com**. Fifty bucks and five minutes later he got the web account details and immediately created a subdomain called **Dexter**. He created an INDEX.HTM page including a simple entry form. He upload the same graphics he got from the official Dexter website into the bogus web site. In less than ten minutes he had a page at **Dexter.SecurePasswordAdmin.com** uploaded that looked identical to the style of the real web site. It even had a "Home" button that took you there when finished. He tested it and within moments received an email back with information he provided on the web page.

Then, he created an official-looking email message, addressed to a single entity: "Students and Faculty." In the blind-copy, he entered Zimmerman's email address. The message was simple: "We have reason to believe that a news bureau has gained access to some email accounts and we are asking that you change your email password within twenty-four hours. If you do not act at once, your account will be suspended and will have to be manually regained by calling 244-4820. We prefer that you use the secure automated method. Thus, this number will not be manned until tomorrow evening. Here is the link: **http://www.Dexter.SecurePasswordAdmin.com**. Please click on it or copy/paste it into your browser."

Atop the message was yet another official-looking logo, and along the bottom were links to various contact, webmaster, and departmental addresses and links.

He sent a test message to himself, then tried it out and realized that he needed a "success" page where Zimmerman would be taken after he successfully changed his password, which took another ten minutes to create and test.

The whole process took about thirty minutes. Charms knew that Steve could have done it in half the time, but was still proud of the finished product nonetheless.

He hit SEND and a message from **PasswordAdmin@Dexter.edu** was sent to Zimmerman. Hopefully he would take the bait. If he did, in fact, bite, then Zimmerman would get a response that said, "Success! Your changes have been saved and will be activated within four hours. Your old password may still be used until the new password takes affect (which will be done in four-hour blocks). Please keep your password safe."

Now, to wait. If Zimmerman decided to not trust the email and contact Cullen, then Cullen would have no choice but to tell him it was a bogus *phishing* email and should not be done.

He set his email software to check for messages every minute. Then he realized that if he was going to make this look real, he'd have to check it not once a minute but ten times a minute. Zimmerman was not the unsuspecting type. Charms would have to log-in quickly and change it manually before Zimmerman became suspicious.

Fortunately, within two minutes he got an email saying the old password was "Lizzi219" and the new one was "Lizzi220."

Ha! For once, he caught a break.

Charms already had the official Dexter Log-In web page ready to go with Zimmerman's email address already entered into the USERNAME block and the cursor set at the PASSWORD block. He quickly entered "Lizzi219" and logged-in. Then he clicked ACCOUNT INFO, then CHANGE PASSWORD, and changed it to "Lizzi220.". Hopefully he did it before Zimmerman had a chance to check it.

Next he quickly logged back in and did a search for all email messages in the past two weeks, then forwarded them to his own Gmail account. Lastly he went to Zimmerman's SENT MAIL folder and deleted them from the history.

Total time: forty-two minutes, including changing his own email from **Password.Admin@Dexter.edu** back to **Charms@Dexter.edu**.

Now he could relax a little and carefully look through Zimmerman's email messages. ✈

Mr. Hellums underestimated the number of investigators who converged on his farm, and it was quite unnerving, though he managed to look more disoriented than anxious and guilty.

A two-square mile area was cordoned with patrol cars. News vans filled the side roads just beyond the protected area. Initially a single helicopter slowly drifted overhead at eight hundred feet above the corn. Within thirty minutes, two additional news copters joined it above the farm, but they circled at fifteen hundred feet. It seemed that half of the town's population was on the Hellums' farm.

When the police first knocked on the door, Mr. Hellums answered the door with a greasy rag in his hand, and welcomed them into his kitchen. They said they were here for Steve Brinkley. Mr. Hellums said Steve had gotten a call about a half an hour ago, said goodbye, and jogged out to the road.

"If need be, we will have a search warrant issued to search your property," said an excited local officer.

"Why go to all that trouble? Search away, but I tell you the boy's gone. You boys must have found out about the plane crash."

"What plane crash?"

"The young man crashed his plane here a while back. Nice kid. Wasn't pilot error. He said the tail came off."

"How long has he been here?"

Mr. Hellums looked over at Mrs. Hellums. "Ma?"

Mrs. Hellums said, "Leroy, it was well after midnight when he called."

Mr. Hellums added, "I get confused sometimes. They got a fancy name for it, but I just call it 'getting old.' I drove out and got him at the airport. Her eyesight ain't too good at night."

The policemen were about to ask more questions when a middle-aged handsome man came in and they actually stepped back slightly. Obviously this guy was in charge.

"Mister and Missus Hellums, I'm Stu Varney."

"Hi, young man. I'm Leroy. This is my wife Ruthie. Have a seat."

Mrs. Hellums said, "Nice to meet you, Mr. Varney. You look hot in that dark suit. Would you like some iced tea? It's fresh."

"Why, uhm, yes. Thank you." Then he looked around and said, "Gentlemen, it's a little crowded in here. Can you please excuse us?" Stu noticed that he was sweating profusely, yet the elderly Hellums weren't the least bit uncomfortable. "Hot day," he said to the Hellums as the other officers filed out.

Mr. Hellums said, "Sure is. We'd turn the air conditioner on, but it always blows a fuse if too many things are running. In fact, we're out of fuses until tomorrow, when the social security check arrives and we can run down to True Value and get some more."

"How do you stand it?"

Mrs. Hellums poured the tea into a glass filled with large ice cubes. "It's actually good, because the electricity bill should be down a lot this month."

"You've been without air conditioning for a month?"

"When it gets really hot, we just turn on the sprinkler in front of the porch and sit out there and watch it fan back and forth. Waters the yard and cools the air at the same time."

She handed him a paper towel. Stu wiped his forehead, took a sip, then asked, "Can I please talk to Steve? I don't want him in any more trouble."

"I told the other policemen, he left a half an hour ago."

Stu shook his head. "I'm so sorry. They were supposed to hold everything in place until I got here. I'll probably ask the same questions again, if you don't mind."

"Sure. But a plane crash sure is a bigger deal than a car crash, given how many police have shown up here."

"Plane crash?"

"That's why you're here, ain't it?" Mr. Hellums canted his head slightly.

"No, is that what Steve told you?"

"He said that you guys had found out about the crash. That you'd be coming for him."

"How long has he been here?"

Mr. Hellums said, "He sure likes her chicken casserole."

Mrs. Hellums said, "Leroy gets confused. Steve got here last night a little before two A.M."

"How did he get here?"

"Leroy went to the airport to get him. You see, I don't drive at night anymore. I figured that if he made it to the airport, then Steve could help him get back home. He has Alzheimer's Disease."

"I do not! I just forget things sometimes. It ain't no disease. What's Steve's favorite dish?"

"Chicken casserole, dear."

"See. Disease? Hmmph."

Stu looked at the table, patiently waiting for them to finish. When they settled down, Stu looked at the greasy parts laid out on a folded tarp atop the kitchen table and asked, "Lawnmower?"

"No, it's a carburetor from a two-horse, nineteen seventy-two Johnson Mallory Outboard."

"They make the Mallory way back in seventy-two?"

"Yeah, seventy-two through nineteen ninety, but they made variants in both the Mallory and the Sierra carburetors throughout the mid-eighties, none of which work with the seventy-two. Parts are hard to come by."

Stu raised his eyebrows. "You sure know your carbs."

Mrs. Hellums said, "Ask him how old his son is."

"How old is your son."

"Twenty-five."

"Good gosh, Leroy, your son is twice that age." She turned to Stu and said, "See?"

Mr. Hellums looked confused, then picked up a small, loose part and started rubbing it with a greasy rag.

Stu turned to her. "Mrs. Hellums, have you been watching the news?"

"Not for a couple of weeks. The living room's fuse blew and it's a twenty-amp. There's three of them in the fuse box: one for the living room, one for the kitchen and bath, and one for the bedroom. The kitchen one blew, and I had Leroy swap it out with the one from the living room. The check should arrive tomorrow and we can go to True Value. Get some more."

"Have you been into town?"

"Not since a week ago Sunday. Church and the grocery store. We should have gone to church yesterday, but some days are better than others for Leroy."

Mr. Hellums rolled his eyes and kept working.

"So you haven't seen the news in the past few days?"

"I guess not. Why?"

"Mr. and Mrs. Hellums, I hate to tell you this, but a friend of Steve's was found murdered on Saturday in Chicago."

"Oh, my Lord! Who?"

"Monica Barnes."

She said, "My goodness. That's awful. Steve didn't mention —wait, her nickname isn't 'MoJo' is it?"

"Yes, ma'am." Stu tried to read her expression.

Suddenly, Mrs. Hellums' eyes watered and her lower lip began to quiver. She put her hand over her mouth. "MoJo? That can't be. Dear Lord, that's Steve's girlfriend. Please don't tell him. Let us be the one to tell him. Oh, my dear. God bless that young child. She was lovely."

"Mrs. Hellums, we need to talk to him. He is a suspect."

She looked at Mister Hellums, then back to Stu, then whispered, "You can't be serious. Well, he got a call from Alan. You know Alan?"

"Yes, ma'am."

"Well, I know it was Alan because I answered the phone. After the two of them talked, he thanked us for picking him up and letting him sleep here. Then he jogged out to the road to catch a ride."

"With whom, Mrs. Hellums."

"Why, with Alan, I guess. Who else?"

"How long ago?"

"Oh, I don't know, twenty, thirty minutes, I guess."

"Did you see the car?"

"No. Dear me. That poor, blessed child."

Stu took a sip of tea and wiped the new sweat off his face with the paper towel. Once again, he was one step behind him.

"Mr. and Mrs. Hellums, do you mind if we go ahead and look around the farm anyway?"

She was quietly crying. He, on the other hand, was trying to unstick an old bolt from the rear housing of the carburetor. He shook his head. "I'd take off that jacket first. It's gotta be nine-eight degrees already." ✈

Charms went through them all and found nothing. Half of the emails were from faculty and students. The others were a mix of emails from professional associations to eBay listings. He looked through the recipients and nothing appeared out of order.

Dead end. Now what?

All he had really done was expose himself in the event that Zimmerman brings up the whole password change request with other faculty members. He was truly at a dead end. Short of bursting into Zimmerman's home and putting a knife to his throat, he was out of ideas.

He was about to close out the email listings when he noticed that an eBay listing had been forwarded to an email address called **Jzimm101@HotMail.com**.

He quickly went to the HotMail home page and clicked on the Login button. He entered "Lizzy" and it bounced, saying the password was incorrect. He tried "Lizzy219." No, not that. He started to try increments from "Lizzy1" onward, but decided to try "Lizzy101" just in case.

It worked! He was in.

This account was filled with purely non-work related material, including coupons and offers from various Casinos, predominantly from the River Royale Casino. He opened one of them. The River Royale was in Caruthersville, a good two hour drive from Kernsville. He closed it and began looking through each of the other messages in greater detail. He noticed one from CherepskiPLLC and opened it. It appeared to be SPAM. Some guy named Ed Cherepski was offering to consolidate Zimmerman's debt. Charms was about to close it out, when he noticed at the bottom that the firm was also from Caruthersville. He took out his phone and dialed the number.

After one ring, a man with a gravelly voice answered, "Cherepski."

"Hello, my name is Jack Zimmerman," he lied.

"Zimmerman. Listen, you got a fuckin' nerve. The laptops are gone for good. Both of them. Okay? You been watching the news? You fuckin' call me again and I'll do more than give you a black eye. I'll rip your damned lips off." *Click.*

Charms watched his phone go dark. What had he just stumbled onto? Now what?

He looked through the rest of the emails for more messages from **CherepskiPLLC@HotMail.com**. There were a few. He opened one and it had a link to an FTP address. He clicked on it and it said, "Page Not Found."

Something must have been there. He tried different combinations. Nothing worked. *Cherepski must have removed it.*

What now? Before closing out Zimmerman's HotMail account, he did one more perusal and found an online receipt for BackUpAllYourFiles.com. He opened up a new page and went there. He put in the Hotmail email address and it wouldn't open. Then he tried the Dexter one and suddenly all of Zimmerman's files from his computer were there. Upon further inspection, he was astonished to find all of the CarbonRenderer's documents in a folder called *Meissa*.

Charms smiled. Gotcha! He knew Steve's wit when he saw it. Meissa is the name of the star that represents the head of the constellation Orion, or The Hunter.

The files looked like pictures—JPEGs—but they would, of course, not open. That's because they weren't pictures. They were spreadsheets, text documents, databases, presentations. Zimmerman didn't even know what he had. Everything related to the CarbonRenderer was there, neatly organized in folders, disguised as beach photos.

Obviously, Cherepski must have sent him the contents of the laptops via an FTP link, then once Zimmerman got them, Cherepski took them off the site and destroyed the laptops taken from the back of MoJo's car last Saturday. The files were the direct link between MoJo's murder and Zimmerman, since Zimmerman had purchased the online backup of his computer's files. Chances are that Zimmerman didn't even know these files were being backed up.

He jotted down "BackUpAllYourFiles.com" along with the access code from the email message, then went back to close it out and a HotMail Login window appeared.

He reentered the correct password and it bounced, stating *Invalid Password.*

Uh, oh.

He tried again. *Invalid Password.*

Crap. Zimmerman must have opened his HotMail account and been blocked by Charms' usage of it. Zimmerman was on to him!

He scribbled a note, then slammed shut the laptop and rushed to the counter, getting the waitress's attention. She wandered over.

He waved the slip of paper, then wheeled it around on the bar top for her to see. "This is urgent. This will be the most important thing you'll have done in your life!"

"What?"

"Call the police. Tell them to get a message to Stu Varney, see right here." He pointed to his name on the slip of paper. "Tell them to tell Agent Varney that all of the evidence is here. Get ready to arrest Zimmerman." He pointed to both the name Zimmerman and the BackUpYourFiles web site. "Here's the username and password. It's in a folder called 'Meissa' and tell him these files are not beach pictures. Okay?"

"Not beach pictures. Okay. But why can't you do it?"

"I've got to go. Please—and remember, ask specifically for Stu Varney."

With that, he ran out of the bar at full speed. ✈

Chapter Twenty-Five

S teve's cell phone buzzed in his pocket. People were moving all around him. He wanted to reach over and stop if from buzzing, but any sudden movements would certainly be noticed. So he let it continue to buzz and remained motionless inside a cramped cavity beneath the combine's hopper. Fortunately, in was in his left pants pocket in his shorts, and he was lying on his left side, atop a crumpled piece of carpet. Due to the intense heat and the men hunting for him, he could barely breath—which was good because he was afraid to breath.

For thirty minutes he listened to the sounds and footsteps just beyond his thick, metal enclosure where he was hiding. Any moment, he would be caught, he just knew it.

The helicopters overhead provided enough noise to mask the buzzing of his iPhone and soon the buzzing stopped, followed shortly thereafter with a single, short buzz, indicating that the caller had left a message. He didn't dare listen. ✈

Charms hung up and picked up the pace. It was awkward trying to run while leaving a message for Steve and carrying a laptop. He rounded the corner of the building, bounded into the law offices of Dan Burge and Associates and fortunately spotted Debbie before the receptionist could catch him. She looked horrified to see him and rushed him into her office.

Once they were inside she asked, "Have you lost your mind? Do you know who I've just spent the last hour with at my house?"

"The police, I'm sure. Listen, it's Zimmerman all right. I just got the proof. I need to borrow the minivan again."

"I can't. As soon as I let you have it, I become a conspirator."

"Come on, Debbie, you already are a conspirator! The police will eventually figure out that you know me. This is Steve's life we're talking about."

"I don't know."

"I don't have time for introspection. If you won't let me have the keys, I'll just steal it."

"Where are you going?" She looked down at her desk. The keys were right there.

"Caruthersville." He picked them up and nodded, demanding her approval.

"Where's that?" She shrugged her shoulders. The approval to take the keys was done beneath the overt questions and answers.

"Missouri. I'll explain later." With that, he opened her office door, jogged over to the main door, and was gone. ✈

"Varney here." He had stood up and politely turned away from the Hellums.

"We have good news."

"Good. I could use some."

"You need to be here."

"I'm there." *Click.*

He pulled up his "brick" and pressed the transmit button. "Put the chopper down now. I need some fast transportation." Then he said, "Mister and Missus Hellums, I apologize. I need to go. It's an emergency of sorts. May I talk with you later?"

"Yes, of course," she replied. He smiled slightly.

He swung open the door to an awaiting Ron Dulaney.

Ron spoke, "Stu, I have Alan Overman in custody. He had been hiding out in—"

Stu interrupted him, "Sorry, but I have to get airborne. Cancel the search for Steve here. Find John Ruess—Charms. He's with Charms."

The police helicopter swooped down and landed in a grassy area beyond the big green combine and the beginning of the corn field.

Ron was insistent. "That's just it. We just got a call from a lady in a bar downtown. This guy Charms wants you to investigate some files on a web site. He said Zimmerman should be arrested."

"Arrest Charms. I want to talk to him."

"He's gone."

Stu stopped and drooped his shoulders. *Again!* "Fine. Call me with the phone number of that lady in the bar. Park patrol cars in front of and behind Zimmerman's house. We're done here."

With that, Varney jogged past the combine and into the waiting helicopter. Steve heard Stu mutter something about "entropy" to himself as he jogged by. Then moments later the helicopter's engines revved back up to speed. Shortly thereafter a rush of air erupted, indicating its ascent. Steve smiled from his darkened confines. He had come to respect the man he was running from. ✈

"Where to?" asked the pilot from the front right seat.

Stu's phone rang. "Jeez. Not a moment's rest," he mumbled, then louder, "Chicago." He flipped open his phone and said, "Varney."

"Stu, it's Dulaney. Listen, I know you're busy but if we're going to catch this guy you need to stay informed."

Really, he thought. He let it go. Four hours' sleep, well into the third day. How long since he had been called during that golf match with his son? Stu thought how lucky Dulaney wasn't within choking range. "I'm all ears." He rested his head on the leather headrest and closed his eyes. The drone of the large police helicopter was a lullaby. All he wanted was some sleep. He thought the helicopter ride northbound would afford him an hour or so.

"Alan Overman turned himself in, but only after he found out we were hunting him down. He was staking out Professor Zimmerman's home when you were in there. In fact, he was on the phone with Steve Brinkley while you were interrogating Zimmerman. Brinkley told him to write the note and leave it on your squad car."

"Yeah." Varney knew this already.

"Then a news crew spots the car and pulls him over and gets him on camera. That's when he decided to turn himself in."

That wasn't completely true, so Stu offered, "After consulting with Steve."

"Yes. But, think about it: he must have been talking with Charms, too. During my interrogation, he said that they all believed the killer was Zimmerman. Charms isn't at his apartment, and he doesn't answer his phone. Someone obviously picked Steve up from the farm. Had to be Charms."

Stu yawned. "What was the last thing I asked you to do, not two minutes ago?"

"Arrest Charms."

"Yeah."

"Well, here's the deal. Charms' car is parked at his apartment. Brinkley's old truck is parked behind the barn at the farmhouse. It hasn't been run in days because grass is growing around the wheels. Question is, what are they driving and where are they staying?"

"Where was Alan staying?"

"He said he rented a house from a lawyer. He was posing as a cameraman from Court TV. You know how there are no hotel rooms to be had around here."

"Did you dust the place for Charms' prints?"

"We can dust all we want, but these kids weren't crooks. What do we match them with? They were Boy Scouts and we don't have any Boy Scout prints on file."

Dulaney was right. Stu wasn't thinking straight. He was so deprived of sleep it was seriously affecting his ability to reason. "You're right, but Brinkley has prints on file from his arrest four or five years ago at M.I.T. I'd hate to find out later that he had been there, too. I don't think any of them would be stupid enough to try to rent a car from Hertz. Your best bet is go back to that lawyer and drill him some more."

"Her."

"Her?"

"Yeah, her. The lawyer is a young woman."

"How young?"

"Young—and gorgeous."

"How much did they pay for it?"

"The house?"

No, the woman, you idiot. "Yeah, the house."

"Two thousand dollars for the house and the car for a week."

Suddenly, a neuron fired. Stu popped open his briefcase and began digging through some documents. His fingers thumbed through several printed pages until he recognized the document he was looking for. Pulling it out, he continued, "Tell me you asked Alan where he came up with two thousand dollars. When I was in college I couldn't afford Cup O' Noodles." He was having trouble flipping the pages while holding the phone to his ear. "So let me get this straight: two college kids with money to burn rent a house from a gorgeous young woman, perhaps only a few years older

than them. Tell me, how did they find her? Did she advertise that
her home was for rent? Here's what you need to do: bring that
woman lawyer in again and put some pressure on her. Use the
phrase 'show me the money.' I'll bet you a Frappuccino she's
involved."

"Will do."

"Oh, and what's the name of the bar where Charms told that
lady to call me?"

"It's called the Puissant Bar. But everyone around here calls
it The Pisser."

"Let me guess. It's within walking distance of this lawyer
lady's office."

"You know, I think it is."

He shook his head. Dulaney was in over his head. Stu
flipped to the last sheet and read the name at the bottom into his
phone, "Deborah Burge."

"Okay, now you're scaring me. How could you possibly
know her name?"

"Ron, she is the lawyer who filed the patent paperwork on
behalf of Steve Brinkley, John Ruess, Monica Barnes, and Alan
Overman. You need to study the case materials. We're a people
business. Call me when you have her in custody." *Click.*

Within minutes, Stu was sound asleep. ✈

Mr. Hellums walked by the combine and spoke just loud enough
for Steve to hear as he passed, "Stay put, in case someone's still
watching, but I think it's safe enough to breath again."

"Thanks." He saw the shadow of Mr. Hellums continue on
towards the barn. Steve's side was killing him. He had been in the
same position for over an hour. His left arm was asleep, needles up
and down the length of his arm. He carefully rotated one hundred
and eight degrees over onto his right side, careful not to let the
carpet unfurl beneath him, exposing him to the jagged machinery

underneath. Once properly repositioned, he reached into his shorts pocket and retrieved his last remaining throw-away phone. The screen was on when he pulled it from his pocket, illuminating a box that said, "10% Battery." *Rats*. He must have been mashing some of the keys while the phone was underneath him, illuminating the screen and discharging the battery the whole time. He had no charger; it was in the hangar in Chicago.

Hopefully he could listen to the message before the phone died. The only ones who knew the number were Alan and Charms, since he put the number on the HotBlackTruck.com blog at about four A.M. If the call had been from Alan it could only be bad news. If from Charms it could be either good or bad. He was relieved to hear the voice on the message belonged to Charms. "Steve, Charms. I hacked into Zimm's email. The operative word is Jackpot. Call me."

Steve smiled and hit the button next to CALL BACK on the phone. It rang once, twice... ✈

Charms hadn't walked twenty paces from Debbie's office when the phone went off in his pocket. He tried to reach for it, but had to step laterally next to the street and lay his laptop on top of a fancy metal public trashcan that the city had been placing up and down the newly-renovated downtown area. It was powder-coated with glossy black paint and the oppressive sunshine had most likely heated it to a hundred fifty degrees already, but he only needed to put his laptop there long enough to reach for his cell phone. He answered it on the third ring, not recognizing the number.

"Hello?"

"Charms it's Steve. You called?"

"Ouch," he said as he lifted the laptop from the top of the hot trash receptacle. "Jeez, you spooked me. That area code was showing from Chicago. I thought it was Agent Varney."

"Yeah, I'm down to my last throw-away phone and no battery left. Make it quick, important stuff first in case my phone dies."

"Meet me at the lone oak out near the crash site. We have an errand to run. Turns out Zimmerman has the files from your laptop, you know—the Meissa folder."

"Mr. Hellums said I need to stay hidden a while longer. He's not sure the coast is clear yet."

"There's more. The thug's name is Cherepski. He's in Caruthersville, Missouri, where the River Royale Casino is. Get out to the tree as fast as you can and I'll—hang on." Just then, a police car appeared from seemingly out of nowhere, its blue lights blazing and approaching quickly. No siren. *Trouble.* Charms lowered his head and casually did a one-eighty, facing Debbie's office when he saw another police car approaching quickly from the other direction. Its lights were on as well. He froze. He was trapped. He hung up the phone without saying goodbye and stuck it in his pocket. *I'm so screwed.*

He was about to raise his hands to surrender. The first squad car whizzed by him and double-parked outside of Debbie's office, lights still on. The other one wheeled into an empty space directly across the street and turned off his lights. Both officers emerged from their cars and looked to be heading towards her office, obviously in a hurry.

Charms slowly—ever so slowly—turned and started walking, innocently, in his original direction again. He held the laptop with one hand and spread his fingers out on the other hand, so they would clearly know he was not holding a weapon, should they spot him and draw their weapons.

He pictured himself being shot in the back, his face smashing head-on into the concrete. He listened intensely for a "halt!" or "hands where I can see them!" command but none came. Another twenty yards and he'd be able to turn down College

Avenue and make a break for it. Ten yards to go. *Be cool. Don't speed up, yet.*

In what seemed an eternity, he finally reached the corner and turned behind the corner shop, then ran with all his might towards the minicamper. Then he thought, *Is this smart?* They were now arresting Debbie. He felt awful. He dragged her into this. She'll have no choice but to confess to everything. Who could blame her?

The minicamper will be targeted now, he concluded. He slowed his pace, then began walking. He was breathing hard, not from the run but from the ensuing panic. Now he was alone, in downtown Kernsville, police closing in on him, no transportation.

If he walked over to the police department and surrendered, he would be leaving Steve alone and abandoned. He stood there for a moment and pondered his options. Did he have enough evidence to nail both Zimmerman and Cherepski? Perhaps. But that evidence was flimsy at best. Maybe he could steal a car. No, bad idea, and quickly dismissed the thought.. If he could make it to his car, he could take it to a used car lot and trade it in on a cheaper car. It might buy him twenty-four hours while the paperwork was processed. It might also expose him if the used car dealer recognized him. No, he concluded, it was really Steve who was the infamous one. Perhaps trading his car was worth a shot.

He took one step and heard, "Hands in the air, John Ruess! You're under arrest!"

He sighed and lowered his head in defeat, nodding once on the way down. The decision was made for him. He raised one arm quickly. He slowly rotated his laptop upward and raised the other arm with it awkwardly, hoping they wouldn't shoot him right there on the spot.

The first officer grabbed his right arm. The other officer was kind enough to grab the laptop rather than allow it to drop onto the pavement from seven feet up. Over the next two minutes, they treated him much rougher than they did his laptop, handcuffing him, frisking him, and hauling him into the squad car. ✈

Steve had to make a decision and had to make it now. His hiding place had worked. Scores of policemen and investigators had been there for hours, scouring every inch of the farm, yet he evaded them successfully. His cloister was hot, dark, reeked of oil and grease, cramped, and uncomfortable. But it was safe.

He also realized that simply hiding was not going to get him exonerated nor catch the real killer. Ergo he had to be proactive. *Jackpot.* That was the word Charms had used. He needed a little more convincing and brought the phone back up to call him back

He hit REDIAL and it started to make the call, then the phone went dark. "No," he muttered, and stuck it back in his pocket.

Likely, Charms was heading out to the lone oak tree at the edge of the Hellums' property, not thirty yards from where he had crashed the plane. It would be a fifteen minute jog through high corn. He had to go.

Painfully, he pushed up on the heavy metal plate. It seemed to weigh twice as much as it did when he lifted it to get into the compartment. On the first try, he didn't have the wherewithal. He was exhausted and had been stationary for who knows how long. He summoned his strength, then pressed up again and in one motion wedged his chest between the bottom of the combine's hopper and the cover plate. The plate must have weight over a hundred pounds. There was no way to do it quietly, so he gave it one last bench press, rolled clear, and let it drop.

The noise it made coming down onto the floor of the hopper rang and resonated so loudly, he thought he might have permanent hearing loss. Even though he was still inside the hopper, it was really just a metal lattice and anyone nearby could clearly see into it. He lay motionless, waiting for someone to rush up and arrest him, guns blazing.

No one came, not even the Hellums. He never saw Mr. Hellums come out of the barn; he must have heard the metal plate drop. It must have been heard a half-mile away.

He sat still and breathed the fresh, slightly cooler air. Fully two minutes passed, then he decided to survey the area around the combine. Slowly he crept to each corner and gazed out.

Nothing. Not a soul around.

Strange.

He figured with all of the commotion earlier that there would be news crews trying to interview them, or a few officers left behind to watch the place.

He looked in the direction of the farmhouse, some fifty yards away. The Hellums' car was gone. What the... He waited, indecisively, for another half minute then climbed out of the hopper, scampered down the back side and made a dash for the corn field at full speed. Once twenty feet into the corn, he stopped and dropped to all fours, expecting at any moment a barrage of bullhorns and gunfire.

Nothing.

Very strange. He took a bearing on where he needed to go. It had to be a half-mile straight down the corn row until he hit the road. Then he'd back up to stay concealed and trudge at a ninety degree angle through the rows until he found the huge tree. Hopefully he wasn't too late. He didn't think Charms could afford to loiter there.

He started jogging, stopping occasionally to listen and look for trouble. The going was rough. Corn stalks are rough and thick. This late in the season they were at their peak both in height and breadth. He soon discovered that he made the best progress by squatting down and jogging low with his hands covering his head. Steve thought that many people who have lived in Kernsville their whole life had probably never wandered through a corn field and failed to grasp just how tumultuous it was. After only a few minutes into the trek he began to sweat profusely. From a practical perspective, he knew he'd need water before too long or he'd get dehydrated or, worse, succumb to heatstroke.

His mind again went back to MoJo, and the rage he felt of her senseless death turned his tired eyes to red and fully teared. It also gave him the strength to continue. Zimmerman needs to be taken down.

He was shocked at how exhausted he had become after the relatively short distance he had traveled. When he finally reached the road, every muscle in his body ached. He was cut and scratched, mostly on his neck and forearms. He receded back into the field far enough to remain hidden, then began the tougher, albeit shorter, part of the journey, and started crossing through the rows southbound.

Stopping several times to rest, he realized he was grunting with every move. Just when he was convinced he couldn't go any further, he spotted the top of the tree directly in front of him and much closer than he thought it would be when he would spot it.

The tree must have been a century old, standing majestically alone at the corner of a rectangular field of green. He remembered the layout precisely, having drifted into the field underneath his emergency parachute not far from here.

Getting to the base of the tree, it was not idyllic and pristine as he had imagined. It was a bevy of weeds, root outcroppings, and bugs of every genus and species. There was no place to really sit. He envisioned that this would be a place where copperheads and possums might reside.

One thing he immediately noticed that was absent was Charms. He knew there were only a couple dozen rows of corn to traverse to get to the crossing road, and decided to head there, hoping to spot a car with him in it. Ten minutes later he reached the edge of the corn and his heart sank. He was hot, exhausted, filthy, and alone. He retracted into the corn again and took a knee. *Cherepski. Caruthersville. River Royale Casino. Zimmerman. Meissa.* Charms had been busy. But where was he now? Did the call fail or was he caught? How long can he last here? Can he hang out at the tree until nightfall? He couldn't lay down. The bugs would eat him alive. He needed sleep.

Heading out to the tree was a bad idea, he concluded. ✈

Charms sat in a clean, but otherwise miserable jail cell for almost an hour before anyone came to see him. The first person to visit was a nicely dressed man in a thousand-dollar, perfectly tailored suit. He looked to be fifty-ish and Charms had never seen such perfectly groomed hair and shiny shoes. He looked strangely familiar.

But this man wasn't smiling.

"You Charms?" He asked, already knowing the answer.

"Yes, sir." He stood and faced the man on the other side of the light green iron bars.

"My name is Dan Burge."

His heart sank. *Uh oh.* "Sir, I know what you're going to say and—"

"Oh, I'm not going to say much. It's my actions that should concern you. You are going to take the fall for every single bit of this. Do you know what my daughter is being charged with?"

"Well, probably a litany of things."

"She's my pride and joy. She's our only child. The very first thing that will happen to her is the state bar will revoke her license to practice law. Then she will be convicted of various felonies and will, most likely be sent to prison. Can you imagine just how much I despise you at this moment? I promise that I will do everything in my power to push the blame solely on you, that you threatened and coerced her into committing these acts. I just want you to take a good look at me, young man. I'm your worst nightmare."

"Mr. Burge. I will help you in every possible way in transferring the entire blame to me. I will testify that I held a gun to her head, if you think it will get her charges dismissed. I'm dead serious. Do not doubt me."

Charms put his hands in his pockets and continued, chest out slightly, challenging the other alpha male in the room, "Three days ago, we were all as happy as we've ever been in our lives. We created and patented a process that will revolutionize parts manufacturing world-wide. We were going to be rich and bring back a manufacturing base to the United States. Our process would create jobs here, helping thousands. Along the way, I met your wonderful daughter. Alan's icing on the cake was winning a world-class band competition in Chicago. Steve could finally put aside the shame of having been thrown out of M.I.T. He and MoJo had never been more in love.

"Then, all of that changed when she was brutally murdered on Saturday. Poor Steve. You know, he has no mother and his father has all but abandoned him since his dismissal from M.I.T. MoJo was the center of his universe and now she's gone. He is devastated and has no one to turn to." He pointed a finger at Mr. Burge. "I want you to know that your daughter believed in me—in all of us—and someday you will see that she is even *more* lovely and wonderful than even you could ever imagine. By enabling me, she will have saved Steve's life and brought about justice without regard to herself. Listen, do you know what you can do for me right now?"

The man stood there, incredulously. "Do for *you*?" He folded his arms. "What would I possibly do for you?"

"Send an investigator in here. Send ten of them in here. An hour ago I uncovered evidence of who and where the real killer is.

Yet in spite of the fact that this is the number one news event in the world, no one seems to want to take the time to interrogate me. I need to talk to the police, and I mean *now*. I need to lay it out for them and if they wait, they're going to lose him."

Burge stared at him.

Charms added, "We catch this guy, your daughter's actions will be seen in arrears as heroic. Your standing here threatening me is not helping her plight, sir."

Burge unfolded his arms and left, expressionless. Charms thought Dan Burge might be a good poker player, because he had no idea if his diatribe had worked. ✦

Dulaney hung up the phone and said, "Still no answer."

The other uniformed officer said, "You know, Agent Varney got pretty pissed when we spoke to the old farmer couple before he got there."

"Yeah. But what are we expected to do, just sit on our thumbs while we have three people sitting in jail cells? One of them knows where Brinkley is."

"How are they doing?"

"Overman is sleeping. The girl is crying. The new kid is yelling 'Attica! Attica!' trying to get our attention."

Dulaney smiled. "He's a real wise-ass, isn't he."

"It's hard to believe that any of these kids could be wrapped-up in this."

"Well, either his helicopter is out of cell phone range or he's just not answering. He might be sound asleep. He's had less sleep than I have. My wife is mad as a hornet that the news crews know more than the police chief's wife does. She's a news junkie and is being hounded by the neighbor wives for information. Dan Burge just bit my head off. The news media is really pissed that I made the farm off-limits to them—the last thing I want is a lawsuit from the Hellums for the ruckus we caused this morning. An hour ago their son, some sort of high-powered lawyer, called me from California, threatening legal action if I don't either charge them with something or leave them alone. I don't know, but I've got enough people fed up with me at the moment. We're just going to have to cool our heels and wait until we get back in touch with Varney." ✈

An hour later, and only halfway back to the farmhouse, Steve heard a car approaching and hit the ground, even though he was a couple of rows deep into the corn. He scurried out slightly to catch a glimpse of who was driving by.

It was the Hellums' car. *Good.* Where had they been? It looked like only Mrs. Hellums was in it. That explained why the car was gone earlier. Mr. Hellums wouldn't have left him in the combine without one of them watching out for him. Mr. Hellums must still be back at the farmhouse.

Suddenly another car approached from behind it. He didn't see it coming. It wasn't a car he recognized. It was a big, black, shiny Escalade. It looked official, like the kind you see in a presidential motorcade. It was following her. He receded slightly, thinking he was concealed. But the car suddenly, almost violently, braked to a stop just beyond him. Then the reverse light came on and it backed up. *Oh no.*

He didn't dare move. Maybe his light-colored t-shirt—as dirty as it was—contrasted with the green leaves of the corn stalks? Maybe they got him with one of those infrared cameras. Then he thought, perhaps it was Charms, but he quickly dismissed it. Where would Charms get an Escalade?

"Steve, I see you there," came from the man emerging from the car, fifty feet away.

He still didn't move, trying to ascertain who was speaking from the big black Escalade. He was *so* caught. Should he just stand up. He'd probably be shot. Maybe they would draw him near, then taze him. That wouldn't be much fun, either. "I am unarmed," he yelled at the top of his lungs.

"Boy, I sure hope so."

At that moment, he recognized the voice. "Mr. Hellums?"

"Yeah, come on. Hop in," he said, walking around to the passenger side of the huge SUV.

Steve emerged from the field, looking warily in both directions. Mr. Hellums had already made the turn into the farmhouse's long driveway from the dirt crossroad. He jogged over, hopping across a small drainage ditch lining the edge of the road. Mr. Hellums had opened the passenger door and was walking around the front back to the driver's side.

"Out for stroll, are we?" Mr. Hellums asked as he hopped in.

"Charms called. Told me to meet him at the oak tree," he said, hopping into the front passenger seat. "Oooh. That feels good," he added, allowing the vent to blow cold air on his face. It was nice and cool inside.

"You would have been waiting for a while. Charms was arrested a while back."

"How did you find out about that?"

"Mrs. Carlock knows all. She's lives next door to the police chief's wife. They have to know everything that goes on in this town. Looks like everyone is in jail but you."

"Charms told me that he found the information that was stolen from the laptop in MoJo's car last Saturday." He put his face closer to the air conditioning vent.

"I bet you could use some ice tea."

"It's way hot today. Where is everyone? I figured after the police left, the vultures from the news media would descend on your farm, trying to get information from you."

"My son saw the live shots of the farm on the news when he got up this morning out on the West Coast. He called the police station and told them that if we were harassed in any way, he was going to sue the city for millions. He mentioned something about my weak heart. That's my boy!"

Steve smiled.

Mr. Hellums gave him a good look from head to toe as he put the SUV in gear and accelerated. "Boy, you need to get cleaned up. Unless you're wearing Grease and Grime aftershave."

"Yeah, I could probably use a shower." Then he changed the subject, "Charms said the guy who killed MoJo is some thug named Cherepski who lives in Caruthersville, Missouri. He's affiliated with the River Royale Casino there."

"Well, this is for you, but for emergency use only," he said, patting the steering wheel.

"This?"

"Yeah, and we stopped by the bank and took out three hundred dollars out of savings to pay for gas. It's in the glove box. This is Mrs. Carlock's car. We got her to offer it to us, so we could get around town without being noticed." He winked. "It has tinted windows and is hard to see inside. As long as you don't get in an accident, you can drive anywhere you wish if you need to leave here in a hurry."

"Like Caruthersville."

"No, not Caruthersville. This is an escape vehicle only. Don't go off half-cocked. If this guy killed MoJo in a busy parking lot, do you think he would hesitate killing you on his own familiar turf? If you have the evidence, you should hand it over to the police. Let them take it from here."

"I have to assume that Charms has done this already. What can it hurt to go there and get a feel for the place?"

"Except for the fact that you're intentionally putting yourself in close proximity to a murderer? Except for the fact that you have no real plan? Nothing, I suppose."

Steve didn't nod in agreement. He didn't have to. Mr. Hellums was right. The police will be there soon enough. The Escalade made the turn into the driveway, then up to the farmhouse and pulled around to the back of the house to let him off, just in case. Steve went into the back door as Mr. Hellums pulled the truck back around to the front to park. ✈

Chapter Twenty-Six

Toweling off, Steve felt refreshed. He needed to shave and he still had bags under his eyes from no sleep, but it was an improvement over fifteen minutes ago. By now, the Hellums would have left for the grocery store. Now that they had two cars, they felt they could leave him alone for a while and let him get some rest. The agreement was that Steve would take a much-needed nap, once he had showered. Just like a mom would do, Mrs. Hellums had waited by the door as he handed her his filthy clothes. They would be ready for the dryer by the time she got back. In the interim, Mrs. Hellums had laid out one of Mr. Hellums' short-sleeved, button-down K-Mart shirts and a pair of new overalls on the bathroom countertop so he would have something to wear while she washed his shirt, shorts, socks, and undies. She even threw his shoes in with the other clothes.

Steve was thin relative to Mr. Hellums, so waist size was not an issue. However, being a good four inches taller, Steve had to lengthen the straps quite a bit to get them over his shoulders and clasped on the front flap. Wearing overalls was a first for him. But wearing them sans undies felt even more foreign. He thought about the line, "Always wear clean underwear in case you get into an accident," and felt a foreboding.

Before swinging open the bathroom door, he was shocked at the person he saw in the mirror. For a brief moment he smiled. How different he looked in farmer clothes. *Not bad.* He thought about the TV commercial and changed the occupation to match the reflection he saw in the mirror. *I'm not a farmer, but I did stay at a Holiday Inn Express last night.*

Flipping off the light to the bathroom, he fumbled around because the bedroom was quite dark. Hard to believe that it was only noon. Mrs. Hellums had pulled down the two window shades and had turned down the bed for him. He stared at it. The room was cool because of the air conditioner wedged in the window, the only unit in the house that was never turned off in the summertime. In fact, the only reason the room wasn't completely dark was because of the light emanating around the air conditioner trim panels. The bed was so inviting, he actually considered taking her up on the offer of rest.

But he reminded himself that he was all alone now. No one else was helping him. All of his friends were in jail, charged with obstruction, aiding a fugitive, et cetera. He also got his second wind, so he opened the bedroom door and walked ten feet to the utility room next to the kitchen. His laundry was only half-done. He stopped the machine, pulled out the underwear, shoes, and socks, wrung everything out as best he could, and tossed them all into the dryer and cranked it on. He had no time to wait for the full cycle. Then he turned it on high heat, walked a few steps through the kitchen and into the living room. The Hellums' computer was in the corner on a makeshift desk. He fired it up.

He was still formulating the details of his plan, but he knew of a few things that were high on the list. The first thing he did was go online to Google Maps to look up the route between Kernsville and Caruthersville. Then he picked a town about halfway there. Next, he opened another window and went to **WalMart.com**. There was one right on the edge of town. *Good.* Then he went to **AnyWho.com** and typed in "Cherepski" and "Caruthersville" and "MO" into the text boxes. Nothing came up. *Rats.* Then he went to Google and typed in the same words. A police report .PDF appeared in the Google list. He clicked on it and a document prepared by the Caruthersville Police Department appeared. He searched through it and quickly found Cherepski as a line item in the arrest report section. Aggravated assault. It listed his address as 13 Rothrock Road. He stared at the address of the man who killed MoJo and the rage resurfaced. He realized he was gritting his teeth and his whole body was tensed. This man needs to die.

' He rubbed his face. Soon, anger turned back to reason. She's not coming back. This is about justice, not revenge. Let the state of Illinois kill him. Still, his heart was pounding.

He looked at his watch and listened to the clunking of his tennis shoes in the dryer. He had a few more minutes. So he went to **FoxNews.com** and verified what he knew already: there had been additional arrests and Steve Brinkley was still on the loose. There was no mention of anything regarding the farmhouse nor Professor Zimmerman nor Mr. Talone. At least as far as the news reports were concerned, he was still the only suspect. If Charms did hit the jackpot, then he must have shared this information with the police and they must have taken Zimmerman in for questioning by now. He needed to call Agent Varney, but the only phone was the Hellums.

He checked the time. He'd give his undies a few more minutes in the dryer, then he had to get on the road. It was a long drive to Caruthersville. ✈

Agent Varney was prone across both rear seats and sound asleep when the helicopter landed. The pilot shut down the two, seven hundred horsepower Turbomeca Arriel 1C engines by pulling the engine levers aft. The noise decreased to an acceptable level almost immediately. To save wear and tear on the rotor brake, he pulled up slightly on the cyclic—not in accordance with any standard practice—to allow aerodynamic braking versus using the rotor blade brakes. He wouldn't do it if anyone were approaching the helicopter. But they were not greeted by anyone. Once the blades almost stopped, he finally applied the brakes, shut down the radios, beacon, then finally the two master switches. He pulled off his white helmet and looked over at the other crewmember who had already removed his helmet. They exchanged smirks. "A lesser pilot would have awakened his passengers."

"How can you be so gifted, yet be so modest?" the other said sarcastically. They both opened their respective doors, yet he still didn't budge.

"Should we let him sleep?"

"I'm tempted to, but he had to get here in a hurry." He turned around and yelled, "Hey! Agent Varney. Time to wake up."

He squinted, opening only one eye slightly. "Sure wish I could hit the snooze button."

"You look like you could have slept for a whole day."

"I could have. Thanks for waking me." He reached for his dress coat, put it on, then rubbed his eyes. That little bit of sleep helped. His phone was in his pocket, messages waiting, but was still a little too groggy and didn't think to check it. Instead, he grabbed his briefcase and hopped out. ✈

Steve laughed at the reflection in his rear-view mirror. He had borrowed a pair of large, round reading glasses and one of Mr. Hellums' old John Deere baseball caps. His ensemble was complete. The photos of him that adorned every channel were of a clean-cut kid with much shorter hair. MoJo had wanted him to grow it out a little and he hadn't had it cut since June. Normally, his hair was perfectly styled. Over the past few months, however, his hair had become ragged and extended below his collar and halfway down his ears. Still not overly long, but much longer than the photos in the news reports showed him.

So, with little advanced planning, he was now camouflaged as a young farmer kid wearing overalls, with longish hair underneath a beat-up baseball cap. The stubble of a beginning beard underneath his round glasses changed his whole appearance. He was unrecognizable, even to himself.

He pulled into the WalMart parking lot, opened the door and the heat from the parking lot hit him like a blast furnace. He hopped down and went straight for the bathroom just inside the door. Emerging minutes later, he managed to bypass the greeter, making a sharp left where he stopped at the McDonalds inside the store to get a double-quarter pounder and a Diet Coke. The young, fat girl behind the counter didn't give him a second glance. *Good.*

Once he downed the meal, he armed himself with a shopping basket and immediately found an automobile charger for his throw-away phone. Dropping it into the basket, he then headed back towards the sporting goods. He had to get a weapon, yet he knew he couldn't buy a gun of any sort. Paperwork and waiting periods. Maybe a fishing knife or something. Then he spotted the perfect weapon. It was a high-powered slingshot, the kind with a wrist brace, thick surgical tubing, and a leather pocket. The thing was almost thirty bucks and was definitely not a toy. He tossed it in the basket, too. Leaving the sporting goods, he spotted some thick, neon-yellow nylon rope, looped and ensconced in an equally bright, printed cardboard wrapper. He grabbed it, too, barely slowing his pace. He stopped in the toy section and bought a bag of marbles, then headed back to the front of the store, making a detour through the office supplies where he grabbed some scissors. Just before he reached the checkout area he grabbed a big bag or corn chips and a couple of big cans of Arizona Iced Tea. He found an empty lane in the automated check out section and paid cash for everything. His total time in the store, including eating the burger and downing the Coke: less than ten minutes.

Walking back to the truck, he thought that was too easy. He reminded himself that though he now had some tools he still had no real plan. Once in the truck, he took the slingshot out of its box and stretched it out a few times. Yes, getting hit with a marble with that thing would be debilitating at least, perhaps lethal. Could Steve do it, he had asked himself during the first hour of the drive. Could he really kill someone? What's the difference between him doing it and leading the investigators to him and letting the state ultimately do it? He reasoned that he would be better served by letting the state do it, but would take matters into his own hands if the situation warranted. The anger in his gut swelled once again. This man, Cherepski, killed MoJo. *Bastard.* He flipped on the radio and switched it to A.M. so he could catch the news at the top of the hour. His anger again subsided, staying just barely suppressed.

Pulling out on the highway once more, he took out a handful of marbles and stuck them in the large pocket of his coveralls. He also took off the reading glasses. They were giving him a headache and affecting his depth perception. He didn't need them behind the tinted glass anyway. ✈

He was about to enter through the double-doors, when his phone went off. "Varney here."

"Agent Varney, this is Ruthie Hellums."

The door sensor detected him and they swung inward quickly. He backed away and they closed. "Yes, Mrs. Hellums. What can I do for you?"

"I'm afraid that I think Steve has gone and done something stupid." ✈

Charms stood up as the chief of police unlocked the steel door and entered the vestibule surrounded by bars. "Finally. I've been trying for hours to have someone, anyone, talk to me."

Ron Dulaney stepped closer to the cell, "Yeah, I've been hearing your wailings. Would you like to have a lawyer present?"

"Can one get here quickly?"

"Probably not."

"Then, forget it."

Dulaney disappeared for a moment. What the... Then as quickly as he was gone, he reappeared, this time with a folding chair and a yellow pad. He clanked it open and onto the painted concrete floor with one motion, then sat down and crossed a leg. "Start talking."

Then another officer appeared, "Sir, can I see you for a moment?"

Dulaney lowered his forehead and closed his eyes. Then he looked up above the top edge of his glasses and said, "Hang on."

As he was leaving, Charms couldn't resist, "I'm your priority. I have the answers you need. I'm going to make your day."

Dulaney stopped at the metal door, twisted his head, and stated, "Just pipe down, boy. You have too high an opinion of yourself."

Then he left, slamming the metal door behind him. The echo was present longer than he had been. ✈

His first clue that he had fallen asleep at the wheel was the buzzing noise coming from underneath the Escalade as it drifted onto the shoulder. He opened his eyes, not knowing exactly where he was. Just as he realized his predicament, the SUV lurched from the road , undulating horribly as it bounded across a shallow drainage ditch and into a soybean field. Steve had long since slammed on the brakes, but at sixty miles an hour and varying degrees of traction underneath, it took a while for the forward motion to cease. Only after the vehicle stopped completely did he feel like he had regained control.

His heart was pounding as he looked up and down the highway for other cars.

He gunned it, tires sending soybean leaves, roots, and mud in every direction. He gained what he thought would be enough momentum, then turned into the ditch, wildly careening down, then back up again and back on the road.

He looked behind and saw the damage: two perfectly aligned ruts leading into the field, and two coming back out. His shiny new black Escalade was now covered in mud and debris.

He tore down the highway as fast as he thought he could go, trying to put distance between him and the damage he had just done. His heart, still pounding, was pumping adrenaline throughout every artery. He gave himself a once-over and realized he was physically shaking. Out of frustration, he pounded the steering wheel. *Idiot! You have no business thinking you can do this alone.*

For another hour he pressed ahead, thinking he would see blue lights in his rear view mirror at any time. He didn't relax until he passed over the Mississippi River across a very impressive bridge that could have handled ten times the traffic that was on it. Between Memphis and Cairo, Illinois, this was the only way to get across the river. However, the population density was so low in this region, the boot heel of Missouri, that there was no such thing as a traffic jam getting over this bridge.

Leaving behind his fears of being pulled over for speeding or reckless driving, he now regained his previous fear of having to face MoJo's killer.

Landing on the western shore of the Mississippi River, he found himself in the town of Caruthersville. Its subsistence was primarily from two old industries and one new one. Farming and a river barge manufacturing company constituted the old. But riverboat gambling was the new business in town. Four floating casinos were permanently moored to the Missouri-side banks. In fact, huge rock breakwaters were constructed around the casinos. Technically they were floating. However, they couldn't move under their own power if they wanted to.

The casinos, however, were not his destination. He drove through town on the same highway that had taken him over the bridge, exiting when he got to the business bypass as he neared the center of town. Another three-quarters of a mile and he was on the edge of town once again. He slowed, knowing the street was approaching, based on his recollection of the Google Map he saw online. Rothrock Road was easy enough to spot. It was the only crossroad for a solid mile once you left the city limits. The road was cut into a thick forest at the northwestern edge of town. Around the forest was fertile cotton and soybean farmland. A few more miles away and you hit Fifty-five, the Interstate leading from New Orleans to Chicago.

You could have renamed Rothrock Road to Redneck Way if you wanted a more descriptive street name. Half the homes were trailers. The other half, tiny framed homes. All were littered with trash, decades old shrubbery, and old cars in various states of disrepair. One was actually up on blocks with the hood up, though no one was working on it. In fact, there was no sign of life at all on the street. He drove his shiny albeit muddy monstrosity through the pot-holed squalor, looking for number thirteen. He drove over pavement that was, most likely, laid before he was born. It was as though the ground had boiled and cooled underneath repeatedly, and the road was slowly surrendering itself back to the earth. The road was pockmarked with huge chunks of asphalt heaved up into shards and massive tufts of thick weeds exploding from various crevasses. Even at a walking pace, the vehicle bounded in every direction like a plane flying through severe turbulence. He drove past the house, stopping when he saw "15" on a mailbox. He backed-up to take a mental snap-shot of the premises. There was no number on the house, but the house before it read "11." That had to be it. He looked around. There was junk everywhere in the carport, including warped old lumber leaning against the back wall and a faded blue tarp over something with small flat tires underneath. But no car. This was the sliver of land that was Mr. Cherepski's, MoJo's murderer. No car on the property. The driveway was simply two worn lanes of mud, with pieces of mud-colored rocks sticking up here and there, indicating that it had been, at one time, at least a gravel drive. Not anymore.

The front yard was overgrown and could easily be interpreted as the front yard of an unoccupied or abandoned house. The only indication that someone actually lived there was the carport light had been left on, even though it was only five o'clock and there were many hours of daylight remaining.

The back yard appeared to have a moldy and rotted archery target leaning up against a tree. However, the untrimmed tree branches seemed to envelope the target, which clearly had not been used in years. A rusted ten-speed bike with curled handlebars was laying on its side, also not serviceable in any way. The backyard had no grass, just pockets of weeds and dirt under a canopy of pecan trees. A rusted and bent wire fence delineated the property line. His was the only fenced-in backyard. This was not just poverty. This was *I don't give a shit about anything.*

He pulled ahead until the road ended another block and a half down a straight line. The woods that corralled Rothrock Road were thick with nondescript trees and heavy kudzu.

This small forest was truly No Man's Land, and probably home to every species of snake, bug, and vermin in the Deep South. From his vantage from the plush interior of the fifty thousand dollar air conditioned SUV, the forest looked completely impenetrable.

The expensive Escalade driving down Rothrock Road was not the only contrast. Steve Brinkley was once among the best and brightest at arguably the most prestigious engineering school in the world, Massachusetts Institute of Technology. Now he was a fugitive and murder suspect hunting down a thug on a decrepit street in a small, poor town in middle America. The anger in him rose again.

This must be the same reconciliation process as when you are told you are dying. First denial, then anger, followed by acceptance. *Well, this is it.* This street is where the anger ends, and it will end today. This is where the transition to acceptance begins —which is also the last stage before dying. Maybe this is where it all ends. Everything. *And maybe that's okay, too.*

He drove to the end of the road, took several back and forth turns, then finally got the Escalade facing the other way back towards the highway, some three quarters of a mile away. There were no homes down at the end of Rothrock. And, if it was possible, the road was in even worse shape there. It was as though the street surrendered to abject poverty before all of the tiny lots were sold, because at this end of the road, there were no man made structures and the forest seemed to be etched closer to the street than at the other end.

He turned left and pulled completely off the road. He could barely tell the difference, except the grass was almost as high as the top of the SUV. He pulled as far off the road as he dared, then stopped and turned off the engine. If Cherepski was home, Steve would be a sitting duck driving up in a car like that. For now, he chose to simply wait at the end of the road to see if any movement was noted from any of the homes and trailers.

After fifteen minutes of waiting for something to happen, nothing did. In those same fifteen minutes, he became more agitated and more enraged at the thought of knowing the man who did this lived just down the street.

He checked his watch: five fifteen. In a moment of reason, he said aloud, "I'm calling Varney." The phone was fully charged, but only one bar of reception. He dialed the number from memory, waited, then it beeped twice, indicating that the call had failed. He tried again. It rang once, then failed again.

"Screw this," he muttered and got out of the SUV, sticking the phone in the left pocket of his overalls. The right pocket was full of marbles. He left his wallet in the SUV deliberately. He grabbed about six feet of rope and cut it with the scissors. He stuffed it behind the front flap of his overalls. Then he cut off another six feet, coiled it, and stuffed it in his back pocket. He was about to toss the scissors back in the front seat when he thought it might be better to take them with him. He stuck them in his right pocket with the marbles.

Satisfied and drenched in adrenaline, he closed the door and headed sideways into the woods. There were large spider webs everywhere, but he didn't care. He could have been walking over copperheads and water moccasins, but his eyes were on the structures ahead. He moved slowly enough and far enough back in the underbrush that he wouldn't be seen. Yet he remembered being spotted earlier in the day by Mr. Hellums. He moved back even further into the woods. After a few minutes he stopped and looked around. He was dripping with sweat. The sound of the myriad of bugs and other creatures in that gawd-awful place was deafening. There was no telling how many thousands of eyes were watching him at the moment, mostly insects, some reptilian and perhaps a few mammalian.

He heard a dog bark in the distance. This was the first domestic sound he had heard since he arrived in Caruthersville. He waited, then the barking ceased.

He started moving again, this time even more slowly.

A few minutes later he was directly behind the house. He stayed there for a good five minutes. The homes on either side of him appeared just as vacant as Cherepski's.

He crept forward beneath the thick underbrush and got as close as he dared.

Squatting there for a few minutes, a thought came to his mind: *Who are the Hellums, really? How well do I really know them? Why did they befriend me so quickly? Why did they trust me without question, particularly in light of all of the news reports? Didn't they go to the same church as Zimmerman? They sure were quick to give me that big SUV. Is this a setup? But why?*

He tried to stay focused on the facts. This was it, the end of the journey to the truth. MoJo was dead. The man living at the house beyond the weeds, underbrush, and fence line killed her. The rage reappeared.

Anyone home? Let's see.

He reached in his right pocket, beneath the scissors, and pulled out a marble. Through a slit in the foliage some fifty yards away, deep in the woods, he pulled back on the super-slingshot and let it fly. He was both amazed and alarmed and the velocity the slingshot produced, because it seemed no sooner had his arms dropped than he heard the crashing of broken glass, followed immediately by a dog barking.

Rats. Wasn't counting on a dog. He remained completely motionless for five minutes until the dog finally quit barking. Then he looked up and continued to watch for any movement for another five minutes. If there were anyone home, anywhere, that would have been plenty of time to either come out, or call the cops. Either way, the street was still calm, except for that damned dog. Why *did* the dog quit barking?

He reached in his pocket and loaded the leather sling with another marble. It was time to move a little closer.

No sooner than he loaded it, an immense creature came at him with teeth glaring and wild eyes. The animal was in mid-air leaping right at him with a guttural, blood-curdling growl. Steve screamed in shock and rotated backwards, pulling back on the slingshot with one arm while holding the slingshot with the other. He let go and it went right into the mouth of the dog and out the back of its head. The dog collapsed on top of him, dead before he impacted. Steve pushed the carcass away as it was descending. Steve uttered another panicked cry, rolled, and ended on all fours, every hair on his body sticking straight out. His head jerked from side to side, looking for others. Relax. It's over. His body was physically shaking, almost convulsing.

He had done it. He had killed. That poor dog was simply guarding the property or protecting his master. He crept over to it. The dog's eyes were open, frozen in time. He examined it and concluded this dog was no ordinary house pet. It was a weapon. It looked to be a thin Rottweiler, but larger than any Rottweiler he had ever seen. He remembered a news report of a new type of terrorizing animal called the Presa Canario. That's probably what this was. Except this on had open sores on its side like it had either been physically abused or malnourished, or perhaps both.

Steve glanced down at his own weapon. He was absolutely shocked at the power of this slingshot. If he had not had a marble in the sling or had been the least bit out of position, that dog would have killed him, no doubt. He grabbed another marble and tried to put it in the sling, but his hands were shaking so badly that he couldn't. His eyes were tearing with all of the emotions of the last few days coming to a head. All the death. All the violence. Did he really shoot Mr. Talone in the leg? What has happened to him. Who had he become? Was this how violent men got this way?

What if he had been a young child playing in the woods? If there had been any doubt that the owner of this vicious animal deserved everything that was coming to him, there was none now.

He felt something warm against his leg. In all the excitement he failed to notice that in falling and rolling the scissors had cut through his overalls' pocket and jabbed him in the leg. Blood was seeping through the thick denim. Trouble. He appeared to be able to walk on the leg but the extent of the damage was unknown.

Enough.

He stood, angrily, and began walking directly towards the house. The marbles began sliding down the inside of his pants pocket and hitting his tennis shoe. *Hole. Scissors.* He shook his leg, gathered four or five marbles, and stuck them in his left pocket where they rattled against his cell phone. He reached in his right pocket and pulled out a bloody pair of scissors, a piece of pink flesh at the tip—his flesh.

Moving on adrenaline only, he glided up to the fence and entered the back gate into the yard. It was still broad daylight, yet no one appeared to be around. He walked up the two old, chipped concrete steps, swung open the old screen door, and broke out the glass pane just above the door handle with the back of the scissors.. He was holding the slingshot in his left hand, pinching the marble in the sling with his thumb and index finger. His right hand reached in, scissors and all, and unlocked the door.

He pulled his hand/scissors back out and in one motion twisted the doorknob and pushed it in. The moment he got inside, a terrific noise, an explosion, erupted and he felt a jolt in his left shoulder, followed by a burning sensation. As he twisted away he leaped and hurled the scissors at the origin of the noise.

Another noise—an explosion—went off and glass broke behind him.

Everything was a blur.

He hit the corner of the room, only to see a gun hit the floor, followed quickly thereafter by a pair of what must have been his scissors.

They must have bounced off of him, because he was now leaning down to pick up the gun.

I'm dead.

Steve frantically tried to turn left but a searing pain came out of his shoulder. Yet he managed to keep his grip on the slingshot. He had only one shot, but he couldn't raise his left hand. so he simply anchored his left arm and with his right arm grabbed the slingshot and pulled it forward, then released the sling. It was a terribly underpowered shot—he knew it—but wasn't about to wait for the results and rolled away.

He heard what he thought was a muffled dish breaking, followed by a gurgle.

He scrambled to his side and fished for another marble as the gun hit the floor, followed by the man, holding his face.

Steve bounded over and grabbed the gun as the man fumbled, unsure of where he was.

Now Steve was in control and pushed the man away with his feet.

"Just tell me why you did it." Steve said, so much adrenaline going through his veins that his voice was cracking.

The man spit blood on the bare, wooden floor. "You knocked out my fucking teeth."

"Why did you have to kill her?" Steve was crying. He was losing control. Just pull the trigger. Don't wait for an answer.

"She was just at the wrong place at the wrong time."

At that moment, the phone rang in Steve's left pocket. He let it ring until it quit. He was shaking wildly, bloodied in both his shoulder and his leg. The disgusting creature five feet away was spitting large volumes of blood onto the floor. Steve pushed himself back against the wall, to allow himself a better target.

The phone rang again. Now he had to make a decision.

He screamed with pain as he reached for it, but managed, "Make one move and I'll do what I really want to do right now, which is blow your brains into the next room."

He struggled to answer the phone, but said nothing. He managed to hit the speaker button and let the phone drop a few inches onto the filthy floor. The world was spinning and he was beginning to feel light headed. He was going into shock.

A voice emitted clearly from the phone's speaker. "Steve. It's Stu Varney."

"Stu. I'm in Caruthersville. I've got him. I have the guy who killed MoJo." He was having trouble talking. Something was wrong. He was seeing double.

"I don't think so."

Did he just say 'I don't think so?' Steve stared straight ahead, trying to focus. The man was still on all fours, spitting blood. "No, I'm at thirteen Rothrock Road. Please have the police come here. I'm. I've been. I've been shot. I have him in cust— custody." The man started to stand up. Steve pulled back on the slingshot and hit him hard in the thigh with a marble. He was alarmed at the recoil of the weapon he held. The man dropped and curled up. Blood instantly appeared through the man's dirty blue jeans. Forcing himself to stay conscious, Steve uttered, "I told you. Can't you listen? Next time, it's between your eyes, you bas..tard."

Steve was starting to see things in the room change colors. He could smell the cordite from the man's gun as though it was being pumped into his nose. He knew he was shot, somewhere on his left chest. *This must be what it feels like to die.* The colors were bright reds and yellows. He knew it was only a matter of time before he passed out. If he passed out, then the man would kill him for sure. Either way, he's dead. He gathered every ounce of energy he had and fought to stay conscious. As he wrapped another marble in the sling, a chill came over him. What had Stu just said: "I don't think so," was it? *My God, have I got the wrong man?!*

Through the phone's speaker, he heard a female voice, "Steve, it's MoJo."

He looked at the man writhing on the floor in front of him trying to make sense of what he just heard.

"Who?"

Just then the door burst open and five men in thick black uniforms stormed in, automatic weapons up and pointing. Steve opened up wide, releasing everything he was holding, assuming the position of a snow angel on the floor. One of them pointed the barrel directly at his head. He closed his eyes. This is it. *I'm dead.* Then he passed out. ✈

Chapter Twenty-Seven

When he woke, he listened closely and convinced himself no one else was in the room. It was so bright it hurt his eyes. Quick glances were all he could manage. There was a lot of activity outside though. His first clue that it was a hospital room was the ancient TV high on the wall and the white chalkboard beneath it with the charge nurse's name written in blue marker. The TV wasn't on.

He was alive. *Good.* He was safe, too. But where? He tried opening his eyes in a different direction. *There's an IV. Yep, hospital all right. Which hospital?*

"Hey champ." The voice was unfamiliar, but it was from a man in charge, and definitely upbeat. Steve opened his eyes and saw a man in a dark suit with a shiny badge, sitting in the corner. "Agent Ron Cardwell, FBI Memphis. Glad you're back. Jeez, you were out for over twenty-four hours. The doctors said it was more from sleep deprivation than anything physical."

"How's Cherepski? I didn't kill him, did I?"

"No. But he's going to need some dental work He'll be sipping prison food through a straw for a while."

Steve quit trying to open his eyes and just talked with them closed. "He admitted to me that he killed her. He did it. He deserves to die. He said she was in the wrong place at the wrong time. Well, too bad for him."

"Well, he didn't kill her. Here. Ask Agent Varney. Just hit SEND." The agent handed him the phone.

"She's—?" *You mean it wasn't a dream?*

"Yep. She made it. You see, the news media just took some bad information and ran with it. We simply chose not to correct them initially. We were so engaged in finding you that we didn't reply to the info requests. At first, we thought you would try to go after her again so we decided to let it ride until we caught you. Thought it would be later that day. Then her murder took on a life of its own. The more we delayed telling the truth, the more the story grew. All I can say is, well, let's just say we are human and should have corrected the press reports. Truth be known, her parents were convinced she was safe as long as you thought she was dead. We thought, 'What's another day or so?' When she woke up yesterday, she told Agent Varney what happened and that's when we put the word out that not only was she was alive but she also confirmed that you were off the hook. We had no idea you would do something so stupid as confront her attackers directly."

Steve nodded. He couldn't move his left arm from the heavy bandaging around his shoulder. He didn't care. He pressed SEND on the phone and brought the phone up to his right ear with his remaining arm.

"Varney here."

"Stu? Is MoJo—"

"For a guy on his way to M.I.T., you sure are stupid."

"Excuse me?"

"I just saw on the news where the Board of Trustees at M.I.T. just held a news conference and have offered you a slot next fall to get your masters degree, if you want to further your education. You know, the world is so fickle. First you're the most wanted man in the country. Next, you're a hero. Hard to keep up. The stupid part is your being a vigilante and trying to do this on your own. You should see the mob of news vans and satellite dishes—"

"Yeah. Yeah. You're right. Whatever. Is it true? About MoJo?"

"Sure. They had her in a drug-induced coma for several days here while they did the reconstructive surgery on her cheek bone and temple. They were concerned mostly about the brain swelling, but after about twenty-four hours she was out of the woods. She's asleep again now, but when she wakes up I'll have her call you."

"Thanks," was all he could muster. This was a miracle. "And thank you for not shooting me."

"How could I? You were always one step ahead. By the way, there were two men who attacked MoJo. We have them both. If you had simply called me, we would have told you to stay put. We were storming the place anyway. Frankly, you're lucky we didn't shoot you, too. You know, things get a little blurry when a raid happens, even with the best people. Looks like the bullet grazed your collar bone. You're going to need some Tylenol for several weeks.

"We also arrested Professor Zimmerman. He sent them up there to steal your information. We even arrested some people at the Casino for their debt collection tactics. Hey, there are some other people here. Hang on."

Steve couldn't believe it. Tears flowed down both sides of his face. Mister No Emotion. Mister I Don't Need a Hug. He didn't care that people were starting to trickle into his hospital room now that he had awakened. The tears were flowing.

A familiar voice came through the earpiece. "Steve, so what's the hospital food like in Memphis? Ribs? Hush puppies?"

"Charms. Have you seen her?"

"Sure. She's all bruised and bandaged. But they said she'll have no scars. They did all the work from the inside of her mouth and through her nasal cavity. Pretty amazing."

"Can you call the Hellums? Let them know?"

"Nope. But I can do this. Hang on." A moment later Steve heard, "Hey, young man. You still got my John Deere hat?"

"Mr. Hellums. You're all there. Thank you so much for everything. You never lost your faith in me." He started to get choked up again.

"Hey, you could have treated us like just a couple of old people. You gave us some purpose, made us feel we still have some value. Thank you, young man. Listen, people are falling all over each other to do good things for you. Agent Varney sent the helicopter back down to Kernsville and gave me and Ruthie a helicopter ride up here to Chicago. Also picked up Alan and Debbie, that skinny girl we saw picking up in the field the day after you crashed. He wanted to get them away from the TV people while they finish pressing charges against the Zimmerman gang. You know she's a lawyer? That skinny girl? That's the first time I've seen the farm from the air. You can have Chicago, though. Nothing but people and concrete."

Steve heard Mrs. Hellums say in the background, "Leroy you've had way too much coffee."

Steve smiled at how talkative Mr. Hellums was. He began to open his eyes. The room was full of other smiling faces. He hadn't seen many smiles lately.

Mr. Hellums continued, "Your dad's around here somewhere. He's so proud of you. And you know that guy at Mahoney Aircraft? He gave that guy Mr. Herrmann—you know the guy you stole the airplane from? Well, he up and gave him a brand new Mahoney S-6. I just talked to Mr. Herrmann out in the waiting room. He said you can keep his Cessna, burned seat and all. Maybe you could use the engine on the next airplane you build. Some guy with a British accent has been talking to Charms on the phone and has him pretty excited about your invention. Wait. Hang on."

Steve heard the phone rustle one more time. A steady flow of smiles drifted into his hospital room. Most looked official. Some looked like hospital staff trying to get a glimpse of the most famous person in the world today. When he thought the room was at capacity, they continued to file in, wordlessly filling any empty space around the perimeter of the room. All eyes were on him. He was still trying to come to grips with the news. He acknowledged their smiles, then rotated his head back into his pillow, looking at the ceiling tiles.

Then he heard the voice he thought he'd never hear again say in a soft, quiet voice, "Hey, who is in control here?"

He closed his eyes and exhaled. "You are."

The woman's voice was soft, but confident. "Who's the luckiest man in the world?"

Steve's lower lip was quivering. His eyes were watering so much he could barely see. He took a deep breath and answered, "I am, MoJo." He closed his eyes and whispered again into the phone, "I am." ✈

✈ About the Author

- Tom Sylvester is a graduate of the United States Air Force Academy, with a BS from the Department of Astronautics and Computer Science.
- ...was a "rocket scientist" and R&D officer for the US's Ballistic Missile Office.
- ...consulted with a Washington DC engineering firm, designing airports worldwide.
- ...developed software for the aerospace industry, including equity claim coding for distribution of over $400M in bankruptcy claims to the pilots and extensive work with the Transportation Security Administration (TSA).
- ...is an inventor and owner of two patents, one the result of his work as a visiting corporate advisor to the bioengineering department at NC State University.
- ...is an airline pilot with over 15,000 hours of flying in his log book. He holds type ratings in the Bae3201, EMB-120, A319/A320 Airbus, and the A330 Airbus. He has flown many other aircraft, including corporate jets, executive charters, organ transplant "life" flights, commuter/regional turboprop aircraft and the Douglas DC-9 and Boeing 757. He is currently flying worldwide in the half-million pound Airbus A330 wide-body airliner.
- ...was a member of the Pilot Merger Committee for the NWA/Delta Airlines merger.
- ...holds over a dozen software copyrights ranging from satellite tracking to music production to aviation management, one being the most popular software of its kind in the country.
- ...is a managing partner with Cerventis, LLC, and head of the design team of the MusicJam mixer for the iPod.
- ...is the co-owner of Cerventis Records, representing a Nashville recording artist.
- ...is an avid but wholly untalented guitar player, playing in various unknown bands such as *Sarah's Uncles* and *Maroon78*.
- ...is married with one daughter, who recently graduated from Harvard.

www.TomSyl.com

www.ingramcontent.com/pod-product-compliance
Lightning Source LLC
Chambersburg PA
CBHW070535260626
47161CB00002B/396